Also by Tarah Benner

The Defectors
Enemy Inside
The Last Uprising
Recon
Exposure

Outbreak

Book Three of The Fringe

By Tarah Benner

To my most enthusiastic readers who love Harper and Eli as much as I do.
I couldn't do it without you.

one

Harper

Everything seems louder when you're the last human alive. Your footsteps echo in the empty spaces, and your whispers linger too long. Your breathing is heavier, but it seems insignificant as it disappears into the air around you.

They're all dead, I think as we shuffle through the empty commissary in compound 119. *Dead.*

The jarring *snap!* of something metal makes me jump, and I wheel around just in time to see Celdon pry open the control panel and flip several oversized switches.

An electric hum fills the deserted atrium, and neon lights flicker on at all the booths around us.

Apart from the lack of people, the commissary looks just like ours back home. The shelves are stocked with anything you could possibly want or need: shoes, lamps, lingerie, computer monitors, children's toys, handheld vacuum cleaners. It even smells the same: a mix of expensive cologne, synthetic coffee, and fruit-flavored lip gloss.

A loud blast of music from a booth on my right nearly makes my heart give out, and an overenthusiastic male voice starts to play through a hidden speaker.

Are you tired of waiting for results in the gym? Are you ready to kick-start your weight-loss journey?

The image of an overtanned male model appears on one of the enormous ad screens and flashes a smoldering grin.

Suddenly his voice is interrupted by upbeat club music as

another ad starts to play two booths over. A peppy female voice joins the din: *All the latest club looks at an affordable price . . . tops, bottoms, accessories . . . you name it!*

Two more ads start, the canned voices melding into an indistinguishable racket as they bounce off the high ceiling. I throw Celdon a sharp look.

"Sorry," he groans, examining the control panel and toggling a few switches. The lights flicker off and back on again. When he finds the correct switch, the ads stop abruptly, and I see spots in my vision as the bright screens shut off. I let out a breath to calm my racing heart.

Celdon and I have walked every level of the compound from Recon up, trying to find someone with a heartbeat to tell us what happened. The supply train departed for our home compound hours ago, leaving us stranded until the next supply run — assuming there *will* be another supply run.

My insides are a tangled knot of dread and disgust. Even though 119's deceased are contained to the dead level, I can still taste the decay of thousands of corpses in the back of my throat.

I don't think I'll ever be able to banish that horrible sight from my mind: thousands and thousands of people — all dead. And we never even heard a whisper of the tragedy back home.

The Operations workers sent to loot supplies from 119 *must* be part of Constance. If the board knew, they must have helped cover it up to avoid a panic.

How long did they plan to keep this up? I wonder. *Until supplies ran dry? Until Bid Day?*

Bid Day. That sends a fresh wave of horror crashing over me. The new recruits who didn't accept their original bids would have been sent here.

"Do you think this was happening last Bid Day?" I ask

aloud.

"Huh?"

"The other recruits — the ones who left 112 . . . Do you think the board would have sent them here if they knew what was happening?"

Celdon snorts as he rifles through a rack of clothing at the next booth over. "I wouldn't put anything past them." He picks up a banana-yellow tank top with the words "Let's Bang" written across the chest. "Wanna stock up while we're here?"

I shoot him a dirty look.

"What? Fire sale. Everything must go."

"What is wrong with you?"

"Well . . ." Celdon shrugs, looking around the empty commissary. "No one here is going to buy anything."

I just stare at him for several seconds, and — before I can stop it — a choked laugh bursts out of my throat. It sounds much too loud in the empty space, and as soon as I hear it, it makes me think of all the people who will never laugh or joke again.

My fit of hilarity triggers something else inside me, and I feel it morphing into a sob.

Celdon's smile disappears when he sees the change in my expression, and he drops the tank top guiltily and crosses to where I'm standing.

"Hey . . . hey . . . it's okay," he murmurs, draping his long, skinny arms around me.

Loud, ugly sobs roll through me, and we sink down together onto the dirty tile in an awkward embrace.

I'm angry at myself for losing it, but I can't stop crying. Everything is hitting me all at once: Our only hope of escaping Constance is gone, we're trapped here for at least another day — maybe longer — and no one at our compound has any clue that one of the largest human settlements in the country has been completely wiped out.

A few hours ago, I was devastated that Eli lied about joining us at 119, but now I'm grateful because it means he doesn't have to confront this horrible reality. Eli would handle it better than I am, but he's faced so much tragedy already. He deserves to be spared this.

"Do you wanna . . . *talk* about it?" Celdon asks. He never really knows what to do when a girl starts crying on him, but he tries.

"N-no."

"Okay, good. Me neither."

We sit in silence for several minutes. I'm desperately trying to pull myself together, and Celdon falls into a strange rocking motion that makes me feel a little sick.

"What if we're stuck here?" I whisper.

He lets out a heavy sigh, and I feel his narrow chest puff out and deflate abruptly. "Well, I guess . . . free T-shirts for life, huh?"

"I'm serious!"

"So am I!" A dark laugh rumbles through him. "I don't know. There's probably enough emergency rations to last us a lifetime. And as long as the solar grid holds out, we'll probably be good on power."

"You're thinking of *staying* here?"

"Well, it isn't ideal. But we might not have a choice."

I shudder. "We can't stay here."

"Yeah, I guess you're right. I'm sure they'll be back. They won't stop until they've picked the carcass clean."

"That's a little harsh."

"No, it's not. That's exactly what they're doing . . . opportunistic bastards."

"How long do you think they're going to keep pretending everything's fine over here?"

Celdon snorts. "Probably as long as they've been pretending that the drifters don't exist."

I take a deep breath and wipe my nose with the back of my sleeve.

"Let's keep moving," I sigh. "We can at least figure out what killed them all."

"Yes, ma'am."

Celdon is purposely trying to keep his voice light, but I can sense his relief. We're both exhausted, and every level we explore without finding another living soul just adds to our despair. Going straight to the source fills me with anxiety, but it also gives me a sense of control.

Celdon hops to his feet and pulls me into a standing position. Now that I've been sitting for a while, my legs feel a little wobbly from all the walking we've been doing. But I take one last gulp of cologne-laced air and force my feet to move.

It's stale and damp inside the stairwell. I know it isn't possible for the stench of decomposing bodies to travel this far, but being in the dark enclosed space intensifies my memory of that odor. As long as I live, I'll never be able to forget the smell of all those dead people.

On the next landing, we hit a small puddle of cloudy water, and Celdon swears as the grime stains his loafers.

"If we stay here, I'm going to have to read up on plumbing. This is fucking disgusting."

"Let's hope it doesn't come to that," I murmur. I can't imagine Celdon trying his hand at compound maintenance. I've never even seen him hang a picture. If the two of us have to keep this place running on our own, we're screwed.

I still want to investigate all the tier-two sections and confirm that there aren't any survivors left, but right now, finding out what killed everyone seems like a more pressing priority.

We keep climbing until we reach the medical ward, and I steel myself for the possibility that whatever killed them could kill us, too.

There could have been a massive radiation leak. Or maybe the groundwater got contaminated. After Owen's warning to stay away from 119, there's a small part of me that wonders if one of the drifter gangs had something to do with it, but there's no sign of an explosion or forced entry — not exactly the drifters' MO.

The deserted medical ward is still just as creepy as it was when we first arrived, but this time my feet lead me confidently around the long line of gurneys pushed against the tunnel wall.

Celdon stays near the front desk to try to boot up one of the computers. If we can gain access to 119's network, we can view the news feeds and possibly hack into the compound's medical records. Then we should be able to discover what killed everyone.

As he works, I check the patient rooms for any lingering evidence of what transpired. Unfortunately, the medical ward staff didn't leave us much to go on.

All the beds have been stripped of their linens, and the waste receptacles inside the patient rooms are empty. There are no medications lying around — no nurses' interfaces conveniently loaded with patient notes.

After a few minutes, I find one supply closet that hasn't been looted yet and feel a surge of relief. If there are things in here we could use back home, there's a strong chance our Operations workers will return for another load of supplies.

I flip on my interface and focus the beam of blue light on the shelf just above my head. Most of the medication bins are fully stocked, but there's one that's completely empty.

A tag on the bin reads "Bartrizol," and I wish Sawyer were here so she could tell me what it's used for. Whatever it was, it doesn't seem to have worked. But if we knew what it was intended to treat, we would know what killed everyone.

"Bingo!"

Celdon's echoing voice jerks me out of my thoughts, and I fly out of the closet to find him.

He's still behind the front desk, swiveling from side to side on the tall stool. When he sees me, a wicked grin spreads across his face, and his eyes flash with pride.

"Are you in?"

He claps his hands loudly and flexes his slender fingers. "Oh, I'm in. Their security ain't for shit."

"It's because they didn't have *you*," I say, feeling free with compliments now that we're one step closer to solving the mystery.

"Damn straight."

"Can you hack into the compound medical records? I want to know what Bartrizol is used to treat."

Celdon looks up at me and quirks an eyebrow. "Riles . . . look who you're asking."

I roll my eyes. "Just do it so we can get out of here. This place gives me the creeps."

Celdon's fingers start flying, and his eyes narrow the way they do when he's deep in concentration.

Time seems to slow down as he works, but then his eyes light up again. "I'm in."

Taking a deep breath, I step around the desk to look over his shoulder. Most of the patients in the admittance log were brought in a few weeks ago, and my heart sinks at the sheer number of them.

Celdon clicks on one of the names — a male patient in his early thirties. His compound ID photo pops up in the left-hand corner of the screen, and I get a chill at how healthy and normal he looks.

There's a hasty physician's note typed into the box under his last visit: *Patient was admitted with more of the same . . . high fever, respiratory problems, chills, and vivid hallucinations.*

The diagnosis: unknown virus.

Before I can say anything, Celdon clicks out of the window and selects the next patient in the admittance log. The symptoms match, and the diagnosis is the same, too. Desperately, he clicks on several more patients.

Unknown virus. Unknown virus. Unknown virus.

Fingers flying, Celdon performs a search for "unknown virus" and clicks on the first patient listed by date. He was from Health and Rehab himself.

This man's file is much more detailed, and it's clear the puzzled doctors were more diligent in gathering a complete list of symptoms. The virus first presented with a fever, progressing into a wheezy cough that began whenever the patient took the stairs.

Within a day and a half, he was having trouble breathing at all. That's when he was admitted to the medical ward, where they put him under observation. The physician thought it was bacterial pneumonia. He prescribed antibiotics, but the patient's condition only deteriorated.

Within twenty-four hours, the hallucinations started. At this point, the physician's notes start to get more frantic. He called in another doctor to consult.

They ran tests. They tried other drugs, but nothing seemed to help.

The patient's lungs filled with fluid, and every breath cost him great effort. They drained his lungs and put him on a ventilator. His heart rate slowed.

Four days after being admitted, patient zero was dead.

Feeling desperate, I nudge Celdon out of the way and pull up the compound news. The current feed is empty, but I scroll down to the week before the last wave of patients was admitted to the medical ward.

All the headlines are just variations of the same message, growing more frantic each day: Unknown virus claims hundreds more lives.

Celdon clicks out of the window and sits back on his stool. He looks just as shocked as I feel.

"It was a virus," he murmurs. "A damn virus killed all these people."

"It doesn't make any sense," I say. "How would a virus like that get in here?"

"It had to come in from the outside. Recon, maybe."

I shake my head. "Recon operatives are always contained in the postexposure wing for a few days at least. They would have caught it."

"Maybe ExCon, then."

"I guess it's possible . . ."

"What about another compound? Do you think it could have passed to 119 during a supply transfer?"

"Maybe."

In one swift motion, Celdon highlights all the entries in the log and beams the data to his interface.

"What are you doing?"

"Saving these files so Sawyer can tell us what the hell is going on."

Why didn't I think of that?

"There was a drug they were using to treat it," I say. "Bartrizol."

"Well, obviously it didn't work so well."

I ignore this comment. "Their supplies were totally depleted, but maybe Sawyer knows what it's for."

Celdon follows me back to the supply closet, and he's tall enough to read the label on the bin without standing on his tiptoes. He takes a picture of the label and saves it to his interface for Sawyer.

"It's pretty bleak, you know?" Celdon mutters. "Whatever this stuff is, they just kept prescribing it even though they knew it wasn't working."

My heart aches as I imagine what it would have been like to be stuck here as my friends and former classmates all grew sick and died.

"They probably just did it to keep people calm," I say.

"It wouldn't have kept me calm. I'd have locked myself in my compartment and never come out."

I shiver. Even though the last infected citizen died weeks ago, being in the medical ward after a viral outbreak puts me on edge.

Logically, I know all traces of the virus must be gone. Our Operations workers have been traipsing in and out of here for weeks, but it still makes me uneasy.

"Let's get out of here," says Celdon.

I nod and shuffle out of the closet behind him. Our footsteps echo loudly in the pristine white tunnel, and a feeling of hopelessness swamps me when I realize how powerless the compound was in the end.

Just as Death Storm wiped out nearly everyone on the outside, a tiny organism brought down thousands of people in a matter of weeks. The best treatment money can buy was no match for nature. She swept through with a vengeance, killing every human nearby.

We bypass the megalift and take the stairs up to Systems. The freedom to move on our own two feet feels reassuring, plus neither of us wants to get stuck on the lift if it malfunctions.

Celdon leads us down the nicest residential tunnel and heads straight for the corner compartment. The door opens easily, and he shoots me a guilty look.

"I went ahead and overrode all the door codes in the compound," he mutters. "Just so we can access what we need."

Any other time, I might chastise him for flaunting his skills, but I can't unstick my throat. We're about to enter a dead family's compartment — the place where they lived and ate and slept.

I bet they never thought that when they left for the medical ward, they wouldn't be coming back.

As soon as I step inside, I'm blinded by daylight streaming in through the tall windows. The stark white walls magnify its intensity, and it takes several seconds for my eyes to adjust.

This place makes Celdon's studio look like a closet; you could fit ten compartments the size of his inside the expansive living area. Sunshine bounces off the polished floor, and all the furniture is sleek, modern, and extremely uncomfortable looking.

The windows stretch all the way up to the vaulted ceiling, which tapers down in sharp lines to a loft with a sitting area and several upstairs bedrooms.

On the second level, I can see a tiny staircase winding up toward the ceiling, and I get a pang of envy when I realize that the compartment has its own private entrance to the observation deck.

"Whose compartment was this?" I ask.

"The president's."

"You're kidding."

"Nope."

I throw him an admonishing look, but I guess it doesn't matter whose compartment we choose. Everyone is dead.

"We should get some sleep," he says.

Judging by the sun's position on the horizon, it's just past noon, but I've been awake for more than thirty hours.

Suddenly that furniture doesn't look so uncomfortable. And if everything in the main living area is this nice, I can only imagine how great the beds must feel.

"You think one of us should stay up to keep watch?" I ask.

Celdon snorts. "Watch over *what?* There's nobody here but us."

That thought should put me at ease, but it just makes me sad. "Right."

We make the odyssey up the narrow staircase, and as soon as I catch sight of the massive bed in the first room, sleep starts calling me.

I should brush my teeth, but I realize belatedly that we left our rucksacks in the medical ward. Without turning on a light or even glancing around the room, I collapse onto the fluffy comforter and fall asleep.

* * *

I awake in total darkness and instantly panic.

I'm not in my compartment. The bed is much too large and comfortable, and there's a huge window to my left with a breathtaking view of the starry night sky — a stark contrast to my streaky window overlooking the Underground platform.

It takes several seconds for my fuzzy brain to catch up to

reality.

I'm in 119, sleeping in a dead stranger's bed.

I reach out for the lamp on the nightstand. When I touch it, a warm glow illuminates the room, and I realize I didn't wander into a guest room as I'd thought. There's a soft-looking sweater draped over a high-backed chair and a cluster of beauty products crowding the bureau.

Whoever lived in this room could have been my age — maybe the president's daughter or a favorite niece. And now she's gone.

I sit up quickly and slide off the bed. Careful not to make a sound, I open the door and tiptoe down the stairs to the living area. A shadow moves in front of the massive window, and I let out a little yelp of surprise.

The figure turns. It's only Celdon.

"Sorry. I didn't mean to scare you."

I take several breaths to calm my racing heart. "What are you doing up?" I ask.

"Couldn't sleep." His voice sounds very far away, but when he turns to me, it's the same old Celdon. "Dead guy's compartment and all."

"They're all dead guys' compartments," I mutter.

"True. But that doesn't make it any less creepy."

I can't argue with that.

Flipping on my interface, I'm startled to see that it's almost twenty-three hundred.

"Do you know what time it is?" I ask, feeling a little frantic.

"Yeah."

"You shouldn't have let me sleep so long! The supply train will be here soon."

"I was going to wake you up, but I thought you could use all the sleep you could get."

"Well . . . we should get moving."

Celdon clears his throat. "Yeah, we should."

The silence that stretches between us is heavy with unspoken fears. Neither of us wants to acknowledge that the supply train might not come. We don't have time to dwell on that possibility.

Taking one more look around the luxurious open floor plan, I promise myself that I won't have to spend another night in a dead man's compartment. And I'm *certainly* not going to be stuck here for the rest of my life.

two

Celdon

I've always tried to avoid silence. Silence feels like death — and there's plenty of death here to go around.

I never quite realized what a long descent it is from Systems to the lower levels. It seems a million times longer in the dark with the strap of my bag cutting into my shoulder and nothing to distract me other than the sound of Harper's breathing.

It's kind of amazing to think we have an entire compound to ourselves, but I've never wanted to leave a place as much as I do now.

We splash through yet *another* puddle of standing water on the middle landing, and Harper quickens her pace. She reaches the next level first and throws her weight against the metal door, bathing the stairwell in the harsh glow of the emergency lights emanating from the Recon tunnel.

Seeing her standing there ankle-deep in cloudy water with her jacket rolled up to the elbows, I realize how much stronger she is than me. Bid Day didn't destroy her. If anything, her time in Recon has made her tougher and more determined.

The telltale rumble of the approaching train echoes down the tunnel, and relief shoots through my body like a hit of surge. We won't be stuck here forever.

"Come on!" calls Harper, throwing the door open wider.

I take the last few stairs two at a time and join her out in the tunnel.

The Recon level in 119 is even dingier than it is back home. The cinderblock walls are a drab institutional gray, the dirty tile is broken in several places, and the metal compartment doors we pass have obscene messages carved into the chipped paint.

The screech of brakes is so loud that it hurts my ears, and my heart speeds up at the prospect of escaping this hellhole.

As we near the "T" in the tunnel that leads to the Underground, I hear the train doors roll open and the slap of workers' boots on the platform.

Harper's breathing has picked up, and her knuckles are white against the wall as she waits for the workers to vacate the premises.

Somebody barks orders that are indistinguishable over the rumble of activity. Dollies roll down the train, and the workers bang around some more, unloading the empty crates. Harper peeks around the corner and then whips around so fast that we nearly bang heads.

"Hey! What the —"

"Move! Move! Move!" she hisses.

"Why?"

"They're coming down here!"

I freeze. Something isn't right. The Operations workers are supposed to be heading up to Health and Rehab — not slumming down in Recon. But I force my legs to move and follow Harper down the dark tunnel at a run.

When we reach a row of compartments, she stops and tries the first door. It doesn't budge.

She jiggles the handle again and turns to me with a wild look in her eyes. "I thought you unlocked all the doors remotely!"

My brain is struggling to connect the dots, but I finally realize what the problem is. "The remote unlock command must have timed out."

She growls in frustration and tries another. I open my mouth to tell her it's futile, but then she turns and sprints down the tunnel away from the Underground.

I follow at a brisk limp. My legs feel heavy and sore after traipsing through the compound yesterday, and I'm definitely not as fit as she is.

We wind through the maze of compartments until we reach a set of double doors. A tarnished placard over the entrance reads "training center."

"No!" Harper breathes.

I glance down. There's a chain threaded through the door handles and a heavy-duty padlock holding it in place.

She wheels around and tries another door, which swings open easily.

"Come on!" she whispers.

I follow her inside. The room is cramped and chilly and reeks of plastic and mildew. I only have a second to survey our surroundings before the door slides closed and thrusts us into total darkness.

Most of the available floor space is occupied by tall metal shelves filled with rubber bins and stacks of gray uniforms. Plastic crates, defunct workout equipment, and overflowing bins of ration packets are scattered haphazardly between the rows.

This must be the supply room.

I take one step forward and trip over something tall and wide, barely saving myself from a face-plant into a metal shelf.

"Shh!" Harper hisses.

I roll my eyes.

Then I hear a door creak open and the nearby rumble of a dolly. Muffled voices float through the wall from the other side, and there's a loud scraping sound as somebody shifts something heavy.

"They're in the weapons room," Harper breathes.

"I kind of wish we were in there and they were in here," I mutter. We wouldn't have to worry about being caught if we were trapped in a room full of assault rifles.

But before I can voice the joke to Harper, a door to my right swings open, and a triangle of light spills onto the floor.

My stomach drops. The weapons room and the supply room are connected, and someone is coming in here.

The Operations worker flips a switch, and the lights flicker on one by one. There's just a single shelving unit between me and him, and I'm barely concealed by a tub of water bags.

I try to make my labored breathing as quiet as possible, but it still seems loud enough for anyone in the vicinity to hear. The worker moves down the row of supplies, and a head of messy brown hair appears.

The worker is preoccupied with a shelf of ammunition. He's reading the labels on the crates carefully, and I can tell this guy's never loaded a gun in his life.

Finally, he seems to find what he's looking for and turns to grab his dolly. I see his ear and then the flesh of his cheek right before a black blur leaps forward and clobbers him on the back of the head.

The guy was still turning when he was struck, and I see the light leave his dark brown eyes. He collapses onto the ground like a sack of potatoes, and I gape openmouthed at the spot where he was just standing.

Harper is hovering behind him, holding a small corroded barbell plate between her hands. She looks horrified.

"Oh my god," she mutters. "Did I kill him?"

"Probably!"

I bend down to check the guy's pulse. It takes me a minute

to find it, and I let out a breath of relief when I feel the steady rhythm of blood beneath my finger.

"He's alive."

"I just panicked!" she whispers, glancing over her shoulder at the door to the weapons room. "I think the other guy left."

"Shit!" *Harper just knocked a guy unconscious!*

"What do we do?" she splutters.

"I don't know! Leave?"

I can't believe she just knocked somebody out and expects *me* to come up with a plan.

"I had to," she says, as though she's reading my mind. "If he saw you, he would have blown our whole cover. Constance would have dragged us in . . . tortured us . . ."

I nod, but my brain is still screaming *What the fuck?*

Just when I think things can't get any more ridiculous, Harper bends down and tugs on the guy's limp arm.

"Can you help me?"

"What are you doing?"

"Getting him up," she says, as though this is obvious. "We can't just leave him here."

"The hell we can't! It's not like he's dead."

"Do you really want Constance questioning why one of their workers is missing? And what's going to happen when they find him?"

"I don't think he saw me."

"We're wasting time!" she groans. "Just help me!"

I'm still staring at her like she's crazy — because she is — but I toss my bag in the corner and bend down to get a grip on Mr. Nosey.

The guy weighs a ton. He keeps slipping off my shoulder, and when I yank his arm more securely around my neck, it feels too weak and flimsy to support his weight.

Together, Harper and I drag him out of the supply room and down the dark tunnel. I'm already sweating bullets, and my hand hurts from holding the guy's wrist in a death grip. If I loosen my hold on him for even a second, he's going to slip right out of my arms like a bag of Jell-O.

Miraculously, we don't encounter another living soul as we make our way back to the Underground platform, but I'm starting to panic again. It's hard enough to sneak onto the train without being seen, and now we have an extra 170 pounds of dead weight slowing us down.

Harper carefully transfers her half of the unconscious guy to me, and his mass seems to triple. My knees shake under the weight, and she checks to see if the coast is clear.

"Now!" she breathes, bending down to take some of the weight back.

I feel no immediate relief, so she must just be holding his hand or something. But we start moving, and somehow my legs manage to propel us forward.

I don't look around. I don't watch where I'm going. I'm pretty sure I black out somewhere between the Recon tunnel and the train, but when I become aware of my surroundings again, I'm lifting up my foot to step onto the car and depositing the Operations worker behind a stack of crates.

I breathe a loud sigh of relief and try to straighten my crushed spine. My shoulders and back are still screaming, but Harper looks energized and alert. She definitely wasn't carrying her fair share.

"Come on," she says, moving toward the end of the car.

"Huh?"

"You want to ride back to the compound with him? What if he wakes up?"

Point taken. He's going to have one hell of a headache —

possibly brain damage — from Harper's psychotic assault.

The voices are back on the platform again, and I follow her frantically to the next car. The workers haven't loaded any cargo in here yet, so we keep moving until we find one with a few stacks of crates to hide behind.

The workers' voices are drawing nearer. There's a loud *clang* as somebody rolls a dolly onto the car, and the dust bunnies near my feet shift as the worker deposits some more crates in front of mine.

My heart is pumping so hard that I can't hear anything except the blood throbbing in my ears, and when somebody slams our car door shut, I nearly cry in relief.

"We made it," Harper whispers.

I lean back against the side of the car and wait for my cardiac episode to end. "Yeah."

We don't speak again until the last car door slams and the train lurches beneath us. I feel the wheels grinding along the track as it slowly picks up speed, and I wait with bated breath for someone to burst in at the last minute and throw us off the train.

No one does.

As the empty platform flashes by and we're swallowed by the dark tunnel, I expect to feel a sweet rush of relief that we're leaving 119 behind.

But with an unconscious Operations worker lying two doors down, Constance gunning for Harper's death, and a compound full of rotting corpses, all I can think is that our problems have just begun.

three

Eli

I t's strange to think that I've seen more of my brother in the past twenty-four hours than in the past thirteen years combined.

I can't stop watching Constance's surveillance footage of the Fringe. It's the only concrete evidence that a member of my family is still alive — that I didn't imagine Owen.

His cameo doesn't even last thirty seconds, but there's no doubt it's him. The crooked L-shaped scar on his left bicep is a dead giveaway — a souvenir from the time he clipped a tree on his dirt bike.

The rest of his features are hidden in shadow, but I can just make out the suspicious arch of his brow and the hard set of a jaw that reminds me of Dad.

He and I could be twins, but we're very different people. We got separated the night our parents were murdered, when I was eleven and Owen was thirteen.

Three years later, I was brought into the compound, while Owen was left out on the Fringe to be raised by drifters.

All those years of hard living have taken a toll on him. Now that he's an adult, he's tormented by suspicion and determined to bring down the compounds.

I glance at the time blinking in the corner of the wall screen. It's oh-seven hundred, which means I've been here all night. Nobody uses the Recon surveillance room after hours, so I knew I'd be safe.

It's nothing compared to Constance's setup — just a glorified closet crowded with monitors. The walls are covered in faded maps of nearby towns, and a leaderboard in the corner of every screen details the date an area was last cleared of drifters.

On screen, I watch Owen stalk out of the frame. Then I smack the keyboard again and rewind the footage.

As far as I know, this is the only video Constance has of Owen, and it seems strange to me that he would get caught on camera after living like a ghost all these years.

The drifters are planning something — something huge — and Owen's appearance makes it seem as though he's taunting the compound. He's had the same smug expression since we were kids: *come and get me, motherfuckers.*

He couldn't have known *I'd* be watching this footage. Recon relies on heat mapping to gauge how many warm bodies are holed up in the towns surrounding the compound. I didn't even know that Constance's reach extended to the radiation-soaked desert — not that I'm surprised. There seems to be no limit to what they're capable of.

All the public areas within the compound and dozens of compartments are under surveillance. They used my computer to spy on me and drained Harper's bank account to keep her from leaving. They probably know where I am right now.

Owen moves out of sight, and I pause the recording again. I'm just about to rewind the footage when a blurry sign behind him catches my eye.

I zoom in on the image and squint at the writing. It's one of those pre–Death Storm novelty signs that reads, "Hog Parking Only — Violators are Cruisin' for a Bruisin'."

I *know* that sign. I've *seen* that sign.

I hastily pull up the file of my deployment history and

pound in my password. I remember the most recent deployments, but the Green Valley mission is a little fuzzy. At least I *think* that was the town with the biker bar.

I didn't leave any descriptive notes about the town itself — just the number of drifters I killed and their locations. Luckily, the person who visited after me was more thorough. He even took a few photos of the town's major landmarks.

Sure enough, I see the biker bar in all its rough-neck glory: weathered wood siding, the rattlesnake emblem burned into the wood, and an outdated sign advertising Mud Wrestling Mondays.

Suddenly, the door to the surveillance room creaks. I hit "escape" to hide the files and spin around in my chair.

I've got an excuse on the tip of my tongue, but it's only Miles. His towering tattooed frame fills the doorway in an intimidating way, but I'm relieved to see him.

"Finally!" he snaps. "I've been looking for you everywhere."

"What?"

"It's almost oh-eight hundred. You're gonna be late for training."

"It can't be." I rub my eyes and glance at the time again. Sure enough, I've pissed away another forty-five minutes, but it felt like five. "Shit."

Miles is staring at me as though I've gone nuts. "Have you been here all night?"

"I . . . yeah."

"Never knew you to pull an all-nighter for Jayden," he says, a suspicious edge to his voice. "What the hell is going on?"

"Nothing, I just . . ."

I trail off so I don't have to make up an excuse. I know I shouldn't tell Miles about Owen — or that Harper ran away to 119 — but all those secrets are weighing on my mind. I've never really needed anyone, but right now, I desperately want to unload my troubles on Miles.

"What's going on?" he prompts.

Miles may be more of a brawler than a strategist in the ring, but he's one of the most intuitive people I've ever met.

I let out a tired breath and swivel around to pull up the footage of Owen. I rewind and hit "enter," and the recording starts to play.

Owen's appearance is over before Miles really has a chance to focus, and when he leaves the frame, Miles looks more confused than before.

"What am I supposed to be looking at? Is this ours?"

"No. It's surveillance footage from Constance."

"Those assholes have surveillance cameras on the Fringe?"

"Yeah."

He swears. "And they've just been sitting on this information the entire time? We could have *used* this."

If Miles weren't my only real friend, I'd be scared shitless. He's terrifying on his best day, and right now, he looks furious.

"That's not what I wanted to show you."

I hit rewind and play the footage again. He watches the recording over my shoulder, and I freeze the video and point at Owen. "Look like anyone you know?"

"How can you tell? I can't even see his face."

"That's my brother."

There's a long pause.

"Huh?"

"My brother . . . Owen."

For a moment, Miles stands frozen. He's staring at the screen in deep concentration, and I realize I only mentioned Owen once — back when we were kids in the Institute.

"The brother who was killed the night your parents were

murdered?"

"That's what I thought."

"He's . . . He's *alive*?"

I nod slowly. Hell, I can hardly believe it myself.

"Shit!"

"Yeah."

"Wait . . . is he a drifter?"

"What else would you call someone who lives out on the Fringe?"

"Oh my god." Miles's eyes grow wide, and he reaches up to rub the back of his head. "Shit, man. I'm sorry . . . But are you sure? I mean, how can you even tell that's him? You can't see his face."

"Because I met him . . . the last time Harper and I were deployed."

Miles's eyes bug out, but his expression quickly turns serious. When he speaks next, his voice is slow and deliberate. "What do you mean you *met* him?"

"I mean he saved my life. A couple gang bangers were torturing him for information, and Harper and I got caught in a shootout. I would have been killed, but he shot one of the other drifters. When I saw his face, I just knew."

"Are you sure he's your brother, though?"

"You don't think I checked?" I ask, a little irritated that he's so reluctant to accept my story.

"Okay, okay. I'm only asking. I mean, it just seems so . . . unlikely."

"I know."

"So you two talked?"

I nod.

Miles jerks his head around behind him, as though he's worried someone might overhear us. "*Are you out of your fucking mind?*"

"What was I supposed to do?" I snap. "I thought he was dead all these years!"

"Dude! If Jayden finds out you were talking to a drifter, you'll be in the cages for the rest of your life! Shit. Treason is grounds for lethal injection."

"You think I don't know that?" I growl. "He's my brother!"

"You're not thinking of trying to find him again, are you?"

I glance at the screen. This conversation is not playing out the way I'd hoped.

"You're going to try to find him!" Miles snaps in disbelief. "Eli, you're gonna get caught! Are you seeing all this?" He gestures around at the monitors. "They're watching you everywhere! They're probably watching us right now!"

"So what?"

Miles shakes his head and then falls silent for several seconds.

"Are you thinking of *joining* him?" he asks in a husky voice. "Going AWOL and turning drifter?"

"No!" I splutter. "No. Of course not."

He looks marginally relieved, but he's still shaking his head.

"I'm not crazy," I add. "You know what's crazy? The board thinking we can protect the compound when we have no fucking clue who these guys are or what they're planning."

"What do you mean?"

"The drifters want to bring down the compounds. To them, we're the enemy. Hell, we've been killing off all their friends for years."

"You sound like one of them."

"I'm not! It's just the truth."

Miles sinks down into the chair next to me as though our conversation has taken everything out of him. He presses his hands together and lets out a hard breath against his fingers. "Eli, I want you to listen to me: They are the enemy. The drifters want us all dead. They're the people you need to be fighting — not Jayden, not the board, not even Constance."

I open my mouth to speak, but he points his index finger at me in a commanding way that makes the words die on my lips.

"I know you've got this crusade against Jayden and Constance because they tried to put Riley six feet under, but people like them exist to keep us alive. The drifters are the real threat. They're the ones we're fighting.

"I know your brother being one of them makes you question everything. Shit, you'd be fucked in the head if it *didn't*. But don't confuse the issue."

When Miles finishes, I'm completely speechless.

Miles — the guy who shamelessly steals extra rations and takes on illegal fights — still believes in Recon's mission. He still thinks the compound has his best interest in mind. He believes we're doing the right thing.

And if he believes it, that means everyone else must believe it, too. In that moment, it hits me just how tight a hold the compound's leaders have on our minds.

When I finally find my voice, it's hoarse with indignation. "What we do is *murder*."

Miles shakes his head slowly, his dark brown eyes serious and unyielding. "No, Eli. We're fighting a war."

"What war?" I yell. "They've got nothing, and we have everything! They're blowing us up with our own mines, for god's sake."

"What has gotten into you?" he snaps, jutting his face forward so it's closer to mine. "You of all people used to understand. You used to hate the drifters more than anybody."

I scoff and look away, but Miles isn't letting this go.

"Eli, those people are the ones who killed all your cadets. They're the ones who killed your parents."

"Don't you get it? *Those people* are somebody else's parents. And we just shoot them like they're not even human."

"Whatever. We wouldn't even be having this conversation if it weren't for Riley. She's got you all turned around."

"I've got it under control," I snap.

"No, you don't. That's your problem. You think you can handle Constance and the drifters on your own like you're some one-man army. But the only way Riley's ever gonna live is if she takes that ticket to 119. Period."

His words settle in my stomach like a brick. "She already did."

"What?"

"I sent her and Celdon to 119. She's gone."

Miles gives me a funny look. "No, she's not."

"Yeah, she is."

Miles's eyes grow wide. "Dude, you need to get some sleep."

"What are you talking about?"

"I just saw her."

My spine goes rigid, and my heart speeds up. "What?"

"Yeah." He glances at the time again. "She's in the training center right now with all your cadets."

Even though I know it's impossible, a bolt of electricity shoots through my chest. It stings with fear and dread, but it also leaves a trail of warmth in its wake.

Harper can't be here. Miles must be talking about someone else who just looks like her, but I have to see for myself.

Without another word, I fly out of my chair and squeeze past the servers crowding the doorway. I shoot out of the surveillance room and down the dimly lit tunnel toward the training center.

The smell of bleach and sweat hits my nostrils before I even open the doors, and when I step inside, my senses are overwhelmed by activity after hours alone in the dark.

It's nearly oh-eight hundred, so the training center is swarming with cadets warming up and waiting along the walls for their commanding officers.

I carve a path around the older Recon veterans stretching on the mats, looking for a dark head of silky hair and a pair of luminous gray eyes.

In my desperation, I almost call out for her, but there's no way she'd be able to hear me over the cadets' chatter and the heavy *clink* of weights. As someone passes above me on the suspended metal track, the loud shaking adds to the din.

Out of the corner of my eye, I catch the flick of a dark ponytail.

If Miles is seeing things, then I am, too. But there's no mistaking Harper's lean profile or her energetic cadence as she jogs around the track.

The fear simmering just beneath the surface spills into my bloodstream and ignites a fire in my chest.

Miles wasn't hallucinating. Harper is back.

four

Harper

The first rule of avoiding murder? Don't go anywhere alone. Stay away from dark tunnels and shady underground fights. Stick to public places with lots of people.

That's the *only* reason I dragged myself to training this morning after Celdon and I returned from 119. I didn't sleep at all last night. My mind was reeling from everything we'd learned about the virus and the danger we'd be facing now that we're back on Constance's radar.

Jayden is going to try to make me disappear — no doubt about it — but I don't plan on going down easily.

As I round the corner of the suspended metal track, I inch closer and closer to Lenny. Her normally creamy complexion is flushed from the run, and her fiery red braid is swinging back and forth between her shoulder blades.

She isn't as fast as I am, but she's pushing herself this morning. She beat me to the training center and didn't even stop to talk when I arrived.

Her impending deployment must have lit a fire under her, and now she's training like crazy in the hope that if she's fit enough, fast enough, and strong enough, she might be able to outrun death on the Fringe.

Blaze is another twenty yards ahead and gaining speed. When I got to the training center, the first thing I noticed was that he'd trimmed his spiky copper hair into a clean crew cut. His normally carefree expression mirrors Lenny's look of panic and determination, and his shirt is already drenched with sweat.

"Hey! Riley!" calls an angry voice from below.

I know that voice. It sends a surge of heat through my chest that quickly spreads to my extremities.

I quicken my pace and glance down to the training floor. Eli is standing in the crowd, staring up at me.

Even though it's only been a little more than a day since I last saw him, I drink in the sight of him as if it's been a year. Those sharp blue eyes are boring into mine, and the severe set of his jaw makes it look as though his face has been cut from stone.

This is not the concerned, compassionate Eli from the Fringe or the intense, fiery version who pinned me up against the wall. This is Eli the asshole, and he looks pissed.

"Get down here!" he yells.

Lenny glances over her shoulder and raises an eyebrow. "What did you do?" she pants, a devilish grin cracking her anxious expression.

"No idea."

I jog around her and take my time coming down the rickety stairs toward Eli. But as soon as my feet hit the floor, he's striding toward me with purpose.

In all his handsome, furious glory, I have the bizarre urge to tear off his uniform and run my hands down his body. His chiseled chest is rising and falling rapidly under his gray fatigues, and his powerful arms are clenched at his sides.

But as soon as he gets close enough to kiss, he clenches a hand around my bicep and drags me across the training center like a disobedient child. I don't look up, but I can feel the other cadets' eyes on my back as Eli drags me toward the exit.

Indignation flashes through me, and a hot flush spills down my neck. As soon as we clear the double doors, I yank my arm out of his grip and shove him in the chest — hard.

Eli looks momentarily stunned but doesn't relax his posture.

"What the hell is your problem?" I snarl.

"My problem?" he repeats, eyes flashing. "What the *fuck* are you doing here?"

"Keep your voice down," I hiss, glancing over my shoulder.

Through the open doors, I can see a few cadets craning their necks to get a good look at us. Eli's sudden fits of rage aren't a secret in Recon, but it's not every day that a lieutenant singles out a cadet and drags her out of the training center.

I'm unprepared for the intensity of my outrage. Eli has no right to order me around — especially after he lied to me about coming to 119.

I'm hurt and humiliated and a little offended that he's so unhappy to see me. I mean, I didn't expect him to sweep me off my feet and kiss me in front of everyone, but a tiny bit of enthusiasm would have been nice.

Eli's eyebrows are furrowed in deep concern. He's *definitely* not working up to a passionate kiss. "Harper . . . why did you come back? You shouldn't have come back!"

"We didn't have a choice."

He frowns. "Did they send you back?"

"N-No."

"Then why are you here? You should have stayed at 119."

I look around again to check that the tunnel is deserted and lower my voice. "We *couldn't.*"

I take a deep breath, steeling myself to voice the horrible reality of the situation. "There *is* no 119. Everyone there is dead."

Eli stares at me in disbelief. Then a look of intense distress flits across his face. "*They're all dead?*" he whispers.

I nod. "We looked everywhere. We couldn't figure out where

they all could have gone. And then we saw the dead level . . ."

A violent shudder rolls through me. Eli twitches as though he wants to pull me into his arms, but then he swallows and clenches his fists.

"We went poking around in the medical ward," I continue. "Celdon accessed the network so we could check the news feeds and hack into their medical records. They all died from some kind of virus, but Health and Rehab didn't know what it was or how to cure it."

"But what about the supply shipments? Why would our people go there if . . ."

"They've been looting from 119 — cleaning out their medical supplies and who knows what else. Those Operations workers *must* be part of Constance."

"And you didn't find out how the virus was introduced in the first place?"

I shake my head. "We didn't get that far. But Celdon snagged all the files. He's going to see what Sawyer can make of them. Maybe she can tell us what happened."

Eli lets out a full-body sigh, and his gaze drifts over my shoulder. Now that I'm this close to him, I can see the deep purplish shadows etched under his eyes. It looks as though he hasn't slept since I left.

"What are we going to do?" he mutters, running a hand through his hair.

His words wash over me like ice-cold water, and the hurt I felt when I found out he lied hits me all over again. I know I shouldn't even say it — his dishonesty is not our most pressing problem — but the words spill out before I can stop them. "There is no 'we,' Eli. Not anymore."

Now I have his full attention. "What?"

"You lied to me," I say, unable to conceal the pain in my

voice. "You never asked for Celdon's help or appealed to bring Owen to 119. You never had any intention of joining us."

"That's not true."

"It isn't?" I snap, glaring up at him. "What was the plan, then?"

"I . . . I was going to follow you. But I had to see Owen first. He was never going to agree to live in 119, but I thought maybe he could relocate to be closer. Then if I was placed in Recon, I'd at least have a *chance* of seeing him again."

I hadn't expected that, but it doesn't do much to dampen the sting of betrayal. "Why should I believe you?"

"I don't know, Harper! Maybe because I've done nothing except protect you since the day I met you. Why would this change anything?"

"It changes everything!" I cry. "I can't trust you!"

Eli closes his eyes and lets out a frustrated growl. "What was I supposed to do? I had to get you out of here, and lying was the only way to make you leave."

"It doesn't matter! When two people are together, they aren't supposed to lie to each other. And you've lied to me *twice* now."

Eli's eyes widen in surprise. I know bringing up his lie about my recruitment is a low blow, but that isn't the part of my rant that captures his attention.

"Together?" he repeats.

Oh god. My face glows bright red, and I try to backpedal. "I just mean . . . it doesn't even . . ." I let out a burst of air. "I know you only did what you did to protect me, but I can't be with someone who's going to lie to me just because it's more convenient than the truth."

"*More convenient?* Are you serious? If I hadn't lied, you could be rotting away in the dead level by now. Would that be better?"

"No!" I splutter. "I know why you did it, Eli, but it doesn't mean it was the right thing to do."

Now he looks truly furious. Those blue eyes I could get lost in for days have turned cold and empty. His warm, kissable mouth has tightened into an angry line, and he's doing his signature "towering over me" thing.

When he speaks, his voice is barely audible — and deadly serious. "It *was* the right thing to do, Harper. I don't *care* if you're too stubborn or pissed off to see it. Go pout about it . . . talk it over with Sawyer or whatever. I don't care. But you need to get out of this compound — with or without me."

He takes one last second to let his words sink in and then brushes past me into the training center. A few mutinous tears are stinging in my eyes, but I wipe them away furiously and whip around to follow him at a distance.

By the time I join the other cadets in line, Eli is already giving instructions in his cool detached way. It's as though the last few minutes never happened.

I find it infuriating that it's so easy for him to compartmentalize, but I'm more angry with myself. I *hate* letting my emotions run the show, and lately I haven't been able to control them. True, there have been some unusual circumstances — getting the rug pulled out from under me with my placement in Recon; finding out that the entire VocAps system was a lie; getting on Constance's bad side; getting shot at and blown up on the Fringe; killing people and nearly getting killed myself — but it's no excuse.

I need to get my shit together. Otherwise, Jayden's going to have no trouble manipulating me.

My own fucked-up fixation with Eli is the reason I was so hurt and angry about his life-saving deception. He's right. It *was* the right thing to do. I never would have left the compound if he'd told me the truth, and there was no question that I needed to.

"Riley!"

I jump at the sound of Eli's voice.

"Yes, sir?" I *hate* that I have to call Eli "sir."

"Did you hear what I just said?"

I bite the inside of my cheek to keep myself from rolling my eyes. "No, sir."

Eli drags in a big breath as though he's gearing up for some big douchey display of authority, but then the fight leaves his eyes. "I said that you'd work with Adams on the sim course today. He needs some extra work there to prepare for deployment."

"Yes, sir."

Eli dismisses us, and I look down the line for Blaze. With his serious new haircut, he looks tougher and more intimidating, yet there's this raw terror in his eyes I recognize from my first deployment: It's the sudden realization that you're woefully unprepared for what you're about to face and that your days could be numbered.

I offer him a weak smile and jerk my head toward the double doors. "Ready?"

Blaze breaks into a grin and follows me toward the exit.

As soon as we're out of the noisy training center, he quickens his stride until he's right at my shoulder. "What was all that about?"

"What?"

"The thing with Parker. I saw him drag you out of the training center. He looked pissed."

"Oh . . . you saw that?"

"Yeah. It was kind of a dick move . . . yanking you out in front of everybody like that."

"Yeah, it was."

"So . . . why did he?"

I sigh and throw my body against the heavy door leading to the simulation course. I don't want to make up some lie to get Blaze off my back, but it's not as though I can tell him what's really going on.

"He was mad that I took the fight with Marta."

Blaze's eyes widen in surprise, and for the first time, I notice they're an unusual blue-green color.

"Why? He does illegal fights. And I thought Parker was in on that whole thing."

"He was at first, but he didn't want me to fight Marta. He thought she was too dangerous."

"Well, he was right."

I try to ignore the twinge of irritation that statement provokes. I still have a black eye to remind me of that fact; I don't need everybody telling me how wrong I was.

But instead of taking my frustration out on Blaze, I slide the bolt into place and flip the heavy switch. The stage lighting flickers on corner by corner in the gigantic open space, and I get a slight pang of nausea when the fake cars and rock formations come into view.

The course is designed to provide realistic target practice, with painted outlines of people jumping out from behind obstacles and returning fire with harmless pellets. I spent a lot of time here before my first deployment — and every week since — but the simulated attacks don't come close to the real thing.

I run over to the door that connects the sim course to the armory and swipe my key card. I select a weapon from the touchpad and check out an extra rifle for Blaze.

As soon as I finish, there's a loud buzzing sound, and the drawer below the counter clicks into place. I open the small metal door and find two rifles and several extra mags ready to go.

I toss Blaze some goggles and don a pair myself. He stretches the band absently, as though he wants to say something but isn't sure if he should.

"Just so you know . . . I'm not as oblivious as everybody else is," he murmurs.

I feel my mouth fall open but quickly school my expression. "What?"

"People forget who my father is."

I bite the inside of my mouth to keep myself from letting out a stream of vial words about Shane. He sent his men to kill me on Jayden's orders. They dragged me to the dead level, bound me, and beat me. They would have finished the job, too, if Eli hadn't intervened.

I know Blaze is nothing like his father, but it still awakens that fight-or-flight instinct inside me. "Trust me, I know who your father is."

"Well, then you understand how being his son would give me a talent for knowing when people are lying to me. Parker wasn't yelling at you because of the fight."

"Sorry to disappoint you," I say, choking out a fake laugh. "But you know how Eli is. Everything has to be his way."

Blaze's eyes flicker up to mine, and he's wearing a knowing look that throws me off balance. It isn't as intense or intimidating as Eli's gaze, but his eyes reveal an unsettling amount of intuition and empathy.

He *knows* there's something going on with me and Eli — he just doesn't know what.

It occurs to me that everybody underestimates Blaze because he's quiet and easygoing, but he's probably the most prepared for deployment. He's fast and fit and surprisingly smart, but it's his instincts that will save him out there.

Blaze lowers his gaze but still doesn't put on his goggles. He seems to be lost in thought, battling some grand internal debate.

"Okay," he says finally. "Just let me know if Parker gets to be too much for you."

"Too much for me?"

He grins. "I know you're tough, Harper. But he's way too intense sometimes, and I don't want him pushing you around just because he thinks he can."

"Eli doesn't —"

"Yeah, he does," says Blaze, an uncharacteristic note of anger in his voice. "He thinks he can push you just because you push back, but that doesn't make it right. He can be a real asshole sometimes."

I can't argue with that. Then again, I can be a real asshole, too.

Staring at Blaze, I suddenly have the feeling that I could tell him everything and he would understand. But I don't.

He pulls on his goggles, and I can tell this conversation is over.

"Let me know," he murmurs. "I'm not scared of him."

five

Eli

"Explode off your feet!" I say for what feels like the hundredth time. "You're gonna keep doing it until I see some real power, Horwitz."

Across the training center, Lenny lets out an angry battle cry and aims a wild kick at the standup punching bag.

"Save it," I say sharply, forcing myself to summon some patience. "You're stuck here until you nail the whole sequence."

Since Harper is working with Blaze on the sim course, today is the Lenny Horwitz show. Jayden plans on deploying Lenny and Blaze within a few weeks, and right now, Lenny is horribly unprepared for the Fringe.

To wear her down and push her to the next level, I set up a hellacious obstacle course that runs the entire length of the training center. Lenny's bum leg has always held her back on running and footwork, and everything on the course is designed for explosive speed and coordination.

I've lined up two rows of tires for her to hop through and a series of progressively higher box jumps. As soon as she sticks the last one, Kindra is supposed to attack her, and Lenny has to deploy one of the self-defense maneuvers we've worked.

Then Bear throws a rope around her waist, and she has to fight his considerable weight to keep moving down the course. It ends with a side kick powerful enough to knock over the standing bag.

That's how it's *supposed* to go, anyway. She hasn't knocked it over once, and the other two kind of suck at tough love.

Kindra advances for the attack as though she's going in for a hug, and Bear is being too easy on her. He throws Lenny an apologetic look as she aims another pitiful kick at the bag, and a stream of angry curses floats back to me.

"If you spent *half* as much time running the course as you spend complaining, you'd be done by now," I yell.

Lenny stiffens. I can't see her face, but I'm sure she's rolling her eyes.

Finally she turns and shuffles back to where I'm standing. I can feel the frustration pouring off her, and her face is beet red from exhaustion. She's making an effort, but she's overthinking everything instead of just blazing through it.

"Nice try, Parker," says a voice behind me. "But even *you* can't fix two left feet."

I turn around and instantly wish I hadn't. Jayden's lapdog, Seamus Duffy, is coming up behind me.

Seamus used to be one of those annoyingly positive officers who went through the motions of training without ever forcing his cadets to make any real progress. All the higher-ups liked him because he did everything by the book, but I always knew he was full of shit.

When I was deployed, he took over training my squad. Then Jayden got her claws into him and started using him as her personal errand boy. The power must have gone to his head, because he went from being Mr. Sunshine to a cocky douchebag overnight.

"Kiss my ass, Duffy," I call as soon as he's within earshot.

"Ooh. Somebody's testy this morning."

"Because I know Jayden only lets you out of your cage to come annoy me. So get on with it. Some of us have work to do."

"I can see that." Seamus eyes Lenny up and down and wrinkles his freckly face into a condescending stare.

She glares daggers at him, which I find hilarious for some reason.

"Working hard, I see," Seamus muses. "That's good. I think your deployment date is coming up pretty soon."

I step carefully between them before Lenny hurls an insult at Seamus and gets herself court-martialed. "Like I said . . . lots to do. So if you've come to *summon* me, let's get it over with."

I should get a medal for my saintlike self-control.

"Who's she going out with?" Seamus asks, referring to her partner on the Fringe. By his tone, he might as well have asked, "Who's getting stuck with her?"

That pisses me off.

"I don't know," I say, acting casual. "I thought maybe I'd ask Miles to show her the ropes."

Seamus's light-blond eyebrows shoot up in surprise, and Lenny looks just as shocked.

"Really?" she asks.

It's no secret that Miles and I are best friends, and I knew Lenny would see that matchup as a major vote of confidence. I'm not sure if I suggested it to make her feel better or to take the wind out of Seamus's sails, but either way, Miles is going to kill me.

"Yeah, why not?"

Lenny smirks at Seamus, and I swear she grows about three inches.

Seamus looks a little taken aback and turns his full attention to me. "The commander wants to see you for your briefing. I already sent Riley."

"Another briefing?" I snap. "We were just deployed!"

He shrugs. "Crazy times."

"I'll be back," I say to Lenny. "Keep running the course until you get it perfect. Then I want five miles from everyone."

Bear and Kindra deflate a little, but Lenny is still glowing with pride.

Seamus leads the way out of the training center, but instead of heading to Jayden's office, he turns down the tunnel toward the escalator.

"Where are we going?"

"The commander has a busy day lined up. She asked that you come to her while she's making her rounds."

"Making her rounds *where?*"

Seamus doesn't answer, but it soon becomes clear as he leads me up to the wing above ExCon. There's nothing over here except the loading bay.

I've never exited the compound from this area, but it's how ExCon accesses the solar fields for maintenance. It's a sparse industrial space with steel walls and heavy-duty shelves stretching up to twenty-foot ceilings.

The entire place is lit by short observation windows running along the outer wall, but work lamps glow over men holding soldering irons and standing at table saws.

"Parker!" barks an impatient female voice.

I hold in my groan and turn slowly.

Jayden is standing by the window looking out on the Fringe, and next to her is a man I recognize as Cole Griffin, Undersecretary of Exterior Maintenance and Construction.

He's a burly, hardworking man with a reddish beard and rough, weathered features. Unlike the rest of the board members who wear their taupe suits everywhere to flaunt their position, Griffin seems to prefer the orange and khaki foreman's uniform when he's working in the trenches — probably so ExCon workers will view him as one of their own.

Jayden holds up her index finger to show she'll only be a minute, and I get a pang of irritation at how much she enjoys having me at her beck and call.

I don't know why Jayden is over here or what she'd need to talk to Griffin about. She spends most of her time antagonizing Remy Chaplin, Undersecretary of Reconnaissance.

As I watch, Jayden's mouth twists into her signature "do what I say . . . or else" sneer, and Griffin's expression hardens. Jayden must be steamrolling him on something, and he isn't happy about it. Then her eyes light up in triumph, and she turns on her heel to come join us.

Seamus hands her the folder tucked under his arm just as Harper shuffles around the corner.

"Thank you, Lieutenant," Jayden murmurs. "That will be all."

I raise an eyebrow at her cool dismissal, but Seamus looks unfazed.

"Ahh, Riley," simpers Jayden. "Nice of you to join us."

I glance at Harper to gauge her mood, but I can't read anything except her naked contempt. Three days ago, Jayden tried to have her killed, so I guess a little bitterness is to be expected.

"What's going on here?" I ask Jayden, eyeing the men in orange moving things around on forklifts. I don't come over here much, but I know there isn't normally this much activity in the loading bay.

"We're updating the land mines," she says. "That was the compromise we reached in our strike negotiations. I assured Undersecretary Griffin that we had absolutely no knowledge of hostile survivors on the Fringe — or any survivors, for that matter. But we agreed to take some extra precautions to ensure that his workers felt safe."

"What about *our* workers?" I ask incredulously. "We're the

ones getting blown up by the repurposed land mines."

Jayden's fake smile twitches. "That's being handled. But in the meantime, I suggest you take a different route."

"So it's *not* being handled."

"Why did you call us?" Harper butts in.

Jayden's gaze snaps onto Harper, and I can see the delight radiating from her predatory eyes. She doesn't care that Harper knows she ordered the hit. I think she actually finds it funny.

"I have another assignment for you. I already briefed Parker."

She moves away from the flurry of activity and motions for us to follow.

"This gang of drifters may be the biggest threat the compounds have ever faced. In the last few years, we've had no trouble crippling their forces, but they are growing in numbers. And, if your reports are accurate, they've also made great strides with their technology. We cannot afford a wide-scale breach of the perimeter — not now when things are so . . . volatile."

I roll my eyes. "Volatile" is the understatement of the century. Control has managed to keep a lid on violence within the compound since the tier-three riots, but finding more drifters in the cleared zone would definitely end the grudging truce between ExCon and Recon.

Jayden whips open the file Seamus brought and hands it to Harper. It's one of the stills Constance captured from Fringe surveillance. I recognize the man in the photo as Malcolm Martinez, the cutthroat leader of the Desperados gang.

"I need you to locate this man and terminate him. He is your number one priority."

I can practically see Harper's wheels turning. She wasn't there when Mina led me to Constance's headquarters in Information. Before now, she had no idea how far Constance's reach extended.

"Also keep a lookout for this man," Jayden continues, flipping to the next photograph. It's Jackson Mills, the man Owen feels he owes for his protection.

"He used to be the leader of Nuclear Nation — another gang — but his crew has been absorbed into the Desperados. The old Nuclear Nation members aren't numerous enough to pose a threat, but some of the Desperados would follow Mills if Martinez was out of the picture."

Harper swallows, still avoiding my gaze. I can almost hear what she's thinking: *If Constance knows about Malcolm and Jackson . . .*

Jayden flips the photo over to reveal the last still. It's the image that's burned into my memory from the hours I spent in the Recon surveillance room.

Harper studies the photo for a moment and then drags in a sharp burst of air. She met Owen in person, so the few distinguishing marks visible in the still allow her brain to supply the rest of the face.

"What is it?" Jayden asks. "Have you seen him before?"

Harper swallows. She's scrambling to come up with a good excuse. "N-no. I just didn't know we had surveillance capabilities on the Fringe."

"That's no accident. Unfortunately, we haven't been able to get a clear shot of this man. He's done a decent job of flying under the radar, but you can identify him by that scar on his arm. He's Mills's right-hand man, and he needs to be dealt with."

Jayden snaps the folder closed and glances around to ensure we haven't attracted any unwanted attention. "Review these tonight. Learn their faces and then destroy the photos. This is your mission."

"You want us to kill them?" Harper asks. Her voice is barely audible, but I can detect the undercurrent of fear and desperation there. She still hasn't taken her eyes off the folder.

"I don't expect it will be easy, but it is necessary," says Jayden. "Don't take too long, Parker. I am not a patient woman."

"This isn't our job," snaps Harper.

I freeze, but Harper just glares up at Jayden with the boldness of someone who's already looked death in the face once. Any normal person would shrink under that hateful expression, but it just fuels Jayden's feelings of superiority.

"It is now."

There's palpable tension in the air as Harper reins in her defiance. I know Jayden doesn't need to threaten Celdon's life again to get her to do what she wants; Harper's already seen what Constance is capable of.

Jayden leans forward — close enough to kiss her — and murmurs, "That is all."

Harper pulls back with a withering stare, and I draw her away before she does something *really* stupid . . . like slap Jayden in front of all these people.

She follows me out of the loading bay at a brisk pace, and we're barely out of earshot when she lets out an exasperated growl. "She wants us to assassinate *Owen?*"

"Keep your voice down," I hiss, lengthening my stride to put a little more distance between us and Jayden. "At least she doesn't know who he is . . . yet."

"Well it's only a matter of time!" she splutters. "You two could be twins! The only reason she didn't see it this time was because half his face was hidden."

"Well, there's nothing I can do about that," I say, feeling a smack of frustration.

My white lie about 119 may have damaged Harper's trust in

me, but it's not as if *everything* is my fault.

"I didn't even know Constance was surveilling the Fringe until the other day," I mutter. "But I guess it makes sense. They have cameras everywhere else."

We take the megalift back down to Recon, and when we disembark, the tide of people rushing in the opposite direction forces us to pause our conversation.

It takes lots of elbowing to break through the crowd, and when the sea of people thins out, I quicken my pace to get back to my compartment.

Then Harper's hand closes around my arm, bringing me to a halt just outside my door.

"We can't go in there. They could be watching."

"They're watching us everywhere," I say. "In the megalift, in the training center . . . I don't know if there's a single place in this compound that Constance can't find us."

"What are we going to do?" she asks in a small voice.

I know she's talking about Owen, but that isn't what captures my attention.

As she stares up at me with those earnest silvery-gray eyes, I realize Harper's faith in me isn't gone for good. She needs me to reassure her, but I have no idea what the fuck I'm going to say. She still doesn't know about the other half of my discussion with Jayden. She doesn't know how much is riding on this.

Jayden promised me that if I took out the gang leaders, she'd call off the attempts on Harper's life. I don't trust her or Constance to leave us alone, but now that Harper's back from 119, I have no choice but to go along with Jayden's plan until I come up with something better.

"I don't know," I murmur.

Harper is still gripping my arm, and in the seconds I was lost in thought, I managed to move even closer.

Her scent is all around me — that sweet vanilla perfume mixed with her hypnotic natural fragrance. I know that if I kissed her right now, her skin would be slightly salty from her run, and I have the sudden urge to bend down and taste her.

Harper's lips part slightly as she watches my gaze, and I know we're both thinking of the last kiss we shared in my compartment.

Without another word, I run my hand softly down her arm and cautiously interlace our fingers. She lets out a little sigh, and the look on her face is a mixture of relief and reluctance.

She's still angry that I lied to her, but she's glad that we're a team again. She isn't shutting me out, and I'm touching her the way I've wanted to ever since I put her on that supply train. This is progress.

I turn toward my door so I can punch in my code and pull Harper inside my dark compartment. She follows silently and nudges the door closed behind her.

I lean down to find her warm, soft lips, and she tastes even better than I remember. To my delight, she kisses me back without reservation, and we stumble sideways in the dark.

I move my hand to her hip to pull her closer, and the unwelcome florescent lights kick on automatically.

A tiny startled yelp escapes from Harper's lips. She yanks her mouth away and jumps back as though she was burned.

At first I think she's come to her senses and decided not to forgive me so easily, but when I turn around, I see the source of her surprise.

Mina — the sexy, terrifying Information girl who works for Constance — is lying on my bed. She's wearing a pair of skin-tight black pants and a geometric tank top that shows off her impressive cleavage. She's lying back so her dark brown hair drapes over my pillow, and she's got her feet up as though she owns the place.

The sight of a beautiful girl lounging on my bed should get me excited, but Mina just makes me feel sick to my stomach.

"What the hell?" Harper chokes.

"Sorry to break up the fun," says Mina, flashing a sultry smile. Her gaze flickers between me and Harper. She isn't sorry at all.

As I watch, she stretches her arms like a cat and lets out a soft sigh, digging the pads of her perfectly manicured fingers into my bedspread.

"What the fuck are you doing here?" I growl. Aside from Jayden, Mina is the absolute *last* person I want to see right now.

"So unfriendly."

Mina pulls herself into an upright position, shimmies her ass to the edge of my bed, and looks up at me innocently through endlessly long lashes. "I just came by to get what's mine."

Beside me, Harper stiffens, and I don't even want to see the menacing look she's giving Mina.

"What are you talking about?"

"My gun, silly," she says, bouncing off the bed and landing on her feet. In her teetering black wedges with orange rhinestone heels, she's nearly as tall as me. "I left it here the other night by accident."

I open my mouth to protest, but Mina cuts me off by holding a finger to my lips.

"You look stressed, baby." Her dark gaze flickers down to Harper. "Is it because *she's* here?"

I can practically feel the shock and fury radiating from Harper, and I smack Mina's finger away to put an end to this bullshit.

I cross to my desk and press my thumb to the drawer sensor. It beeps, and I reach inside to grab Mina's compact handgun.

"Here," I say, shoving it into her hand. "Now leave."

Mina lets out a pouty little huff of air and juts out her bottom lip. "You're not as fun as you were the other night." She glances down at Harper and then back to me and cracks a dirty grin. "I'll see you later."

As she turns to pass between us, she scratches four long tangerine fingernails down my chest and brushes her bare shoulder against mine.

The door snaps shut behind her, and I run a hand down my face. "That wasn't what it looked like," I mutter, waiting for the stress to recede. "Mina is part of —"

"Fuck you," Harper snaps.

I pull my hand away from my face and see Harper staring at me with a look of such intense betrayal that it breaks my heart.

"Harper, no," I say quickly. "There's nothing going on between me and Mina."

She lets out a derisive laugh and gestures toward my pillow. The imprint from Mina's perfect ass is still visible right next to it, and I realize just how bad this looks. "Oh, please, Eli. She was lying in your bed!"

"Yeah, because she's an evil little sl—"

"Save it!" she snaps, wheeling around.

"Harper!"

I reach out and grab her arm, but she loads up her fist and shoots it out toward my nose before I even realize she's going to hit me. I slip the jab purely on instinct, but Harper follows up with a nasty overhand right we worked on just last week.

Hot pain radiates from my nose to the back of my skull, and Harper takes the opportunity to yank her arm out of my grasp and stalk out of the room.

The door slams shut behind her, and almost on cue, I feel the hot trickle of blood gushing from my nose.

Under any other circumstances, I'd be thrilled by that punch, but now I don't know how I'm going to fix things with Harper.

Jayden must have sent Mina to my room to remind me in no uncertain terms that Harper's life depends on me killing the drifter leaders. I hate hiding that detail from Harper, but I don't think she'd be able to live with the guilt if she knew I was trading their lives for hers. I still don't know what I'm going to do about Owen, but killing Malcolm and Jackson to save Harper is a no-brainer.

Even though I'm only lying to protect her, Harper has every reason not to trust me. And after today, I doubt she's ever going to trust me again.

six

Harper

The heat of the Fringe isn't enough to counteract the icy vibes I'm sending Eli's way.

I didn't say a single word to him after I left his compartment yesterday, and I barely made eye contact when he brought me my gun from the weapons room.

I could feel his eyes on me as Remy Chaplin read our deployment disclosure, but as soon as the compound doors shut behind us, I began to feel sick for an entirely new set of reasons: the fear of getting shot and the creeping dread that I may have to shoot someone else.

We barely make it ten yards before Eli broaches the suffocating silence of the desert.

"Will you just let me explain?"

"Now really isn't the time," I snap, scanning the horizon for any sign of movement.

I don't know why Eli thinks it's still a good idea for us to be partners. I feel off balance and distracted every time we're together, and all our emotional baggage doesn't exactly make for a healthy partnership.

"Nothing happened with Mina. She literally broke into my compartment the night you left and brought me up to Constance's headquarters to see Jayden."

"She seemed pretty cozy on your bed," I mutter.

What is wrong with me? I am not this girl. I don't want Eli to think I'm hurt and bitter — even if I am. I don't want to give him that power over me, but my emotions are not cooperating.

"That's just the way she is," he growls. "She's like Jayden. She just uses that shit to manipulate people."

"Then why did you have her gun?"

"She *gave* it to me," he sighs in exasperation. "She knew I wouldn't come with her otherwise."

"You expect me to believe that a woman from Constance — a woman Jayden trained — would just hand over her gun?"

"Yeah. I guess."

I scoff in disgust. He can't expect me to believe that.

"Do you *really* think I'd go down to Neverland and find someone to sleep with the night you go off to 119?"

I know he can't see my full expression behind my mask, but I give him my best sideways glare.

Eli's eyebrows shoot up in surprise. "*Really?* Wow. Thanks."

Now he's pissed. Good. He deserves it after all the shit he's put me through.

"Well, I guess that clears a few things up," he growls, uncharacteristically flustered. "Only, I'm not sure why you'd even *be* with me in the first place if you thought I was such a scumbag."

That strikes a nerve.

"I guess I didn't know," I say lamely.

"That's bullshit, Harper. You know the type of guy I am. You know me better than anyone. What you see is what you get, so if you think I'd do something like that, you must have had a low opinion of me for a while."

I open my mouth to retort but close it quickly. I *do* know him — at least I thought I did. It never crossed my mind that Eli might cheat on me until I saw that bitch sprawled out on his bed. If I hadn't seen it with my own eyes, I never would have believed it.

"You should know I'd never do something like that," he says, filling the heavy silence with his reassuring voice. "There's no one else I want to be with."

Those words are enough to break through my wall of anger and confusion. A pleasant warmth starts to spread from my chest to my extremities, and I feel my jealousy-induced icicles start to melt.

"Well . . . that's good to know, I guess," I say, fighting a smile.

He stops walking, and I stiffen, instantly on high alert for drifters. I don't see anyone approaching, so I chance a look at his face.

He's got a playful twinkle in his eyes, but I can't read his full expression. Slowly, he turns toward me and runs his hands up and down my arms.

"You didn't know that?"

His gentle touch is incredibly distracting, but I manage to blurt out a muffled "no."

Eli's breath hitches behind his mask, and he lets his hands wander up to my neck. It's as far as he can go with my mask in the way. "This is when I'm supposed to kiss you," he whispers.

I nod and try to pull myself together. This isn't the time or the place, but Eli's looking at me with so much affection and desire that I know if he pulled off his mask to kiss me right now, mine would be gone in a second.

Watching him watch me behind the heavy piece of plastic, I get the sudden urge to laugh. It rumbles up my chest and bursts out of my mic before I can stop it, and Eli's eyes narrow.

"I'm sorry," I choke, unable to contain my laughter. "I'm sorry! It's just . . ." I reach out and tug on the bottom of his mask. "We're having a moment out on the Fringe. It's kind of funny."

At first I think I might have ruined everything and that Eli is going to become sullen again, but then his eyes crinkle in amusement, and he starts laughing, too.

I decide it's my favorite sound in the whole world.

Our little moment doesn't last long enough. Eli regains his focus within a few seconds, but when his laughter subsides, he's still staring at me with a disarming fondness that makes coherent speech impossible.

He redirects his gaze to the horizon, and we start walking again.

As we approach the land mines, I pull up my interface and study the three-dimensional map that shows where they're buried. Dozens of new red dots crowd the path in front of me, which makes charting a safe course more difficult than usual. I can see the freshly packed dirt where ExCon installed the new ones, and I wonder if they'll be able to keep the drifters at a safe distance.

By the time we clear the mines, the sun is beating down with fierce intensity. My long-sleeve overshirt is soaked with sweat, and I fight the urge to strip down to my tank top and shorts.

I'm still replaying Eli's words in my mind, and I'm so distracted that I barely notice him leading us in a completely different direction from last time. Instead of the imposing sandstone formations looming in the distance, all I see is open desert.

"Where are we going?" I ask in alarm. Surely I couldn't have thrown Eli off his game so much that he lost his way.

"We're taking a different route into town. It's a longer walk, but there's nowhere for the drifters to hide."

"Oh . . . good."

"And I doubt they would rebury our land mines all the way out here. Nobody from Recon comes this far north."

I nod.

"Did you think we were lost?" he asks, clearly amused.

"No. Well . . . maybe a little."

He chuckles, and it strikes me just how different this deployment seems. Our little moment made everything feel deceivingly light, but it's more than that. After provoking Constance's ire, I might actually be safer out here than I am in the compound.

Eli wasn't kidding about the roundabout path being longer. My throat is parched from thirst, and I can feel the heat making an imprint on the top of my forehead and the bridge of my nose. I could really use a water break, but something about Eli's purposeful stride makes me think he doesn't want to slow down.

When I finally emerge from my bubble of discomfort, I see the fuzzy shape of a town looming off to our left. On our right, the highway carves a gentle path through the rugged terrain, the blacktop swimming in and out of focus in the sunshine.

We walk faster as we approach the town, and I grip my rifle a little tighter. There aren't any rock formations to provide cover for a sniper, but the drifters probably still have lookouts stationed near the edge of town.

Then I hear a high-pitched rush of wind. It's a sound I've heard twice before, but it takes me a second to recognize it.

Eli grabs me around the shoulders and pulls me to the ground. My elbows burn as they scrape pebbles and grit, but he pushes me down farther. He shimmies along next to me, trying to conceal himself in the slight slope of the land, and I copy his movements until we're lying side by side.

That's when I realize that the sound I heard was a car.

As the vehicle approaches, I tuck my head and focus on lying absolutely still. My heart is pounding against my ribcage, and I can feel Eli's ragged breathing as his chest expands and contracts against my side.

There's a sharp *whoosh!* as the hunter-green SUV blazes past us, and I let out a low breath of relief.

"It's headed into town," says Eli. "That has to be the Desperados."

We lie in the dirt for several minutes, steeling ourselves for the possibility that we could encounter Owen's gang.

"You think he's with them?" I ask.

Eli lets out a long breath. "Only one way to find out."

"What are you going to do if we find him?"

He shakes his head. "Hopefully get close enough to talk to him — tell him to get the hell out of here."

"And you think he'll listen?"

I don't mean for the question to come out so indignant, but it does.

I only spent a few hours with Owen on our last deployment, but that was enough time to realize he was even more stubborn than Eli. I can't imagine he'd cut and run just because his brother asked him to.

Then again, I never thought Eli would admit he had feelings for me, so it's possible the Parker brothers aren't as incorrigible as they like people to believe.

Once the SUV has disappeared from view, Eli helps me back up, and we continue our trek toward the town.

"Stay alert," he mutters under his breath.

I nod and hurriedly wipe my sweaty palms on my fatigues.

That old fear of the Fringe is back in full force, and it feels like my first deployment all over again. At the sight of the SUV, all my training melted away — leaving me with nothing but my basic instincts. I try reminding myself that Eli is here, but that does little to quell my panic. He's had so many close calls on the Fringe already.

Luckily, I don't have much time to dwell on the horrible thoughts running through my mind. We've reached the outskirts of town, and unfamiliar buildings are popping up all around us.

Once we break through the sparse industrial area, we emerge onto a street that looks much nicer than the pit-stop side of town. The sidewalks are lined with old-fashioned street lamps and wrought-iron benches, and artsy shops and restaurants stretch all the way down the block.

We cut through the alleyway between a rustic-looking brewpub and a stationary store, but just as we step off the sidewalk into the street, male voices drift over on the wind.

I hear the scuff of their boots, but there's no way to tell where the men are coming from.

I duck down between a trashcan and an empty newspaper stand, and Eli does the same. There isn't a lot of room in our little hiding place, so he has to practically fold his body over mine.

The men round the corner, but they're still too far away for me to discern what they're saying. They're in their midthirties and look less intimidating than most of the drifters I've seen guarding the town. They aren't dressed in black T-shirts and bandanas like the Desperados; they're wearing faded jeans, T-shirts, and button-downs. The two I can see are armed, but their handguns are tucked into holsters.

The men seem to decide something as a group, and one of them rubs his forehead, looking agitated. They talk for a few more seconds and then head out in opposite directions.

For several minutes, the only sound is Eli's uneven breathing against the back of my neck. Then he rises into a standing position and pulls me up, too.

"Come on."

Glancing around to make sure the men are really gone, I

follow him across the street toward one of the touristy clothing stores. Its windows are still intact, and the wooden sign hanging over the door reads "Mountain Man Outdoor Emporium."

Eli pulls a tool out of his belt and uses it to jimmy the lock. The door swings open easily, and I follow him inside.

The shade is a welcome relief, but it's still hot and stuffy inside the store. I pull off my mask and take a huge drink of water, surveying the racks of outdoor clothing and sporting equipment.

"Who were those guys?" I ask, wiping my mouth with the back of my hand.

"No idea."

Eli removes his mask and hangs it from a hook near the cash register. Then he heads straight for the men's clothing.

Judging by the barren walls, the store owner must have sold off or taken anything valuable with him, but there's still plenty of clothing hanging from the metal carousels.

"Pick out something to wear," says Eli. "Our uniforms are too recognizable."

"We're changing?"

"Yeah. I don't know who those men were, but they weren't Desperados. There's bound to be plenty more where they came from, and I'm not taking any chances."

Eli doesn't look up from the clothes, but the anxiety in his voice is palpable. He selects a light blue shirt from the rack, and the full meaning of his words finally sinks in.

"You want to pretend to be drifters?"

What he's suggesting is brilliant, but it's also treason. Recon operatives don't go undercover. They work by staying out of sight and shooting drifters.

"We're not going to become best friends or anything. We're just going to blend in."

I stare at the clothes. Something tells me we'd have a tough time passing for drifters up close. We're too pale and much too clean. But these clothes would help us avoid attracting unwanted attention as we make our way across town.

I wander over to the other side of the store, where there's a small selection of women's clothing. I rifle through the first rack of shirts I find and pull out a plum tank top that looks about my size.

As I hunt around for some shorts to match, I look up to ask Eli if we should grab jackets, too.

I never get the words out.

Eli has his head bent low, unbuttoning his shirt on the other side of the store. There's something intimate about watching him undress, and I can't stop staring.

His discarded overshirt hits the floor. He pulls his black T-shirt over his head, and the sight of his broad muscled back makes me forget what I was going to ask.

A loud zipping sound breaks the silence, and Eli's upper body disappears behind the clothing rack. That's enough to make me come to my senses.

I rip my gaze away from the spot where he was just standing and turn around. But in my haste, I stagger into another rack of clothes and almost impale myself on a rogue hanger.

Eli shoots back up at the rattling noise and lets out a low chuckle.

I jerk my head over my shoulder. "W-what?" But my red face gives me away.

Slowly, deliberately, Eli navigates around the rack and makes his way up the aisle between the men's and women's clothing. His low-slung khaki shorts are half unbuttoned, and he takes his sweet time sidling over to where I'm standing.

He's still shirtless, and the low light filtering in from the dusty windows throws shadows over his magnificent chest and biceps.

When he's barely two feet away, he jerks his head up and cracks a wicked grin. My breath catches a little, and I silently berate myself for being so enamored with him.

"Did you enjoy the show?" he whispers.

I feel myself blushing more, but I shake my head and return to browsing. "I don't know what you're talking about."

"*O-kay.*"

I feel him edge closer, and I fight the urge to step back into his arms.

"You're wearing this?" he asks, spotting the tank top hanging sideways on the rack.

"Mm-hmm."

Out of the corner of my eye, I see him reach out and finger the thin strap. He lets out a low sigh, and my heart beats a little faster.

Then, without warning, he wraps his arms around my waist and pulls me back against his bare chest. The shock of it knocks the wind out of me, and he rubs his palms low against my stomach.

"I feel like you have an unfair advantage now," he murmurs, his breath disturbing my hair.

"Oh, yeah?" I choke. "What's that?"

"You've seen *me* half-naked."

My entire body feels as though it's on fire, but I attempt a nonchalant shrug. "It's nothing I hadn't seen before," I say, thinking of him in the ring.

He chuckles and squeezes me tighter. "Still counts."

I can feel his heart hammering against my back, which is comforting and a little disorienting. His breathing is shallow and hungry in my ear, and his hands seem to be traveling lower with every pass.

At least I'm not the only one losing my shit.

I'm not used to this version of Eli — the guy who flirts and says what's on his mind — but now is *so* not the time to test the boundaries of our weird relationship.

I clear my throat loudly and try to squirm out of his grip, but he doesn't let go.

"I need to get changed."

"I know." I can hear a laugh on his lips, and he situates himself so his rough, bristly cheek rests against mine. "I think we need to even the score."

Any semblance of composure I just gained evaporates instantly. I know I must be beet red from the roots of my hair to the tips of my toes, but I don't fight him when he pulls away and pivots me around.

When I meet his gaze, my nervousness dissipates slightly. It's the same old Eli — same probing blue eyes. But they're filled with a desire that makes me nervous and excited at the same time.

My hand has a mind of its own when it reaches out to touch his chest. He drags in a labored breath, and his eyes follow my hand as it trails down to his tight stomach.

I stop for a minute to brush my thumb over the smooth skin between his abs and his hipbone, but he grabs my hand away and pulls me into him.

This time when our lips meet, there's no careful exploration. Eli's kiss is frantic and a little out of control. My pulse is racing, and his skin feels unusually hot.

My brain completely abandons the situation, and all I can do is grab hold of him and try to take everything in.

For the first time, I have the chance to run my hands all over his firm chest and beautiful arms, and I take full advantage of the situation.

But before I've finished memorizing every line of him, Eli draws back. There's a slight smirk playing on those skillful lips, and his eyes crackle with mischief as they flicker down my body. "Fair's fair, Riley."

If I weren't so flustered, I might give him a playful punch right in those delicious abs. But when neither of us moves, everything becomes much more serious.

His smile fades slightly, and his gaze becomes very intense. It feels as though he threw down a dare and I didn't blink.

Slowly, his hands travel up my arms to my collar, and he starts unsnapping my overshirt. He's trying to take his time, but his breathing grows a little heavier with every button.

When my shirt is hanging open, he meets my eyes again, and I shrug my shoulders so he can pull it off my arms.

Things have gotten real.

I tilt my head up to kiss him again, and he opens his mouth for me right away. His kiss is deeper — hungrier than before. Then he puts a few inches between us and tugs on the hem of my tank top.

In one sharp motion, it goes up and over, bra and all. A slight chill prickles up my spine, and when my clothes hit the floor, Eli's eyes widen.

His rough hands travel down my arms and back up my bare waist, and I shiver when the tips of his fingers brush my spine. We lock eyes, and he brings his lips down again to kiss me softly.

A slow burning heat is making its way down my body, and I'm surprised at the thoughts that flash through my mind.

Then a tiny, annoying voice in my head reminds me that this isn't the time or the place.

What did we come here for again? Oh, that's right: We're on an assassination mission.

Eli seems to read my mind. I can feel his hands slowing down, tracing slow circles on my back as though he's savoring the last touch.

"We should probably get going," I mutter against his neck.

"Yeah." His voice is low and rough.

I start to pull back, but he holds me just a few inches away and takes one last lingering look. I flush under the intensity of his gaze, but then he threads his fingers in my hair and places a kiss on my forehead that makes all my anxiety disappear.

"I guess you need this," he says, grabbing the thin tank top off the hanger.

I clear my throat. "Bra."

"Oh, yeah."

He turns away a little as I get dressed, and I mentally shake myself to clear the fog clouding my senses.

Now more than ever, I understand why romantic entanglements are such a bad idea in Recon. It's going to be tough to focus on the mission after what just happened.

Eli pulls the shirt he found over his head backwards, and I fight a laugh as he twists it around to the correct position. Things are about to get interesting.

seven

Eli

As soon as the blazing sun hits my shoulders, I'm a dead man walking. I'm on high alert for the sound of approaching footsteps, but I'm pretty sure if a drifter jumped out in the street and aimed a gun at me, I'd just stand there and eat lead.

My mind is consumed by thoughts of Harper: her body, her eyes, the way she felt against me . . .

I hadn't expected that to happen. I was ninety percent joking about evening the score; I never thought she'd go for it — especially after the Mina incident.

Seeing her staring at me shut off that part of my brain that acts as a filter, and the words just slipped out of my mouth. And seeing that she wanted me as much as I've wanted her, well . . .

"Shouldn't we go this way?" asks Harper, calling me back to reality.

"Huh?" I stop, trying to get my bearings before she realizes that I was completely lost in thought.

She points down a side street. "The restaurant . . . don't you think we should start there?"

"Oh." My brain lurches as it tries to refocus on the mission. "Yeah. Owen could show up to deliver a message from Jackson."

I try to make it sound as though the idea just occurred to me so she doesn't think I was about to lead us in the wrong direction.

What is the matter with me? I know where the restaurant is, but something about her skimpy purple tank top is completely screwing with my internal compass.

"Sorry. I just got turned around for a second."

She gives me a funny look over the top of her mask but turns down the street.

Harper is way more alert than I am. Her posture is casual, but her right hand keeps inching toward the handgun at her hip. We can't shoot anyone without blowing our cover, but the instinct is automatic.

We left most of our supplies back at the store. Our compound-issued rifles and rucksacks would have been a dead giveaway that we were with Recon, but traveling so light makes me feel naked.

If we were really committed, we would have ditched our masks, too, but blending in perfectly isn't worth breathing in all those radioactive particles.

Luckily, the place is swarming with out-of-towners like the men we saw near the outdoor supply store, so the masks shouldn't attract attention. For all anybody knows, we could have traveled here from Salt Lake City or another red zone.

To avoid having to speak to any drifters, we stick to side streets and make our way slowly toward the old abandoned restaurant the Desperados use as their base. Every so often, the voices of approaching drifters float toward us, and Harper turns down another street to avoid a face-to-face encounter. If anyone gets too close or asks the wrong questions, they'll be able to tell we aren't drifters.

Seeing so many reinforcements puts me on edge. They must be part of Malcolm's grand plan to bring down the compound, though I still have no idea what that could be.

Even if he gathered all the drifters within a 100-mile radius and rushed the compound, they wouldn't be able to make so much as a dent in the structure. The founders anticipated being attacked after Death Storm, so they built the compounds to be able to withstand anything from a hail storm to a storm of bullets.

Any drifter siege would end in bloodshed. But then again, a bunch of hostile survivors at our doorstep would raise a lot of questions the board doesn't want to answer.

The closer we get to the restaurant, the more my discomfort grows. Near the outskirts of town, the buildings are spaced farther apart, which means there's very little cover.

A few abandoned cars are still parked along the street, gathering dust and sand and getting buffeted by tumbleweed. Every building we pass looks more dilapidated than the one before.

When we reach the fast-food restaurant with the creepy dancing burger mascots, I know we're getting close. Harper draws her gun and leads us toward the filling station just across from the restaurant, and I pick up the pace.

We duck down behind one of the defunct gas pumps, and Harper glances up at me. I know she's waiting for me to take charge and formulate a plan — which is what I'm here for — but I still feel off-kilter and nervous for reasons that have nothing to do with the Desperados.

Trying to regain my composure, I clear my throat and flip on my interface, zooming in to see the entrance to the restaurant more clearly.

The last time we were here, the drifters had a lookout posted up on the weathered wooden porch, but I don't see anyone. An Indiana license plate has come loose from the mosaic of rusty plates and street signs decorating the front of the restaurant, and when the breeze kicks up, the faded scrap of metal rattles against the wood siding. It's the loudest thing for miles.

The last time we were here, we left five dead drifters behind. There's no reason the Desperados would leave the base unguarded. It feels like a trap.

"Do you see anyone?" Harper whispers.

I shake my head, staring at that loose license plate.

"No one?"

"Nope. And I don't like it."

"You think it's a setup?"

"Could be." I flip off my interface and do one more scan of the deserted restaurant. "Let's go around back."

Harper rises into a crouch and surveys the wide stretch of concrete where the crumbling parking lots meet the road. Then she takes off at a run.

I brace myself for the crack of a rifle, but nothing happens.

We skirt around the dumpsters and the old rusted-out pickup truck and reach the back exit without incident. I try the door handle, expecting it to be locked, but I'm surprised when it turns in my hand.

My heart rate picks up a little. I glance down at Harper. She meets my gaze unflinchingly, which gives me the strength to draw my gun and fling the door wide open.

The sudden gust of air stirs the dirt lining the kitchen shelves, and for a moment, it's impossible to see anything through the cloud of dust shimmering in the late morning sunlight.

I step inside, keeping my gun aimed at head height, and Harper takes my other side.

The cramped kitchen looks just the way I remember it, except for the pots and pans lying on the ground. Then there's the trail of smooth tile gleaming through the layer of dirt where someone dragged the dead bodies up from the basement.

Harper closes the door behind us, and it takes a few seconds for my eyes to adjust to the dim lighting. I listen hard, but

I can't hear anything going on down below.

Nodding at Harper, I inch toward the basement door and pull it open. It creaks a little, but there's nothing I can do about that.

As soon as I step onto the narrow staircase, I can hear Harper's ragged breathing in my ear. It mixes with my own thunderous heartbeat and becomes a single frantic cadence as we make our way down.

When the wall dips and opens onto the landing, I flatten myself against the battered drywall and take several deep breaths. This is it.

In one motion, I whip around the corner and take aim, but there's no one to shoot.

Behind me, Harper lets out a disappointed sigh.

Everything is gone. The wooden tables from upstairs are still scattered around the basement, but all the drifters' computers and equipment have disappeared.

Other than the dried blood staining the dirty floor, a few bullet casings, and the chair lying on its side where Owen was bound, there's no evidence that the drifters were ever here.

"Back to square one," I mutter. "Jayden isn't going to be happy."

"Their new base has to be nearby," Harper says in a tired voice. "Why else would they still be hanging around this town?"

"It doesn't matter. It could be anywhere. It would take us *weeks* to check out every building."

"Do you think Owen is still around?"

The sound of my brother's name causes a painful tug in my chest, and I drag in a deep breath to alleviate the dread building inside me. "I don't know."

I don't want to voice my worry that Owen is gone for good. The thought of having a brother out there whom I'll never see again is almost worse than thinking he was dead all these years. Seeing him again stirred some long-buried hope inside me that maybe I could have a family again. I don't want to face the horrible possibility that Owen is just the Desperados' cowardly yes-man.

"Let's check out his house," I say, eager for a new plan to focus on. "We can't exactly start poking around random buildings with all these drifters around."

I can tell Harper thinks it's a long shot, but she nods and leads the way up the stairs and out the back exit.

As we make our way down the street toward the little row of houses where Owen was staying, the conspicuous lack of people makes me think we should have guessed that they'd relocated.

We don't encounter a single drifter all the way to Owen's street, and when the cluster of ramshackle houses comes into view, it almost looks like a movie set. Shutters are hanging by a single hinge. Loose pieces of siding are flapping in the breeze, and Owen's windows are all boarded up.

We go around back to the door he led us through the last time we were here, and my heart sinks. It's locked.

"Wait here," I whisper.

I stow my gun and walk around to the side of the house, trying to fight the sinking feeling that Owen left without intending to return. A few garbage bags are strewn across the yard in tatters, as though he just dumped the trash outside to be scavenged by desert animals.

I don't even want to think how he disposed of the bodies we hauled out of his place last time. Instead, I focus on the windows, counting from the back of the house until I reach the one leading to Owen's bedroom.

When we were kids, he always slept with the window open.

If he were still living here, he'd want to nail the boards so that he could slide it up and down at night.

It's a long shot, but it's worth a try.

As soon as I reach Owen's window, somebody knocks on the other side of the glass. I stumble backward in surprise and draw my gun, my heart nearly beating its way out of my chest.

Then Harper's muffled voice floats through the wall. "It's okay. It's just me."

I let out a burst of air when her face appears between the boards. The window groans as she pries it open, and I get a big whiff of musty old house.

"What the hell?" I ask, unable to contain my excited smile. "How did you get in?"

"One of the boards was loose around back, and the window was unlocked."

"Seriously?" Now I feel like a moron.

"It was a tight squeeze, but . . ."

Without warning, the two-by-four in front of my face shudders. I realize Harper aimed a kick at the bottom board to drive it loose, but her kick wasn't quite strong enough.

"Careful . . ."

She doesn't listen. She grunts and aims another side kick, and this time, it splinters the wood. I'm impressed, but I have a bad feeling about this.

The third kick breaks through the board, and, sure enough, she nearly tumbles out of the window. I grab her leg to stop her momentum and catch a glimpse of her proud smile as she bends down to offer me a hand.

There's no way she can hoist me up and over the sill, but I find a foothold on the protruding water spigot and manage to pull myself through the window.

I summersault into Owen's bedroom, and when I sit up and

get a good look at the place, disappointment trickles into my stomach.

The room looks completely abandoned. The twin bed shoved up against the wall is draped in a torn yellow sheet, and four empty drawers are hanging out of the beat-up dresser.

"Eli . . ."

"Yeah?"

Harper's eyes crinkle in sympathy. "The house looks sort of . . . empty."

"Empty?"

I can't believe it — I won't. Owen can't *really* be gone.

Pulling myself into an upright position, I turn away from Harper and go to check the rest of the house for myself. The floor responds to my footsteps with loud, tired creaks, as though it's stretching after a long nap.

The living room looks the same as it did the last time we were here — shag carpeting, scratchy couches, creepy cat figurines from the previous tenant — but there's a definite feeling of abandonment hanging over the place.

Wandering into the kitchen, I'm startled by the loud *snap* of floorboards and the tick of the cat clock hanging near the stove. It's unbearably loud.

There are a couple empty glasses scattered around the porcelain sink, but the dusty film inside tells me they've been there for a while.

I open up a few of the cabinets. There's no food, no whisky — no clue that Owen was ever here.

"Eli . . ."

I don't turn around. I can't face Harper yet. I don't want to accept that Owen left without so much as a goodbye. I *won't* accept it.

I tear past Harper without looking at her and head back to

the bedroom.

I pull apart the dresser and ransack the closet, looking for something of Owen's to latch on to. I find a few stray socks and a ragged feather duster — probably from the house's original inhabitants — but no evidence to suggest that anyone was living here recently.

"Eli, he's gone," says Harper in a soft voice. "I'm sorry."

The thickness has returned to the back of my throat, and it's making me feel trapped. Harper is hovering right behind me, but I don't want to see her feeling sorry for me. I can't stand it.

"This is *just* like him," I sigh. "Running as soon as things get . . ."

I snap my mouth shut and clench my jaw. All my resentment toward Owen has built up like poison in my system, and I know if I keep letting it stew, I'm going to lash out at the only person nearby.

I sink down on the stained carpet and lean against the scuffed wall. I want to get out of this house. It's dirty and depressing — nothing but a painful reminder that my one living family member is gone again.

"He probably had to leave," says Harper quietly, kneeling down across from me and trying to catch my gaze. I can read her concern in my periphery, but I just can't look into those warm gray eyes.

"You mean run."

"Well . . . we did kill those drifters. Malcolm's crew might have been suspicious. If they thought Owen had something to do with it, he might be on the run."

"Owen's been on the run his entire life," I snap. "That's why he joined the Desperados in the first place — to escape any real responsibility to find me and build a life for us."

"You can't tell me he didn't want to find you," says Harper.

"You're his brother. And you can't blame him for joining Nu-clear Nation. He was only *thirteen*. He was looking for a family . . . same as you."

"Yeah. But he *stayed* with them. Even after everything . . ."

"It might not have been as bad as it was for you. From what he said —"

"They're still a bunch of thugs, Harper. And now he's in trouble, and he's run off."

I know I'm being harsh and juvenile, but Harper reaches over and puts a hand on my arm. "We'll find him, okay?"

I finally meet her gaze, and the earnestness in her expression catches me off guard. There's no doubt in her mind that we'll find Owen. Even though he could be anywhere and we're pretty much restricted to a ten-mile radius around the compound, she has absolute faith that he'll surface and that we'll be here when he does. I wish I shared her optimism.

Trying to keep my spiraling helplessness in check, I pull my eyes away and stare at the saggy twin mattress and box spring. Mom would flip. The bed doesn't have a comforter or one of those stupid bed curtains that hangs down to the floor — just that sad, dirty sheet.

Then something else catches my eye. I reach down under the bed, and my fingers brush something hard and smooth. It's about the size of a shoebox but much more solid. Gripping it around the edges, I pull it into the light.

It's a small cedar box with delicate flowers carved along the sides. The lid is held closed by a brass latch, and something about it feels achingly familiar.

I brush my hand over the top, and the pads of my fingers come away completely dust free. Someone must have handled it recently.

"Is that Owen's?" Harper whispers.

It *has* to be, but I don't say a word. I have the crazy suspicion that voicing the possibility will make this last shred of hope slip right through my fingers.

Slowly, carefully, I undo the latch and open the box.

The first things I see are Owen's old army men. I know they were his because they aren't the green plastic kind that every kid had growing up. These are the cast-iron men that our grandfather gave Owen when he turned eight, with nearly indiscernible features after decades of play. There's also an Indian arrowhead that Owen and my dad found on a walk, but that's not what catches my attention.

Underneath Owen's trinkets are a few photographs. They're slightly bent from being stuffed inside the box, and the edges are worn from years of handling. But as soon as I see them, my heart speeds up.

The first two photos are blurry snapshots of our golden retriever Millie, but there's another one of me and Owen holding up two fish we caught on vacation.

As soon as I pick it up, I feel another picture stuck to the back. And when the photo paper snaps apart, the lump returns to the back of my throat.

Staring down at the photo, I can hardly believe what I'm seeing: Owen has one very tan arm slung around my shoulders, and he's smiling with that easy grin he used to have. I'm squinting in the sunlight, utterly oblivious to the fact that I should make this picture a good one. Owen and I could be carbon copies of the same kid, except he's about four inches taller and broader around the shoulders.

But what really captures my attention is my mom. She isn't looking at the camera — she's looking up at my dad and smiling. He has one arm tucked around her waist, and his other hand is slightly blurry where it trails out of the frame.

By the way he's leaning, I can tell he set the camera on a rock, started the timer, and ran back to pose for the shot.

I can almost hear my mom telling him to take his hat off for the picture. She was always in charge of the staging: finding the perfect backdrop, making Owen put on a shirt, and trying to get my dad to separate from his baseball cap long enough to see his bright blue eyes — same as Owens, same as mine.

This has to be the last picture ever taken of my family. I remember this day. We'd taken a trip down to Fishlake National Forest — part of our parents' endless crusade to give me and Owen a normal childhood — and we'd had the whole place to ourselves. It would have been eerie a few years before, but it was normal after Death Storm.

"You guys look really happy," Harper whispers, leaning in and resting her chin on my shoulder. It's such an intimate gesture that it startles me a little, but I try not to move because I don't want to ruin it.

"That's just the picture," I murmur. "You can't tell, but the mosquitos were murder that year."

Harper chuckles and points in the box. "What's that?"

I look down and tilt it slightly. Something metallic shifts along the bottom, and I see that it's a necklace nestled in the corner — a tiny piece of turquoise and a silver hare hanging from a thin chain.

As soon as I realize what it is, I can barely control the burning in my eyes.

"This was my mom's," I say finally. "I can't believe Owen kept it."

My mom had worn this necklace for as long as I could remember. She'd gotten it on a road trip with my dad before Death Storm, when he'd deviated from GPS directions because he thought he knew a shortcut.

They got lost, and when my mom grew so irritated that she stopped talking to my dad, he finally stopped to ask for directions. An old Native American woman was selling jewelry near a scenic overlook, and my dad bought the necklace as a peace offering.

When he came back to the car, he handed her the necklace and said, "Please forgive the hare's cockiness. It was just in a hurry to get there so he could enjoy the weekend with you."

"You know what this means?" Harper whispers, breaking through my wandering thoughts. "He has to be in the area."

"What?"

"Owen wouldn't leave all this here if he didn't plan on coming back."

"Oh. I guess."

I don't want to get my hopes up, but Harper's right. Owen's never been sentimental, yet he went back to the house to save these last pieces of our family. There's no way he'd leave the box behind after carrying it with him all these years.

Harper leans back against the wall, and I realize I haven't put down the photograph or stopped worrying the turquoise stone between my fingers. I clear my throat again and tuck the photo into my back pocket.

I'm not going to risk losing the one picture of my family in existence. I let the silver chain run through my fingers and pool around the hare resting in the palm of my hand. I want this piece of my mom, too, so I tuck the necklace into my shorts for safekeeping.

Suddenly there's a loud banging on the back door. I jump, and the box tumbles out of my lap. Army men spill out everywhere, and Harper throws me a panicked look.

The banging outside intensifies, and it sounds as though someone is trying to break the lock on the back door.

"What do we do?"

I don't answer. I just scoop up the scattered trinkets, replace the box under the bed, and pull Harper into the closet.

A few seconds later, there's a loud *crack* as the door slams against the wall, followed by the sound of thunderous footfalls.

"Parker!" yells a voice.

My upper body twitches in response to my name, but the intruders *have* to be looking for Owen.

"Parker!" the man yells again.

At least two more sets of footsteps join in the search, and the loud whine of floorboards tells me they've entered the kitchen. There's more banging as they follow my search pattern, throwing open cabinets and knocking chairs around in their haste.

The heaviest footsteps pick up speed, and I cringe as they move closer. Harper's breathing hard and fast against the back of my neck. We're trapped, but I'll be damned if they get the jump on me. I draw my handgun and point it at the gap in the accordion doors, waiting for the drifter.

He's coming toward the bedroom, and I get an idea that could either save our lives or get us killed. I only have a split second to make the decision.

Throwing open the closet door, I step into the room and pull a very reluctant Harper out behind me. She's giving me a "What the fuck?" sort of look, but I yank the bedsheet down and shove her onto the mattress.

In one motion, I yank off my shirt and toss it carelessly into the corner. Harper's ponytail is already disheveled from our earlier activities, and she's splayed on the mattress in shock.

I raise my gun just as the drifter flies around the corner and catch him looking at me like a deer caught in the headlights.

"*What the hell?*" I shout, sizing up the drifter quickly to see if

I recognize him from Jayden's surveillance pictures.

He's a couple inches shorter than me — very tan, with light brown hair and a mouth that looks as though it spends most of its time swearing.

It isn't Malcolm or Jackson. I have no fucking clue who he is. He knows who I am, though — or at least he thinks he does.

From what Harper said and from what I could tell with my own eyes, Owen and I are virtually identical. And someone who doesn't know us that well might not be able to tell who's who.

This guy can't. A look of relief passes over his face, followed swiftly by anger.

"Where the *fuck* have you been, Parker?"

"Dude . . . do you mind?" I ask, feigning irritation and throwing a pointed glance at Harper.

She's still sitting on the rumpled bed with a startled expression on her face that's not inappropriate for the scenario I tried to create. If I'd had a couple more seconds, I could have faked it better, but I think the guy is convinced.

His gaze shifts to Harper, who quickly straightens her tank top and pulls on a bashful expression.

What can I say? The girl can roll with the punches.

The drifter clears his throat. "Oh. Er . . . sorry. I'll give you a second."

And just like that, he looks away and backs out of the room.

As soon as he disappears around the corner, Harper throws me a look that says, "Are you out of your mind?"

I shrug and bend down to retrieve my shirt, straining my ears to pick up on the drifters' conversation in the kitchen.

"Yo, Jay . . . is he here?"

"Oh, he's here, all right . . . doin' it with some hot little piece of ass."

"What the hell? He knows we don't have time for that shit."

"You wanna tell him? Be my guest."

After a few seconds, it occurs to me that they're waiting for us to emerge, but I haven't even formulated a real plan yet. These guys clearly don't know Owen that well, but I'm sure they expect him to know why they're here.

If we play our cards right, we might get them to lead us to the drifters' new base. But if they ask too many questions, we're dead for sure.

I toss Harper one more look, and she nods. I know she's thinking the exact same thing, but she's ready to go along with it.

Taking a fortifying breath, I step out of the bedroom and follow the men's voices into the kitchen.

Just as I thought, there are two other drifters standing around the small table. One is a tall, flabby guy with a painful-looking sunburn; the other is a scrawny Hispanic man with a goatee.

"You ready?" asks the one called Jay.

"I guess so," I say, maintaining an irritated tone.

From what I've seen of Owen, he gets by on intimidation, so maybe if I keep that up, they won't ask too many questions.

The big boy shifts uncomfortably and stares at Harper. "She comin'?"

"Is that a problem?"

To my delight, Big Boy backs down. "No." He lowers his head. "Just . . . you know how Malcolm feels about all that . . ."

By "all that," I assume he means bringing random-ass girls along on gang field trips, but I doubt Owen would care.

"Well, then he can take it up with me when I see him," I say, putting an arm around Harper's shoulders and glaring at the men. "Let's go."

eight

Harper

The walk to the base with Owen's posse is the longest of my life.

My heart is pounding so loudly I'm sure Eli can hear it, and I get a sick, slimy feeling in the pit of my stomach every time the men's eyes pass over me.

Finally, the one called Jay addresses me directly. "So what's your name?"

"Harper," I murmur, immediately wishing I'd given a fake name. *What the hell is wrong with me?*

"That's a nice name," he says in a lazy drawl, falling into step beside me. He looks me up and down, his eyes settling on my mask. On the way out, Eli had the good sense not to grab his. Owen never wears a mask, but there was no way I was stepping outside without mine.

"Where you from?"

"Salt Lake City," I lie. Maybe that will put an end to his line of questioning.

"The radiation real bad there?"

I swallow nervously, afraid of getting caught in a lie. "Isn't it bad everywhere?"

"Well, it's a lot better here, I'll tell you that. But whenever we drive up there, I always see people wearing masks like that."

I give a noncommittal nod.

"Still, I don't think it does much. The cities are in real bad shape."

"Real bad," echoes the bigger guy.

"Sure are."

Jay seems to approve of my agreement, but he's still staring at me curiously. I inch closer to Eli, who glares at Jay until he falls back.

"So where you been hiding, Owen?" he asks.

Is this guy the damn spokesman for the group?

"Around," says Eli in a tone meant to put an end to the conversation. He's playing with fire pretending to be Owen, but it's not as though he had another choice. If the drifters had found us hiding in that closet, bullets would have started flying for sure.

"Malcolm's not happy with you," says the skinny guy with mocha skin.

"Well, Malcolm can kiss my ass," growls Eli. "After all the messes I've been cleaning up for him, I deserve a vacation."

I throw a nervous glance at Eli, silently begging him not to stumble into a conversation involving Owen's whereabouts.

"Yeah, you tell 'im," mutters the big guy.

"Don't give him any ideas, Tony," warns Jay. "If I were you, I'd be real apologetic. Malcolm's pissed that he had to send out a search party to find you."

I stifle a shudder. Clearly the Desperados' leader commands quite a bit of fear. It sure doesn't make me excited to meet him — especially not when I'm posing as Owen's fake girlfriend from Salt Lake City.

"Why did you run off, anyway?" asks Big Tony.

"I didn't run off," snaps Eli. "I just had some other things to take care of."

"What other things?" asks the third guy.

This man makes me nervous. He's quieter than the other two, but his eyes are calculating and suspicious.

"None of your goddamn business," Eli snarls.

I throw Eli a pointed look to tell him to tone it down. I know he's acting brash to capture Owen's charming personality and fend off further questions, but I worry that he's going to push it too far and make the drifters turn against us.

The third man quickens his pace until he's walking right beside Eli. He tilts his head up in defiance and throws him a menacing look. "If it concerns Malcolm, it *is* my fucking business."

I swallow. My palms are sweaty, but my mouth is as dry as the desert. I don't know what Eli is going to say next, but whatever it is better be good.

Slowly, he turns his head and glares at the man. "It's done, okay? Don't go making trouble where there isn't any."

Damn. If I didn't know him, I'd be terrified by the expression on Eli's face. It's the type of look that makes people stop asking questions, and it's enough to get Malcolm's biggest fan to back down.

As we approach the next intersection, Eli and I hang back so the others won't be able to tell that we don't know where we're going. They lead us through the nicer downtown area, past the block of buildings that look relatively untouched, and back to the fringes of town.

I recognize some of the businesses over here: a dilapidated mini mart, a Quik Loans place, and a dirty-looking gyro restaurant with a metal cage door secured over the entrance.

We continue walking to the corner of Shell Street toward a shop with a faded yellow exterior and a sign that reads Master Pawn. A few of the windows have cardboard and plywood duct taped over the frames, and several people have tagged the place with spray paint.

Upon closer inspection, I see that the windows aren't broken; someone just covered them to hide whatever is going on inside.

Instead of entering through the front door, Jay leads us around through the alley to a side door that's partially hidden by an overflowing dumpster. He bangs on the door several times, and my heart beats a little faster.

What if Malcolm realizes that Eli isn't Owen? What if he asks the wrong questions? What if he's so angry with Owen that he hurts Eli?

All these thoughts flash through my mind as I scan the building for an escape route. Unfortunately, the drifters have done a good job securing the place. Thin metal bars cover the windows in the back, and I'd bet money there's a lookout stationed on the far corner of the block.

As soon as we walk in, we'll be trapped.

Eli seems to be thinking along the same lines. He keeps glancing up and down the alley, as though he's annoyed that Malcolm is making him wait. But I can tell he's looking for exits.

We both still have our handguns, but those will be no match for the number of drifters we're facing. Blowing our cover isn't an option.

Finally, a deadbolt scrapes in the lock, and the door creaks open slowly.

A cute burned-looking guy with bleached-blond hair and a lip ring sticks his head out. As soon as he spots Eli, he breaks into a fond smile.

"Well, I'll be damned. Look who the cat dragged in."

His voice is hard to place. His accent reminds me of those I've heard in old Western movie clips, but it's a mix of a Southern drawl and a slur.

"Hey, Gunner," says the third drifter with us.

Gunner flips his long blond bangs out of his eyes and nods slowly. "How's it goin', Mouse?"

"Better now that we finally found this son of a bitch." He

jerks his head toward Eli in a way that's meant to be lighthearted, but I can tell he genuinely resents Eli/Owen.

Eli shifts angrily, which puts me directly in Gunner's line of sight. As soon as he sees me, his pale green eyes light up in interest.

"Ooh, who is this pretty lady?"

"Parker's girl from Salt Lake City," says Jay.

"Mmm," says Gunner, drawing his lip ring into his mouth and nodding appreciatively. "How you doin', Mama?"

I raise an eyebrow and scowl, but my heart's not really in it. I'm too nervous about meeting Malcolm to care about the come-on, and Gunner's flirting seems pretty harmless — almost as if that's his way of relating to people.

"How can you even tell she's hot?" Jay mutters, his gaze bouncing between my fading black eye and my mask.

"I can tell," says Gunner, drinking me in appreciatively. "Mmm-hmm. Eyes are the windows to the soul."

Big Tony snorts. "You can cut the crap, man. That shit's not gonna get you laid out here."

"I don' know, Tones. I don' know. There's lots of pretty mamas from out of town. They might need a little somethin'-somethin' to keep them cozy."

Eli glowers at him and follows the others inside, looking at me in a way I know means to stay close — as if I'd go anywhere.

It's a little bit dark inside, but as my eyes adjust to the light of a single bulb hanging from the ceiling, I can tell we've stepped behind the counter in the front room of the shop.

I was right in thinking this place had been badly looted in the aftermath of Death Storm. All the electronics and weapons are gone, leaving the far wall nearly bare. All that's left is a hodgepodge of used movies, a busted guitar, some tarnished jewelry in a glass case, and a few other odds and ends.

Jay, Tony, and Gunner lead the way through a beaded curtain to the back room, which is much more spacious. I take off my mask, but it does little to cool me down. It's dark and sweltering hot behind the curtain, and as soon as I look around, I see why.

All the computers and equipment that went missing from the restaurant basement are arranged in the back room. A handful of drifters are plugged in to whatever they're watching on the monitors, headphones in place and completely oblivious to their surroundings.

The sight reminds me so vividly of Celdon that I get a pang of homesickness. I have an urge to step around the mound of cords to see what they're working on, but I force myself to stay right at Eli's side.

"Holy shit!" calls a voice from the shadows.

The drifters' body language changes instantly, and I know the voice must belong to Malcolm.

"The prodigal son returns!"

Eli's fists clench and unclench nervously at his sides. Every muscle in his forearm is tightly flexed. I place a covert hand on the small of his back to calm him down, but when the man emerges from the shadows, Eli stiffens as though he plans to launch himself straight at Malcolm.

The man standing in front of us is definitely the guy from the surveillance photos. The Desperados' leader is tall and wiry — about Eli's height but much scrawnier. His face is pointed like a rat's, and he's got heavy black eyebrows that are furrowed in constant suspicion.

"Where the hell have you been?" he asks.

"Well, hello to you, too," says Eli, feigning offense.

"Hello?" Malcolm's face falls. "*Hello*? Don't fuckin' 'hello' me. I've had search parties out hunting you for days, Parker.

You strut in here after god knows how long, looking like you fucking own the place, and all you have to say to me is '*hello*'?"

I can't breathe.

For a moment, Eli and Malcolm just stare at each other, and the mood in the room becomes very tense.

Even though Eli and Malcolm have never met, there's a deep sense of history and resentment between them. Clearly Owen had a habit of challenging Malcolm, and Eli came equipped with that same boldness.

Then Malcolm's furious expression slips, and he falls into an easy — if somewhat off-putting — smile. "I'm just fuckin' with you," he says, flashing a pair of pronounced canines and extending a sideways handshake to Eli.

Eli lets out a stiff chuckle that does little to convince anyone, but he takes his hand anyway.

I release a slow sigh of relief, and Malcolm's heavy gaze shifts to me.

"And you brought a *friend*." He pronounces the word with clear double meaning.

"This is Harper," says Eli.

"Nice to meet you," says Malcolm, extending a hand.

"Likewise."

His palm is surprisingly cold. He envelopes my hand with both of his, and when we shake, I feel Eli shift a tiny bit closer.

I glance around the room, trying to keep my nerdiness in check. "You've got an impressive setup here," I say in an attempt to be gracious.

"It's coming along," says Malcolm. "We're able to keep pretty close tabs on the compound rats . . . not that it's done much good."

"Oh, no?"

Malcolm shakes his head. "We've lost a lot of men recently."

I nod, fighting the bile rising up in my throat. I think back to the men at the body shop — the man I killed — and the trail of dead bodies we've left in our wake since.

To distract myself, I wander over to the wall behind the computers, where they've tacked up a map of the town and the surrounding desert. Several routes are hand drawn over the terrain in blue marker, and I recognize one as the path Eli and I took last time.

To the left of that map, there are eight grainy photographs that look like mug shots — six men and two women staring blankly at the camera. I don't know any of them personally, but I recognize their photos from the compound news feeds. They're the AWOL Recon operatives.

I drag in a shallow breath and try to focus on something else. My hands are shaking so badly that I have to shove them in my pockets to avoid attracting attention.

"Are these them?" I ask, touching the edge of one of the photos.

"What?"

"The compound workers who've been killing your men," I say, more harshly than I meant to. "Are these the ones?"

"No," says Malcolm. "Those operatives are . . . Well, let's just say they're no longer a threat."

I swallow twice to wet my parched throat. "What about the workers from 119? How are you managing them?"

As soon as the words leave my mouth, I realize I've gone too far. I'd been fishing to see if the drifters knew that 119 had been wiped off the map, but when Malcolm's mouth twists into a sneer, I realize I probably just got Eli/Owen into even more trouble.

Malcolm chuckles. "I see Owen has been sharing."

Then something in his expression changes, and his amusement makes an almost imperceptible shift to suspicion. "Where did you say you were from?"

I swallow, trying to keep my expression neutral. "I didn't. I'm from Salt Lake City."

Malcolm points between me and Eli. "And . . . how do you two know each other?"

I let out an embarrassed laugh to hint at something scandalous and glance at Eli. It's time for him to start fielding some questions.

"We ran into each other between here and Fort Sol," says Eli. "She was having some car trouble, and I stopped to help."

"Huh," says Malcolm. He rubs his chin, his expression pensive. "Was this before or after you ran off and sold me out to Jackson?"

I freeze. A heavy silence falls over the room, and I realize all the drifters are staring at Malcolm and Eli, bracing for the storm.

Eli recovers quickly. "*Sold you out?* Is *that* what you think?"

"I don't really know what to think, to be honest," says Malcolm in a low, threatening voice. "All I know is that you have Nuclear Nation tattooed all over your fucking forehead. You've made it clear from day one that you're Jackson's man through and through.

"I thought he and I were going to work together on this. I've been more than generous and accommodating with his people. I brought them into the family like they were my own. Then he sends me you to deliver a progress report, and five of my men turn up dead. The base was almost compromised. Three of my enforcers are still missing — the men I sent looking for *you*.

"What am I supposed to do with that, Parker? Am I supposed to believe you work for *me* now?" He shakes his head. "It just doesn't sit well."

Eli lets out a long sigh and rubs the back of his head. Part of me wonders what the plan is. I'm ready to pull out my gun and start shooting my way out of here, but he doesn't look as though he's in a hurry.

"I knew this would come up eventually," Eli sighs.

I can tell he's choosing his words carefully because he knows whatever he's about to say is going to put us at enormous risk.

"I'm not going to deny killing those thugs you sent to question me. I showed up in good faith to tell them what I knew — which, by the way, wasn't much. Then your men tied me to a chair and started beating the shit out of me to get information that I didn't have. What the hell was I supposed to do?"

Behind him, Mouse makes an angry noise in his throat and glowers at Eli as though he wants to curb stomp him, but Malcolm throws Mouse a warning glance. Then he shifts his eyes back to Eli, sizing him up as though he's trying to decide whether to have him shot on sight or mess with him some more.

Then, to my enormous surprise, he nods.

"Thank you for telling me, Parker. It takes a man to admit what you did. I won't apologize for doing my due diligence, but I can't say you're entirely to blame for the unfortunate events that took place at the restaurant."

Mouse looks as though he's about to explode with rage. His shoulders are hunched in a fighting stance, and he's breathing hard through his nose like an agitated bull.

"Are you serious?" he asks Malcolm. "He killed Santiago and the others in cold blood, and you're just gonna let him get away with it?"

Malcolm snaps his head around and fixes Mouse with a piercing glare. "I will decide on an appropriate punishment later, but right now, we have more pressing matters to deal with."

Mouse opens his mouth to retort, but Malcolm cuts him

off. "This discussion is over."

Just then, I hear heavy banging from the side door, and Gunner clatters through the beaded curtain to answer. Urgent male voices drift back to us, which seems to capture Malcolm's attention.

Gunner reappears a moment later, slightly out of breath, with two more men trailing behind him.

"Compound rats about two miles out," says a dirty-looking man in a yellowish wife beater. "They're moving fast. Kill or capture?"

"Can you tell who they are?"

"We've identified one of them," grunts the man. "He's good. The other one is brand new."

"Shoot them."

A wave of nausea rolls through me when I realize they're talking about two Recon operatives — one of whom has to be a cadet.

Everything moves very fast after that. Jay, Mouse, and Tony cross to a cage of rifles in the corner and start grabbing their sniper gear. One of the drifters working at the computers gets up and points to the large map on the wall. He tells them the Recon operatives are approaching from the south side, charting the same path Eli and I took when we got shot at. Jay and Mouse argue briefly about the best place to position themselves, and then they turn to leave.

"You comin'?" Tony calls to Eli.

I'm sure I'm wearing a look of pure terror, because Eli clears his throat uncomfortably and glances down at me. "I don't think so."

"I need to take care of something," Malcolm says to Eli. "But you and I still have a lot to talk about."

Eli nods.

Malcolm slaps him on the shoulder. "Don't go too far. I may need you."

"Right."

Malcolm follows the others out, and something tells me it's time to go. I pull on my mask, and Eli starts moving toward the door.

"Hope to see you again real soon, Mama," drawls Gunner as we leave.

I glance over my shoulder and attempt an awkward smile, but Eli yanks me around the corner so fast that Gunner is just a blur. His hand finds mine, but it's not a romantic gesture; he's very close to ripping my arm out of the socket as he strides through town in the opposite direction of the approaching Recon operatives.

"Wait!" I gasp. "Where are you *going?*"

Eli doesn't answer. It's as if he doesn't even hear me.

"Eli, stop!" I yell, digging in my heels and yanking my arm out of his grasp. "We have to help the Recon guys."

"Help them how?" he asks, rounding on me with a look of desperation. "The Desperados have them in their crosshairs as we speak. If we go out there, we're as good as dead."

"We have to try!"

"How? They all think I'm Owen. If I turn against them, what do you think's gonna happen the next time Owen shows his face? I'm not going to put him at risk again. I won't do it."

"We don't even know if Owen's coming back!" I yell. "But we *do* know our friends need our help."

Eli lets out an exasperated growl and drags a hand through his hair. He knows I'm right, but at the moment, he's single-mindedly focused on protecting Owen.

"Fine," he says, resuming his long strides in the wrong direction. "But we can't do anything without our rifles. We need to get our stuff and get into position."

"We don't have time!"

"It's the only way, Harper. You want to do this or not?"

I want to argue, but he's right. We can't very well take out the drifters from afar with a handgun.

We half walk, half run up to the store where we left our rucksacks and weapons. Eli rummages around for some extra ammunition, and I see him place the photo of his family and his mother's necklace inside the bag for safekeeping. Then he flings the rucksack over his shoulder, loads his rifle, and jerks his head toward the door.

I wish he'd put on his mask, but I'm not about to waste time nagging him when our friends could be in jeopardy.

The trip across town goes much more quickly. I know we must have run most of the way there, because my heart is beating wildly against my ribcage. The sun is starting to sink lower on the horizon, but I don't know if nightfall will help the situation or make it worse.

As Eli leads us back through the bad part of town, I try to conjure up a mental image of the drifters' map to remember where exactly they planned to station themselves.

Then I hear a gunshot, and my mind goes blank.

nine

Eli

At the sound of gunfire, my heart drops to my knees. The look on Harper's face is one of utter devastation. We may already be too late.

I stop in the street and tilt my head up to scout the buildings around us. Most of them are only one story, but there's a rundown old apartment building that stands taller than the rest.

Nearly all the windows are broken, giving the building a menacing smile. My eyes follow the brick ledge about ten feet up and catch sight of a rusty fire escape.

I turn to Harper. Her face is flushed from running, and her eyes are full of terror. I kneel down in front of her, and she gives me a bewildered look.

"Climb onto my shoulders."

"What?"

"I can't reach the fire escape. I'm going to lift you up so you can grab the ladder."

She gives me a shaky nod and swings her leg over my shoulder. I hold out a hand, and she uses it to steady herself as she puts all her weight on my back.

Harper's light, but she's trembling so badly I'm afraid she's going to slide right off. I stand up, gripping her legs, and she latches her ankles around my body as I position her under the ladder.

She wobbles a little, but then I hear a loud *creak* as she yanks on the rusty ladder.

When I kneel down, Harper slides gracefully off my shoulders and clambers up ahead of me.

We've barely reached the halfway point when another gunshot shatters the silence.

I feel the vibration inside my rib cage, and the image of a bullet ripping through the air paralyzes me on the ladder.

The gunshot came from far away — and the bullet wasn't meant for us — but I still feel death deep in my bones.

Every nerve in my body is stretched to the breaking point. My hands are gripping the ladder so tightly that my palms are numb. I can't move.

"Eli!" Harper calls.

"Yeah."

"What's wrong?"

I'm gritting my teeth so hard that my jaw hurts. "Nothing," I choke. "I'm coming."

My hands are slow and shaky as I continue to climb. The ladder feels a thousand feet long, and I keep having to stop to steady my shaky limbs.

Every second I delay is a second we don't have, but after dodging death time and time again, my body is finally turning on me.

When I clear the edge of the roof, the sharp gust of desert air clears my head, and I feel more like myself.

The roof isn't as high as I would like, but it offers a much better vantage point than we could have gotten on the ground. To my right, I can see most of the sleepy town stretching off into the distance. To my left, there's nothing but desert and sky.

I have a good view of the rock formation where Jay and the others are shooting from. It's very far away, but if the wind dies down, I might have a shot at taking out the drifters before they kill one of us.

I kneel down on the roof and prop my rifle up on the low brick wall running around the edge of the building. Then I zoom in on my interface and scour the rocks for the drifters.

"Can you see them?" Harper asks. She's kneeling behind the adjacent wall with her body oriented toward the desert. She's looking for our people — not the snipers — but I don't have the heart to tell her that searching for the source of the gun-shots would be more productive.

"Not yet," I murmur, still scanning the burnt-orange rocks.

Just then, a tiny flicker of movement catches my eye — a white T-shirt or a face.

I can't tell if it's Jay or not, but someone is definitely con-cealed behind a jagged piece of sandstone.

A mirage is blurring my view of the rocks, so I focus my scope on a building about 200 yards away and place it back on my target.

When you're shooting through a mirage, you can't rely on your eyes; they'll lie to you every time. You have to shoot where you *know* your target's going to be — not where your eyes are telling you to.

I adjust for the wind and focus on my breathing, waiting patiently for Jay to show himself again.

Several long seconds pass, and the wind kicks up. I swear loudly, debating whether I should readjust or just wait for the wind to subside. Jay could show himself at any moment.

I watch a tattered flag flap in the breeze and then settle into a gentle unfurling rhythm.

Come on. Come on. Come on.

That's when Jay reappears. I adjust my aim and focus on my breathing. *In and out. In and out.*

I can see his mousey brown head and the barrel of his rifle. He's getting ready to shoot again, but he's struggling. His target must be on the run. Mine's not.

Without thinking, I let out my breath and pull the trigger.

Jay's body shudders, and then he slips out of view.

Then there's just silence.

My slow sigh of relief is cut short by another gunshot. This one didn't come from Jay.

One of the other drifters is shooting, and I have no idea where he could be hiding.

A surge of adrenaline shoots through my body as I search frantically for the source of the gunshot. There are a million places the second sniper could be concealing himself, and I never heard where Tony and Mouse were supposed to be stationed.

My eyes quickly scan the buildings near the edge of town, but I don't see anyone. That can only mean that the shots are coming from one of the other rock formations.

I look through my interface at the cluster of sandstone rocks to identify the shooter. Then I spot Mouse's black bandana as he ducks down for cover.

"Shit!"

I line up my shot, waiting for him to reappear. I don't think he hit his mark, so he has to show himself eventually if he wants to finish the job. I focus on my breathing to keep my hands steady and wait.

It happens so fast I almost miss it.

Mouse's head appears above the large sandstone rock, and he fires as I pull the trigger.

His head drops out of my line of sight, and I swear.

It's impossible to tell if I hit him or not. But then Big Boy jumps out from another little alcove and starts hoofing it back toward town. *What an idiot.*

I zoom in with my interface and see his beet-red cheeks and

flabby arms pumping in the air.

I must have hit my mark. Now that his buddies are dead, he's abandoning his post and making a break for it.

I readjust my aim and get Big Boy in my crosshairs. My finger is hovering over the trigger, ready to eliminate the threat, when a choked sob makes my heart stop.

Suddenly, every thought of the drifters is wiped from my mind. I'm no longer on the Fringe. Time becomes something physical that my body can inhabit as the second stretches out and I turn around in horror.

Harper is standing on the edge of the building, hovering like a statue with her hands gripping the low wall.

"Oh my god," she breathes.

She turns, and I half expect to see blood blossoming from a gaping wound in her chest. There's no reason for me to think the sniper shot Harper, but my first instinct is to protect her always.

When I see that she wasn't hit, my first feeling is pure relief. I drink it in greedily, but the look on her face shatters my elation.

Her silvery eyes are wide like two pools of fresh water, but they're quivering with unshed tears.

That expression tears my heart in two, and cold dread spills into my chest. She must have located our people.

"What is it?" I ask in a hollow voice.

I don't want her to tell me, but I have to know.

Harper opens and closes her mouth several times, breathing hard. She clicks out of her interface and presses a shaky hand over her mouth to stifle a wave of sobs. When she speaks, her voice is muffled, but I still hear her loud and clear.

"It's Lenny and Miles."

ten

Sawyer

I have no idea what time it is when my interface wakes me up from my nap. It takes several seconds for me to reenter the land of the living. The frantic beeping means someone is paging me, but the sound is so ubiquitous in the medical ward that sometimes I imagine it.

I finally locate my interface and sit up on my bunk. The page is short: *Emergency Fringe Retrieval.*

Those three words make my blood go cold, and I lean forward and place my head between my knees to ward off the panic.

When Harper's been deployed, *any* Fringe retrieval is enough to set me on edge, but the fact that they added "emergency" to the phrase means I have genuine cause for concern.

Get it together, I breathe. If Harper can go out there after she's been blown up and shot at, the least I can do is hold it together long enough to do my job.

Before my mind can jump to the worst conclusion, I roll out of my bunk and nearly twist my ankle on a stray shoe.

"Shit!"

Another interface starts beeping.

The flashing blue light illuminates Caleb snuggled under the blankets in the bottom bunk, still blissfully unaware that we have a job to do.

I have the urge to pick up the shoe and whip it across his freckly face, but the beeping wakes him before I have the chance.

"Emergency Fringe retrieval?" I ask, turning my back to him and replacing my sweat-stained T-shirt with fresh scrubs.

"Yeah," he yawns, pulling on his shoes.

I'm not sure why I bother turning around — it's nothing he hasn't seen before. As two of the four interns with level-A security clearance, we practically live together in the temporary bunk room.

Between our regular twelve-hour shifts and all the extra research hours we've been logging to impress the Progressive Research Unit, we've been running ourselves ragged. Most of our conversations consist of yawns and impatient snapping in the tunnels.

Part of me thinks Health and Rehab makes the internship program a pressure cooker on purpose. Forcing interns competing for top positions to live in close quarters with very little sleep must be good training for the demands of being a full-fledged doctor.

Back in higher ed, the competition would have thrilled me, but right now I just find it tiring and a little gross. I could really use a shower — or at least a little deodorant — but there's no time. I just run my fingers through my hair and yank it up into a messy ponytail.

Without waiting for Caleb, I fly out into the brightly lit tunnel and try not to look as though I just rolled out of bed.

"Lyang!" barks a voice from behind me. "There you are! What the hell took so long?"

It's Dr. Watson, the most impatient asshole in the medical ward. Of course he would be on call tonight.

"Sorry, sir. What's going on?"

"Emergency Fringe retrieval," he snaps.

No shit.

"Did they say if they've been injured?"

"No. They're still too far out to know for sure, but Eagle Eye says they'll be chambered in just a few minutes. You and MacAvoy should head down there to get them. Page me immediately if you need assistance."

"Yes, sir."

I know I'm supposed to wait for Caleb, but I'm just too anxious. I grab the first gurney I can find and summon an automatic wheelchair to follow me onto the freight lift. You never know which one you're going to need.

Just as the doors start to close, I spot Caleb running frantically around the ward and roll my eyes.

It's not that he's a bad guy. In a less competitive section, we might even be friends. But since there's only one spot available in Progressive Research, that makes him just another kiss-ass who needs to be eliminated.

On the ride down to the ground level, it's all I can do not to think about a wounded Harper draped over Eli's shoulder. She got lucky the time he was shot, but I'm not sure how long her luck can possibly hold out with such frequent deployments.

As soon as the lift doors open, I rush down the tunnel toward the postexposure chamber. There's already a hazmat suit and a mask waiting for me. I unzip the thing in one motion and pull it off the hook to slither inside.

It's much more difficult to get it zipped back up once I'm wearing it. My fingers feel clumsy in the attached rubber gloves, and I can't see what they're doing outside the suit when my face is encased in plastic.

Finally I secure the hood and rush into the secondary chamber to meet them. Through the small window in the door, I can see several shadowy figures crowded in the radiation chamber. It's too dark to distinguish their faces, but it looks as though there are more than two people in there.

When I press my face closer to the glass, I hear frantic shouts and a high-pitched whimper.

Harper.

I wait with bated breath for the compound doors to shut. As soon as the green light flashes on my side of the chamber, I frantically stab the door release to let them inside.

Three people rush toward me, and I press myself against the wall to make room. All the movement and body heat is a little disorienting, but I try to focus on the awkward shape to my right.

"We need to get her to the medical ward!" somebody yells.

The voice is male — low and terrified — but it isn't Eli. The man is stooped to avoid bumping his head on the low ceiling, and he's hunched over as if he's carrying a heavy bundle.

Then he steps into the light, and I see that the voice belongs to Eli's tall, hulking fighter friend — Miles, I think.

He doesn't look so tough right now, though; he has the same helpless look I've seen on the faces of people in the medical ward who are about to lose their loved ones.

Cradled in his arms is a small redheaded girl with milky white skin. She's trembling and breathing hard, and sweaty curls are clinging to her forehead.

I scan her body for signs of injury, and my eyes land on a dark bloodstain spreading near her abdomen.

"Gunshot wound?"

"Yeah," says Miles, looking at me as though I hold all the answers to the universe.

Somebody brushes past me, and in the harsh blue light, I can just make out Harper's ashen, tear-stained face. I give her a quick once-over and feel a tiny surge of relief that she seems unharmed.

"It's my friend Lenny," she says, choking back a sob. "You have to help her. She's lost a lot of blood."

My heart feels as though it might beat right out of my chest, and my breathing speeds up.

They warned us about this — getting sucked into the panic. They train us to stay calm and respond to an emergency with a clear head, but nothing could have prepared me for the paralyzing fear and pressure.

From the look on Harper's face, it feels as if I'm single-handedly responsible for the life of the girl in Miles's arms, and the prognosis doesn't look good.

Suddenly, my mind flashes to one of the first operations I assisted with after the explosion in Systems. A man who'd been buried in the rubble was bleeding out on the table. I was having a panic attack in the operating room, and my overseeing physician had said, "When we don't have peace, we rely on process."

A calm feeling washes over me as I picture Dr. Fey's kind, capable face, and I know what I have to do.

"We need to decontaminate you first," I hear myself say to Harper.

"Are you *serious*?"

"The gunshot wound is *her* most pressing problem — not yours."

Harper looks as though she wants to put up a fight, so I push the button for the shower and shove her under the spray. She cringes as icy water pounds down on her, soaking her to the bone.

"Give her to me," I instruct Miles.

He gives me a skeptical look but transfers Lenny to my arms. I nearly buckle under her weight, but it's manageable. She's smaller than me, and the rush of adrenalin helps.

As my arms close over her small frame, her breathing starts

to come a little faster — as though she fears I might drop her. But I stab the door release with my foot and stagger out to place her on the gurney just outside the chamber.

"Decontaminate," I shout to Miles, not taking my eyes off Lenny as I lay her on the crisp white sheet. Maybe it's the sickly light from the chamber, but she looks much too pale. She needs to go through the decontamination shower, too, but I worry she doesn't have time.

I can't see her abdominal wound clearly, but the blood is seeping through her uniform at an alarming rate. I press my hands down and apply pressure to stem the bleeding, and a look of agony flashes over her face.

"It's okay," I tell her. "You're okay."

I hear the shower running again. Yanking down the zipper on my suit to access my interface, I page the medical ward for immediate assistance upon arrival. I don't bother stripping off the suit completely. I'm going to be in trouble, but I can already feel process breaking down.

I'm not ready for this.

"Help me push," I yell to Harper.

I can't see her, but the gurney starts moving toward the megalift.

The doors open, and Caleb rushes out — nearly careening into our gurney.

"What's going on?" he splutters.

"GSW," I pant. "Take care of the others."

Caleb freezes on the spot, but I don't have time to worry about him.

Miles appears on my other side wearing just his shorts. Droplets of water are sliding off his tattooed chest, and he's trembling slightly.

The sight of a man his size on the verge of a breakdown

causes a lump to form in my throat, but I shove it down and keep moving.

"I can take it from here," I say gently. "Go with Caleb."

"I'm comin' with you," he growls.

"Just until we get up to the medical ward. Then they'll take her into surgery."

We crowd onto the lift, and Caleb just stands there — paralyzed by the responsibility that's been thrust upon him. I hear some garbled instructions coming through my interface, but all I can think about is the warm gush of blood under my gloves and the pale, broken girl on my gurney.

As the lift doors close and we shoot up toward the medical ward, I give Lenny a cursory examination. Then her eyes drift closed, and I start to panic in earnest.

"Lenny. Lenny! Stay with me."

She doesn't move.

Harper's face blanches, and I swallow down the bile burning in my throat.

Lenny is still bleeding profusely, and she's dangerously pale. I can't lift my hands to check her pulse, but I can tell she's in serious cardiac distress.

After what seems like an eternity, the lift dings, and Harper shoves the gurney forward into the ward.

That's when all hell breaks loose. Nurses rush forward to usher Harper and Miles into separate exam rooms, and another pack of them shove me aside to rush Lenny to an operating room. There's a flurry of hands unsnapping her shirt and sticking monitors onto her chest, but I already know she's in serious trouble.

I feel the sting of separation as the gurney rolls away. I start trailing after them, but a sharp yell calls me back to reality.

"What in the *hell* are you doing?"

I freeze.

"*Are you out of your fucking mind?*" Dr. Watson growls, striding toward me with his white coat billowing behind him like a cape.

That's when I remember I'm still wearing the hazmat suit and I'm elbow-deep in Lenny's blood.

I open and close my mouth several times, but no words come out.

His watery blue eyes flash. "Lyang! You're contaminating this entire unit!"

"I had a gunshot victim!" I splutter. "I couldn't decontaminate her without delaying treatment, so —"

"She hasn't been decontaminated either?"

"N-no."

Watson swears loudly, and those telltale angry creases appear on his forehead. They're the lines he gets just before he berates someone in a very humiliating public fashion. "She hasn't been decontaminated? She hasn't been —" He sighs. "Is this your first day, or are you just *stupid?*"

"I'm sorry, sir."

"You're sorry? You're sorry. You just put this entire ward at risk! And for what? One first-year Recon operative who's just going to die on the table?"

An alarming amount of heat is radiating from my body, and I clench my fists together to stop them from shaking. I can barely see Watson's livid expression through the tears accumulating in my eyes, but I can hear the hatred in his voice.

I'm going to be put on probation for sure. I might as well say goodbye to Progressive Research. If Watson has his way, I'll be taking urine samples for the rest of my life.

"I have half a mind to tell you to hand in your scrubs and hoof it down to Operations right now."

Horror flashes through me. I couldn't have screwed up this badly — not badly enough to get me thrown out of Health and Rehab, surely.

But then the lift doors fly open, and an eruption of shouts forces Watson to put his rant on hold.

Eli strides out of the lift, followed by a frazzled-looking Caleb. He's stripped down to a pair of boxer briefs, and Caleb is just in his scrubs. Eli is clutching his rucksack to his chest like a life preserver, and I'm caught between the urge to laugh, cry, and check out Eli.

"We have to get you to an exam room," says Caleb.

He tries to pull the rucksack out of Eli's arms, but Eli twists out of his reach easily.

"And you can't take that with you. It hasn't been decontaminated!"

"That's my cadet you just wheeled off!" yells Eli. "I want to see her."

"You can see her when she gets out of surgery," says Caleb, an annoyed edge to his voice.

"What the hell is this?" Watson splutters. "Can none of you do your job?"

Caleb whirls around. As soon as he sees me and Watson, his face goes bright red.

"Uh . . . he's just a little hysterical, sir."

"I'm not hysterical," snaps Eli.

"I need to take this," says Watson.

Eli jerks out of his grip, but between Watson and Caleb, they manage to successfully peel the rucksack out of Eli's death grip.

"Who the hell are you?" Eli barks at Watson. "And where's Harper?"

"Cadet Riley was just admitted, but I'm afraid you'll have to wait to see her."

"This is *bullshit*."

Under any other circumstances, I'd find it hilarious that a patient was standing in the tunnel in his underwear yelling at Caleb and Watson. But this is Eli. In the few interactions I've had with him, I've learned that he's a little unpredictable when it comes to Harper. And right now, he looks frantic.

"Eli, I'll take you to see Harper as soon as she's been debriefed," I say, trying to keep my voice steady.

His steely gaze softens a little, but I can feel Watson's cold glare burning a hole in my back.

Finally, Eli yields and allows Caleb to steer him toward an exam room. He should be in a wheelchair. It gives me some satisfaction to know that Caleb is going to get a lecture later, too, but it's nothing compared to the browbeating I'm about to receive.

"Decontaminate *now* and scrub up for Riley's exam," Watson snaps. "Then meet me in my office at twenty-two hundred so we can talk about your dangerous stupidity."

He breezes away, leaving me standing there in my hazmat suit.

For a second, I don't think I'm going to be able to move, but I force my feet to shuffle down the tunnel toward secondary decontamination.

I lock myself in the little shower and try to extricate myself from the suit. But as soon as I'm alone, all my scared, angry tears start pouring out.

My sobs echo back at me off the white tiled walls, and my gloved fingers fumble uselessly at the zipper running down the front of my suit. Usually we pair up to take these off, but I can't have anyone witnessing my meltdown.

I keep struggling with the zipper long after the shower cycle has stopped, and once the last water drains from the sloped floor, I cringe at how pathetic I must look.

Sinking down onto the cold tile, hopelessness swamps me.

Maybe I'm not cut out for this. After months and months of work, I don't feel any closer to being considered a legitimate doctor or researcher. All those sleepless nights, extra shifts, and dirty bed pans were for nothing. One stupid mistake was enough to destroy my job prospects.

Then I think about Harper and how she's going to react when she learns that she's lost her friend. I don't know for sure that Lenny's heart stopped, but she didn't look good. And if she does die, Watson's going to make me break the news to Harper and Eli myself.

After all that, nothing I did mattered. Lenny was always going to die.

A soft knock on the shower door pulls me briefly out of my misery, but the voice on the other side is the absolute last one I want to hear.

"Sawyer?" calls Caleb. "Are you okay?"

"Go away, MacAvoy," I blubber. "I'm not in the mood."

The door rattles briefly, but then he stops. "I'm coming in," he calls, a note of hesitation coloring his determined voice. "You decent?"

I groan.

There's a brief pause, but then the door opens. Caleb is standing just outside the shower, looking exhausted but not unsympathetic.

"You shouldn't be in here," I say, gesturing to my suit. "You're going to have to decontaminate and rescrub all over again."

"I don't mind," he murmurs, kneeling down next to me and reaching for the zipper.

His expression is warm and calm as he tugs it down, and my overheated body welcomes the rush of cool air filtering through my scrubs.

Caleb takes my hands and helps me into a standing position so he can pull the suit down to my ankles. It's much trickier than putting the suit on, since the plastic suctions to every inch of exposed skin.

"I heard Watson yelling at you through the lift doors," he murmurs.

"Who *didn't* hear that? Now everybody thinks I'm an idiot."

"Are you kidding? You're the smartest intern here *by far*. No one thinks you're an idiot . . . least of all me."

From the tone of his voice and the set of his jaw, I can tell he isn't just saying those things to make me feel better. He genuinely believes them.

I let out a long sigh and deflate against the shower wall. "Why are you being so *nice* to me?"

"Because you had a shit day," he answers quickly. "And because I think you did the right thing."

"Not according to protocol."

"Fuck protocol," he snaps. "That girl would have died if you'd followed protocol."

My heart sinks. "I think she did die."

"No, she didn't." He sounds surprised. "They're still working on her in suspended animation."

"*What?*"

I don't want to believe him. It seems too good to be true. And I can't allow myself to feel any false hope. That will just make the blow of failure that much more painful.

"Yeah. I saw them wheel her in there with the crash cart. They're going to try to bring her back after they operate."

My heart rate picks up a little, and despite my best efforts, hope beats down on me like a warm ray of sunshine.

I'm also a little bit excited. I've never seen this procedure performed, and I want to be there when they do it.

"You wanna go watch?" Caleb asks, correctly interpreting the eagerness in my eyes.

I glance back up at his face and crack a smile.

"Okay. Hang on."

Caleb reaches up and hits the button to run the decontamination cycle again. I cringe as cold water pelts us both, and a strange feeling of intimacy creeps over me as I watch the water soak through his scrubs and rain down on his face.

He grins at me through the blast of water, and I feel myself go a little red as I stare at the tiny droplets clinging to his blond eyelashes and ruddy lips.

Then the water stops, and he turns to open the door on the other side. There's a stack of fluffy towels that smell like bleach and a bunch of scrubs in odd sizes waiting on the shelf. I hurriedly dry off my hair, and we turn away from each other to change.

I don't know what that was, but a new excitement is thrumming through my veins that has nothing to do with the medical miracle I'm about to witness.

Maybe I don't have to hate Caleb after all.

eleven

Sawyer

I've watched dozens of surgeries from the gallery above this operating theater, but I've never had the urge to fall right through the glass and shout in the patient's ear, *Come on! You can do it!*

I've always been a detached observer, as though it was a staged production where the nurses, doctors, and even the patient knew exactly what was about to happen.

This is nothing like that.

The doctors put Lenny in suspended animation — a procedure I've read about but never actually seen. She's lying on the operating table under layers of scratchy blue paper with her arms at her sides. The surgical lighting makes her look even more like a corpse: Her hair is a bright, unnatural orange, and her skin is practically translucent.

She looks dead because she is, technically. When her heart stopped, the doctors pumped all the blood from her body and replaced it with a saline solution. Chilling her body should delay brain death and buy the doctors a few hours to fix the damage to her organs and repopulate her body with blood.

"That's incredible," breathes Caleb.

The look on his face captures the way I'm feeling exactly. His nose is barely an inch from the glass, and I can see Lenny's body reflected in his wide eyes.

"She still might not make it."

He glances over at me. "She definitely wouldn't have made

it if it weren't for you. Her heart stopped right when she got here. A few more minutes, and . . ."

I swallow, trying not to focus on the "what ifs."

Caleb turns back to watch the operation, and his face falls into a scowl. "I just can't believe it."

"What?"

"That it's all true. I thought ExCon was making everything up about the hostile survivors in the cleared zone, but *someone* had to shoot her."

"Oh." I hurriedly school my expression. "Yeah . . . you're right."

I cringe. I'm horrible at lying.

Harper told me that Recon was fending off Death Storm survivors near the compound, but most interns aren't privy to that type of information. The doctors and nurses who work with Recon patients inevitably discover bits and pieces of what's going on out on the Fringe, but they're trained not to ask questions that aren't directly related to the patient's health.

Because Health and Rehab is understaffed and Caleb and I have security clearance, we've been called upon to work a few Fringe retrievals. He's had a taste of what Recon workers go through, but this must be his first time seeing patients after a deployment went badly wrong.

"The board's been lying to us all this time," he continues. "I'm honestly surprised they've been able to keep it quiet for so long."

"What do you mean?"

"It's just . . . how have people not wondered why so many Recon workers just disappear?"

"Well . . . you never did before now."

I realize too late that my comment may have sounded like an accusation, so I clear my throat and add, "I never did, either."

"I know." Caleb shakes his head, looking angry with himself. "It isn't right. Nobody even cares. It's like they're *invisible*. You can bet if a bunch of tier-one workers started disappearing, people would ask questions. Hell, it would be all over the news feeds."

"I think you might be overestimating how much the other sections care about us."

"Shit. You might be right. Everyone's just in their own little bubble around here."

A heavy silence falls between us, and I feel the heat of shame creep over me. It's so strange to be standing here having a real conversation with Caleb MacAvoy. I've spent so much time and energy hating him for trying to take what's mine that I never bothered to get to know him. It's almost as bad as no one caring what happens to Recon workers.

"She's our age, you know," he murmurs, staring down at Lenny. "I saw her chart. God. It's unbelievable what they expect their first years to do."

I open my mouth to agree, but my throat feels too tight. Beside the operating table sits a stainless steel tray with a dozen tiny bullet fragments that they pulled from Lenny's lifeless body. Suddenly my own problems seem embarrassingly shallow.

What have I been doing? For the past few months, my entire existence has centered around getting ahead in Health and Rehab. I've barely seen Harper other than when she was injured or being detained here in psychiatric holding, and I haven't so much as grabbed dinner with any of the other interns. It's as though I've put my entire life on hold and refused to think about all the big important things going on in the compound.

"They're reviving her," Caleb breathes.

His voice is a welcome relief from my own guilty thoughts. I lean forward slightly, and I actually feel my nose hit the glass.

Lenny's blood flows through the curled tubes hanging off the operating table, making a graceful loop that looks like a signature. We watch in awe as it courses back into her veins, shooting through the tubes as though it's in a hurry to return home.

Within minutes, a faint pinkish hue begins to color her skin as her cold corpse transforms into a warm, almost-living body. They wait.

Then the surgeon bends over her, says something to the nurse, and attempts to restart her heart.

We hold our breath as the seconds tick by.

Then the unthinkable happens: Lenny comes back from the dead.

The first beep on the monitor is so faint it could have been my imagination, but then her heart rate picks up and resumes its slow but steady rhythm.

I let out a breath I didn't realize I'd been holding, and Caleb's triumphant laughter shatters the tension. My laugh comes out choked with emotion.

I turn to him, and he throws his arms around my shoulders. The atmosphere of celebration inside the tiny gallery overwhelms the awkwardness, and we laugh and murmur our relief until the moment passes.

When I pull away, Caleb is still grinning, and I have a fast, fleeting thought that he's actually really good-looking. That's enough to make the easy smile slip from my face.

"Thanks for watching with me," I say, feeling uncomfortable. "And for . . . you know."

"Sure."

Am I imagining how strange his voice sounds?

"I better go tell Harper the good news. I have to examine her anyway."

Voicing my plan surprises even me. In the aftermath of the retrieval and my own emotional turmoil, Harper's exam had completely slipped my mind. I shake my head and leave the gallery, angry with myself for losing focus.

Luckily, the ward is busy today, so no one will notice that Harper has been waiting in the exam room for an awfully long time. I take a deep breath to collect myself and rap loudly on her door.

"Come in." Harper's voice sounds oddly nasally, and I get a pang of guilt when I realize how worried she must be.

I push the door open and rush inside.

As soon as I see her, my heart breaks in two. Harper looks tiny and childlike, shivering on the table in her thin hospital gown. She's got a mountain of damp tissues piled up beside her, and her eyes are red and bloodshot.

"I'm so sorry," I say, putting an arm around her.

"H-how's Lenny?" she gasps, her glassy eyes filling with tears again.

"She's fine. I'm sorry. I should have been in sooner. I was watching her operation. Her heart stopped, but it looks like they were able to fix the damage from the bullet and restart it. They had to put her body in hibernation mode to do it, but she should wake up in a few hours."

"Oh my god," Harper whispers, her head dipping down in relief. "I can't believe it was her. I saw it happen, and I still can't believe it. She wasn't supposed to be sent out yet."

"Jayden's speeding up deployment?"

"I don't know what she's doing. Lenny wasn't ready. None of us were."

I know I shouldn't ask, but I'm in so much trouble as it is, and my conversation with Caleb just magnified my curiosity.

"Harper . . . what the hell is going on out there?"

There's a long pause, and when Harper looks up at me, her expression is haunted.

"Oh my god, Sawyer. It's so much worse than we thought." She shakes her head in disbelief. "There are so many of them. They're congregating just a few miles away, and now they have the technology to pick us off one by one."

"Hang on. How do you know that?"

Harper's eyes widen, and she glances furtively at the closed door. "Eli and I found their new base. We . . . we pretended to be drifters, and they let us inside."

The heaviness of that statement falls over me with a crushing force. "*What?*"

"There's more."

I don't know how there could possibly be more, but judging by the frantic look in Harper's eyes, it's something huge.

She opens her mouth to speak, but she's interrupted by the beep of my interface. It shakes me out of my trance, and I glance at the message flashing in front of my eyes.

"Shit."

It's from Watson, reminding me of our meeting in a few minutes.

Dread settles over me, and I immediately remember that I'm supposed to be examining Harper and taking a blood sample.

"I have to draw some blood," I say, grimacing when I realize that the sample is going to be late. I am *really* off my game today.

She holds out her arm, and my hands are a little shaky as I tie the tourniquet around her bicep. I've done this a million times, but I'm still on edge from the Fringe retrieval.

Harper makes a fist, and I stick the needle in her vein. It's not my best work, but the pain barely registers on her face as I fill two vacutainers with blood.

"How are you feeling?" I ask.

She shrugs. "Okay, I guess. I'm just tired."

"I'd be surprised if you weren't."

I finish drawing her blood and hold a piece of gauze to the needle prick to stop the bleeding.

"I'll get these to the lab. They're going to want to keep you under observation for a couple of days to monitor your white count and look for signs of radiation poisoning."

"How's Eli?" she asks. "He wasn't wearing his mask when we went with the drifters, and —"

"He took off his mask?"

I can't imagine how Eli could be so stupid. Going out onto the Fringe is dangerous enough, but doing it without a mask is suicide.

Harper shakes her head impatiently, and I can tell she's getting ready to launch into whatever she was about to tell me. "He —"

My interface beeps again — more frantically this time. It's from the lab, wanting to know where Harper's blood samples are.

I sigh. "I'm sorry. I have to run this over for analysis. But I'll be back. And I'll check Eli's dosimeter to see how much radiation he was exposed to."

Harper purses her lips together, trying not to cry. I feel bad for adding to her worries, but Harper is my best friend. I can't lie to her.

If Eli went without his mask, there's a strong possibility he's going to have serious radiation poisoning.

"It's going to be okay," I whisper, squeezing the arm I didn't draw blood from. "Eli's strong."

Harper nods without meeting my gaze, slowly gathering her

composure and regaining some of that inner toughness I wish I could summon.

"I'll be back."

* * *

I always dread making a handoff at the lab. The technicians in the Progressive Research Unit have an inflated sense of self-importance, and the one called Marge gives me a condescending sneer as I roll the vials of blood across the steel table.

"You're late," she snaps.

"I know. I'm sorry, Marge. There was an emergency with one of the other Recon patients."

"I need this within the hour after exposure, and this sample is late."

I nod quickly. I'd agree to anything to avoid a full-blown lecture. "I'm sorry. It won't happen again."

She gives me a stern look but doesn't say anything else.

For some reason, the lab techs are very particular about the samples collected from Recon operatives just returning from the Fringe. It seems strange, considering how little they care about every other aspect of their treatment. I know they need properly timed samples to watch for a sudden drop in white blood cells, but once radiation poisoning is confirmed, the techs aren't as quick to process patients' lab work.

I only have a few minutes before my meeting with Watson, so I head straight to the supply decontamination room in the hope that they haven't cleared Eli's dosimeter yet.

An enormous radioactive symbol fills the center of the dented metal door. I stop to don a hazmat suit and then punch in the door code and wait for the tired *beep*. The SDR is just a glorified storage area, but you need security clearance to access it.

The walls are a dull grayish white, and the concrete floor dips near the middle for drainage. Shelves line the back wall, and a long stainless steel table gleams under the bluish light running down the center of the ceiling.

I'm relieved to have the place to myself. It's unusual for anyone who doesn't work the decontamination unit to be in here, and it could lead to some awkward questions. Most physicians just wait for the decontamination workers to post the dosimeter readings to the patient's file, but then again, most physicians aren't friends with any Recon operatives.

Eli's rucksack and uniform are stuffed in a rubber tub at the end of the table, as though someone just dumped it there and ran off to erase the trail of radioactive particles I left behind.

His dosimeter is still clipped to his holster, and I press the button on the top to beam the readings straight to my interface. I turn to go as soon as I hear the low *beep*, but then I remember Eli clutching his rucksack to his chest like his first-born child.

I've only spent a limited amount of time with him, but Eli doesn't strike me as the type of person to lose it after a deployment. He's too experienced for that.

There's something important in his rucksack, and I'd bet it's related to whatever Harper was trying to tell me.

I pause for several seconds, listening intently for the sound of footsteps coming down the tunnel. Hearing nothing, I reach over and grab his rucksack and open the flap hanging over the drawstring.

There's nothing unusual inside — just a dozen or so ration packets, a half-empty water pouch, a first aid kit, and extra ammunition. I lay it all out on the table and stare at the items as though they might tell me something.

What was it that Eli wanted to protect?

He could have just been scared and flustered, clinging to

something solid to reassure himself that he was alive. But it doesn't fit.

Frustrated, I tip one more stray ration packet onto the table and hear a tiny metallic *clink*.

Holding the bag up to the light, I see a little zip pocket sewn into the lining. I stick my hand inside and retrieve two items: a silver charm necklace with a bright blue stone and an old photograph.

My heart beats a little faster. I've never held a physical photograph before. People had them before Death Storm, but I never saw a need for one. This picture is crinkled around the edges and slightly discolored, but those things just make it seem more real.

It's a picture of a woman in her late thirties, a man who looks a few years older, and two young boys — probably the couple's children.

I'm not sure why Eli would have this photograph in his possession. He knows better than anyone that it's illegal to bring pre–Death Storm relics in from the Fringe. It's also kind of bizarre that he would want a random picture from someone else's life.

Still, it could be important, so I carefully fold the photo along the deep crease in the middle and go to stick it in my pocket. But something on the back catches my eye. It's a line of faded cursive handwriting scrawled along the edge in blue ink: Camping at Fishlake; Owen age 12, Eli age 10.

That's when I stop breathing.

I unfold the photo again and stare at the two little boys. The younger one is squinting in the sunlight, but his features are clearly visible. He's got brown, almost black, hair and big blue eyes. He's small and lanky, but it's definitely a ten-year-old version of Eli.

Now that I know it's him, I can't believe I didn't see the resemblance before. That must mean the older boy is his brother.

He could be Eli's twin, only he's taller and has a little more meat on his bones. There's also something in the eyes that sets them apart: His brother has the look of a born troublemaker.

That's when I realize that the photo and necklace are probably all Eli has left of his family. That would explain why he was guarding them with his life, but not why he brought them along for his deployment. They'd be much safer in his compartment — unless he brought them back from the Fringe today.

That can only mean one thing. It seems so unlikely, but the evidence is undeniable.

Somehow, somewhere, a member of Eli's family is still alive.

twelve

Eli

Growing up in the Institute, there were times I used to think Miles was telepathic. He always seemed to have a sixth sense for when I was getting the shit beat out of me, and he'd turn up just in time to help. When we'd turn back to back to fight our way out of a corner, we moved around each other as though we shared one brain.

Unfortunately, Miles seems to have lost his talent for telepathy.

As soon as Jayden strides into the room for my debriefing, I can tell from her air of irritation that she's already spoken to him. He must have let it slip that I'd been shooting at the snipers who got Lenny to make me look good, but Jayden isn't happy.

"I just received word from Cadet Horwitz's doctor," she says. "Apparently, they were able to repair the damage to her organs in suspended animation and restart her heart."

An odd sense of relief cuts through my dread, and I let out the breath I'd been holding since she walked in. "Is she going to be all right?"

"She'll need several weeks to recover before she can train again, but yes." Jayden flashes a tight smile. "She'll be fine."

I nod and meet Jayden's cold, dark gaze.

"Congratulations," she whispers. "Once again, you manage to fend off death on the Fringe and return from your mission early with absolutely nothing to show for it."

Indignation flares through me, and the spark ignites all the pent-up rage I've been suppressing. "I took out one of Malcolm's men who was shooting at *our* people. And I wouldn't have needed to return early if they hadn't been sent out in the first place!"

"Parker —"

"What were they even doing out there?" I ask, cutting through her protests. "Miles wasn't due for deployment, and I never cleared Horwitz for combat."

Jayden makes a small jerky movement with her head — a gesture of superiority that's become something like a nervous tick.

"Do I need to remind you who's in charge around here? I've given you free rein in training your cadets in the past, but that ends now. I believe I've made it clear that the speed at which you're preparing them is *unacceptable*, so now I'm forced to intervene."

"They aren't ready!" I say. "And sending them out isn't going to *make* them ready. You give me a bunch of twenty-one-year-olds who have never fired a gun or thrown a punch in their lives and expect me to turn them into trained operatives in three months? It's fucking ridiculous."

"That's not your call to make anymore."

"I need more time with them!"

"We don't have time!" snaps Jayden. "The Desperados have five hundred people waiting just a few miles from this compound. Do you have any idea what would happen if they attacked us?" She tucks her chin and glares up at me with menacing eyes. "Let me put it in terms you can understand: Your little cadets would be the first bodies the board throws outside to take care of the problem."

She leans forward — so close I can see through her heavy

layers of makeup to the tired bags under her eyes. "I need — to know — what they're planning."

"Well, I can't help you," I say, trying to keep my expression neutral.

It's half true. I *don't* know what the Desperados are planning. I might know the location of their new base, but I'm not giving that up before I have a chance to find Owen and warn him.

"Don't lie to me, Parker," she says in a deadly whisper. "Don't you fucking sit there and lie to my face."

Something in Jayden's expression changes, and I realize suddenly that this is no ordinary debriefing. Jayden has come unhinged.

I swallow. I'm not sure what she knows, and I don't want to speak first and risk revealing more.

"Let's watch a movie," she says.

The uneasy feeling in my stomach intensifies, but I try to look nonplussed as Jayden clicks her interface and projects an image onto the blank wall across from my bed.

She taps her interface again, and another clip of surveillance footage appears. It shows me and Harper following the drifters to the pawn shop.

My heart sinks. She knows we found their base.

We disappear down the alleyway, and Jayden fast-forwards several minutes. When she hits "play" again, Malcolm strides into view, and Jayden's expression sours into pure, unadulterated fury.

"You and Riley went on a little field trip today, I see. You played dress-up and pretended to be drifters?" she growls indignantly. "It's not enough that you completely abandoned standard operating procedure. You were in the same *room* with Martinez, and you let him walk right out the door!"

She shuts off her interface, and the image on the wall disappears. "I've grown used to your bullshit, Parker, but you've outdone yourself this time. You've got to be the most worthless, irresponsible lieutenant I've ever trained."

I take a deep breath, trying to separate my feelings of loathing from what I'm about to say. "We didn't have a choice. That town was *crawling* with drifters. We only dressed like that so we would blend in, and it worked. They led us right to the base.

"We would have killed Martinez right then, but there were way too many of them. We never would have made it out alive if we'd opened fire in that store."

In one swift motion, Jayden picks up the vase of flowers from the table behind her and chucks the entire thing at my head.

I slip out of the way, and the vase hits the wall behind me. I hear it shatter into a million pieces, sending a splash of cold water down my back and showering my bed in flowers.

"I don't give a *fuck*! News flash, Parker! One dead drifter is worth *ten* of you! I gave you direct orders, and you completely disobeyed them."

"I'll get it done," I growl, balling the blanket in my fists to prevent myself from grabbing Jayden by the throat.

A second later, a petite blond nurse rushes through the door looking alarmed. "What's going on in here?"

Her head snaps back and forth between me and Jayden, and the crease in her brow deepens as she tries to figure out what happened.

"Get out!" Jayden whispers, turning her piercing glare on the nurse.

The poor thing clearly isn't one of the regulars in the post-exposure wing — everybody who normally works with Recon operatives knows to steer clear of Jayden. The nurse opens and closes her mouth a few times and then backs awkwardly out of the room.

Jayden slams the door behind her and wheels around to face me again. Her slim chest is rising and falling rapidly, and the dread in my stomach intensifies.

"I'm done messing around, Parker. Our intelligence tells me Martinez has disappeared again, and Jackson hasn't showed his face around that town in weeks. Our mystery man has gone off the grid, too.

"The *second* one of them shows his face again, you and Riley are going back out. And when you do, I don't want to see either of you again unless you've got a dead drifter to show me."

"Got it," I snap.

"I don't think you do, so listen closely," she snarls. "I want you to stay out there until you get the job done, Parker. I don't care if it takes six days or six months. If you come back from deployment with nothing to show for it, Cadet Riley is going to take another trip to the dead level. And this time, she won't come out. Do you understand me?"

At those words, my blood turns to ice in my veins. Jayden can't possibly mean what I think she does. She plans to send us out to the Fringe indefinitely. And the only way we can come back is to deliver Jackson, Malcolm, or Owen.

"And don't even think about lying to me again," she murmurs. "I have eyes *everywhere*."

I don't say anything. I can't speak. I can't think. My hands are trembling with fury and indignation — just itching to reach out and wring Jayden's scrawny neck.

She struts past my bed in her too-tight uniform, snatching up a wilted orange lily with a seductive sweeping motion. "I heard about Riley's little trip to 119, so I know you know she doesn't have anywhere to run."

Jayden pauses and turns toward me with a cool, half-disinterested look in her eyes. She holds the petals to her nose, inhales deeply, and then shifts her grip on the stem and whips it across my face like a switch.

My face stings as the stem cuts across the skin just below my eye, but I just grit my teeth and glare up at her.

Jayden offers me a cold smile and then cups her hand gently around the flower.

At first I think she's going to start yelling again, but she just sighs and plucks lazily at a stray petal. "If you fuck up and lie about it again, I'm not just going to kill your little girlfriend." She closes her fist and twists her hand so all the petals fall away in shreds. "I'm going to enjoy it."

thirteen

Harper

The medical ward is never completely quiet. Nurses' hushed voices float between the seams of the frosted glass walls. The metal cabinet across from my bed rattles as a gurney blazes by my room.

Every few minutes, the air kicks on. It fills the room with a low whirring noise and makes me shiver under my thin, overbleached sheet.

But around oh-three hundred, everything grows eerily still. The air conditioner shuts off. The nurses trickle out of the postexposure wing.

I can't sleep. The small amount of light coming through the six-inch window in my door is enough to stimulate my senses. After spending three days in the medical ward for "observation," I've had about all the rest my body can take.

A dark shape moves across the wall. Then the light from the tiny window vanishes, throwing my room into total darkness. Through the curtain of hair falling over my eyes, I can see someone looking in, blocking my view of the rest of the tunnel.

Someone is watching me.

I hold my breath, waiting for the nurse or doctor to see that I'm sleeping and leave. But a moment later, I hear the door handle turn.

The visitor steps inside and shuts the door quickly. I don't move a muscle.

It *could* be medical ward personnel, but they always flip on a light and apologize profusely when they come by to check my vital signs in the middle of the night.

Suddenly, a horrible thought pops into my head: What if Jayden sent someone to finish the job? Maybe she doesn't plan on giving me and Eli a chance to complete the mission; she intends to have me killed before I even leave the medical ward.

"Harper?"

I jerk up in bed at the sound of the whisper. "Who's there?"

"It's me!"

Sawyer.

The figure in front of the door moves closer, and the side of Sawyer's face comes into view under a shiny curtain of hair.

I let out a sigh of relief and put a hand over my racing heart. "Shit. You scared me half to death."

"Sorry."

"I thought you were Jayden or . . . some assassin Jayden hired to get rid of me."

"Oh my god. I'm so sorry. I shouldn't have sneaked in here like that. I didn't even think."

"No, no. It's okay. What's going on?"

Sawyer plops down on the edge of my bed, and I scoot toward the headboard to make room.

"I need to tell you something."

This sounds serious, but I can't read her expression in the dark. "Okaaay . . ."

She hesitates. "I'd like to tell you and Eli together."

A slight surge of panic ripples through my body. "Is Lenny okay?"

"Lenny's fine," she says quickly. "She's regained consciousness, and her vitals look good. She's just a little groggy."

"Did you find out more about the 119 virus?"

"No, not yet."

"Jayden hasn't been pushing to keep us here longer, has she?"

"No, no. Come on. Let's just go get Eli."

I climb out of my bed and follow her into the tunnel. I'm not used to this side of Sawyer — the Sawyer who sneaks around the medical ward in the middle of the night and breaks all the rules.

I kind of like it. It feels as though she's finally coming into her own, rather than lying down and taking whatever crap people throw her way.

Back in higher ed, the other students would constantly ask to borrow Sawyer's notes or to get "help" on assignments. They weren't her friends, and they didn't want her help; they just wanted to copy her work. Sawyer was too naïve to realize it back then, but this new Sawyer doesn't take shit from anybody.

She leads me around the corner to the room where Eli is staying, and we let ourselves in without making a sound. I open my mouth to announce our presence, but the words die on my lips when I hear a low groan from across the room.

I squint through the darkness. A lumpy shape is thrashing around on the bed, but I can't tell what's going on. Then Eli cries out.

I panic and run over, ready to body slam his attacker. But when I flip on the light, I just see a shirtless Eli sprawled across the bed with the sheets tangled around his ankles.

A deep crease appears in his forehead, and his eyebrows scrunch together. His free hand grips the bed tightly, creating deep indents in the cheap mattress.

I glance at Sawyer, feeling guilty about intruding on Eli's nightmare.

She throws me an awkward shrug and gestures at the door. "Maybe I should . . ."

"Yeah. Just give us a minute."

Eli's going to be upset enough that *I'm* seeing him like this. I don't know what he would do if he woke up with Sawyer staring down at him.

Once she's gone, I lower myself carefully onto the mattress and reach for him. My left hand skims over the warm, soft skin of his taut stomach, causing his abs to tighten reflexively. That sends a little jolt of electricity through me, and I continue my trail up his chest. He stiffens at my touch but doesn't wake up.

A tiny, selfish part of me just wants to sit here and look at him for a few more minutes; it's less intimidating than doing it when he's awake.

But then his jaw stiffens in pain, and I reach out with my other hand to touch his cheek. I stroke my finger gently down his face, feeling his smooth skin disappear under a fine layer of stubble.

"Eli . . ."

He jerks awake, and I tighten my hold on him.

"Eli."

On instinct, his arm flies up to snatch my hand off his face, and a jolt of fear shoots through me. He's in full attack mode, and I'm in a very bad spot.

Luckily, his eyes snap open, and his harsh gaze softens at once.

"Harper?"

"Hey," I murmur, not sure what I originally planned on saying.

He loosens his death grip on my wrist but doesn't let go.

"What's going on?"

"What were you dreaming about?" I ask, my voice barely a whisper.

He closes his eyes for a brief second, as though he's suppressing a shudder. "Nothing."

I tilt my head in disbelief and caress his smooth stomach absently with my free hand. He glances down, distracted, and I tighten my grip on him a little. As though my touch has magical powers, he begins to talk.

"It was just a nightmare . . . about the Fringe . . . you and Owen. I could only save one of you."

That tugs at my heart. Without thinking, I reach out and run my fingers through his dark hair. He relaxes into my touch but still doesn't let go of my other wrist.

"It was just a dream."

"Yeah, I know."

We're startled by a soft rap on the door, and Eli shoots into a seated position.

"It's okay. It's Sawyer."

He looks puzzled, but I don't have time to explain. A moment later, the door opens halfway, and Sawyer slips inside.

Eli clears his throat and straightens up, trying to look all tough and imposing even though he's still sitting shirtless in bed. I smile to myself and have to fight a full-on grin when he shifts his grip from my wrist and threads his fingers through mine.

"Hey," says Sawyer, looking painfully awkward. She has the good sense not to stare at our interlaced fingers, but Eli's move wasn't lost on her.

"Hey," says Eli. His voice is the deep one he uses in training, but his gaze is attentive rather than harsh.

"Sorry to do this in the middle of the night," she begins. "But I needed to talk to both of you, and I didn't see another way. The attending physician is discharging you tomorrow, but there's something you should know . . ."

Eli and I glance at each other, both of us wondering what

news could possibly top everything we've discovered in the past few weeks.

"You know we've been taking lots of blood samples to check for signs of radiation poisoning . . ."

Dread settles in the pit of my stomach. This is it. This is when Sawyer tells me my life is about to be cut short. It just doesn't make sense.

"I *feel* fine," I murmur.

Sawyer nods. "Your latest test results came back, and neither of you is showing signs that the radiation affected you at all."

Eli's eyebrows shoot up in surprise. "That's good, right?"

Sawyer opens her mouth, closes it, and opens it again. "It *is* . . . except it's weird because it should have. I pulled your dosimeters right after you were admitted. Both of you were exposed to extremely high levels of radiation, and Eli went without his mask for a good part of the time. Anyone else definitely would have suffered some adverse effects."

"Just got lucky, I guess," says Eli.

The crease under the bridge of Sawyer's glasses deepens, and she bites down on the inside of her cheek.

I can tell she's caught in a struggle between what she *wants* to tell us and what she's *allowed* to tell us. A few months ago, I think rule-following Sawyer would have won that battle, but tonight, she's in full badass-Sawyer mode.

"Look. There's a branch of Health and Rehab that spends a lot of time looking at patient data . . . especially *unusual* patient data. It's called Progressive Research." She looks at Eli. "You've been on their radar for a while. You've been exposed to as much radiation as anyone, yet you've never gotten sick. Not many Recon operatives your age can say that."

Eli shrugs. "I grew up out there. Maybe I'm just immune."

"That's the thing. You aren't the first person brought in from the Fringe Program who doesn't seem to be affected by this. I looked into it. Progressive Research has, too."

"What do you mean?" I ask, my nervousness manifesting as impatience.

I don't like the sound of this research branch Sawyer is talking about. They sound an awful lot like Constance, and I don't think we'll survive being on yet *another* shady organization's radar.

"Your results prompted them to reexamine your VocAps health data — all the genetic markers and risk factors that go into your viability score," explains Sawyer. "Your risk factors for things like cancer were elevated, which is why you scored so low and ended up in Recon."

"But the radiation isn't giving us cancer?"

Sawyer shakes her head. "It's not affecting you at all. See, the data they use to determine those risks dates back to before Death Storm. And your viability results go straight from the DNA sequencing machine to Systems so their supercomputer can pull in your aptitude scores and rank you for each section.

"When they process all the higher-ed kids' genome data, they don't have time to go through the results by hand. No human even looks at it. But when Progressive Research took a closer look at yours, they found some gene mutations that we haven't seen in humans before."

"Mutations?"

"What mutations?" pipes in Eli.

"They're still looking into it, but they think the mutations are helping your bodies repair DNA damage after exposure to radiation."

As soon as her words sink in, it triggers a storm of questions.

"What do you mean they haven't seen it in *humans* before?" Sawyer's eyes light up the way mine do in a room full of computers. "Scientists have mutated bacteria and smaller organisms to develop radiation resistance, but they've never tried it on humans."

"Whoa, whoa, whoa," says Eli. "Are you saying this is something they can *control?*"

"Not right now. We don't know all the mutations that cause it. But if they figured out exactly how your bodies were doing it, it's possible they could try to edit other people's DNA."

Eli looks a little sick, but I'm still too intrigued to be truly spooked by the idea of compound scientists tinkering with people's genes.

"But why us?" I ask. "Why Fringe babies? Is it because our parents were exposed to high levels of radiation?"

Sawyer shakes her head. "That's not why you're resistant. Evolution doesn't work that fast. This is the sort of thing that would take *generations* to develop. But this gene is probably the reason your parents survived after Death Storm and why you were both perfectly healthy when you were admitted."

Now that we've got her talking, I can tell Sawyer is more fascinated than creeped out by this mutation stuff. I'm equal parts intrigued and nervous.

"Back when they first started experimenting with this, they bombarded bacteria with radiation," she continues. "They used the survivors to breed a hardier generation and repeated the process a bunch of times."

"But when would our ancestors have been bombarded by radiation?" interrupts Eli.

"People were exposed to radiation all the time before Death Storm," says Sawyer. "Radon seeping up from the ground . . . cosmic radiation . . . X-rays. There's no way to tell where it came from — only that your ancestors survived and passed their resistance on to you."

My brain is running on overdrive as I struggle to wrap my head around this information. "So you think my parents had these mutations?"

"They must have."

"But that's impossible. My parents died of radiation poisoning a few weeks after coming to the compound."

Sawyer shrugs. "I mean, radiation resistance doesn't make you one hundred percent *immune*. I suppose extremely high levels could have caused too much damage for their bodies to repair."

I shake my head. "It just doesn't fit."

"I know. I tried to pull your parents' file to look at their medical records. Only . . ."

"Only what?"

Sawyer sighs. "Only there *was* no file. There's no record of your parents ever being admitted to the medical ward, which makes no sense. Anyone brought in from the Fringe is required to undergo extensive testing before they're integrated with the general population. We used to keep Fringe babies under observation here for *weeks*."

I shake my head. "They told me my parents got really sick right after we came here. There *has* to be some record of them being admitted."

"That's what's so strange. There should be. But don't worry — I'm looking into it."

"Don't worry?" snaps Eli, rejoining the conversation after several minutes of tense silence. "You just told us that we have some radiation-repelling superpower. Do you realize we're going to have to spend the rest of our fucking lives on the Fringe when Jayden finds out?"

"Jayden isn't going to find out," says Sawyer. "Progressive Research doesn't share their findings outside of Health and Rehab. Their research could have too many ethical ramifications."

"Never?"

"Well . . . I guess if there were extenuating circumstances. But they would need a unanimous vote to release any of their research."

"And are there any circumstances that would make them vote to share this information with the board?" Eli prompts.

Sawyer shrugs. "I don't know. It's too early to tell. And we don't have a large enough sample to perform any kind of conclusive study anyway. You guys are kind of a scientific anomaly."

Eli doesn't look convinced, and in truth, neither am I. I've seen too much corruption within the compound to believe any ethical agreement is ironclad. For all we know, Constance could have people planted in the Progressive Research Unit.

But my fear and uncertainty are quickly being overtaken by suspicion. It doesn't make sense that Health and Rehab wouldn't have any record of my parents being admitted, and the fact that they probably shared these genetic mutations just makes the situation even more questionable.

"Are you *sure* I have what he has?" I ask Sawyer.

"I'm sure. I pulled your records, and your file is huge. They've been studying you since you took the VocAps test, which means something in your genome raised a red flag. And all your blood tests look like Eli's. You've been exposed to high levels of radiation, but your body isn't reacting the way it should. I'm going to see if I can get ahold of the raw data."

Suddenly, a new thought occurs to me. "You said lots of people brought in from the Fringe have this. Does that mean Celdon has the mutations?"

"I don't know. He hasn't been exposed to radiation, so there's no way to tell other than pulling his raw viability data. When I go in to retrieve yours, I'll pull his, too."

"You shouldn't be poking around in this. If you get caught —"

"It's okay!" says Sawyer, clearly excited by the prospect of solving a medical mystery. "If I play my cards right, I'll get into Progressive Research anyway. I'm not breaking any rules by digging into this — not really."

I shoot her a look of disbelief. I love the bold new Sawyer, but I don't want her jeopardizing her future in Health and Rehab or putting herself in danger.

"I'm not breaking *many* rules by digging into this," she concedes. "And anyway . . . don't you want to know why your body can heal its own DNA? Don't you want to know if your parents were super mutants?"

She grins, and I feel myself wavering. I can't deny that I'm curious, but it's driven by a morbid fascination with the Fringe Program more than hope.

I refuse to feel relief that my time on the Fringe hasn't affected me physically. Being immune to radiation can't undo the things I've done or help me unsee the horrors I've witnessed. It doesn't mean Eli and I won't be shot or blown up. And if Jayden finds out that the two of us have some special immunity, she's going to send us out even more frequently.

But I desperately want to see my parents' missing file. Something just doesn't fit.

Eli is quiet, and the faraway look of concern in his eyes tells me he's deep in thought. Sawyer has fallen silent, too, but her eager expression is awakening the Harper who loved breaking the rules and wreaking havoc in the Institute.

I *really* want Sawyer to stay out of this, but we can't do it without her.

I nod slowly and take a deep breath. "Where do we start?"

fourteen

Eli

The next day, the attending physician comes by to discharge me from the medical ward. He tells me I'm showing no signs of radiation sickness, but nothing about his demeanor indicates that he knows about my unusual test results.

I can't wait to escape the nauseating stench of disinfectant mixed with sick people, but I'm also dreading getting back to training. As soon as Harper and I return to Recon, Jayden will be itching to deploy us again — indefinitely this time.

I've been racking my brain to come up with a plan, and the one I have isn't great. There's a pretty high chance I'm going to fail, and Harper's going to hate me. But right now, it's the only thing I can think of to protect her *and* Owen.

On my way to check out, I pass by a cracked door in the ICU. I peek inside and see Lenny lying in the bed with her red curly hair fanning out in every direction. She's regained some of her peachy coloring, but she still doesn't look like herself.

Squeezed into one of those little waiting-room chairs next to the door is Miles. He's nodding off under a canopy of "get well" flowers and looks more out of place than I've ever seen him. He's got dark grayish bags under his eyes and the strain of worry around his mouth. His shirt is stretched out and wrinkly, which makes me think he hasn't left Lenny's side in days.

As I watch, his head dips forward toward his hand, and he jerks it up at the last second as he teeters on the brink of sleep.

"Hey," I murmur, leaning against the door jamb and patting him on the shoulder.

Miles jumps and opens his eyes. "Hey!" He clears his throat and shifts around in the chair, but he can't quite muster up his trademark swagger sitting at Lenny's bedside.

"How's she doing?"

"All right, I guess," he sighs, dragging his palm over his face. "She got pretty lucky. A few more minutes, and she would have been a goner."

His tone is light, but when he turns back to face her bed, I can tell he's replayed that horrible day over and over, thinking about what he could have done differently. It's how I felt after Harper made her first kill, and it's why I have to do this my way.

"It's not your fault," I say in a firm voice.

"The hell it isn't." Miles shakes his head. "I *led* her that way. I led us straight into a fucking firing squad."

"You couldn't have known."

"I should have, though. You guys were attacked along that route. I just thought if we were real quiet, maybe we wouldn't attract attention."

"Well, she ought to be grateful she was with you. I doubt any other private would have gotten her back to the compound so fast."

"Man, stop trying to make me feel better, all right?" Miles snaps. "I fucked up. You asked me to take her out and show her the ropes, and I fucking *failed*. I don't even want to think about what would have happened if you hadn't taken out that drifter."

I swallow down the guilt rising up in my throat. I don't want to tell him that I could have gotten into position a lot faster if I hadn't been so preoccupied with protecting Owen.

"Stop blaming yourself," I say. "Some of this shit is beyond your control."

I let out a burst of air. "And you didn't fail. I wouldn't have wanted to send her out with anybody else, and I stand by that decision."

Miles shakes his head. "You shouldn't. I'm not cut out for this babysitting shit."

"Yeah, you are." I pause, hesitant to lay everything out there. "In fact . . . I think you should keep going out on her deployments. She's going to grow into a good partner for you, and I want you to keep an eye on her . . . and the rest of my cadets."

Miles scoffs. "You planning on taking a vacation or something?"

"Not exactly," I murmur. "But I . . . I may be going away for a while, and I just want to make sure somebody's looking out for Harper and the others."

"Harper?"

"Yeah. Jayden came to my room the other day for a little heart-to-heart."

I close the door and sit down in the empty chair beside Miles, unloading the story of how the drifters caught us in Owen's house and led us back to their base. I tell him about the confrontation with Malcolm and how Jayden saw us leave him there alive.

When I finish, Miles is staring at me as though I've completely lost my mind.

"You went into their base pretending to be Owen?" he repeats incredulously. "Are you *insane*?"

"I wasn't sure what else to do. If they knew we were Recon, they would have killed us for sure."

He scowls. "That's why you don't stick around to have conversations with drifters! You shoot them and get the fuck out!"

"I couldn't," I groan. "They caught us by surprise, and I had no idea how many there were."

"And what do you think is gonna happen when Owen comes back?" he asks. "How's it going to look when he has no memory of hanging out with those guys?"

"Bad," I admit. "Which is why I need to find him."

I clench my fists and grit my teeth, gearing up for the lecture I know I have coming.

"As soon as one of the gang leaders shows his face again, Jayden is going to deploy me. I'm going to find Owen and fake his death. So long as Jayden never sees him again, she'll have no choice but to believe me."

"How are you going to fake his death?"

I raise an eyebrow. "I have an idea. I just need to call in some reinforcements."

Miles shakes his head in disbelief. "And you think Owen is just gonna go on the run because you *tell* him he should?"

"He doesn't have a choice. He's as good as dead anyway, now that Malcolm is questioning his loyalty."

"Because of you."

"That's beside the point. Owen can't stay here . . . not with Jayden *and* the Desperados after him."

There's a long pause as Miles considers my logic.

When he looks up at me, there's a pained expression in his eyes — as though he knows he's looking at a dead man.

"Why are you putting yourself through this?" he asks. "Just tell Jayden you aren't going to be her little bitch anymore."

"I can't," I groan, staring down at my hands and willing him to understand. "If I don't go along with this, Jayden is going to kill Harper."

"So tell Harper to leave! Send her to another compound the way you planned."

My stomach drops. I completely forgot that Miles hasn't heard the news about 119.

"That's not really an option anymore. I don't want to go into it right now, but trust me . . . I would if I could."

"So what if Jayden sends you out there and you can't find Owen? What then?"

"I *have* to find him," I say. "No matter how long I have to stay out there."

It takes several seconds for the meaning of my words to sink in, and when they do, Miles's expression goes blank. "Are you telling me you're planning to stay out on the Fringe until you find your brother?"

I nod. "Jayden's orders. She says she doesn't care if it takes six days or six months. I can't come back without a dead drifter . . . which is why I'm putting in a request for a new partner."

Hearing those words aloud and seeing Miles's expression intensifies the horrible guilt that's been eating at my stomach all day.

"*You're dropping Riley?*"

"I have to. She's not cut out for the Fringe, and it wouldn't be right dragging her out there with me."

"Wouldn't be right? What about the other poor bastard you rope into your suicide mission? How is *that* right?"

I grit my teeth. "It won't be a suicide mission if we pull it off."

"Yeah, but that's a pretty big 'if.'"

"I don't expect *you* to do it," I say, feeling defensive. "I just can't put Harper through that."

Miles opens his mouth to argue, but our conversation is cut short by a soft knock on the door. It's Sawyer.

By the look on her face, she didn't catch the tail end of my last statement, but she still looks uncomfortable.

"Glad I caught you before you left," she says, scooting into the room and glancing at the empty tunnel behind her.

"Is Harper okay?" I ask.

"She's fine. She's being discharged, too."

Sawyer glances down the tunnel again, and I get an uneasy feeling in my gut.

"Can we talk for a second?" she asks, glancing bashfully at Miles. "In private?"

I can't imagine what she could say that I don't want Miles to hear, but I get up and follow her out into the tunnel anyway.

Sawyer leads me out of the ICU and through the postexposure wing. Then she turns down a short dead-end tunnel that's just for storage, where a few extra gurneys are lined up along the walls. As soon as we enter the little alcove, the ambient noise from the wing fades to a low hum.

"What is it?" I ask. "Did you get your hands on the raw viability data?"

She shakes her head so her shiny black hair swooshes around her chin. "Not yet."

I look at her expectantly. She shifts her weight from one foot to another, carefully avoiding my gaze.

"Don't be mad," she says, "but when I went to read your dosimeter, I snooped around in your bag a little."

That's probably the absolute *last* thing I expected her to say. Now I know why she was acting all shady, but after everything Sawyer's done for me and Harper, I'm too grateful to be pissed.

"When Caleb brought you up to the ward, you were guarding that with your life." She gestures to my rucksack. "I figured something was up, so I had a look inside."

Sawyer jerks her head over her shoulder once more to make sure we aren't being watched and then reaches into her back pocket to pull out something I can't see.

She passes me the picture as if she's making a drug handoff, and I take it reverently.

The photo paper has a warmth I can't explain, and the crinkled edges feel reassuringly familiar.

"I also found this," she says, reaching into her front pocket and withdrawing my mother's necklace.

I hold out my other hand, and she lets the chain spill slowly into my outstretched palm.

"I shouldn't have taken them," she says quickly. "But the decontamination unit inspects everything that comes back from the Fringe and blasts it to get rid of radioactive particles. I didn't want it to get confiscated or ruined."

"Thank you," I say, a little shocked that Sawyer has been harboring my contraband all this time. "Really."

She jerks her head dismissively, as though she's not used to being thanked. "I thought you would be mad."

"Why would I be mad?"

"Because it seems like something you might want to keep secret." She gives me a pointed look. "I read the back of the photo."

I nod. Sawyer knowing about Owen definitely puts her at greater risk, but I'm not worried that she's going to go blabbing to Jayden or anything. And, to my relief, she doesn't seem to expect any sort of explanation. I can see why Harper trusts her.

"Anyway, I'll let you get going."

"Thanks for this," I say quickly. I hope she knows I mean it.

"No problem."

Sawyer turns to go but stops short of the main tunnel. She doesn't turn around to look at me, but I can tell she's debating with herself about something.

"Just be careful, Eli," she says in a tremulous voice. "Harper's my best friend."

"I know."

Sawyer nods and then turns and disappears around the corner.

When she leaves, I get the feeling that I should have said more. I should have told her to watch out for Harper after I'm gone. I should have told her that I'd do anything to keep Harper safe — even if it means making her hate me.

fifteen

Celdon

Whenever I'm especially fucked up, a cold shower is about the only thing that can bring me back to reality. After a night in Neverland, I'll stand in the narrow glass box and run the shower cycle on repeat until my skin is pink and numb all over.

It usually makes me feel like I've been given a fresh start, but not today.

I could shower for a hundred years and never be able to wash the stench of dead bodies off me. I haven't stopped smelling the thousands of rotting corpses since Harper and I returned from 119.

Frustrated, I grab my damp towel from the hook on the wall and forcefully scrub my wet hair so it sticks up in a million different directions. I rub it down my face, wrap it around my hips, and begin my search for clean clothes.

I need to do laundry. Hell, I need to do a lot of things.

I grab a pair of pants from two nights ago that have a suspicious pinkish stain on the thigh and hear the familiar siren call of a pill bottle rattling in the pocket. It's got half a dozen fun-looking yellow uppers sliding around in the bottom, and my hands shake a little when I toss the bottle onto the couch.

Must find clean pants.

Wrinkled slacks are scattered all over my closet floor like crumpled tissues. But just above my head, I find a neatly folded pair still fresh from the laundry service.

"Score," I mutter.

My search for a clean shirt is interrupted by a sharp knock at the door. I'm expecting Harper, so I throw it open without looking through the peephole first and jump back at the sight of her six-foot-tall lieutenant.

He looks all serious and sexy as usual, and I'm suddenly very aware that I'm a little bloated from drinking all night. Meanwhile, Lieutenant Sexy is probably hiding a perfect six-pack under that uniform.

"*Heeeey*," I slur, drawing out the word to defuse the awkward tension.

"Hey," he says, glancing over my shoulder at my compartment. He's probably here looking for Riles. How adorable.

"What's up?"

"You have a second?"

I clear my throat and redirect my gaze so he doesn't think I'm staring at him. "Yeah. Sure. Come on in."

This is weird. This is weird. This is so weird.

I turn around and leave my door wide open, frantically scanning the compartment for a clean shirt. I grab one hanging off the back of a chair and pull it on, wondering what this could *possibly* be about.

When I turn around, I can tell Eli feels just as awkward as I do. He's taking in my compartment with a grim expression — probably thinking that Systems people are spoiled douchebags.

"So what's up?" I prompt, hoping to move things along. The guy might be good-looking, but a conversationalist he is not.

"I actually had a favor to ask you."

He glances up at me so those piercing blue eyes can do their thing, and I realize very quickly why Riles has such trouble with this guy.

"Go ahead," I say, crossing my arms as if I can somehow shield myself from the sexy vibes he's putting out.

He glances around my compartment, and his eyes land on my computer setup.

"Don't worry about Constance," I say. "Those code monkeys can't get past the booby traps I set for them. It's safe to talk."

Eli still looks uneasy, but he meets my gaze again and starts talking. "Harper told you about my brother Owen, right?"

"Yeah."

"Well, I had a talk with Jayden the other day, and she told me I have to assassinate him . . . or one of the other gang leaders who are rallying the drifters."

I blink, feeling a little sick for reasons that have nothing to do with my hangover. "Rallying drifters? Where?"

"Just a few miles from the compound."

"Shit."

"Yeah. And Jayden has gone completely off the rails. She told me that if I don't come back with a dead drifter, she's going to kill Harper."

By his matter-of-fact tone, I can tell he's given this so much thought that the threat has lost its sting. But this is new information to me, and it feels as though someone just punched me in the stomach.

"So take them out," I snap. That probably came out harsher than I intended, but I don't care. Apart from Owen, Eli doesn't know these guys from Adam. And if assassinating one will keep Harper safe, I'm all for it.

"That's the thing. Owen is MIA right now, but as soon as he shows his face, Jayden and the drifters are going to be looking for him." Eli takes a step forward so he's towering over me in an intimidating/hot sort of way. "I need to be the one who finds him."

Now I'm annoyed. It's bad enough that Eli recruited Harper for Recon, but now it seems as though he just drags her into one dangerous situation after another.

"Look, Eli, I'm not trying to be a dick here, but if Jayden wants Owen dead, I'm not sure you're gonna be able to stop her."

I kind of expect him to react by punching me in the face, but Eli just nods. "Exactly. Jayden wants Owen out of the picture, and Jayden hates it when she doesn't get what she wants." He pauses for dramatic effect. "That's why I'm going to fake his death."

For a second, I just stare at him. He can't be serious. Faking a drifter's death sounds like the dumbest fucking plan in the universe. Eli might be the best lieutenant in Recon, but he's no match for Constance.

"How?"

"This is what I need your help with."

Oh, joy.

"Constance has surveillance cameras planted all around the towns closest to the compound. I need to know where their blind spots are."

"And you want my help hacking into their feeds."

"You got it. I need to know where to tell Jayden I killed Owen and the areas he'll have to avoid once it's done."

"What does Harper think about this plan?" I ask. I'd bet money she thinks it's dumb as hell, too.

Eli looks suddenly guilty. "She doesn't know."

That doesn't sit well with me, but I choose to ignore it for the moment. "And you think Owen is gonna go along with faking his own death?"

Eli sighs and drags a hand through his hair, rubbing his

scalp and grimacing in a way that tells me he isn't completely sure. "I don't know. I hope so. If he won't, I'll have to find another drifter to kill for real."

"What if you can't?" I splutter. Eli really hasn't thought this thing through.

"I don't have a choice."

"What do you mean?"

"I mean I'm not coming back until I have a dead drifter for Jayden."

I stare at him, mouth agape. "*That's* your big plan?" I choke. "Just stay out there forever? Harper's never going to agree to that! She *hates* the Fringe."

"I know," says Eli, his voice deadly calm. "That's why Harper isn't going."

"Does she know that?"

"No." He lets out a long sigh. "I just put in a request for a new partner, but I need your help making sure it goes through."

"I'm not doing that!"

For the first time since he got here, Eli looks as though he's gearing up for a serious confrontation. He draws himself up to his full height and fixes me with a pointed stare.

"Listen. I chose to make Harper my partner, and she's the best one I've ever had. I wouldn't trade her for anyone if it weren't the best thing for her.

"You haven't seen the look she gets on her face every time we have to go out on the Fringe. I'm not going to drag her along for a mission that has no end date. I won't do it."

My first instinct is to smack Eli upside the head, but his words give me pause.

I imagine Harper stuck out in the desert, spending the rest of her life dodging bullets and struggling to survive. The thought makes my heart ache. It's not what I'd choose for her either.

"She's gonna be pissed when she finds out," I say finally.

"But you aren't going to tell her, are you?"

I stand there silently for a minute, conflict raging in my chest.

Harper is my best friend. She's going to be heartbroken when she finds out that Eli dumped her for a new partner — regardless of his reasoning — and she'll be furious with me for hiding it from her.

But then I look at Eli standing there all worried and determined, and I feel my resolve start to crack.

Eli might be moody and sullen, but there's no doubt in my mind that he cares for Harper. He'd do anything to keep her safe, which includes opting her out of a never-ending mission on the Fringe.

Against my better judgment, I find myself shaking my head. "I won't tell her. And I'll make sure you have a new partner in the system. But don't expect me to help you when she finds out."

* * *

I get a perverse thrill from using Systems' resources to do something illegal. I don't know if it's because Systems rejected Harper for totally bogus reasons or because they're my employer — which technically makes them "the man" — but I really, *really* enjoy using their equipment for illegal purposes.

I could have hacked into Constance's feeds from my own computer, but it would have been much more difficult to cover my tracks than getting to the feeds from Systems.

Because a penetration tester's work involves hacking into sensitive databases and testing our network security, I have my own private glass cube with auto-frosting walls along the back wall of HQ.

From there, I can see everything going on in the bull pen. Usually the workstations are alive with the clack of keys and the creak of swivel chairs, but tonight the only sounds are the quiet tick of all the servers blinking in the darkness and the gentle purr of the air conditioning.

"I'm in," I murmur, my voice dying quickly in the silent room.

"Oh, good," says Eli, trying to look alive. He's been watching me from his slumped position against the wall for the past hour, and I know he must be bored to tears.

I pull up the feeds on my little semicircle of monitors, and Eli's eyes widen in amazement.

"Just like that?"

"Just like that."

I try to sound casual, but I find myself sitting up a little straighter at his tone of awe. It's nice to have your skills admired — even if the person doing the admiring doesn't know shit.

Eli comes up behind me and peers over my shoulder. "Damn."

I don't say anything. I'm too busy staring at what looks like a town from our history textbooks.

The place is completely desolate. There are roads and buildings and street signs but no people in sight. Everything is covered in a thick layer of dust, and the scraggly desert foliage seems to be overtaking the streets and parking lots.

I have no memory of living outside the compound, and I'm completely blown away. I knew what was out there, of course, but it's different *seeing* it. It's as though I just stumbled into a video game and discovered that everything happening in the game was real.

"There," says Eli, pointing at one view of an abandoned street. The curb and sidewalk are lined with trash, and the run-down buildings look as though they haven't had any visitors in a hundred years. Most of the windows are broken or boarded up.

Eli points at the image of a yellow building on the monitor. Its faded sign reads "Master Pawn," and the place seems to be the sort that was a little sketchy even before Death Storm.

"What's that?"

He lets out a long breath through his nostrils, studying the building in frustration. "That's the gang's new headquarters."

"No, I mean, what's a Master Pawn?"

"It's a pawn shop," says Eli. "People bring in their old stuff, and someone pays them for it. Then the owner turns around and sells it to someone else for a lot more."

"Seriously?"

"Yeah."

I glance over at Eli, filled with a new sense of respect. He really has been *out there*, but up until now, I'd never really considered what that meant.

"If Malcolm comes back, this is where he's going to be," he mutters, more to himself than to me.

In the harsh blue glow of the monitor, I can read Eli's frustrated expression. He looks as if he wants to reach through the screen or somehow teleport to the Fringe, though I can't even imagine how terrifying it would be to encounter drifters in person.

Something about venturing outside the compound scares the shit out of me. It's irrational, considering I was *born* out there, but it just seems so vast and so dangerous.

"Where would Owen be?" I ask.

"No idea. I don't know if he'd meet up with the gang or not. He's in trouble, thanks to me. But if he shows his face and doesn't report to Malcolm, it's going to get even worse." He sucks in a burst of air through his teeth and glances down at me. "If you see him, let me know right away."

"Will do. And I'll try to compare the camera positions to the maps in Constance's confidential files to find a blind spot."

"Thanks."

Eli crosses awkwardly to the door, but before he leaves, I say, "And I took care of the other thing."

"Oh, yeah?"

I nod, hating myself for it. "Harper is no longer your default partner for deployment. It's this kid . . . Derek Something. He's a private. Middle-of-the-road scores on everything. I doubt he'll be missed."

Eli doesn't turn around, but I see him clench and unclench his fists a few times. "Thanks."

Watching him go, I get the overwhelming sense that I made the wrong decision.

No good can come from Eli heading out to the Fringe to fake his brother's death. In all likelihood, he's going to get himself killed by the drifters or get caught in a lie and be killed by Constance.

I hate being part of a plan that's destined to fail. But more than anything, I hate that I helped Eli lie to Harper.

sixteen

Harper

Getting ready for a night in Neverland always gives me a nervous thrill. There's an element of danger that comes with venturing into the underworld, but there's also something freeing about being down there.

The drugs, the sex, the illegal fights — Neverland lends a sense of anonymity you can't find anywhere else in the compound. Sure, all the regulars down there know each other, but since everyone is up to no good, what happens in Neverland tends to stay there.

Tonight I'm wearing tight black pants and knee-length boots. I've squeezed my boobs into a sleeveless top that cuts low in the front, with straps that crisscross to form an X across my back.

Anything less sexy would draw attention down there, but I still want to feel capable and in control — no skimpy dresses tonight.

My heart beats a little faster as I descend the emergency stairwell. When I reach the bottom, the stench of sweat and urine is overpowering, and I breathe through my mouth and try to calm down.

The heat of hundreds of gyrating bodies is emanating through the steel door, and I can already feel little beads of sweat springing up along my chest and face. I lift my hair off my neck for a second and focus on my breathing.

Everything's fine, I tell myself. *You can leave anytime you want. No one is going to hurt you.*

In truth, I can't be sure. I've only visited Shane once, and I was with Eli at the time. After that, Jayden paid Shane to have me killed. Eli would *freak* if he knew what I was doing, but I really don't have a choice.

I'm positive no good would come from Shane and Eli being in the same room together, and Shane is one of the few people I know who is old enough to remember the Fringe Program in its infancy.

Based on the illegal nature of Shane's business ventures, there isn't much that goes on around here that he doesn't know about. He might be privy to some information the board has tried to cover up.

And anyway, it isn't as though he's going to try to kill me *here* — not with all these witnesses.

Pushing the door open, I'm instantly overwhelmed by the flashing lights and the heavy beat of music blaring from the speakers.

Even though it's Sunday night, there seem to be more bodies jammed together down here than usual. I have to turn sideways to squeeze through the ring of people crowded around the door, and I still feel their bodies pressing in all around me.

If it was hot in the stairwell, it's sweltering in here. There are just too many people packed together in the collapsed tunnel and not enough ventilation.

Suddenly, a wave of dizziness hits me — my body's automatic response to crowds. My lungs constrict, and I clench and unclench my fists to fight the panic rising up in my chest.

I can't afford to lose it — not here. Not tonight.

Everything's fine, I tell myself. *You can breathe. It's all in your head.*

Feeling slightly better, I start pushing through the mass of sticky, sweaty dancers and make a beeline for the stairwell. I jut out my elbows to peel apart the cluster of people grinding against each other and get several dirty looks directed my way. The women are wearing microskirts, plunging leotards, and what look like suspenders attached to neon underwear, but the men are mostly shirtless or wearing mesh tank tops.

It's a relief when I break through the crowd and reach the stairs. But just as my feet hit the bottom step, a hand closes around my arm.

An old fear flashes through me, and I swing around with a hammer fist to knock back my attacker.

"Hey!" shouts a familiar voice.

The head behind me is just a blur as the stranger dodges my fist, and I wind up again and prepare to fight.

I won't be taken again. I won't.

"Whoa, whoa. Easy!" says the voice. "Harper, it's me."

Fighting the surge of adrenalin that's giving me a mad case of tunnel vision, I focus on the face swimming in my periphery. It's Blaze, but I didn't immediately recognize him with his new short hair.

"Oh. Hey!" I pant. "I'm sorry. I didn't know it was you."

"It's okay," he says, releasing my arm. "I shouldn't have grabbed you. It was a dumb thing to do."

I wince, still embarrassed that I almost punched Blaze.

"What are you doing here, Harper?" he asks. His question sounds polite enough, but I read the hidden meaning behind his words: *You shouldn't be here.*

"I need to talk to Shane — er, your dad."

Blaze's usually happy-go-lucky expression shuts off like a light. Strangely, the grim look he's giving me now seems more natural than his hazy smile. "Why do you want to talk to Shane?"

I open my mouth and close it immediately. I can't tell Blaze what I know. I can't tell anyone.

Sawyer would be in huge trouble if anybody found out she was using her position in the medical ward to look into old records. And even though my instincts are telling me I can trust Blaze, my resolve to protect Sawyer is stronger.

"I just need to ask him a few questions," I say, hoping he'll take the hint and let me go.

"About what?"

No such luck.

I sigh. "About the Fringe Program."

Instead of looking suspicious or confused, sympathy warms those blue-green eyes.

The only really good thing about getting placed in Recon was that my old identity seemed to melt away as everyone adjusted to their new roles. It's easy to forget that most people in higher ed knew me as a Fringe brat who grew up in the Institute.

I hate that Blaze is feeling sorry for me.

"It isn't worth it," he says finally.

"It is to me."

Blaze shakes his head. "You don't get it. Shane doesn't give anything away without expecting something in return. If you ask him for a favor, you need to be prepared to grant one yourself. And I don't think you are."

A shiver rolls through me as I imagine the types of favors Shane might have in mind.

My first thought goes to my fight with Marta Moreno. It's possible he could ask me to fight again, but I suppose that's one of the tamer requests one can hope for from a crime lord.

Still, I can always walk away.

I shift from one foot to the other, trying to decide how much I should tell Blaze. Throwing caution to the wind, I let out a little of the truth.

"Look, this isn't just me needing to know why I was brought into the compound. I need to know what happened to my parents. Something isn't right."

It's vague, but Blaze is smart enough to understand why I can't say more. He studies me for a long moment, quiet and pensive. It's tough to read his expression in the intermittent flare of the strobe light, and I realize there's much more to him than the easygoing guy I thought I had pegged.

It occurs to me that Blaze might not be quiet and agreeable in training just because he's a nice guy; keeping his head down and not making waves is probably how he survived Shane.

"Okay," he says finally. "But I'm coming with you."

"You really don't have to —"

"I know you can take care of yourself, Harper," he cuts in. "But you aren't used to doing business with people like Shane. I don't want him trying to pull you into anything that you don't want to be a part of."

I open my mouth to protest, but then I remember the way it was last time — how I immediately agreed to fight Marta without knowing I was *way* out of my league.

"Okay."

Blaze seems surprised but turns and leads the way up the stairs, squaring his shoulders as if he's preparing to walk into battle.

The same muscular bodyguard who was there the last time I visited is standing next to the door. He and Blaze greet each other with a friendly head nod the way all guys do, but then the bodyguard shifts to block the door.

"Now's not a good time," he rumbles.

Blaze glances at the door. I can hear the crescendo of angry voices coming through the thin metal, but he looks nonplussed. "What do you mean?"

"McMannis is in there right now."

Blaze swears under his breath and glances anxiously at me. "Is it going well?"

The bodyguard lifts two bushy eyebrows and widens his eyes. "Does it sound like it's going well?"

I tug on Blaze's arm. "What's going on?"

"Nothing we want to be a part of," he murmurs. "Let's go. I'll bring you back tomorrow."

Suddenly the voices coming from inside the room go quiet. "Is that my son out there?" someone yells through the door.

Panic flares through me when I recognize Shane's voice. I glance up at the door and spot a tiny security camera pointed directly at us.

The bodyguard sighs and touches his earpiece to speak. "Yessir."

"Well, don't just leave him standing there, Hector!" yells Shane, not bothering with *his* earpiece. "Bring him in, for god's sake."

Blaze and the bodyguard exchange a meaningful look, and then Blaze grimaces and turns to me. I nod once — nervous but determined — and we navigate awkwardly around Hector's enormous frame.

When we step inside the cramped private room, Shane is hunched over a dainty glass liquor cart, pouring himself a drink.

With his back to us, I have an unobstructed view of his fantastically hideous mullet. His hair is black and glossy in the front, but it tapers down into a deep violet in the back. He's wearing black slacks, a black shirt, and a black jacket, but my eyes go immediately to his illegally sourced ostrich-skin boots.

There are two more bodyguards standing in the corners of the room, and right next to us is a menacing-looking man with leathery skin and bleached-blond hair buzzed close to the scalp.

He shoots Blaze a look of pure loathing, and his eyes linger curiously on me.

"I can come back," says Blaze. His voice is deeper than usual, and his gaze is cold on his father's back.

"Nonsense," says Shane, still fussing over his drink. "We're finished."

"Like hell we are," growls the man I assume is McMannis.

Shane pauses over the drink cart, one hand still swirling a tiny plastic straw. He sighs, removes the straw, and then whips around in one motion and flings the glass tumbler at McMannis's head.

Blaze shoves me behind him, but I still feel the splash of cold liquid as the drink collides with the man's head and shatters on the floor.

"Holy shit!" he yells, clutching his head where the glass hit him. I see blood trickling from a cut under his brow, and he slams his hand onto the wall behind him for support.

"Maybe you've taken one too many punches to the head," says Shane in a low, deadly voice. "I said we're finished here. That means we're finished."

McMannis looks up at Shane with a pitiful expression. His eye is already beginning to swell, and he can hardly get the words out. "What am I supposed to tell Bellett?"

"The truth. My connections to 116 are down. I haven't heard anything in months. On top of that, my Fringe connections are all dried up. Nothing's going in or out." He shoots McMannis a withering glare. "Now get out of my office."

McMannis doesn't have to be told twice. He slinks out of the room, still clutching his bleeding head, and Blaze clears his throat loudly.

"What was *that* all about?"

"Just business," says Shane. He sighs, looking perplexed.

"Damn. I spilled my drink."

The bodyguard in the far right corner clears his throat. "I'll get it, sir."

"Thank you," says Shane, all traces of his earlier fury gone.

"Did you say you can't get ahold of someone at 116?" I ask, more curious than afraid after Shane's outburst.

But then his eyes snap onto me, and my bravado evaporates. A muscle in Shane's jaw tightens. His fury is back in full force, and this time it's directed at me. "You're awful ballsy, girl . . . showing your face around here."

I clench my fists at my sides, refusing to let Shane intimidate me.

"You remember Harper Riley?" asks Blaze, a hard edge to his voice.

"Oh, I remember. Your little friend here created quite a big mess for me a little while ago." Shane takes a step toward me, and his silver spurs clink against the tile. "And I don't like messes."

"I'm not going to apologize for not letting your men murder me in the dead level."

Blaze whips his head around in shock and then looks back at his father with wide eyes. Clearly he isn't privy to *all* of Shane's business activities.

"You sent your men out to get her?" he asks incredulously.

"Watch your tone, boy, or I'll smack you right here in front of God and everybody. Don't think I won't. It's none of your business to begin with.

"I have half a mind to keep her right here so I can get what's comin' to me." He rubs his fingers together greedily, and I wonder just how much Jayden offered to pay him if he succeeded in killing me.

"You aren't going to touch her," Blaze growls. "She's with

me."

Shane raises an eyebrow and lets out a harsh, barking laugh. "With you?" He shakes his head, breaking into a mocking smile. "No. She's with Eli Parker — Boy Wonder who lost his last fight. So as far as I'm concerned, there's not much standing in my way."

Blaze goes red in the face but doesn't back down. I feel a little bad for him, but there are more important things to worry about.

The bodyguard hands Shane a fresh drink, but he doesn't take a sip.

"Jayden never had any intention of paying up," I say, feeling bold. "She was just using you because she can — just like she uses everybody else."

In truth, I have no idea whether Jayden would have paid out for the assassination, but neither does Shane. Judging by the way his gaze hardens, though, he believes me.

"Figures. I've never trusted that bitch as far as I could throw her." He tsks loudly, more to himself than to us. "Fool me once, shame on you. Fool me twice . . ."

"So why take the deal?" I prompt, curious about the hold Jayden could possibly have on the scariest guy in the compound.

Shane raises an eyebrow. "Let's just say she and I go way back. Well, not her *specifically*. I was in business when Jayden Pierce was still pissing her bed, but I knew plenty of people like her."

"Constance?"

As soon as I speak, I know it was a mistake.

Shane's face turns to stone. "You'll shut your damn mouth, if you know what's good for you."

Blaze looks momentarily confused, but he's quick to pick up on the fact that I just stepped in something major.

"Let's go," he mutters.

"No!"

I know I'm pushing my luck, but I didn't come all the way down to Neverland just to leave without any answers. "I'm sorry. We don't have to talk about Constance or Jayden. But I need to know something."

"Harper!" Blaze squeezes my arm and gives me a warning look.

Shane lets out a deadly chuckle. "You just don't know when to quit, do you?"

One of the bodyguards in the corner takes a step forward, and fear flashes through me. I know I'm running out of time, but at this point, it can't hurt to ask. The damage is already done.

"Please!" I say, taking a step back and holding out my hands in what I hope is a nonthreatening gesture. Blaze is practically hyperventilating next to me. "Just tell me what you know about the Fringe Program."

A puzzled look flashes across Shane's face. That's definitely not what he expected me to ask. "The Fringe Program?"

"My parents brought me into the compound when I was just a baby. My guardian in the Institute told me they died of radiation poisoning a few days later, but there's no record of them being admitted to the medical ward. What do you know about that?"

A grim smile cracks Shane's fierce expression. "Well, I'll be damned. Sounds like you already know more than what's good for you."

He glances over at the bodyguard who advanced on us and holds up a hand. "Maybe you should come work for me — put those powers of deduction to better use. I can't imagine you get to use that big brain of yours much in Recon."

I don't say anything. The only thing that's going to come out of my mouth is some snarky refusal, and I have a feeling that's not going to get me very far with Shane.

His gaze clouds over again, and I can tell he does know something — he just doesn't want to say. "Wish I could help you. But I don't know anything about that."

"Please," I prompt. "I just want to know what happened to my parents. You don't have to tell me anything. Just point me in the right direction."

That's when I know I've pushed him too far. Something changes in Shane's expression, and he takes several steps toward me until he's hovering just a few inches above my head. Every fiber of my being is screaming to get the hell out of there, but I stay rooted to the spot.

When Shane speaks next, his voice is so low I can barely hear him. "I told you. I don't know anything about that. And even if I did, it's not the sort of information you give away for nothin'. That's the sort that gets you six feet under. Do you understand me?"

At this point, Shane is so close that I can see every pore in his face and the pieces of silver embedded in his teeth. My heart is pounding so loudly I'm sure he can hear it. But I'm not ready to give up.

"I didn't say I wanted something for nothing," I murmur, trying to come up with an appropriate bargaining chip.

"Is that so?"

Shane glances from his son back to me, and I can practically feel Blaze's warning look burning a hole in the side of my neck.

I nod, desperately searching for something to make my bluff more convincing.

I take an involuntary step back, and a piece of glass crunches underfoot. My mind goes to McMannis and the broken connection to 116.

If our compound can't get ahold of anybody at 116, it's possible that everyone there is dead, too. The realization sends a chill through me, but I realize I've found my bargaining chip.

"Well, out with it, then," he snaps. "I haven't got all day."

I glance around at the two bodyguards in the corners as if they're making me nervous, but really I'm just buying myself some more time to think. I don't want to lay all my cards on the table — not when I don't trust Shane to tell me after I reveal what I know.

"Oh." Shane turns to the bodyguards. "Leave us for a moment, will you?"

The man who advanced on us opens his mouth, but one look from Shane is enough to kill the protest on his lips.

The bodyguards emerge from their corners and slip past us through the door. Shane's bloodshot eyes follow them in the video feed on the screen mounted to the wall, and when they're gone, his eyes snap back onto me like a hungry wolf's.

"So go ahead. Tell me what you have to offer."

"I might have a source who can find out what's going on at 116," I say.

His expression doesn't change much, but the brief flicker in his eyes tells me I've got his attention. "Miss Riley, even if that information interested me, your weak promise isn't much for me to go on."

I can practically feel the anxiety radiating from Blaze. He probably thinks I'm talking out of my ass, but I at least know why the supplies flowing from 116 are at a standstill. Our workers probably haven't even made the trip there since the virus annihilated 119.

"You need insurance?" I ask, feeling bold again.

"I always like insurance."

"Well . . . you tell me what you know about the Fringe Program and my parents, and I'll see what I can find out about the other compounds. If I can't bring you anything useful, I'll do another fight. You can pick the matchup."

Now that light in Shane's eyes blazes into a full-blown twinkle. This deal intrigues him. I just have to hope he finds the obliteration of 119 relevant.

"I like you, Harper Riley," he says, breaking into a smile that puts me on edge. "You have a way of making things . . . interesting."

He glances at his son again and then strides over to the fake black leather sofa and makes himself comfortable. He swirls his glass so the ice clinks around noisily and settles into storytelling mode.

"So the Fringe Program . . ." he muses. "Forgive me, but are you sure you want to know? It's part of the compound's more . . . *unsavory* history."

Blaze throws me a sideways glance.

"I'm sure."

"Suit yourself. Why don't you have a seat?"

Sitting down across from his father looks like the absolute *last* thing Blaze wants to do, but I feel as though I'm not in a position to be rude by refusing. Shane's already proven that he has an unpredictable temper, and there's no harm in humoring him.

I sink down onto a low-backed chair with very little cushion, and Blaze perches on the edge of the armrest. Normally it would be weird to have him this close, but right now I find it strangely comforting.

"The Fringe Program was not the systematic initiative the board wants people to believe," says Shane. "At that time, the compound leaders brought in babies and children any way they could."

"What do you mean?"

He shrugs. "Sometimes they would lure in parents with healthy infants with the promise of a place for the whole family. Other times, they would pay off poor families that were trying to make a living in nearby towns."

Shane takes a brief sip of his drink and then smacks his tongue over his teeth as though he tasted something sour. "But the board had no interest in the adults."

"How come?" asks Blaze.

Shane nods. "To keep population counts on track so the compound could sustain itself without overloading the system, the founders figured that a certain number of babies had to be born each year. The year the Fringe Program took off had been a particularly low birth year.

"After some crops failed, there was a major food shortage in the compound. This had happened before, and it made people very nervous."

He turns to his son and raises an eyebrow, as though he's about to throw down some fatherly wisdom. "Uncertainty and nervousness do not put people in a baby-making mood. The board tried everything. They even increased stipends for tier-three workers so some of them might decide to start a family, but it wasn't going according to plan."

"So why wouldn't they just bring in adults who wanted to live in the compound?" I ask.

"It all goes back to the first generation," says Shane, making a faraway gesture with his drink. "You have to remember that they grew up on the outside. The founders . . . they were all smart, educated, progressive people. But despite all that, a lot of them had trouble adjusting when they came into the compound.

"It's like you take an eagle that's been soaring over the

mountains, clip its wings, and put it in a cage. It's unnatural. The animal is unhappy. It goes crazy and claws out its insides and then hangs itself with its own intestines."

I cringe at the grisly image.

"They were worried the adults wouldn't adjust?" Blaze clarifies.

"And that they could cause a disturbance among the general population," says Shane. "They'd seen it before. A woman gets it in her head that she'd rather be out there than in here. She tries to escape. Well, of course, they aren't just going to let people run off, so they throw her in the psych ward.

"But then people start asking questions. They start to feel trapped. Suddenly, you've got yourself a full-blown panic. People want to know why they can't leave. It's ridiculous, but it's what happened. It was a real problem for the founders before Death Storm."

"So what happened to them?" I prompt. "The parents who brought their babies into the compound, I mean."

Shane pauses for a long time, and I start to wonder if I've gotten everything out of him that he's going to give. But then he sets his drink down and makes a jerking motion with his hand that cracks all his knuckles. "Are you sure you want to know?"

"Yes!" I say, feeling impatient. Shane clearly enjoys hearing himself speak, but when it gets down to the important details, he becomes evasive.

"I only ask because this isn't the sort of thing you can just forget. Once you know, you're going to wish you didn't. Once you know, it's going to change the way you see *everything* around here."

Blaze and I exchange a look, and I get the feeling he would rather not know. But he wanted to come up here with me, so he's just going to have to deal. "I'm sure."

Shane dips his head so he's looking me straight in the eye. "If your parents were ever here, they weren't here for long. The day they entered the compound, they signed their own death certificates."

seventeen

Harper

I t takes a long moment for Shane's words to sink in.

"You mean . . . the board had them killed?"

"It could have been the board, or it could have been the Fringe Program Committee. Who knows?"

"But how could they get away with that?" Blaze asks, glaring at his father in disbelief.

Shane throws his son a derisive look as if to say, "Are you *really* asking me that question?"

"Seriously," I say. "How did they explain a new baby to people without accounting for the parents? There's the medical ward staff, the Institute, the child . . ."

Shane shrugs. "Think of it this way: Two people enter the compound with a baby in the middle of the night. Nobody knows they're coming or what condition they're going to be in.

"Someone from the Fringe Program Committee meets them in postexposure and rushes the baby straight to the medical ward for an exam and observation. The parents think that's a good idea. They're told they need to wait there to fill out some paperwork. Your parents probably never even made it to the medical ward."

That floors me. It seems too medieval to be true.

"They just killed them on sight?"

Shane nods. "It was easier that way . . . no one would ask questions. Once the baby was declared healthy and passed off to the Institute, the Fringe Program Committee would make a note in its file that the parents died of radiation poisoning or influenza a few weeks after entering the compound. Maybe the committee would tell the medical ward that they found the baby on the Fringe. Who's going to ask questions? They have no reason to believe it isn't true."

It sounds ridiculous, but Shane is right. I never questioned my parents' death. I believed my guardian in the Institute when she told me they died a few weeks after arrival. She probably never even knew it was a lie.

"How long did this go on?" pipes Blaze. "It can't have been widespread. Someone would have gotten suspicious."

Shane shakes his head. "It wasn't. The Fringe Program didn't last. Only a handful of kids were brought in each year during the pilot program. The funding dried up twenty years ago, and the board just chalked it up to another failed experiment."

"Why do you say that?" asks Blaze.

Dread settles in my stomach.

"Later, they found out that those children weren't as healthy as children born in the compound. They were exposed to too many toxins and high levels of radiation, which put them at risk for all kinds of health problems. Not to mention they were — How should I put this? — *not* part of the compound elite."

Shane spits out the last two words with uncharacteristic contempt.

"*Compound elite?*"

"You have to remember that the compound's founders were a bunch of eugenics nuts. They screened themselves for disease and genetic deficiencies before signing on. They recruited across the genetic spectrum to add diversity to the herd. And when the second wave of people came to the compound, only those with top-notch genes were even considered."

"And the Fringe babies were genetically inferior," I murmur.

"It doesn't really matter whether they were or not," says Shane. "It's all about perception. If people believed others were genetically inferior, it would have made it that much more difficult to convince people that the compound was a meritocracy, wouldn't it?"

My mind flashes to the spreadsheet of VocAps data, with its endless columns of health- and genetics-related scores. *Meritocracy, my ass.*

"But that's ridiculous," says Blaze.

"Is it? How many third-gen kids do you know in Recon? Hmm? What about Fringe kids who ended up in tier one?"

"Celdon," I murmur. As far as I know, he's the only one — an outlier among Fringe rejects.

Blaze's expression hardens. He must be feeling all the outrage I felt when I found out about the VocAps test.

"And what about the babies who didn't come with their parents?" I ask.

According to Celdon's guardian at the Institute, a couple of Recon operatives found him just outside the compound. But that has to be a lie, too.

Shane shakes his head and waves off the question as though it explains itself. "After Death Storm, it was *chaos* out there. People were desperate. All the committee had to do was find a drug addict or prostitute who had a baby. The mother got some cash, got to feel good about giving her kid a better life . . ." Shane lets out a derisive laugh. "Believe me . . . it wasn't a tough sell."

Shane's words feel like a sucker punch. Celdon always thought his mother abandoned him outside the compound, and it sounds as though his theory was not too far from the truth.

After a few seconds, Shane grows bored with my shock and dismay. He kills the rest of his drink in one gulp and fixes me with a grim stare. "I know your first impulse might be to run and tell the world about this, but if you know what's good for you, you'll forget all about it."

I glare at him. "Don't want to be sent to kill me again?"

Shane shakes his head slowly. "It's not a task I enjoy, believe me. It's just business."

"*Just business?*"

"Don't look at me like that. I'm just warning you because it's the gentlemanly thing to do. And it's not just your life, either." Shane looks pointedly at his son and back to me. "They might just start picking off the people close to you."

I have the sudden impulse to jump out of my seat and slap Shane. I'm sick of Constance's threats — even indirect ones. The fury is bubbling in my chest, and I get up to leave before I can act on the violent thoughts flashing through my mind.

"Whoa. Whoa. Whoa," slurs Shane from behind me.

When I turn around, he slides his familiar smug expression back into place. "Now, don't forget . . . you owe me for that little piece of information. And I'm not going to come shake you down for it."

I glare at him. "What's *that* supposed to mean?"

"It means that if I have to remind you, you aren't going to like the way I send the message."

* * *

It takes me about half an hour to lose Blaze after our meeting with Shane. His shocked expression stays firmly in place all the way from Shane's private room to my compartment.

It's strange that the son of a man who runs the black market and orchestrates all organized crime within the compound would find anything surprising, but Blaze must have lived all this time by ignoring some of the more heinous crimes his father commits.

While it was comforting to have Blaze by my side in Neverland, I don't have time to bring him up to speed on everything I know. Once he recovers from the news, I tell him I'm exhausted so he'll leave.

When I hear his door click shut a few compartments down, I check to make sure the coast is clear and head up to Systems to find Celdon.

I still haven't decided what I'm going to tell him about his mother, but I need to share Shane's information with *someone*. He isn't in his compartment, so I go straight to Systems. It's kind of a long shot, but I never saw him down in Neverland, and this is the only place I can think where he would be.

To my relief, Celdon answers the door right away when I buzz headquarters. I can tell he hasn't left this room in hours. His eyes are tired from staring at his computer screen, and his blond hair is sticking up in odd directions from running his hands through it in frustration.

"Hey," he says, taking me in with a furtive expression and glancing down the tunnel. There's no one else around. The only people who live this close to headquarters are Systems retirees, and they're all in for the night.

"Hey. Do you have a minute?"

He looks back over his shoulder and tries — unsuccessfully — to pat down his messy hair. "Sure, sure."

Stepping into Systems headquarters, I get a familiar pang of envy. Station after station stretches before me in a honeycomb configuration, each one tricked out with the latest equipment.

I run my hand over the back of a swivel chair, marveling at the butter-soft upholstery and trying to keep my tech lust in check. All the electronics give the stations a pleasant warmth, and it feels as though I'm stepping inside a living, breathing organism.

"I don't think I'd ever get tired of this," I whisper.

"Yeah, I know."

Celdon's voice sounds strange to me, but I'm not sure if that's because he feels guilty about his Systems status or because his mind is elsewhere.

"You never showed me your new station," I say, trying to buy myself some time before I have to deliver the bad news.

"Oh, well, uh . . ." Celdon trails off, running a hand nervously through his hair. "I would show you, except . . . it's kind of a mess right now."

I throw him a skeptical look. "Like you've ever cared about a mess. Come on! I want to see it."

Celdon lets out a puff of air from between his teeth, looking genuinely agitated. "No, it's like *really* bad at the moment. I don't want anybody to see it."

"I don't care if you were watching porn in there," I say, only half joking. "I just want to see your setup."

He opens his mouth to retort, but no words come out.

Something isn't right.

Before he can stop me, I make a beeline for his station — the only glass cube that's lit up along the far back wall.

As soon as I step inside, I know he was lying about the mess. There's only one canteen takeout container lying next to the keyboard, and it hasn't even begun to smell yet. He's got three top-of-the-line monitors facing away from the bull pen, and they're filled with square after square of Fringe footage.

"Oh my gosh," I murmur.

Celdon steps into the cube behind me, looking very guilty. "Now, before you freak out, let me explain."

"O-*kay.*"

He holds up his hands and releases a quick burst of air. "Eli asked me to do this."

"What?"

"He filled me in on everything that's been going on and asked . . . asked if I could hack into Constance's surveillance to keep a lookout for his brother."

"He did *what?*"

I could smack Eli for dragging Celdon into this.

"Are you insane? Do you know how dangerous this is?"

"Chill, Riles. I'll be fine. They won't even know I'm here."

"You can't fool Constance!"

Celdon tilts his head sideways and cocks an eyebrow. "Actually, I can. Their security really sucks."

But my panic has already reached a boiling point. I keep seeing Celdon as he was after Constance dragged him in to get to me: battered, broken, and afraid.

"No! This is too dangerous! I don't want you involved."

"More involved than I already am?" he snaps. "Because if knowing Constance's dirty little secret at 119 doesn't make me involved —"

"That's different. We got back here without anyone knowing, and we were lucky. What do you think would happen if they noticed someone hacked into their system? Huh?"

"Please. Those amateurs don't even know I'm watching."

"It doesn't matter!" I cry. "I can't let you do this."

"I'm already doing it. And it's not your choice. I'm a big boy, Riles."

I want to shake him. I want to scream at him. I want to tell him that he doesn't understand how dangerous this is, but he does. Celdon knows better than anyone.

Celdon was the one Constance tortured. *Celdon* is the one who continues to be threatened because of me. Who am I to tell him he can't help?

"You're right," I sigh. "You're right, okay? Just please, *please* be careful."

He seems legitimately surprised that I caved so easily. "What's going on with you?" he asks, sinking into his chair. "Why did you come here?"

"I just paid a visit to Shane."

Celdon's eyes bug out, and his mouth falls open. "No, you didn't."

"I know, I know. It was stupid and dangerous, but —"

"Are you serious? You come in here and start lecturing *me* for being reckless, yet you wander right into the den of a guy who tried to *kill* you?"

"I needed his help."

"What could you possibly need Shane for?"

I hesitate. I want to tell Celdon everything, but that would mean confirming all his worst suspicions about the woman who gave birth to him. So instead I start by unloading everything Sawyer told me and Eli about our radiation resistance.

As I talk, Celdon's expression changes from disbelief to excitement. I leave out the suggestion that he might be resistant, too, but Celdon doesn't miss a beat.

"Does that mean I'm a super mutant?"

"There's no way to know," I say. "You haven't been exposed to radiation as an adult, so there's no way to tell how your body would react."

"So I *could* be a mutant."

"I guess," I say, suddenly overcome with exhaustion. "But that's not what I came here to tell you."

Celdon tilts his head to the side and gives me a look of dread. Any news bigger than super-mutant radiation resistance can't be good.

I pause, debating for the hundredth time if I should tell him the truth. It certainly won't put his mind at ease knowing his mom was paid off, but I know if it were me, I'd prefer closure — even misery — to a lifetime of uncertainty.

"Sawyer told me there was no record of my parents ever being admitted to the medical ward."

"What?"

"They have my records from my exam and admittance, but there's nothing on my parents."

"That makes no sense."

"I know. They'd have to be examined before they were integrated into the compound. So I went to Shane. I knew if anyone here would know what really happened, it would be him."

Celdon smacks a hand to his forehead to emphasize my stupidity but doesn't argue. "And?"

I drag in another breath. This is it — my last chance to back out and spare him the awful truth. Maybe he would be better off not knowing, but he'd never forgive me if he learned I lied to spare his feelings.

"There's no record of my parents being admitted to the medical ward because they never got that far," I murmur. "They were probably killed as soon as they got to the compound."

Celdon's hand drops into his lap. "They killed your parents? Just invited them in, took you, and . . . *killed* them?"

I nod.

He sinks back against his chair to process that information and then looks up at me with a twinge of sadness in his eyes. "Do you think . . . do you think that's what happened to my mom? Was the 'finding me outside the compound' thing just a story they made up?"

His hopeful tone breaks my heart in two. And despite my earlier resolution to tell Celdon the truth, I find myself waffling.

I have the rare opportunity to tell a lie that could make his life better, not worse. I know he would probably prefer to think his mother was killed unjustly than think she handed him over for a little bit of cash. Plus, there's no way to know for sure what happened to her.

"Most likely," I choke.

"They just killed her?"

I nod slowly, feeling a rush of relief that drowns out the guilt. "They killed my parents to get to me."

To my surprise, Celdon grabs the takeout container sitting on the desk and chucks it at the wall. It hits the glass with a dull *splat*, and the green-and-yellow mush smears down the wall in slow motion.

"They can't *do* this," he growls, shaking with rage.

"But they have."

"Who the hell do they think they are?" he yells.

I don't know what to say. I've never seen Celdon this angry, so I have no way of knowing how to calm him down.

"Is there any part of this compound that doesn't run on a bunch of fucked-up shit? Everything they've ever told us is a lie!"

"I know."

"We should just let the drifters bring down the compounds," he snarls. "It would certainly even the score."

"You don't mean that."

"The hell I don't! We shouldn't even be here, Harper. This place only exists because the founders decided who deserved to live and said 'screw everybody else.' I can't stay here! I can't live here knowing that other people had to die so I could live the good life."

"You can't tell anyone," I warn.

"Why not?" he yells. "People deserve to know! This is bullshit. If people knew the truth, that would solve all our problems. Constance couldn't just kill us to keep it quiet. There'd be no containing a story like this."

Suddenly, I wish I hadn't said anything. Celdon deserved to know the truth, but I hadn't expected him to react like this.

"Stop! Stop! *Listen* to yourself. Are you out of your mind? Of course they would kill us!"

"Not if it's all out in the open!"

"Even if we got the story out there, they'd just lock us up and pretend we were insane," I say. "Constance controls Information. We'd never get the story out on the feeds. Telling people isn't even an option."

"How can you be so calm about this?" Celdon huffs. "Doesn't it bother you that they murdered your parents? Or are you so deep in this that you don't feel anything anymore?"

"Of *course* it bothers me!" I yell. "I never even got to know them! I could have had a family, and now I have *no one*."

A look of hurt flashes across his face, so I try to rein in my furious tone. "There's nothing we can do."

Celdon just stares at me, breathing hard, and I look away so I don't burst into hot, angry tears.

For several minutes, I just stare at the monitors, watching the scenes of the Fringe change one by one.

Every once in a while, I see a building that seems familiar, but then I realize it's just another abandoned town that looks remarkably similar to the one Eli and I visited.

Then the screen flickers, and a new scene starts to unfold.

A lone figure is striding purposefully down the sidewalk toward the pawn shop, wearing a faded gray baseball cap. He has a pronounced five o'clock shadow that obscures most of his features, but there's something familiar about his confident stride.

He stops at the door to pull his hat down lower, and I catch a glimpse of his face.

It's Owen.

eighteen

Eli

There's no getting that orange dust out of your clothes. It clings to your boots and your pants and your hair — even in a dream.

I've left a trail of the stuff across the shiny black tile floor all the way through the tunnel and into this room.

Everything in Information is painted tuxedo black. The walls and ceiling of my ten-by-ten chamber are as dark as it gets, and the only source of light is emanating from the sharp lines of the crown molding.

It's barely bright enough for me to see the outline of a door directly across from the one I came through. Every nerve in my body is tingling — screaming at me to turn around and leave.

Someone from Constance must be nearby, but a muffled cry from beyond the door captures my attention.

My hand closes on the smooth handle, and I yank the door open before I have a chance to change my mind.

I'm instantly blinded by the harsh light of a single florescent lamp hanging from the ceiling. I have to blink several times before my eyes adjust, and when they do, horror flares through me.

I'm standing in another chamber about the same size as the one I came through, but I'm not alone. Harper is seated in the very center of the room with her hands bound behind her back. She's got a piece of tape covering her mouth, but I can read the terror in her quivering gray eyes.

I move toward her automatically, and the door slams shut.

Before I can even utter Harper's name, Jayden materializes from the corner to my right.

"Nice of you to join us, Parker."

"What the hell is this?" I growl, bending down to check on Harper.

"You left your partner here . . . remember?"

"To give you what you wanted," I say, tugging on the tape to free Harper's wrists.

"I wouldn't do that if I were you."

"Why the he —"

A slight shock zings up my arm, but Harper's muffled whimper means it must have been *much* worse for her. My heart starts pounding from the adrenaline, and my palms break out in a cold sweat.

I tilt my head to examine Harper's neck and see that she's wearing some kind of shock collar. *Bastards.*

I reach out automatically to remove it, but Jayden's harsh *tsk* stops me.

"Careful . . ." she croons, holding up a tiny plastic fob.

"What is *wrong* with you?" I snap. "I did everything you asked. I killed them, and I stayed away until the job was done."

Jayden bats her long eyelashes once in what I can only interpret as a "Gotcha!" gesture.

"Yes, you did," she says slowly. "You were a good boy — a good lieutenant. But you left your partner here . . . after all you've been through together. What does that say about you? Huh? How much could you really care for Cadet Riley if you just abandoned her at the first sign of trouble?"

I make a grab for the fob in Jayden's hand, but she's too fast. She whips her arm out of reach and hits the button again.

Harper makes another pitiful sound, and I feel her pain as

if it were my own.

"Stop!" I scream.

Jayden just smiles.

I throw Harper an apologetic look, and a lone tear rolls down her cheek.

Something inside me cracks, and I have the sudden heart-breaking realization that I'm not going to be able to save her.

Constance never intended for Harper to leave this room. Jayden is going to torture and kill her right here in front of me so I'll never step out of line again.

"That's what I thought," she whispers. "You're a coward, Parker. And now Riley sees it, too."

Just then, there's a knock at the door.

Jayden doesn't move a muscle, and Harper's still staring at me with that hopeless, pained expression.

The knocking becomes more insistent, and I realize faintly that the noise isn't coming from my dream at all. It's coming from my compartment door.

My compartment?

Suddenly, Harper and Jayden disappear. I'm no longer standing in the stuffy chamber, but I still feel overheated despite the cool air of my compartment. My sheets are tangled around my legs like shackles, and I can feel a fine sheen of sweat all over my body.

I'm alone in bed, and someone is knocking frantically on the door.

I spring to my feet, nearly tripping over my sheet in the process. I yank the door open and see Harper standing there wide-eyed. Her gaze snaps down my bare torso and back up to my face, and a slight flush creeps over her cheeks.

She's wearing a sexy black getup I've never seen before that shows a lot of skin. I'm not wearing anything except a pair of boxer briefs, but I'm too relieved to care.

Before Harper can get any words out, I pull her into my arms and crush her against my chest. She lets out a little breath of surprise and then snakes her arms around my waist. I squeeze her tighter and drag her inside.

Darkness envelops us as soon as I close the door, but I don't want to let go of Harper even for the second it would take to turn on the light. I know I'm about to lose her, but it's the right choice.

Even if she hates me for lying to her and leaving her behind, she'll be safer here than she would be out on the Fringe.

"Eli . . ."

I can't make out her features, but she feels so warm and so good that I don't even bother asking why she's here.

Caressing her bare arms from where they're locked around me, I forge a trail to her neck and cup her face between my palms. She shivers, and I have the sudden urge to wrap myself around her and keep her here forever.

Her skin feels unbelievably soft. And when I bring my lips down on hers, I'm overwhelmed by sensation. Her lips are hot — almost feverish — and her breath is coming in uneven little spurts.

She kisses me back slowly, and I can tell there's something else weighing on her mind.

I should ask her what it is, but I don't want to think about anything else — not when this could be the last time I hold her in my arms.

She's here. She's alive. She's with me.

I deepen the kiss, and she opens her mouth with a tiny groan.

There's nothing I like better than tasting her. After a workout, there's a faint hint of salt on her upper lip, but right now, I taste the sting of artificial strawberry. She must have been wearing lip gloss, though I'm not sure why.

I take her lower lip between mine and suck a little, pulling away with a tiny bite.

When she tilts her head back, I tug gently on her silky hair and trail kisses down her neck and throat.

I can feel her pulse racing under my mouth, and I pull away for a second to nuzzle her neck. Her breath catches, and that spurs me on. My hands wander through her hair and down her back, finally settling on the hem of her shirt. I can feel an inch or so of velvety skin between her tank top and her pants, and I slide my hands back up to feel her smooth stomach.

Harper's lips caress mine once again, and this time, she teases me with her tongue. Her hand moves from my cheek to the back of my head, and I see stars when she drags her fingernails against my scalp.

Her other hand burns a trail down my chest, and her thumb finds the groove in my side between my hip bone and my waistband.

She pulls her lips away and breathlessly says my name again. I know she wants to talk, but I'm desperate to reassure myself that this is real.

I kiss her again — softly this time — and whip her tank top over her head with an impatient tug.

Harper lets out a soft note of surprise but quickly closes the distance between us.

When she pulls me into her and crushes her chest against mine, a tremor rolls through my body. Something about the dream has awakened a new desperation inside me, and the skin-to-skin contact is almost too much.

Without hesitation, I pull her off her feet and deposit her onto my bed. She kicks off her boots and inches sideways to make room, but I position myself directly above her so I can feel every part of her body.

I suddenly wish I had a window looking out onto the Fringe so I could see her sprawled out on my bed, drenched in moonlight. I want to memorize every part of her, but I can only see her eyes reflecting back the sparse light, so I take her in the only way I can.

This time when I kiss her, she arches up to grind her hips against mine. I groan and push them down onto the bed, holding her in place.

I want to take my time tonight, and that's not going to be possible with her doing that.

I leave a trail of kisses from her jaw to her neck, and a wild desire flares up inside me. My lips have a mind of their own as they skip down to the soft skin between her belly button and her waistband. I tug down her pants and slide my hand slowly up her leg, but then she disappears.

In the dark, I can see Harper's shape moving toward the headboard, and confusion swamps me as she withdraws.

"Eli, wait," she gasps.

A new kind of panic spills into my stomach.

Shit, shit, shit.

I should have stopped to *think* for a second before I ripped off her clothes and threw her onto my bed. I came on too strong, and now I've wrecked everything.

"Sorry," I say in a raspy voice. I clear my throat and try to slow my pounding heart. "I'm sorry. Was that too fast?"

"No, no. It's just . . ." She sighs and takes a second to collect herself while I teeter on the brink of a heart attack.

"What is it?"

If I didn't ruin things by jumping her as soon as she walked in here, something else must be bothering her.

I reach over to turn on the lamp, and it's all I can do not to let my mouth hang open when I see her sitting on my bed practically naked. She's perfect.

Luckily, Harper doesn't seem to notice my gawking. She's still flushed and a little winded from our exchange, but her head is clearly someplace else. She takes several more breaths and then says, "I came here to tell you that I know about Celdon's little assignment."

My stomach drops.

I can't believe Celdon told her already, the little shit. It's bad enough that I lied to Harper; I also dragged her best friend into it.

I grimace, searching for the right thing to say, but Harper keeps going.

"I don't like that you got him involved with this . . . hacking into Constance's feeds . . . but we just saw Owen on camera."

It takes several seconds for that information to sink in. I wait for Harper to start yelling at me for cutting her out and planning to fake Owen's death, but she seems to be waiting for *my* reaction.

Finally she grows impatient and continues. "He was at the pawn shop."

"You saw Owen on the feed?" I repeat.

God, I sound like an idiot. But I'm still confused as to why she's taking the news so well.

"I looked at the time stamp. It's live footage."

"Was there a clear shot of his face?"

"No. I just got a glimpse. He looked like he didn't want to be spotted, but it was definitely Owen."

That's reassuring. If Harper didn't get a good look at him, it's unlikely that Jayden will see the resemblance and put two and two together. And judging by her casual attitude, it's possible Celdon didn't tell her everything.

"How long do you think it will take for Constance to identify him on the footage?"

"I don't know. But I'm sure they have someone monitoring it twenty-four/seven. Jayden is desperate to find the gang leaders."

"So we'll probably be sent out soon . . . won't we?"

Harper's use of "we" feels like a round kick to the stomach. It breaks my heart to drop her as a partner, but I don't want to break the news to her now.

"Yeah," I murmur. "Soon."

In that moment, she looks so crestfallen it makes my chest physically hurt. I remind myself that I'm only doing this so she won't have to face an indefinite deployment. It's the right decision, but it's still going to hurt her.

Then there's the issue of Owen showing up on the feeds. Knowing he's in that town sets me on edge. He's in serious danger, and by the time Jayden sends me out, there's no telling where he'll be.

I just wish I'd had a little more time to prepare for deployment — time to figure out the right way to break the news to Harper.

Suddenly the mood shifts. Harper's probably wondering if tonight will be her last night in the compound. Impersonating Owen raised the stakes, and now the town is crawling with drifters who probably want us dead.

I'm thinking about how tonight could be the last I spend with Harper.

She shivers and crosses her arms over her chest, glancing up at me from under thick, sooty lashes. I don't want this to end, but I don't know what to say.

"I better go," she whispers, moving toward the edge of the

bed.

Talking about Owen and the impending deployment effectively killed the mood, but I don't want her to leave.

"Stay," I hear myself blurt out.

Harper freezes. I'm not sure if that was the right thing to do, but I don't want her to go.

"Stay with me."

I expect Harper to refuse. I expect awkwardness. I expect to spend the rest of the night alone, wishing I hadn't said anything. I *don't* expect her to nod and crack a smile, but that's what she does.

Surprise and elation surge through me, and suddenly I don't know what to do. It's not as though we haven't slept in the same bed before, but this feels different than it did out on the Fringe — more real, somehow. There's no immediate danger — no reason for her to lie down in my arms other than the fact that she wants to.

Harper scoots back across the bed, and I move toward her slowly.

When I reach her side, she seems to melt into my sheets, and I lean over so I can feel her against my bare skin.

I place a soft kiss on her lips, and she returns it with gentle pressure. I let my hand drift down toward her belly button, and her body responds to my touch.

Then a heaviness settles over me, and Harper's movements become more lethargic. I lie down beside her, and she rolls over onto her hip. I reach over to turn off the lamp and pull her toward me so our bodies are flush against each other.

I invited her to stay with me, and she did.

The thought makes me so happy and so unbearably sad at the same time.

I squeeze her tighter and crane my neck to place a soft kiss on her cheek. She lets out a contented sigh, and that little sound sends an overpowering warmth through me.

I take a mental snapshot of this moment, trying to commit every detail to memory. Then I match my breaths to hers and drift into a peaceful sleep.

nineteen

Celdon

It's easy to lose time in Systems. There are no clocks on the walls and no windows.

Only the small geometric skylights filter in daylight, so one hour seems to bleed into the next until there is no more daylight. Once night falls, it's easy to work until dawn without even meaning to.

I glance at my interface. It's oh-three hundred, which means Harper should have been back by now. When she left to tell Eli, I thought she'd be gone an hour tops, and I'm starting to feel the faint prickle of unease.

I should have warned Eli that Harper knew about the surveillance but nothing else. He probably slipped up and told her everything and then spent the next few hours riding out her storm of fury. Poor guy.

I sit back in my chair and force myself to blink slowly. I haven't left this spot since the Owen sighting. My eyes have been fixated on the pawn shop door, but Owen has yet to emerge.

Maybe he's dead, I think. *Maybe Eli's little stunt out there got him killed.*

My thoughts are interrupted by a soft *click* out in the bull pen. I stare out through the glass at the hundreds of empty stations, waiting for some indication that I didn't imagine the noise.

"Harper?" I call, knowing full well it can't be her. She couldn't get into Systems without a key card.

It's *way* too early for even the most brown-nosey programmers to show their faces, but it could be an Operations worker here to clean. I'm on a first-name basis with the night guy, Mitchell, so I need to be ready to kill the footage if he wanders in here to chitchat.

The place looks empty, but I still have a strange feeling that I'm not alone.

I slide my chair out from the desk and walk out onto the main floor, careful not to make a sound.

Instantly, the warmth from all the computers envelops me, and my jittery feelings intensify. Between the tiny fans on each monitor and the soft buzz of the server lights, it's impossible to pick out any human noises. The little rounded stations throw shadows over the chairs, so I can't tell if anyone is lurking in one of the egg-like enclosures.

My nerves are stretched to the breaking point, which is strange, considering I've never gotten the creeps in here before. But my senses are tingling, telling me something isn't right.

"Hello?" I call out.

Suddenly, a low chuckle breaks through the mechanical hum and nearly sends my heart into overdrive. I whip my head around in the direction of the noise, but it dies on the air as quickly as it appeared.

"Who's there?" I call, trying to sound casual. If it's just another Systems worker, I don't want to come off like a total psycho. But then again, starting a middle-of-the-night conversation with maniacal laughter is kind of psycho, too.

Just then, a monitor at the nearest station flickers to life. The welcome screen floods the half-moon station with harsh blue light, but there's nobody in there.

Now I'm *really* freaking out.

It's fairly easy to take over any one of the computers from

inside headquarters to share what's on your screen, but that means someone is actually in here messing with me.

I look around at the stations again, searching for the telltale blue light of another live monitor. But before my eyes have made their way to the far corner, a bank of about two dozen computers bursts to life.

My pulse begins to race, and I'm having trouble controlling my breathing.

"Very funny," I call out, all traces of normalcy gone. I don't even care that the visitor can hear the panic in my voice. I'm fucking scared.

Then a window pops up on the computer to my right. It's a video-chat window, but the background is completely dark.

"Celdon," says a man in a taunting voice. "*Yoo-hoo . . .*"

That voice. I *know* that voice. It sends a shiver down my spine and makes every part of me recoil.

"What do you want?" I ask, keeping my feet firmly planted and my gaze on the bank of stations. Clearly he knows where I am, but I refuse to look into the camera and give him the satisfaction of seeing my terrified expression. I also don't want anyone to get the jump on me while I'm distracted.

Out of the corner of my eye, I see a close-up of a handsome, menacing face fill the screen. My blood goes cold in my veins, and my hands ball into fists.

"You're no fun," the man whines. "I was hoping to play around a little more . . ."

Without meaning to, I glance down at the video chat. He gives me an easy grin, and it's even creepier that his smile appears genuine. "Did you like my little trick with the monitors? I thought it would add drama."

I scoff. "Kid stuff. Why don't you come out here like a man instead of hiding behind your monitor?"

He looks vaguely surprised, and then his eyes whip around in my direction. I know I'm out of range of the camera, but it still feels as though he's looking right at me.

"I was just going to say the exact — same — thing."

At that moment, he shuts off the monitors, thrusting me into total darkness. My eyes struggle to adjust to the sudden change in light, and my unease intensifies when I realize I can't see him approaching.

"Boo," says a soft voice behind me.

My heart stops, but somehow I manage to keep my expression neutral.

I pivot slowly in the aisle, my body primed to run, and come face to face with Devon Reid.

Devon is tall and trim, but I still tower over him by at least two inches. He's got smooth, handsome features; dark, smoky eyes; thick chocolate-brown hair that twirls into a wave at the front; and a smile that would kill if he didn't constantly use it to make creepy declarations.

Even though it's the middle of the night, his white slacks are pressed to perfection. His blazer is hanging open casually, revealing a low V-neck that frames a few tendrils of dark hair. He moves toward me like a white panther, and I get a whiff of expensive cologne.

"Like what you see?" he asks in a silky voice. "I'm sorry to say I'm here on business."

Right. Like that *would ever happen.*

"What do you want, Devon?" I sigh.

He looks taken aback, as if he always wanders into Systems in the middle of the night.

"What do *I* want?"

He takes another step forward, and I recoil automatically.

"Is that any way to treat an old friend?"

I squeeze my fists together so forcefully that I hear my knuckles crack. Beads of cold sweat spring up all over my forehead, and I get a flash of Devon's face between two prison bars.

I could never forget that face as long as I live. It was seared into the back of my eyelids as Devon electrocuted me and dumped bucket after bucket of freezing water into my airways.

"Why are you here?" I manage to choke.

"I'm here to extend another offer," he says, cracking a genial smile as if he's offering me a regular job.

I glare at him.

"Oh, don't be like that. You should feel flattered. I don't like having to repeat myself, and I almost never beg."

"Well, you're going to have to beg," I growl. "I don't want any part of whatever sick bullshit you people are planning."

"Don't say that," he says, feigning a pouty expression that makes his face look strangely inhuman. "You're bound to hurt my feelings. And when my feelings get hurt, I get mean."

"What are you going to do?" I ask, acting more ballsy than I feel. "Kill me right here? Drag me in to torture me some more?"

"Oh, no. You're much too valuable. Constance could use somebody with your particular skill set . . . but you already knew that."

I *do* know. Their security sucks. But I resist the urge to throw that in his face.

"I *have* a job, Devon. Thanks for the offer."

"So do I," he says, gesturing around at Systems. "And it's a very good job. Good money. Fulfilling work. Fun, smart coworkers. Sexy uniform." He flicks his blazer open and lowers his chin so his eyes smolder when he looks up at me. I wonder how much he's practiced that move. "But Constance gives me something else."

Devon leans forward so he can whisper in my ear, and I get

a whiff of his overly minty breath. "I'm untouchable."

"You only *think* you're untouchable," I growl.

He shrugs. "You know what they say . . . as long as you just *believe.*"

"I'm not interested."

Devon's smile widens, and my stomach does a nervous little flip. I've positioned my body between him and my cube with all the monitors displaying Fringe footage, but it wouldn't be difficult for him to blaze past me and get a good look at what I'm up to.

"See, I think you're just playing hard to get. I think you *are* interested. In fact, I think you have a very specific interest in what Constance is up to."

"Why do you say that?"

"Because you're hiding something. Whatever you're doing, you've gone to an awful lot of trouble to cover your tracks. You wouldn't do that unless you were working on something truly juicy.

"So I'm curious. What is it that you're trying so hard to hide? Or would you prefer to tell me on our little jaunt over to HQ?"

It takes me a moment to realize that he's talking about Constance's headquarters, and I get a perverse flash of excitement at the thought of checking it out.

But clearly it's a trap. There's no way they'd let me take a field trip down there and then walk out without pledging my allegiance.

"No, thanks," I say. "My answer is final. If you want to torture me, go ahead. But my answer will still be the same when you're done."

"Torture?" Devon looks mildly offended. "No, no, no. I'm sorry. I think we got off on the wrong foot." He raises his hands in surrender. "I'll be the first to admit that was probably not the best approach. But you have to understand that those orders came from up top. My hands were tied. If it were up to me, we would have tried a different tactic."

"I don't know what you mean."

He quirks an eyebrow. "I think you do."

"Get out. You're disgusting."

"Oh, get your mind out of the gutter!" he says with a wave of his hand. "Please don't take this the wrong way, but I meant what I said: I'm here on business. And I believe I have some information that you might find . . . *interesting.*"

"We're done here, Devon."

"We are not done here," he says, half angry, half flirtatious. It's a weird combination. "Not until you hear my full offer."

"I don't need to. I already know what my answer will be."

"No, you don't."

"Look. There's nothing you could possibly offer me that would make me want to join your sick organization. You've done nothing except hurt my friends. You nearly got Harper killed."

"Oh, please. That was just a little stunt to shake up Lieutenant Parker. No big deal."

"Get out, Devon! I mean it."

I've lost all patience, but he's just warming up. "Are you telling me you really don't care to know what happened to your mother?" he asks, leaning heavily on the M word.

That's when I lose track of everything. My vision goes all fuzzy. I can't feel my legs. I almost forget to breathe.

"Hmm? I know that question has haunted you your entire life."

I don't say anything for a long time. My mind is still trying to catch up to my ears. *How could he possibly know?*

"It hasn't, actually," I say too late, nervous excitement humming in my veins.

"That's not what your file from the Institute shrink said."

Suddenly, that excitement dissolves into rage. It's so intense and so sudden that it feels as though an electric current just surged through my entire body.

I take a step forward — ready to deck him — but he steps out of the way easily and lets out a low, infuriating chuckle.

"Easy now. Don't want you hurting yourself . . ."

"You read my file?" I growl.

"I apologize. It was a *flagrant* invasion of your privacy. But it's my job to know my subjects." He shrugs. "You understand."

I let out a loud, crazy laugh. "Well, you know, that almost tempted me. The thing is, it might have been a different story if you'd come in here yesterday, but I just found out everything I need to know. You really should cover your tracks better."

The second I blurt it out, I know I said something really stupid. Devon's eyes light up in satisfaction, and he can barely contain his gleeful smile.

Now he knows that we were digging into our parents' history.

"And what happened to her?" he probes, undeterred by my ballsy declaration.

"You people — or the board or the Fringe Program Committee or whoever — brought her in and *killed* her. It's how you got *all* the Fringe babies."

To my immense surprise, Devon doesn't seem put out that he just lost his only bargaining chip. He's wearing a wicked smile that compounds my unease. "Did Harper tell you that?"

"I —"

"You know, it really is a shame that your best friend would *lie* to you."

"What are you talking about?"

"The compound leaders didn't need to have your mother killed. They never had to get rid of her at all."

"What are you saying?" I ask, more desperate sounding than I would like.

"Your mother . . . How should I put this?" He purses his lips as though he's considering the most delicate way to phrase it. "Let's just say the likes of her would have traded her baby for a hot meal."

I stare at him in disbelief, unable to process the words spilling out of his smug mouth.

"I'm sorry to be the one to tell you this, Celdon, but your mother was, well . . . a whore."

"No."

Devon frowns and shrugs. "She gave you up."

"You're bluffing," I croak. My throat is so dry the words are barely discernible.

But I'm not so sure that he is.

I'd like to believe Harper's version of events, but it doesn't quite fit. For one thing, the compound guardians gave her a completely different story than they gave me when it would have been so much easier to explain my mother away with radiation poisoning.

Hell, it would have been better for my well-being to tell me I had a mom and a dad who loved me enough to bring me into the compound — not that I was found by some Recon worker with nothing and no one.

"You're just pissed that you've got nothing," I say finally.

"On the contrary. I've got more than *that* little tidbit of information."

"No, you don't."

He smiles.

"What is it, then?"

Devon's expression melts into delight. "Now, why would I show my entire hand before you agreed to join Constance?" he asks in a flirtatious voice.

This is actually fun for him, I realize. What a sick bastard.

"You've got nothing," I growl.

Devon's smirk grows, and something about his expression tells me he might not be bluffing after all.

"Actually, I do. Your dear whore mother is still alive, Celdon. And I can take you to her."

twenty

Eli

An interface buzzes from the bedside table, and I roll over to stop the noise. The overhead lights in my room are turning on slowly to mimic natural daylight, and as the room swims into view, I'm surprised to see the perfect gentle line of Harper's back disappearing under the covers.

Memories of the night before hit me all at once, and it takes a moment for me to believe they were real.

It doesn't feel like a Monday morning — not with Harper in my bed.

I can't believe I'm starting the day with Harper in my bed.

Careful not to disturb her, I reach out and stroke the skin above her spine with the pad of my thumb. Her skin is *so* soft.

Then I hear another interface buzzing, and Harper stirs. She turns off the alert, checks her messages, and groans.

"Did Jayden summon you, too?" she asks.

"Uh-huh."

The blankets shift as Harper rolls over, and my mind goes completely blank when I see her lying there in front of me. Her eyes look brighter than usual against my charcoal blanket, and her hair is tussled in a sexy, natural way.

"She wants us to come to her office for a briefing in, like, twenty minutes," she says.

"Yeah . . . wait, what?"

"A briefing. They must be getting ready to deploy us."

I freeze.

Something is wrong. Jayden should have summoned me for a deployment briefing, but not Harper. I let out a burst of air and drag a hand over my tired face. *What the hell is Jayden up to now?*

Harper looks at me as though she's suppressing a laugh.

"What?"

"Nothing."

"No, you're laughing at me," I say, feigning offense and throwing an arm over my eyes.

"You're cute in the morning."

I peek out from under my arm, and she sprawls across my chest to plant a kiss on my mouth. My neurons seem to be firing slowly this morning, but I kiss her back, savoring the feeling of her skin on mine.

It doesn't last long. As soon as she pulls away, anxiety starts to set in. If the briefing isn't about the mission, who knows what sort of curveball Jayden's about to throw at us.

Harper slides out of bed and proceeds to prance around my compartment, looking for something to wear besides the slinky black outfit she came here in.

She grabs a pair of my uniform pants from the closet and shimmies into them in a very feminine way. They're way too long for her, but it won't be noticeable once she tucks the legs into her boots.

The uniform shirt is more problematic. All of my over-shirts have my name embroidered on the chest, and they're way too baggy.

"I have some old beaters on the top shelf," I say. "One might be small enough to fit you."

Harper stretches up on her tiptoes and grabs a black tank I haven't worn in years. She slides it over her head — no bra — and I suddenly wonder what I did in my life to deserve this.

When she pulls her long hair into a ponytail, she catches me watching her and goes a little red.

"What?"

I shake my head, trying to hide the fact that I was just checking her out. "Nothing."

Her questioning look lingers for a moment, and I get out of bed to find a fresh uniform for myself. Harper watches me nervously for a second and then clears her throat and turns to peer out of the peephole.

"How are we gonna do this?"

I come up behind her and plant my palms on her stomach. I act like I'm moving her out of the way, but I really just want to touch her some more before we have to pretend that this never happened.

Harper makes room for me, and I squint through the peephole. The officers' tunnel is teeming with people — mostly stragglers trying to get to their early meetings on time.

"I'll go out first," I say. "I'll knock on the door when the tunnel is clear."

I want to say something else — something to solidify our time together — but everything that comes to mind just feels too weird. Instead, I place a gentle kiss on her forehead and slip out into the tunnel.

Nobody pays me any attention as I kneel down next to my door and pretend to lace up my boot.

The other officers look stressed and preoccupied. I never knew the rest of them to care much about what happened to their cadets, but I'm sure Jayden has been leaning hard on everyone.

Even though a higher rank buys a few extra days between deployments, the more cadets and privates who die or go missing, the faster deployments come for officers.

Finally the tunnel clears, and I straighten up to rap on my door. It flies open, and Harper slips out into the tunnel and walks right past me.

I follow a few paces behind her, and we arrive at Jayden's office with barely a minute to spare. Harper and I exchange a look of dread, and I pound on the heavy door.

"Come in!" she barks.

I take a deep breath to keep my temper in check and throw the door open. Jayden is chatting on her interface, pacing her office like a caged animal.

Right away, I notice she doesn't look like her usual self. Pieces of hair have fallen out of her tight bun, and she's left the officer's overshirt draped over the back of her chair. The white blouse she wears underneath is slightly rumpled and open at the collar as though she's been here all night.

"Mm-hmm. All right," she says to the person on the other end. I can see the reverse image of the man in her interface's projection, but he's no one I recognize. "All right. Thank you very much."

She taps her interface to end the chat, and the holographic bubble disappears.

"Thank you for coming," she says.

Harper and I exchange a sideways glance. The only reason Jayden would be this courteous is if she's about to make our lives a living hell.

"What's going on?" I ask.

"We've had a sighting of one of the leaders," she says breathlessly. "We only got a partial face, but the scar matches. Our image specialists are working on a full facial mock-up as we speak, but we're confident we've located Jackson's right-hand man."

Fear flashes through me. I didn't know they could do a facial mock-up or whatever, but I hope the technology isn't good enough to piece together exactly what Owen looks like.

"You sure it's him?" I ask, trying to sound annoyed despite my pounding heart.

"Yes," she snaps. "Now. He's on the move, but I think we can still catch him. The cameras picked him up heading west. There's another town about twenty miles from here. It's possible he's meeting Martinez there."

"Twenty miles?"

She nods. "I want you two headed out now."

I stare at her, positive I must have misheard. If Jayden is ordering a deployment, that means she had to put it through the system to ensure we were medically cleared for duty. She *must* have seen my new partner assignment, yet she's still talking as though Harper and I are going out together.

"How the hell are we supposed to catch him if the town is twenty miles away?" asks Harper.

"You'll take one of the rovers."

That's new. The compound keeps a small fleet of self-driving vehicles in its hangar, but Recon has never been permitted to use them. They're earmarked for transporting the board in the event of an extreme emergency — not shipping out Recon operatives for assassinations.

"How is that even —"

"I spoke to the board," snaps Jayden. "They agreed that the threat the drifters pose to the compound warrants a special-use permit. Now get your things together and meet in the hangar at oh-nine hundred."

"Both of us?" I ask.

"Yes, Parker! Are you deaf?" Jayden is too distracted to put any real effort into her insults, so I just walk out of her office in stunned silence, wondering what could have possibly gone wrong.

Harper and I are being deployed together indefinitely, and Harper still has no idea.

It doesn't add up. Celdon *told* me I had a new partner. The only thing I can think is that he must have hacked in and denied my request so I'd still be paired with Harper.

"What now?" she asks, calling me back to reality.

"I'll meet you in the hangar," I say. "Go pack. Bring some extra uniforms."

"But you always tell me to travel light."

"I know. I'll explain later."

I hear her start to say something, but I'm already halfway down the tunnel, headed for the supply room. I need to get our provisions together for the mission, and we don't have much time.

I know I should tell her to say goodbye to Celdon and Sawyer, but that will just make her panic.

As I round the corner to the training center, I see Miles standing just outside the doors. He's hovering over a petite girl with mousy brown hair whose face is streaked with tears.

"It's gonna be fine," he says as I pass. "It's just one extra deploy—"

He pauses when he catches sight of my face and then murmurs something else to the sobbing first-year private.

"Psst!" he hisses behind me. "Where's the fire?"

"Can't talk," I say, hoping I'll be able to lose him before he can launch into another lecture. "What's with your private?"

"Jayden's amped up deployments for privates and sergeants. It's fucking ridiculous."

"What else is new? We're losing cadets every week," I say, swiping my key card into the supply room. "It's gonna get worse before it gets better."

"Well, you're just a ray of sunshine, aren't you?"

I don't say anything, but Miles follows me inside. "You're leaving again, aren't you?"

I glance around to make sure we're alone. "They spotted Owen on the feeds," I murmur. "He's on the move."

"Shit. And they didn't see the resemblance?"

"So far so good."

Miles watches in thoughtful silence as I fill four rucksacks halfway with ration packets. I'm all out of clean uniforms in my compartment, but the laundry service drops off all the fresh Recon fatigues here.

I rifle through the labeled bins until I find three uniforms with my name embroidered on the chest. Then I grab a tub of water bags and dump those in the rucksacks as well. They won't last us more than a week, but we need to bring as much as we can.

"Hold up," he says. "Why are you packing four bags? And why are you making them so heavy?"

"Jayden's sending us in a rover."

"No shit?" The look that comes over Miles's face is one of pure boyish delight. "That's awesome!"

I shake my head. I'm sure I'd think the chance to ride in a rover was awesome, too — if I weren't being sent out on a never-ending mission. But right now, all I can think about is finding Owen and keeping Harper from killing me when she learns the truth.

"You know how to work one of those things?" Miles asks, completely oblivious to my anxiety.

"They're self-driving. You just plug in the coordinates."

"That's so cool. Hell, if you've gotta be deployed, go in style."

I wish I could join in his enthusiasm, but a bitter feeling is tugging at my insides.

This deployment feels vastly different from all the others. I've always gone out onto the Fringe prepared for the possibility that I wouldn't come back, but now it's more than a possibility — I *can't* come back until we complete the mission.

"What's up with you?" he asks.

"My request for a new partner didn't go through."

"So Riley *is* going?"

"Yeah," I breathe. "And she still has no idea what's happening."

"Shit. You've got some explaining to do."

"Tell me about it."

I finally manage to yank the last rucksack closed, and a heavy dread settles over me. This is it.

I hoist two bags over each shoulder and turn to Miles.

"Take care, man."

Miles is giving me a look that says he doesn't think he's ever going to see me again, and I'm sure my expression is exactly the same.

"You, too."

We don't hug or shake hands. We don't need to. Miles knows that shit just makes it harder to leave.

I only have half an hour before I'm due in the hangar, so I hop on the megalift and head for Systems. I have to find Celdon before I leave and hope that Harper isn't with him.

When I left headquarters Saturday night, he was busy mapping out all the cameras' blind spots. I have no idea if Constance has cameras in the next town over, but I need to find out. Without knowing where Constance has surveillance, I don't have a hope of maintaining the illusion that Owen is dead.

As I approach the upper levels, I get a message on my interface: *Meet me on the observation deck.*

It's from Celdon.

Relief pours through me, and I wait impatiently for the lift to stop. When it reaches Systems, I get out and head for the stairwell leading up to the deck. It's one of the few places in the compound where Constance doesn't have any cameras, so there's little chance of anyone spying on us.

As soon as I emerge from the stairwell, I'm blinded by daylight. The giant glass box seems to magnify the sun's rays, and it's uncomfortably hot.

A path of fine gravel winds its way through the fluffy grass, which is punctuated here and there by little clusters of plants. There's also a koi pond, a Zen garden, and a few scantily clad higher-ed kids sunning themselves in the grass. I really stick out in my full uniform.

Across the deck, I spot Celdon. He's tough to miss with his all-white outfit and glow-in-the-dark skin. Even though he's far away, I can still read the panic in his eyes.

"Finally," he breathes as soon as I'm within earshot.

"Finally? You just messaged me."

Celdon shrugs, his eyes darting around. "Yeah, well, I shouldn't even be here right now. Harper's been pinging me nonstop for the past thirty minutes."

"Yeah. We're being deployed."

"I know."

"What the hell happened?" I ask, suddenly angry. "You said I had a new partner in the system."

"You *did*. I don't know what happened. It was all good Saturday night, but when I checked a few minutes ago, Harper was set as your default partner again."

"Fuck."

Celdon doesn't meet my eyes. "She still has no idea, does she? About the mission . . ."

"No. I was going to wait to tell her."

"Good plan." His voice is dripping with sarcasm, but that's not what captures my attention. Celdon is watching the sunbathers on deck and cracking his knuckles over and over again.

Something doesn't feel right.

"Did you manage to map the blind spots?"

"Yeah." He reaches into his breast pocket and withdraws a folded piece of paper. "I figured it would be better not to leave a digital footprint."

"Good thinking."

I take the paper from him and unfold it carefully. It's a black-and-white printout of the town closest to the compound with patches of red drawn over random street corners in a radar pattern.

"The red marks the camera's line of sight," he mutters, still watching the sunbathers with suspicion.

I groan. "Owen's on the move. He's headed for the next town over. Were there any cameras over there?"

"It's hard to tell. The feeds are just labeled by streets. They could be pulling footage from anywhere."

I let out an exasperated sigh. He doesn't seem to be paying attention, and this is some crucial shit. I can still give Owen the map to use in case he needs to return to his house, but if Constance does have eyes elsewhere, I need to know.

I touch my interface to check the time. I only have fifteen minutes before I need to report to the hangar.

Celdon has already checked out from the conversation, and I can tell I'm not going to get any more information out of him.

"Thanks," I murmur, nodding once before turning back toward the exit.

Celdon doesn't respond, and his odd behavior gives me a bad feeling. I'm not sure why he would ignore Harper's messages — especially since he knows she might not be coming back. But I can't think about that right now.

I'm so distracted that I barely notice the trip down to the hangar. Harper and Jayden are nowhere in sight, but several ExCon guys are milling around with heavy tools and carts of solar panels.

A man I don't recognize is standing next to one of the rovers, and my heart speeds up.

I've never seen a rover up close before. Compared to pre–Death Storm SUVs, it's a hideous, boxy thing that looks sort of like a toy robot. The tires are huge, and the aerodynamic nose is pulled forward so the rover seems to be tucking its chin and gritting its teeth.

"Hey!" says the man, coming around the vehicle toward me. He's got on gray pants and a white-and-blue striped shirt that puckers around his midsection. He must be an independent mechanic from EnComm.

"You Lieutenant Parker?"

"That's me."

"I'd like to go over a few things with you before you head out, if that's all right — just to make sure you have a good feel for her." He gestures reverently toward the rover.

"Okay."

I feel as though I shouldn't be allowed near the thing, but I reach around him anyway and pop the cargo hatch. I slide the rucksacks inside, belatedly realizing that I left Owen's picture and my mom's necklace in my compartment. The thought gives me a pang of sadness, but there's no time to get them now.

"Hop on in."

The mechanic's voice draws me back to reality, and I move around to the driver's side and slide into the captain's chair.

Whoever designed the rovers clearly spent more time on

the interior. The driver's seat is insanely comfortable and hugs my body like a glove. There's half a steering wheel directly in front of me and a bunch of toggles I wouldn't even begin to know what to do with.

The dashboard is sleek and modern — a gentle sloping line that gives the driver an unobstructed view of the Fringe. An enormous screen cuts down to the center console, displaying a map with a highlighted route. The image flickers, and the rover's computer hums loudly as it processes all the data about the nearby roads and landscape.

A second later, I hear a soft *ding*, and a robotic feminine voice comes through the speaker.

Good morning, Lieutenant. Please enter the coordinates of your desired destination.

"How does it know who I am?" I ask.

"It's pulling data from your interface."

Suddenly, my chair starts to move. The backrest squeezes me more tightly, and the whole unit settles farther into the floor.

"What's it doing?"

"Just adjusting to your specifications — height, weight, eye level."

I glance behind me at the back seat and see that it's just as luxurious as the front. It could comfortably seat six or eight more people, but the steering wheel is making me nervous.

"I thought this was supposed to be self-driving," I say. I never had one driving lesson growing up, but most people in this compound have never even *sat* in a car.

"It is. This is just your backup wheel in case the rover veers off course."

The mechanic points to the floorboard, where two small pedals are tucked just out of reach. "Brake left, accelerator right. You shouldn't need to use the manual driving feature at all, but if the GPS goes out, just use the steering wheel to keep from hitting anything."

Hitting what? I wonder. Clearly this guy has never ventured outside the compound. It's just empty desert for miles.

"She does fine on all terrestrial surfaces, so don't worry about going off road. Commander Pierce told me how far you'd be traveling, so you should be fine with the fuel that's in the main tank.

"If not, you've still got plenty in the auxiliary tank to get you there and back, and you can always fuel up at the Recon checkpoints. It's an algae-based biofuel, and this baby is pretty efficient. But if you run into trouble out there, just hit your SOS button."

He points to a red button on the dashboard encased in a tiny plastic cover. "Even if the comms are out of range, we should still receive this signal. That'll flag someone in Recon to send out another rover to come get you."

I want to laugh out loud. I doubt very much that Jayden would send out a rescue party if Harper and I got stranded out on the Fringe. Hell, that would probably make her week.

"That's about it," he says cheerfully. "You should be good to go."

"Thanks," I mutter, getting an odd surge of power as I palm the steering wheel.

The man leaves, and I just sit there staring out the windshield, lost in thought.

When I finally look up into the rearview mirror, Harper is striding through the hangar toward me.

As soon as I see her face, my heart plummets. I jump out of the vehicle and wait for her to reach me.

"Everything okay?" I ask as soon as she's within earshot. I already know it's not, but I'm hoping she's just worried about deployment.

She purses her lips and looks away — an expression I've only ever seen when Harper is trying to conceal her panic.

"What is it?"

She takes a deep breath, eyes darting around as though she's trying not to cry. "I messaged Celdon that I wanted to meet up and say goodbye, but he never answered. I messaged him three times. Then I went to Systems to find him, but his supervisor said he didn't show up for work today."

"Relax," I say, reaching out to squeeze her arm. "Celdon's fine. I just saw him."

Glancing around to check that no one is watching us, I pull out the map and unfold it halfway. "He gave me this. It shows where all of Constance's cameras are. He probably just didn't have time to come find you."

"Oh. Well . . . good." Harper looks surprised, relieved, and then hurt. She nods slowly, swallowing down her tears. "But . . . why did he message *you* to meet him? He could have given that to me. I was planning on meeting him in Systems anyway."

"I don't know. Maybe he just wanted to give it to me directly since I was the one who asked him for it in the first place."

Harper nods, but she doesn't look convinced. "Still. He should have messaged me back. It's not like him to ignore me — especially since I told him I was being deployed today . . ."

I stare at Harper for a moment and then shrug. I'm not sure what to say to make her feel better, so I just keep my mouth shut. I can't afford to get sucked into their best-friend drama today; I have enough drama of my own.

But I can't get Celdon's strange behavior out of my head. Between his panicked expression, Harper's ignored messages, and the dangerous work I had him doing, I can't shake the feeling that something is horribly wrong.

twenty-one

Harper

"Let's go!" barks a voice to my right.

Jayden is striding toward us, her overshirt buttoned all wrong and her hair still askew. She's got a file tucked under her arm and heavy bags under her eyes.

I'm too keyed up about Celdon to engage in a power struggle right now, but luckily she's interrupted by the mechanic in charge of the rovers.

He pulls her off to the side to show her something on his tablet, which gives me a chance to take everything in.

The rover looks more like an animal than a machine, with enormous wide tires and a body style that makes the vehicle look as though it's ready to pounce. But it's the paint job that perplexes me. When I'd first spotted it under the florescent lights, it had looked burnt orange. Up close, though, it's more of a rosy pink. Squinting at the pearly finish, I realize it has multiple hues embedded in the paint — probably to help the rover blend in with the desert terrain.

I slide into the passenger seat, and the cushions instantly form to the shape of my hips and back. My brain is still running on overdrive, so I lean against the headrest and focus on the details of the interior to distract myself from Celdon, Owen, and our daunting mission.

Eli seems to notice my anxiety. He reaches over my lap to fasten my seat belt, brushing his other hand down my leg so fast I could have imagined it. But then I feel the telltale flutter low in my stomach and catch his brief smile that says, "Everything's going to be okay."

"All right," says Jayden, crossing to the open driver's side window and handing Eli a clunky plastic device. "I just entered the coordinates of your destination. The comms can't pick up your interface out there, but if he's gone by the time you arrive, call me immediately. If we spot him somewhere else, we'll enter the new coordinates remotely."

"It might take us a while to locate this guy," says Eli in an irritated voice. "We don't have much to go on other than this scar on his arm."

Jayden nods as if she expected this and whips out the file she was carrying. She opens it up and shoves a still image from the surveillance footage under Eli's nose.

"Look for a guy wearing a hat like that. It's gray with some sort of emblem on the front."

"It's a Colorado Buffalos hat," says Eli automatically.

Jayden gives him a blank look. I don't know what he's talking about either, but it must be some pre–Death Storm reference.

"Gray hat. Got it," he sighs.

At first I think Jayden might let us leave without her usual power trip. But then she leans down and rests her forearms on the edge of the door, fixing Eli with a steely glare.

"Don't even *think* about trying to ride off into the sunset." She taps the rover's GPS screen. "I'll know if you do. Once you complete the mission, hit the home button, and it will drive straight back to the compound."

"Got it," says Eli in a terse voice.

"I expect you to do the best with what you've got, Parker," she adds. "I denied your request because I think being stuck out there with this one will be extra motivation to get the job done quickly."

Jayden straightens up, signaling the mechanic that we're ready to go. The driver's side window retracts back into the top of the rover, and the engine roars to life. I can feel the vibrations through my seat and sense the sheer power humming beneath us.

I turn Jayden's strange comment over in my mind, utterly lost.

What request would Eli have made? And what did she mean by being "stuck out there" with me?

Suddenly the rover starts moving toward the hangar doors. An EnComm man waves his arm to someone out of my line of sight, and the enormous doors start to open.

The rover slides smoothly into the staging area, and we're left waiting in another large chamber. An ExCon man in orange streaks past us and unlocks the second set of hangar doors. I hear the first set clang shut behind us, and the chamber is flooded with light.

I squint automatically, but then the rover beeps, and a pattern of tiny dots blossoms on the inside of the glass. As I watch, the dots darken, spreading over the windshield to form a translucent layer that makes the light easier on our eyes.

"That's cool," murmurs Eli.

I glance over at him and suddenly get the feeling that there's something he isn't telling me. I'm about to ask him what it is when the rover jerks forward and thrusts me back against my seat. The engine groans as we pick up speed, and I feel my pulse start to race.

The wide tires navigate easily over the rough terrain, but the speed and bumpiness is still disconcerting.

When I look out the window, the desert is flashing by in a blur — all blue and orange and shell pink. I'm amazed by how much ground we've covered already.

Strangely enough, the Fringe doesn't feel nearly as frightening when we're encased in a metal monster and flying at a breakneck speed.

I chance another glance at Eli and see that he's wearing a nervous grin. "This is it."

I nod, still turning Jayden's words over in my mind. Why would Eli make a request to Jayden? He knows better than anyone that she'd never give him what he wanted.

In the distance, I see the winding black ribbon of highway swimming in and out of view. From far away, the heat haze looks like steam rising off the pavement, but as we draw closer, the blurry waves disappear.

As we approach the scrubby tufts of desert foliage lining the road, the rover decelerates to a crawl. It navigates easily over the uneven ground, and when it reaches smooth pavement, we start picking up speed again.

"I can't believe you've never ridden in a car," Eli murmurs with a grin.

Despite all my worries, I can't suppress a smile. "I never knew what I was missing."

"I wish we could roll the windows down to give you the full experience."

I look over at him, and his wistful expression gives me a little pang of tenderness. I'm not used to this side of Eli, and part of me still hasn't processed the fact that I woke up in his bed this morning.

He seems to be thinking along the same lines. When our eyes meet, his lips part slightly, and he gets the look he had in his compartment when I was lying in bed beside him.

I'm not sure if he moves or if I do, but all of a sudden, we're both leaning over the center console, and my lips are tasting his warm, inviting mouth.

I don't think I could ever tire of kissing Eli. The hungry way his lips move over mine sends an electric current through my entire body. And when his rough hands find my neck, my heart automatically speeds up. His fingers tangle in my hair, and I tilt my head to the side so he can kiss the spot just over my racing pulse.

As his lips work their magic, I briefly open my eyes and get my first good look at the rover's cargo area. I notice there are five rucksacks back there — not two — but in my heady state, it takes my brain a few seconds to catch up.

"What are those for?" I ask breathlessly.

Eli pulls away, looking a little flustered. "Just some extra supplies."

"I thought we were only going to be out here for a few days . . . a week at most."

He opens his mouth to reply, but the words seem to get stuck in his throat.

"Eli . . . what's going on?"

"I just thought it would be good to have some extra food and water in case we get delayed."

"Eli . . ."

He averts his gaze, staring purposefully out the windshield as though the road might suddenly disappear.

"Why did you bring so many extra supplies?"

"I just thought it would be smart."

"In case . . ."

Eli sighs and drags a hand through his hair. When he meets my gaze again, I can tell he's gearing up for something big. "Listen. Jayden has her heart set on eliminating the drifters' leaders."

"I know. That's why she got us the rover."

"We have to find Owen."

I nod.

"No, I mean, we *have* to find Owen. We can't go back to the compound until we do."

I roll his words around in my head for a moment, positive I must have misheard.

"What do you mean 'we can't go back'?"

"I mean Jayden told us not to come back until we had a dead drifter for her."

That's when my mouth goes dry. I can't speak. I can hardly process what Eli's trying to tell me.

"But that's ridiculous. We don't even know if we're going to find Owen. Jayden spotted him heading toward this town, but he could be gone by the time we get there."

Eli nods but doesn't say anything. I watch him carefully for a moment. I know there's a part of this he's leaving out — some crucial factor he doesn't want me to know.

"Why would you go along with this?" I prompt. "You've never cared about following Jayden's orders before."

"We just can't go back, okay? Can we drop this?"

"No!" Something still doesn't seem right. "Why can't we go back, Eli?"

He lets out a stream of air through his nose and looks away. "If we come back empty-handed, Jayden is going to kill you."

That statement causes a nervous laugh to bubble up inside me, which isn't the reaction Eli was hoping for.

"It isn't a joke."

"Oh, please. Jayden's been threatening my life for months now. If that's all you're worried about —"

"Damn it, Harper! This isn't a game!" Eli yells, slamming his fist against the steering wheel.

His outburst startles me. He's gone a little red in the face, and all the veins in his arm are sticking out. "She knows you ran off to 119, and she's unhinged. You're just a cadet to her."

He turns to look at me with his familiar hardened expression. "Have you *seen* what she's been doing with cadets lately? Do you want to end up like Lenny or worse? Because believe me, she got lucky. Do you know how many went out last month and didn't come back?"

"N-no," I stammer, taken aback by Eli's angry tirade.

"Four."

That shocks me into silence. I'd heard a few cadets had died, of course, but I didn't know how many. I'd been so concerned with which of *my* friends were being deployed and all the drama with my parents and Constance that I wasn't paying attention to the cadets who were disappearing from other squads.

But I *do* remember how Lenny looked in the medical ward — so small and pale. She almost died on that mission, and Jayden wouldn't have cared.

I've faced so many near-death experiences and threats in the past few months that I've grown complacent. But I'm completely disposable to Jayden. In fact, she'd probably enjoy killing me.

"Why didn't you tell me?" I ask, suddenly angry at Eli for hiding the truth. "I didn't get to say goodbye to any of my friends. I didn't get to *plan*."

"You should *always* say goodbye when you're deployed," he snaps. "You know what's out here, Harper. So don't put that on me."

That pisses me off. Eli screwed up big time — the least he could do is take some responsibility.

"You still should have told me!" I cry. "All last night when I was with you . . . you didn't say a word."

"I didn't think you were coming, okay? I thought I had a different partner assigned for this mission. It wasn't even supposed to affect you."

"Wasn't supposed to *affect* me?"

Eli's outburst was so abrupt and so unexpected that it takes me several seconds to catch up. It hurts that he assumes his deployment wouldn't affect me if I wasn't going with him. He knows I see him as more than a partner, and I thought he saw me that way, too.

But that's not the biggest surprise.

"Wait. What do you mean you thought you had a different partner?"

Eli doesn't answer. He won't even look at me.

Suddenly, Jayden's words come crashing back down: *I denied your request . . .*

"Did you . . . Did you *ask* for a new partner?"

He lets out a slow, dread-filled sigh, and embarrassment washes over me.

Eli asked for a new partner. Eli tried to replace me.

"Harper . . . I didn't do it because I don't *want* you as my partner. I did it so you wouldn't have to be stuck out here hunting drifters indefinitely."

"But . . . we're always partners."

"It's only been a few months," he says gently.

That stings more than I'd like to admit.

"You hate the Fringe," he adds.

"Everybody hates the Fringe!" I snarl. I'm working so hard to hold in my tears that I sound a little hysterical.

"It's different for you," he says. "I've seen what it does to you . . . being out here . . . having to shoot people."

"I can handle myself."

"I know you can, but —"

"Eli, if you didn't want me as your partner, you could have just said so!"

I can't keep the tears at bay anymore. I'm so angry and humiliated. The worst is knowing that my inability to keep my emotions in check only confirms Eli's choice to find someone new.

"Harper, no. It's not that at all. I love having you as my partner. It's just —"

Eli's words are cut short by a sharp *crack!*

"*What the hell?*"

Eli jerks down under the dashboard and yanks me down, too.

For a second, I don't understand why, and I fight against his tight grip. Then everything seems to slow down, and I realize the crack I heard was a gunshot.

With all our bickering, I hadn't been paying much attention to the scenery, and judging by Eli's panicked look, neither had he.

There's another shot, and the metal body of the rover sings as the bullet ricochets off.

"Holy shit."

Eli is fumbling with the touchscreen, cranking up the rover's cruising speed. The engine groans as we accelerate, but then the rover swerves.

We're whipped sideways, and my stomach shoots into my throat. My body strains against the seat belt, and out of the corner of my eye, I see Eli fumbling with some pedals on the floor. Everything outside the rover is a blur.

"Shit! Shit, shit, shit!"

There's a slight squeal of rubber on road, and the glass behind me shatters.

A scream escapes my throat, and I hug my knees.

"They blew out one of our tires," yells Eli, clear panic in his voice.

"Can you fix it?"

"Not without getting shot."

The rover comes to a jerking halt, nearly giving me whiplash. Eli unclicks his seat belt and reaches for mine. "We have to move. We're sitting ducks here."

I jump as another bullet cracks the window and lands in the upholstery just inches from my head. Eli pushes my shoulders down and reaches behind me, dragging out two rucksacks and flinging one into my lap.

"Come on. We're gonna make a run for those rocks."

I didn't see where Eli pointed. I can't think. I can barely move.

Fighting every natural instinct to stay in the rover, I push the door open with some difficulty and nearly fall out onto the pavement. My hands are shaking so badly I can't get the rucksack over my shoulder. Instead, I run after Eli on wobbly legs, dragging it by the strap.

I hear another gunshot and jerk down automatically, but we're too far away for the shooter to hit his mark.

Dry brush clings to my pant legs as I scrabble up the embankment after Eli. My limbs feel clumsy and uncoordinated, and I trip several times before I reach the cover of the orangish-red rocks stretching up toward the sky.

My vision has narrowed in on the path right in front of me, and somehow I lose sight of Eli.

I glance around in a panic and yelp when a hand shoots out of nowhere and locks around my arm.

"It's okay," says Eli, his face swimming into view.

My heart is pounding so fast I'm amazed it hasn't given out yet. My breaths are coming in uneven gasps, and it's hard for me to focus on his face.

"Are you hurt?" he asks.

I think I shake my head, but then again, every part of my body is shaking. Eli's rough hands roam my arms and torso anyway, checking for gunshot wounds. I have the sudden, inappropriate urge to laugh, but it's on the verge of a sob.

"You're just in shock," murmurs Eli.

Those deep blue eyes pull me back to reality. Eli is staring at me with such intensity and concern that it grounds me in place and helps my breathing return to normal.

"We can't stay here," he says, glancing up at our rudimentary hiding place. "They'll come looking for us."

"Right," I say, clasping my hands together to keep them from trembling.

"You're okay," he murmurs, rubbing his hands down my arms again.

I give a shaky nod and hoist the rucksack over my shoulder.

I realize neither one of us is wearing a mask, but I guess it doesn't matter if Sawyer's correct about our superhuman radiation resistance. We can't return to the rover anyway.

I'm not sure how far we are from the town where Owen was headed, but we don't really have any choice but to keep moving.

Eli tugs on my arm, and we start to jog along the highway, staying in the shadow of the rock formation. It's difficult to move gracefully with the weight of the overstuffed pack on my shoulders, and I stumble several times on the uneven terrain.

"How far behind us were they?" I pant.

"Hard to tell. But the town's not too far off," huffs Eli, tugging on the straps of his pack and picking up the pace a little.

Thankfully, the looming wall of solid rock opens up to a narrow pathway, and Eli leads us through. The reddish glow of the sunlight reflecting off the rock creates a hypnotic effect in the shelter of the cliff, and I follow Eli without noticing if we're even moving in the right direction.

Something about being enveloped between two enormous sheets of rock gives me a disproportionately high sense of security. But then the gap between the cliff and the outshoot of rock narrows, and Eli swears.

I nearly career into his back as I round the bend. Eli is standing at the end of the tunnel in front of the opening — a fissure in the rock no more than six inches wide.

"Shit," he mutters, glancing behind us for the approaching drifters.

"Should we go back?" I pant.

He shakes his head, looking panicked. "If they followed us, we'll run straight into them."

But he squeezes past me anyway and starts moving back through the tunnel. At first I think he's doubling back to face them head-on, but then I notice his eyes are fixated on the top of the rock formation some forty feet above us.

"There," he mutters, pointing to something I can't quite see.

"What?"

Eli pulls me closer and moves my chin to where he's pointing — a break in the cliff about halfway up the wall. I squint harder and see a narrow ledge that runs for about four feet before disappearing into a small opening.

"We're going to wait this out," he says.

I shake my head, lost for words. "Eli . . . how the hell are we going to get up there?"

"We have to climb."

Now I *know* he's completely lost it.

"It's okay," he says, correctly interpreting my panicked expression. "I used to do some free-climbing with my dad and Owen. It's not a big deal."

I open my mouth to say that it's a *very* big deal, but I don't see another solution. If we stay where we are, the drifters are sure to find us.

Eli has already started searching for something to grab on to. "I'm going to climb up first and tell you where the handholds are."

"What?"

I've never climbed a rock wall in my life — let alone a fucking cliff. But as I watch, I see what he's talking about: There seem to be small crevices and imperfections in the otherwise smooth rock formation. Eli's hands and feet find the cracks easily, and he slowly propels himself up the wall.

At one point, he gets stuck and has to backtrack to find a new path. That's when I hear footsteps and faraway voices echoing off the cliff.

Eli freezes on the face of the rock, sprawled like a spider with one arm extended over his head and one leg poised for his next ascent.

I can't make out what the drifters are saying or how close they are, but if they followed our path on the other side of the tunnel, it's only a matter of time before they double back and find the path we took.

The pool of light spilling from the opening in the rock suddenly darkens, and my heart thunders in my chest. I hold my breath, and the drifters leave. Unfortunately, I can't tell if they're still nearby or if they kept moving toward town.

A scuffing sound draws my attention back to Eli, and everything slows down as I watch his leg slip off a protruding rock.

I clap a hand over my mouth to muffle my gasp and watch in horror as Eli fumbles to find his footing. He's hanging by his arms and breathing hard, legs flailing uselessly in midair. I can't fight the terrifying images that come to mind, and when his forearms flex, I worry he's going to lose his grip.

"Harper!" he gasps, still unable to slow his momentum as he swings against the wall. "Can you see another foothold?"

Scrambling over to stand under him, I spot a small bump near his left foot. "Up and to the left," I whisper.

His foot clumsily searches for the bump, but after a minute, he makes contact and rights himself.

Taking a second to breathe, he reaches up for the ledge and hoists himself over.

"There's a cave," he calls in a loud whisper. "Hurry."

Glancing down the tunnel for any sign of the approaching drifters, I reach for the first handhold Eli used and pull myself up. I find the first few protruding rocks easily with my feet, but halfway up, my brain falters.

"Up and to the right," calls Eli.

Suddenly, I hear voices bouncing off the cliff again, and my heart speeds up.

Focus, I tell myself. *Don't think about them.*

Careful not to shift my center of gravity, I crane my neck to search for the handhold Eli is referring to.

I can just make out a tiny hole in the rock. It's barely big enough for three fingers, but it provides some stability as I shift my right foot awkwardly to the next rock jutting out about an inch from the cliff.

The voices in the tunnel are growing louder.

"Hurry!" Eli hisses.

"I'm trying," I choke, floundering as I reach for the next crack with my left hand. Eli reached it easily during his climb, but he's much taller; I can't even brush it with my fingertips.

"Stretch!"

"I can't reach," I say in a shaky voice.

I'm starting to lose it. The adrenalin from the shootout, my tiring muscles, and the stress of being spotted are a bad combination. I'm quivering against the rock, completely frozen as I will a crack to appear.

Jayden's words echo in my mind. *Being stuck out there with this one . . .*

It doesn't matter what Eli says. No matter how pure his intentions were, there still must have been some small part of him that thought I was incompetent as a partner. And maybe I was, but I'm not going to be weak anymore.

The drifters' individual voices are discernible now, echoing loudly in the tunnel. I don't have much time.

Craning my neck, I finally spot another tiny imperfection in the rock — a gap just big enough to slide my hand through. I get a good grip, but when I place my right foot, it slips right off the tiny ledge.

My right cheek smashes into the rock as my downward momentum throws me against the cliff. The sharp handhold cuts into my left hand as all my weight shifts to my arms.

With every ounce of strength I have, I stretch my leg up to find the slippery bump again, but I've fallen too far and don't have the strength to pull myself up.

I can hear the scuff of the drifters' boots. They're going to see me. I just know it.

I'm in the worst spot imaginable — too high to jump down and make a run for it, but too low to make the final ascent to the ledge.

A shout reverberates off the rock — just a few yards down the tunnel.

Then a warm hand grabs my wrist and tugs.

twenty-two

Eli

With my body splayed across the narrow ledge, I'm just tall enough to reach down and grab Harper by the wrist. I've hooked my foot around a rock inside the cave, but my position isn't good. If I slip even an inch, there's nothing to stop me from sliding off the ledge and pulling Harper down with me.

The drifters are right around the bend, and she's too short to reach the last good handhold.

"Harper, listen to me," I pant. "I need you to pull yourself the rest of the way."

When she finally responds, her voice sounds very small. "I don't have anything to grab on to."

I let out as big a breath as I dare and tighten my hold on her thin wrist. My grip definitely isn't strong enough to support her full weight, and there isn't room on the ledge to hoist her up and over.

"Listen," I whisper, closing my eyes and trying to conjure up a mental picture of the cliff. "There's a rock a couple inches above your right hand. I'm going to pull, and I need you to let go and grab it. Can you do that?"

"I . . . I don't know."

Harper's arm trembles. She must be losing her grip.

"You have to try. It's not that far. Then you can put your left foot on the rock by your hip and push yourself up to the ledge."

How I plan to pull her up that far when I'm splayed on my

stomach is beyond me, but our options are limited.

"Okay," she chokes.

"One . . ." I squeeze her wrist.

"Two . . ." I clench every muscle in my core and brace my foot against the rock holding me to the ledge.

"Three!"

In one motion, I yank Harper up as hard as I can. My knee screams in protest as I raise up awkwardly on my little rock shelf, but Harper doesn't scream, and I don't hear the telltale scuff of her boots floundering against the cliff.

Cautiously, I peer over the ledge. She reached the small, slippery rock, and her left foot has found purchase on another bump. She grits her teeth, and I pull. Sweet relief flares through me when I see her upper half clear the ledge.

We nearly bump heads as I half pull, half fall back toward the cave. She gets a knee on the ledge, and I immediately look down.

From our lofty position, I see the drifters round the bend. There are three men toting guns, moving down the tunnel to where we just were.

"They aren't here," says the man leading the group.

"Well, they didn't disappear."

Don't look up. Don't look up. Don't look up.

"I *said* . . . They. Aren't. Here."

"Well, we gotta keep lookin', then, don't we?"

I freeze on the ledge, afraid to pull Harper into the cave. There's a layer of dust and small rocks covering our path, and one wrong move could make a noise that catches the drifters' attention.

I hold my breath, watching them deliberate.

Finally, the men turn around and start heading back down the tunnel. I wait until they disappear around the cliff and the sounds of their voices fade into nothingness.

When they're gone, I shift my grip to Harper's upper arm. She's frozen on the ledge like a bird on a wire, and I have to give her a gentle tug.

Once Harper starts inching toward me, I scoot back into the cave and pull her down to duck inside. She's breathing hard and looks a little shaken, but other than that, she's okay.

I can't believe how quickly everything unraveled. Less than half an hour ago, we were cruising along in the rover. Now, thanks to me, we're stranded in a cave with a good twenty miles of desert between us and the compound.

Looking around, I'm surprised to see that it isn't completely dark. I'd thought the opening was just a hole in the cliff, but there's light filtering through from the other side.

Crouching low to avoid scraping my head, I start climbing over the rock jutting out of the cave floor.

Finding another exit would be ideal. For one thing, it would help us avoid a possible ambush from the drifter search party down below. But more importantly, I don't think we'll be able to descend from the cave the same way we climbed up.

The sound of shifting rocks makes me jump, but it's just Harper coming up behind me. We follow the light back about ten yards up a steep incline to a two-foot-wide opening that's beckoning us to freedom.

I climb through the hole and emerge on a flat slab of rock, grateful for the burst of fresh air against my cheek. I breathe deeply and try to take everything in, but the view is too magnificent to absorb all at once.

"Wow," murmurs Harper.

That's an understatement.

What I'd thought was a protrusion in the cliff from down below is actually another rock formation entirely. The one we're standing on is taller, but the cliff closest to the road continues for another five hundred yards.

The winding ribbon of highway cuts through the rugged brown landscape, disappearing where the desert meets the breathtaking blue sky. There are about two miles of open land between us and the town, and I can just barely discern the shape of buildings on the horizon.

In another life, I'd be thinking about how beautiful the desert is. Maybe Harper and I would have climbed up here to admire the wide expanse of nothingness and gorgeous sandstone rock formations. We wouldn't be thinking of the men down below who want to kill us or the minefield of danger surrounding the small town.

Harper is studying the cliffside with the same wary admiration. A few strands of hair have come loose from her ponytail, and when they blow back, I can see my own anxiety reflected in her luminous gray eyes.

Now that we're out of immediate danger, I realize just how thirsty and exhausted I am. We have plenty of water right now, so I settle down on the cliff, pull out my water bag, and drink greedily.

Harper follows suit, and for several minutes, we just sit there in silence.

"How are we going to get down?" she asks finally.

I glance over the edge. We're about thirty feet up, with nothing but jagged rocks and rough brush below us. It's possible we could climb down, but one slipup would be catastrophic. Shifting to my hands and knees, I crawl to the edge of the cliff and peer toward the ground.

On the other side, there are a couple tiers of rock leading down to the base of the cliff. This descent looks much less treacherous.

"We can make it down over here."

Harper gives me a look that can only be described as pitiful, and I settle against the large rock I've been using as a backrest. "In a minute."

She nods gratefully and continues to sip her water. I can tell she's exhausted. She's got a nasty skid mark across her right cheek from where she slammed into the cliff and dirt all over her hands and knees. Yet even in her bedraggled state, she still looks so pretty.

Watching her triggers a pang of regret in my gut. I can't believe I almost left the compound without her.

Who was I kidding anyway? I wouldn't want anyone else for a partner. I just hate that she had to find out that I tried to trade her in for someone new.

After a while, she seems to return to her old self. I tighten the drawstring on my rucksack and move toward the edge of the rock formation.

Choosing my handholds carefully, I grip two rocks protruding from the ground and lower myself down to the first ledge. Harper follows, and I watch her closely to make sure she doesn't slip.

The next two drops aren't as easy. The surface of the ledge we're standing on is smooth and flat, which makes getting a firm grip next to impossible. But Harper's looking up at me with that heart-wrenching "What now?" expression, which forces me over the edge and gives me the last push to drop to the next rock.

The protrusion was narrower than I thought, and it's all I can do to stop myself from stumbling right off the edge. I swear loudly and steady myself on the uneven surface, feet aching from the jump.

"Eli!"

Harper's panicked face appears above me.

"I'm all right," I call, forcing myself to breathe normally. "It's just a little narrow. You're gonna have to dangle and let yourself drop. You'll feel like you're going over the edge when you land, but you won't."

"I don't know . . ."

"You'll be fine."

"*You* barely made it."

I sigh and drop my head, debating what I should tell her. It's a dangerous jump — no doubt about it — but there's no time to look for another possible descent point. We've already lost hours. Owen could be on the move right now, and every moment we waste is a moment we risk losing him for good.

"You'll be okay," I say, trying to sound more convinced than I feel. "I'll catch you."

"You can't catch me."

"Just jump."

Harper sighs, and her face disappears from view. Then I see the bottoms of her boots and her legs as she lowers herself slowly over the rock. When it's just her forearms holding her, she tries to find a footing on the edge of the cliff and slips.

"Harper!" I yell.

Dirt and rock rain down on me as she scrambles to get a better grip, but she's sliding off the edge of the slab without even getting the right handholds. She's dangling a good six feet over my head with no way to gauge distance or plan her landing.

"Easy!" I call. "Easy."

Harper makes a strange noise that sounds like a gurgle, and my mind races to give her some kind of instructions.

The problem is that she can't see where I am, and there's barely enough room on the ledge for the both of us.

I can't catch her now. She's just going to have to drop and

regain her balance on her own.

"Harper?"

She makes another sound that isn't a word, and fear hits me like a train.

"You just have to let yourself go," I say, trying to keep my voice calm. "You're only about six feet from the ledge. If you fall straight down and catch yourself, you'll be fine. You're going to land right in the middle of this big rock."

I step into the shadow of her ledge and close my eyes to summon the strength to let her drop.

Harper can do this. This is what we train for . . . sort of.

"On the count of three," I call.

Silence.

"Come on, Harper. One . . . two . . . three."

Harper lets out a little yelp and falls.

Suddenly she's right in front of me. She grins in relief, but then she starts to stumble backward off the rock with no way to catch herself. She must have placed all her weight right on the outer edge, and now the rock is crumbling away.

Harper falls in slow motion, and I make a grab for her. Terror flashes through her eyes, but my hands close around her arms, and I yank her forward.

She slams into my chest, and we both tumble back against the cliff. Her heart is hammering frantically against my ribcage, and I disturb her hair as I let out a breath of intense relief. I squeeze her harder than I should, just to reassure myself that she's safe.

"I thought I was going over," she murmurs into my chest. "I thought . . ."

She pulls away and glances over the edge of the rock. I expect her to turn back with a haunted look in her eyes, but they're wide with adrenaline and excitement.

She lets out a sharp laugh and breaks into a smile. I stare for a moment in disbelief, but her face is frozen in a grin so ridiculous that there's nothing to do except smile back.

The next descent is much easier. There are a few sturdy rocks to use as handholds, and when our boots finally hit solid ground, relief surges though me.

The drifters have probably abandoned our trail by now, but we don't waste any time charting a straight course toward town.

Now that the adrenaline rush is over, I realize I'm hot and thirsty again. Harper seems to be slowing down, too, but I'm reluctant to stop out here in the middle of nowhere without cover.

"Just a little bit farther," I say.

Harper nods, always willing to go along with my terrible plans.

To distract myself from the sweltering heat, I focus on what I'm going to say to Owen when I see him. There's no way he's going to agree to my plan without putting up a fight. Owen is as stubborn as I am, and faking his own death means he would have to leave the area.

The thought gives me a pang of sorrow. If Owen does leave, there's a good chance I'll never see him again. I'd never want him to put himself at risk just so we could stay within close proximity of each other, but it's still hard to accept the fact that I'm going to have to mourn his loss all over again.

Anyway, what sort of relationship could we hope to have if he stayed? Owen is a drifter. There's no way around it.

My sad train of thought is interrupted by the first signs of civilization: a sagging barbed-wire fence, a defunct telephone pole, and a shredded plastic bag blowing in the breeze.

Scrubby desert bushes jut up against a dry, desolate field, and there's a narrow road leading off to a few warehouse-style farm buildings in the distance.

We step over the collapsed fence and make our way down into the shallow canyon where the town is situated. The farther down we walk, the greener the land becomes. Clumps of trees pop up along the side of the road, and a city starts to take shape.

We pass a partially demolished filling station that's missing half its pumps and slowly approach the main thoroughfare.

We pass an old pizza parlor, a nail salon, and a tavern that looks as if it's seen better days. Most of the store windows are still intact, and several abandoned cars line the streets as though the owners just ran into the bank for a few minutes.

There's something odd about the cars, though. While the shop windows are covered in a thick layer of dirt and grime, the cars are relatively clean.

I glance around the street. Nothing.

I walk toward an ancient BMW and peer inside. The backseat is completely stuffed: Old laundry hampers are overflowing with blankets and clothes and cooking supplies. On the floorboards, I spot boxes of ammunition and jars of what looks like food.

Somebody was living out of this car recently. Harper seems to come to the same conclusion, and we both draw our handguns.

The drifters are nearby — we just don't know where.

Then I hear voices echoing off the concrete, growing louder with each passing second.

Harper throws me an apprehensive look, but we keep moving down the street at a crouch.

As we near the end of the block, I can hear the voices as clearly as if the speakers were standing right next to us.

There's only a rundown sandwich shop between us and the drifters, with large picture windows on each side to provide a panoramic view of the street.

I press my face against the glass and squint through the shop to get a look at the people on the adjacent street, but I can't see anyone.

Harper and I exchange another look, and I step around the corner.

Five or six drifters are standing between a beat-up tan Buick and an old white Ford Taurus less than twenty yards away. I hadn't been able to see them standing on the other side of the shop, but if one of them so much as glances over at the little brick building, we're as good as dead. I can feel the warmth radiating from Harper's body, and I reach back to pull her behind me.

The drifters are engrossed in a heated argument, but I can't make out what they're saying. Half of the conversation is in Spanish, with a string of English words thrown in here and there.

Two men standing in the middle seem to be causing the problem — an older guy with coppery skin, long black hair, and heavy eyes, and a tall man I can't quite make out.

The fight seems to reach a breaking point, and the second man scoffs and shoves past the others.

My heart stops. I want to grab Harper and get the hell out of here, but as soon as the drifter in the middle shows his face, I know that isn't going to be possible.

Owen looks different from the last time I saw him — older, darker, and meaner. Only his eyes look exactly the same.

He glances over at the sandwich shop, and for a moment, he seems to stare right through me. Then his gaze narrows.

He shakes his head once, and I know that means we need to move. I back up, bump into Harper, and nearly send both of us crashing through the large shop window.

Finding her hand, I pull her back around the corner in the direction we came. She drags her feet, but I quicken my pace until we're both running at a full-out sprint.

"Eli! Where are we going?"

"Away from here!"

"But Owen —"

"We can't get near him now. We're just going to have to lay low for a bit."

"But —"

"Just trust me on this."

"I do, but —" Harper lets out a note of exasperation and yanks back her arm to force me to stop. "We can't stay here!"

I glance up at the sparse buildings on the block. She's right, of course. They're all one- and two-story brick structures that don't offer much cover, and any one of them could be the drifters' home base.

Unsure what to do, I pull her into the tiny alleyway between Tasty Bakery and an antiques store, breathing hard and trying to formulate a plan. Then, without warning, a blurry figure in a gray baseball cap shoots around the corner. My hand tightens on my gun, but he's on top of us before I can even react.

In one rough motion, Owen throws out an arm and slams me bodily against the brick wall.

"What — are you — *doing here?*" he snarls.

I cough, shocked by the sudden pressure on my throat and the fact that Owen is standing right in front of me.

"That isn't an answer, little brother . . ." he says in the taunting voice he used to reserve for when he was beating me at video games.

This close, I can see every piece of stubble along his jawline and a few unfamiliar lines around his eyes. Owen may be my brother, but right now he's looking at me the way I'd look at a drifter — like something repulsive that must be dealt with.

Before I can catch my breath, Harper lets out a low growl. I don't see her pounce, but there's a minor scuffle in the vicinity of my right elbow, and her ponytail whips me in the face.

I try to move my head to see what she's doing, but as soon as I change positions, the pressure of Owen's forearm against my windpipe intensifies.

Then a fist flies out of nowhere and connects with Owen's temple. It's an impressive punch, but he's a big guy. All it takes is one medium-sized push, and he sends Harper careening right into the brick wall.

Ouch. That does it.

Grabbing my brother around the neck, I use the leverage to drive a knee up into his stomach. He grunts and doubles over, but before I can put any real distance between us, he shoots forward again and pins me against the wall with both hands.

I've still got one arm extended to keep him from really laying into the choke, but the other is wedged between my body and a rusty pipe.

"Let — go — of him — you fucking — *asshole!*" Harper growls, punctuating each word with a vicious kick to the knee-cap.

She's mad he got the best of her, and now she's gonna make him pay.

"Fuck! All right!" he snarls, gritting his teeth and letting go. The pressure on my windpipe disappears, and I cough.

As soon as I'm free, Harper jumps between us and shoves Owen against the opposite brick wall. He looks momentarily stunned by her ferocity, and I take the opportunity to regain my voice.

"What the hell is wrong with you?" I hiss.

Owen looks annoyingly surprised. "What the hell is wrong

with *me*? What the hell is wrong with *you*?"

"I need to talk to you."

"Not here," he snaps. "In fact, if you know what's good for you, you'll take her and get the hell out of town right now."

"I'm not leaving until you talk to me."

"Ain't gonna happen, Eli."

"The hell it isn't!" I yell. "I'm deep in some fucked-up shit right now, and it all has to do with you."

"You wanna talk about fucked-up shit?" Owen snarls. "How about I come by the compound and pretend to be you? Because that's *my* life right now, Eli. That's the shit I'm dealing with."

"I'm sorry about that, okay? But you need to listen."

"You shouldn't have come here at all!"

"We didn't have a choice," says Harper.

Owen shoots her a dirty look, but I step between them. "You need to come with us."

He scoffs and turns away, dragging a hand down his face. "I can't be seen talking to you. Do you have any idea what would happen to me if they knew we were even having this conversation? I'd be shot on sight."

"Well, you're gonna be shot regardless if you don't listen."

I can tell he doesn't believe me, but at least I've got his attention. He's pacing in a tight circle like a caged lion.

"I can't do this right now," he sighs. "Meet me at the rocks after dark. There's a cliff you can climb up that's pretty protected from the desert patrols."

He points in the direction of the rock formation we just came from.

"We've been there," I mutter.

"Then go now. Turn around and walk away. I'll meet you there."

"How do I know you'll do it?" I ask. "How do I know you're

not just gonna cut out of town as soon as we leave?"

"I said I'll be there, Eli."

From the tone of his voice, I can tell the discussion is over. He's got Dad's stubbornness and Mom's abrasiveness, which is a really annoying personality combo.

Our eyes lock, and I realize I have no choice but to take his word for it.

"All right," I sigh. "We'll be there."

"Fine."

Owen turns and leaves without so much as a backward glance, and I feel my whole body deflate.

Letting him walk away feels like the wrong decision. I don't know if he'll keep his word, but I have no choice but to believe him.

"Do you think he'll be there?" Harper asks as we make our way slowly back through town.

"I don't know."

It's the truth. I used to know my brother as well as I know myself. I could always tell what he was thinking and predict with stunning accuracy when he was going to get into a fight or sneak into the woods after dark.

But this Owen — drifter Owen — is a completely different person, and I don't know him at all.

twenty-three

Harper

The trip back to the rock formation feels a lot shorter than our walk into town. Maybe it's because we found Owen or because we're both deep in thought, but the steep rocks are right in front of us before we know it.

I have a bad feeling that Owen is going to stand us up, but I don't share these thoughts with Eli. I'm sure he's thinking the same thing, which makes me feel indescribably sad. Eli found Owen after believing his entire family was dead, only to discover that his brother is completely different from the boy he grew up with.

We take our time climbing up to a small overlook on the west side of the cliff. We've got nothing to do but wait, and I'm in no hurry to sit in awkward silence.

Getting our tire blown out, running from the drifters, free-climbing, and finding Owen distracted me from the argument we were having in the rover, but once things settle down, I know all that hurt and humiliation are going to come rushing back.

We reach the overlook too soon, and Eli lays down a blanket and busies himself in his rucksack.

I sit down, and the full force of my fatigue hits me all at once. My shoulders and legs ache from climbing and running, and my sunburn makes my skin feel too small for my face.

Eli passes me a water bag and then sits down and starts jiggling his foot to a nervous rhythm.

"He'll be here," I say.

"I wish I believed that."

"*He'll be here*," I repeat.

Eli groans and rubs both hands over his face in frustration. "I just need this plan to work. I can't live like this anymore."

I turn to look at him, surprised by his choice of words.

"Like what?"

Eli sighs and shakes his head. "Scared shitless all the time. Being in there . . . wondering if he's still alive . . . being out here . . . wondering how *we're* still alive. Worrying that you've been hurt by Constance every time you don't answer your interface . . . It's brutal. I can't take it anymore."

I want to be angry with Eli for lying to me, but his words tug at my heart. And when I chance a look over at him, it's as though something has shifted between us.

Eli is staring at me with such fierce protectiveness that I suddenly understand why he put in the request for a new partner. He could have told me a hundred times that he only did it for my benefit, but I wouldn't have believed him until now.

"I don't know what I'd do if something happened to you," he says in a husky voice.

"Nothing is going to happen to me."

He throws me a skeptical look. "You can't promise that — you of all people. I thought maybe we'd actually get out of Recon, you know? I thought if we just went to 119, maybe things would be different." He lets out a disappointed sigh. "But that's not going to happen."

"Things can still be different."

"How?"

I shake my head, desperately trying to find something positive to latch on to. "I don't know . . . but we're different."

He raises an eyebrow in bewilderment, and I feel my face turn red.

"I just mean . . . you and I would never have been sitting here having this conversation a few months ago."

He concedes with a smile, looking at me out of the corner of his eye. "I guess you're right."

"We'll think of a way to get out from under Jayden's thumb. We will. We just need to get through today first."

Eli nods, but he's still looking at me sideways as though he wants to say something.

"What?"

"I'm sorry about before. I shouldn't have lied to you, and I shouldn't have tried to keep you out of this."

"It's okay," I murmur. "I know why you did it."

"You do?"

I nod, my throat sticking. "You were just trying to keep me safe . . . like an idiot."

He lets out a short laugh. "Yeah, I was an idiot. But it wasn't just your safety; I know how miserable you are out here."

Eli gestures out at the desert, and for the first time, I really take it all in. Up here with Eli, away from the drifters, it's actually kind of beautiful.

Eli's face turns serious. "There's no one else I'd want as a partner, Harper. I hope you know that."

His earnestness catches me off guard. I tilt my head to the side, unsure what to say, and Eli reaches over to grasp my face with a rough, calloused hand.

My breath catches in my chest as his fingers thread through my hair and find a home on the back of my neck. I melt into him, and then his lips come crashing down onto mine.

He kisses me slowly — leisurely — letting his tongue explore my mouth. Between the heat of the afternoon sun and the warmth enveloping us, my face feels as though it might combust at any moment.

His other hand cups my cheek, and I let my face rest in his palm as he teases me with soft, disappearing kisses.

Then he lets out a surprising little growl and pulls me into his lap. Before I even know what's happening, I'm straddling his hips as his hands work their way up and down my back.

Feeling bold, I grind against him and deepen the kiss. He lets out a low groan and pulls me impossibly closer. I can feel every part of him pressed up against me. Then his fingers brush my collarbone, and a light desert breeze alerts me to the fact that he's unsnapping my shirt.

I pull back, suppressing a chuckle. "What are you doing?"

"Nothing," he says in a rough voice, cracking a roguish grin and continuing to work his way down.

I bite my lip to keep from smiling but let him open my overshirt. My tank top is riding low in the front, and I have to hold in a gasp when he yanks down the fabric and bends his head for a kiss.

My breathing has gone completely haywire, and when his soft kiss becomes a tiny, painless bite, I can't quite hold in my laughter. "Eli!"

He nuzzles me playfully, and by the time he comes up for air, he's laughing, too. It's a spectacular, full-body laugh that makes his deep blue eyes crinkle with joy.

I rarely get to see this side of him, and I don't want him to stop. It's amazing to think that just a moment ago, he seemed to be carrying the weight of the world on his shoulders. Now at least I know how to make him lighten up.

We stay like that for several delicious minutes, neither of us willing to return to reality.

Finally, I swing my legs around and fix my shirt, and we watch the sun sink lower on the horizon until it's just an orange orb casting a coppery glow over the entire desert.

Eli's warm hand finds mine, and he threads our fingers together and squeezes. I look over. He isn't staring at the sunset; he's looking down at our locked hands almost wistfully — as though he's thinking of what might have been.

I don't know what's gotten into him, but I don't want to lose the loving, happy Eli. I have a feeling this part of him has already come back from the brink of death once before — when he lost his entire family and shut out the world to protect himself.

While most people in the compound were raised to think of what's possible, Eli entered adulthood expecting nothing but one loss after another.

Without thinking, I lean over and place a soft kiss on his cheek. His eyes snap onto mine, and he gives me a look more intense than anything I've ever seen from him.

"Ugh! Aren't you two nauseating . . ."

I jump at the familiar voice, but Eli doesn't let go of my hand.

"Nice of you to show up," he says to the air.

Then a head appears over a small boulder, and Owen pulls himself up to our overlook. "I told you I'd be here."

As long as I live, I'll never get used to seeing Eli's doppelgänger. Owen is slightly stockier and extremely tan, but other than that, they're practically identical.

Today Owen's wearing a tight gray beater that shows off his jagged scar and a pair of baggy camo shorts. His hat is stuck bill-first in his back pocket, so I can finally get a good look at his entire face. He's sweaty, covered in dust, and has a few ugly bruises marring his left eye, but he's just as good-looking as Eli.

He straightens up, and we get to our feet.

Before their earlier encounter, I might have thought the brothers would go in for an awkward hug or at least shake hands, but there's no love lost between these two.

Instead, they just stand there staring at each other.

Owen is the first to break the awkward silence. "So what's this about?" he asks. "I'm risking a lot just being here."

Eli glares at him. "And you think we *aren't*?"

Owen sets his jaw in a way that tells me he's holding back some major attitude. "Then why are you here, Eli?"

Eli takes a deep breath and glances down at me. I know he'd rather cut off his own arm than get into this argument with Owen, but he doesn't have a choice.

"My commander gave me an assignment," he says slowly. "She's asked me to take you out . . . you and Malcolm and Jackson."

"So you're here to assassinate me?" Owen scoffs. "That's classy, Eli. Mom and Dad would be so proud."

"No, you idiot. I'm here to warn you that people back at the compound want you dead. And my commander is throwing a lot of resources into this to make sure it happens."

Owen rolls his eyes. "Tell your commander to get in line."

"This is serious!" Eli growls. "I don't think you understand how much reach they have."

"I understand the compounds have been trying to exterminate every surviving human who gets too close for decades. I don't really know how this is any different."

A low rumble rolls up Eli's chest, and I know his frustration has reached its breaking point. "They're *watching* you."

"You mean *you're* watching me."

"No. I mean they have you on surveillance footage. They're tracking your movement, hoping you'll lead them to Malcolm or Jackson."

Owen raises an eyebrow. "Well, luckily they sent you to take me out, huh?"

"No! It isn't *lucky!*" Eli shouts. "Do you know what a mess this has been for me?"

"Don't ask me to lead you to the others," says Owen quietly. "Because the answer is going to be no."

"I don't need you to lead me to the others," says Eli in an imploring voice. "I need you to let me fake your death. If I can just —"

Owen looks up to the heavens as though he's begging for strength. "Are you out of your mind?"

"Just listen for a second. I'm not asking you to do anything crazy here. You just have to leave the area."

"Look, Eli. I've got enough of my own shit to deal with right now."

"And you think I *don't?*"

"Let's just say you won't have to fake my death if I don't get this smoothed over," Owen snaps. "I don't know what the fuck you were thinking when you pretended to be me, but —"

"I didn't have a choice."

"You could have chosen not to put the heat on your own brother! You told Malcolm you'd stick around, and then you disappeared. Jay and Mouse got shot, and now Tony is swearing up and down that there's some double agent super sniper out there. They think I can't be trusted!"

"I shouldn't have let him go," Eli mutters.

"That's beside the point. This isn't the compound, Eli. They don't *talk* about having you killed. You just wind up dead."

"You're gonna wind up dead anyway if you don't listen."

"No offense, but the compound is not my main concern right now. I'm sorry if that puts the heat back on you, but I can't make this my problem, too."

"You don't get it," Eli growls. "If I don't produce a dead drifter, Jayden is going to have Harper killed."

For the first time since he climbed up here, Owen turns his attention to me, and I know I'm not imagining the subtle shrug of his shoulders that says he couldn't care less if Jayden traded my life for his.

"Please," says Eli, oblivious to his brother's indifference. "Just do this one thing for me, and I swear I'll never ask you for anything else."

"Eli, I can't go off the grid right now. I'm sorry, but I can't."

"You're such an asshole," I blurt.

Eli and Owen snap their heads around to stare at me, looking genuinely surprised that I'm weighing in on their discussion.

"Do you realize we could have killed Malcolm?" I ask, getting up in Owen's face and stabbing a finger in his chest. "We were right there. He *trusted* us. And Eli didn't do it because he knew it would bring the drifters down on you. Now he's asking you for a favor, and you can't be bothered. You're just a selfish little coward."

By the time I finish, Owen is breathing hard and staring down at me with such intense dislike that I physically recoil. Just a moment ago, I was marveling at the brothers' resemblance, but I can't imagine Eli ever looking at me the way Owen is.

There's a long pregnant silence, and Owen finally speaks. "Where are the cameras?"

"All around the base," says Eli. "You can't go back there. They've got that area completely covered." He reaches into his back pocket and pulls out Celdon's map. "Just study this. If you stay out of the red zones, I'll take care of the rest."

Owen takes the folded piece of paper and stares at it as though he's trying out his X-ray vision.

"Oh, and I need your hat," Eli adds.

"My hat?"

Owen looks just as confused as I feel but pulls it out of his back pocket. He holds it out to Eli but doesn't let go. "I'll do this for you on one condition."

"Name it."

"I want to show you something."

"What?"

"I can't say. Just meet me at the big church on the far side of town tomorrow at twelve oh five. You can't miss it. There's a big-ass cross out front. Just don't come early, and stay out of sight."

"Okay," says Eli, just as surprised as I am that Owen's agreed to go along with the plan.

"I have to get back." He turns to go but stops short. "Listen . . . if you get caught, we don't know each other. You're just some guy who happens to look like me. I can't have this coming back to haunt me, Eli — not right now."

Owen has his back to us, so he doesn't see Eli's expression harden. But I do.

"Got it," he says.

Owen lowers himself over the edge of the cliff without another word, leaving a sour feeling in the pit of my stomach.

I'm not really sure what to think now. It sounded as though Owen was prepared to go along with our plan, but I have a hard time believing that my little speech could have prompted a change of heart when he was so against it before.

"I'm sorry," I murmur.

"What do *you* have to be sorry for? My brother is the one who won't do something for me without asking for something else in return. Families, right? What a load of bullshit."

"Eli, no. Don't think of it that way."

"How should I think of it?"

"I don't know."

"He doesn't even trust me enough to listen! I'm trying to

protect him, but he looks at me like I'm a total stranger."

"But he agreed," I reason. "That has to count for something, right?"

"It's not what he did; it's the way he did it. He only agreed out of guilt . . . or because he wants something." He sighs. "Dad would be rolling over in his grave if he could see the man he's become."

"Eli . . ."

When I look over at him, the sight is enough to break my heart. He's slumped forward over his knees, both hands clasped together. His hunched shoulders are big and muscular, but those eyes make him look like a little boy who's been let down too many times.

Without thinking, I reach over and extricate one of his hands. It's rough and dusty from all our rock climbing, but it folds easily around mine.

I take a deep breath. "Did you ever think that maybe Owen's reaction is normal considering everything you two have been through?"

"What do you mean?"

"You two lost everything when you were kids."

"Yeah, I know, Harper. I was there, remember?"

"I'm just saying that it affected Owen."

"Hey, it affected me, too," Eli growls. "I was younger than him. I didn't have *anybody*. Then I went to the Institute and I still didn't have anybody. But I remember what family means, so what's his excuse?"

"I'm not saying he has an excuse. But I do think it's pretty remarkable that you still have that love inside you after everything that's happened. I'm not sure many people would be able to hold on to that."

Eli doesn't answer me, but his hand squeezes mine a little

tighter. I can tell he's mulling my words over and maybe trying to dig up a little bit of compassion for Owen.

By now, the sun has set below the horizon, throwing a faint purplish hue over everything. The sweltering heat has broken, and the temperature is starting to plummet. I shiver at the sudden lack of sunshine, and Eli gets up to build a fire.

I join in the search for wood and brush, and it's strangely gratifying when the dry kindling blazes to life. Eli moves our blanket over to the pocket of warmth by the fire, and the mood lifts a little when he starts to heat one of our "just add water" meals.

He moves with such confidence that it's hard to believe he could be so deeply affected by his brother's treatment. But if I've learned anything in the past few weeks, it's that Eli still has deep wounds from growing up without a family. It's the reason he's always pushing people away.

The dried noodle-and-bean concoction starts to boil over the fire, and Eli settles down next to me. We sit there watching the flames dance over the dark desert, and when he puts an arm around me to draw me close, all I can think is how glad I am that he let me in.

twenty-four

Eli

Owen couldn't have picked a worse meet-up spot if he'd tried.

According to my interface, the church is on the far side of the town, which means we either have to take a wide path near the highway or risk showing our faces downtown.

The highway is definitely the safer choice, but it would take at least twice as long. Going through town seems to be the better option.

After a hasty breakfast of half-cooked noodles boiled over the dying fire, Harper and I start making our way down the cliff. By the time we reach the outskirts of town, the heat is back in full force, and it feels as though I'm melting into the cracked earth.

We pass the block with the sandwich shop where we found Owen, and I begin to get a strange prickle of unease on the back of my neck.

We haven't encountered a single drifter yet, and it seems too good to be true.

On the next corner, we stumble upon a brown clapboard tavern with "McNally's" spelled out along the side in cheery white letters. A few faded posters advertising different beer brands are plastered inside the dusty windows, and there are half a dozen cars parked in the crumbling lot out back.

It's too bright to see if there are people inside, but my skin is tingling with nerves.

Just then, the tavern door flies open, and a flurry of male voices escapes. I pull Harper behind a dumpster and crouch down out of sight, hoping the drifters don't hop in their cars and drive around the block.

"No screwups this time."

"Malcolm said everything is in place."

"But last time —"

"Last time we didn't have a contingency plan."

"I'm just saying . . . the whole project was delayed because we lost our man on the inside."

"Well, Travis was a dumb motherfucker."

"If you say so."

My breath is caught in my lungs, and my grip on Harper's shoulder is so tight that she eventually squirms free.

Three drifters stride into view, heading down the street in the same direction we were going. They're all dressed like Owen and toting serious-looking rifles, their heads bent in conversation.

"You think they were the only ones in there?" breathes Harper.

"No. But we can't wait around to find out."

I glance nervously up at the sky. The sun will be directly overhead in less than an hour, which means we need to hurry if we want to reach Owen on time.

I wait a few more seconds to make sure there aren't any stragglers leaving the tavern and make a break for the rear of the building. Harper follows me down the next street, and we continue our journey to the far side of town.

We catch sight of a few more drifters loitering outside of buildings, but they're all too preoccupied to notice the scuff of our boots or our shadows moving behind parked cars.

Finally, the downtown gives way to blocks of older homes

with chain-link fences and dried-up lawns. There's a donut shop on one corner and a dry cleaner on another, but there's little else in the way of businesses.

Slowly, the historic neighborhoods with presidential street names turn into cul-de-sac after cul-de-sac of nearly identical houses.

Here, the streets all have nature names like "Bear Creek Court" or "Alder Drive," but there are no alder trees or bears in sight.

We seem to have entered some sort of pre–Death Storm development. Every house is built from the same palette of light beige, hunter green, and burnt orange, with clean lines and archways meant to appear modern and luxurious.

The perfect emptiness gives me a shiver. These houses don't feel abandoned — they feel as though they were never lived in.

Harper must be getting bad vibes, too, because she picks up the pace and cuts through the dead yards with a purposeful look in her eyes.

We reach the edge of the development, which is flanked by a low stone wall that reads "Cactus Ridge." That's when I see the church.

Owen sure wasn't kidding when he said we couldn't miss it. It's one of those crescent-shaped megachurches that takes up the span of an entire city block.

If it weren't for the twenty-foot copper cross adorning the glass entryway, I might have mistaken the place for a shopping mall. There's a massive parking lot out front and a dried-up fountain flanked by overgrown desert plants.

Harper and I exchange a puzzled look. I'm not sure why Owen would have dragged us all the way out here, but I suppose it's as good a landmark as any. I'm just about to move out when Harper grabs my arm.

At first I don't understand why she stopped me, but then I hear voices. Two husky drifters stride into view. They're moving toward the church at a brisk pace, and we watch them cross the parking lot and go inside.

What the hell?

I glance at my interface. It's five 'til noon. *Why would Owen tell us to come here if the place was crawling with drifters?*

"I have a bad feeling about this," Harper murmurs.

"Yeah. Me, too."

"Do you think there are more inside?"

"No idea."

She doesn't say it, but we're both thinking it: This feels like a trap.

Harper doesn't take her eyes off the courtyard in front of the church. Minutes pass in tense silence, but we don't see any more drifters. I check my interface. It's five after.

"You think he meant another church?" she asks.

I raise my eyebrows and swivel my head toward the enormous cross. "I think it's safe to say he was talking about this one."

"Then why —"

"I have no idea. Let's just check it out. If the drifters are inside, we'll turn around and head back to the cliff for the night."

"Are you crazy?"

I sigh. "I know it looks bad, but Owen wouldn't set us up. If we stay out of sight, we can go up to the church and just see if he's there."

Harper still looks wary, but she nods and draws her weapon. I know she's only going along with it to humor me, and I love her for that.

Stepping over the low stone wall, we leave the shelter of Cactus Ridge and jog across the empty four-lane road. As our feet slap against the reddish flagstone, I can't help but feel as though the cross is throwing an extra-large shadow over me.

The entryway is all glass, but from our angle of approach, we can see directly into the lobby without showing ourselves. There's no one inside, but that deep feeling of unease is still weighing on my chest.

I reach for the handle, but Harper nudges me in the shoulder.

"Are we really doing this?" she whispers.

I hesitate. This situation smells like ten miles of bad road, but Owen is expecting us. And as dangerous as this meet-up seems, it was his one condition for going along with our plan.

I sigh and grip my gun tighter. "We don't really have a choice."

Judging by the look of dread in Harper's eyes, I can tell she thinks this is a trap. But Owen is my brother, and that has to mean something.

"Let's go."

The glass door slides open without a sound, and Harper and I slip into the lobby.

Every muscle in my body is poised for an attack, and Harper seems just as tense. Our footsteps echo in the vast empty space, bouncing off the high ceiling and the shiny tile floor.

Then I hear a low buzz coming from the sanctuary. The heavy oak doors are closed, but there's no way I'm imagining the hum of a crowd.

I signal Harper to stay behind me and approach the doors slowly. My hand closes over the thick handle, but before I open the door, I hear a muffled *thud* and a slight scuffle behind me.

I wheel around — prepared to shoot whomever I see — and nearly have a heart attack.

Harper is engaged in a struggle with a man I can't identify.

He's doubled over from a nasty elbow to the face, and Harper just back-kicked him in the groin.

She winds up to strike him over the head with her gun but stops short when she catches sight of his face. It's Owen.

"*What the hell?*" she hisses, turning bright red.

"I was about — to say — the same — thing," Owen moans quietly, trying to hide the pained expression on his face.

"That's why you don't sneak up on people," Harper growls, fixing Owen with the defiant look she usually reserves for training.

I can't help it. I grin.

"Christ," Owen spits through his teeth.

"Watch it," I say, glancing around at all the crosses adorning the doors and walls.

Just then, the hubbub behind the door grows louder, and I remember why we're here.

"You wanna tell me what's going on?" I ask, jerking my head toward the doors. "You asked us to come knowing there would be Desperados here. So what's the deal?"

Owen shakes his head, still recovering from Harper's defense maneuvers. "It'll be easier to just show you."

He straightens up with a grimace and starts walking stiffly toward a smaller side door I didn't see when we walked in. I still have a bad feeling about this, but now that we're here, I have to admit I'm curious.

This no longer feels like a trap; it feels like some sort of initiation. And as distrustful as Owen is, his inviting us here is a big deal.

The door swings open, and the wave of sound intensifies. Owen leads us up a narrow flight of stairs and turns to face us.

"Stay out of sight," he breathes.

Then he pushes the door open, and the wave of sound almost bowls me over.

Owen disappears around the corner, and I move a little closer to Harper before following him through.

We emerge onto a balcony with enough extra seating to accommodate everyone in Recon. There's no one on this level, but Owen finds a seat in the shadows so he can observe the congregation without being seen.

The room more closely resembles a stadium or amphitheater than a church. The seats are staggered the way a movie theater's would be, arranged in a sloped semicircle around a stage. Another enormous cross takes up half of the far wall, and judging by its pearly finish, I'd guess the entire thing lights up.

The lower level of the sanctuary is half full of drifters, who look very out of place. I'm sure the residents of Cactus Ridge never wore tank tops, bandanas, or cutoff shorts to church, but those seem to be the only pieces of clothing the Desperados own.

Some of the drifters are chatting happily like old friends, but others are arguing in clusters of five or six.

Then I hear the large doors open again down below, and a hush spreads over the disorderly group. Owen yanks on my arm, and I move into the shadows on the other side of Harper.

A tall, wiry man strides toward the stage, and the drifters scramble to find their seats.

When the newcomer turns to face the crowd, my heart thuds loudly against my ribcage. I'd recognize that pointed, rat-like face anywhere: It's Malcolm Martinez.

The chatter dissipates quickly, and Malcolm raises his arms out to his sides like the damn Messiah.

"Welcome, everyone. Thank you for coming."

There's a soft rush of murmurs in the crowd.

"It's so good to see you all here." Malcolm pauses dramatically, surveying the group like a proud father. "Today is a day for celebration. We have disenfranchised American citizens gathered here from as far east as Kansas . . . as far west as California . . .

"I want to thank you for your bravery . . . your determination . . . and your commitment to our family."

I want to puke and roll my eyes at the same time. This feels like some sort of drifter brainwashing summit, and Malcolm is clearly the puppet master.

Leave it to Owen to throw in his luck with these people rather than trusting his *real* family. I'm not sure whether he's trying to convert me or just demonstrate the drifters' strength, but either way, he brought me here for a reason: He doesn't plan on holding up his end of the bargain.

In that instant, everything becomes extremely clear. Owen might not want to cooperate with my plan, but I don't need him — not really. Jayden would be equally happy with another dead drifter — the man standing less than a hundred yards away.

I glance over at Owen, who's watching Malcolm with a sort of grudging respect. I wonder if Jackson is somewhere in the mix or if it would be too dangerous for him to show his face in the crowd of Desperados.

I'm leaning against a square pillar, which provides just enough of a barrier to block me from Owen's view.

Slowly, I draw my gun and point it at Malcolm's head.

I am *so* going to hell for this. I probably won't make it ten yards before I'm struck by lightning for shooting a drifter in a church. But at least Malcolm will be dead, and Harper will have a chance of escaping Constance's threats.

One shot — one shot is all I have to take out Malcolm, grab Harper, and get the fuck out of here.

If Owen doesn't want my help, he's on his own. He'll probably be blamed for the shooting, which means he'll have to disappear whether he wants to or not.

This solves all our problems.

But then a sharp shock reverberates up my arm. Two strong hands redirect my gun, and before I can react, Owen is shoving me against the wall. I grunt as we struggle for control of the weapon, but he twists my hand painfully until the gun clatters to the floor.

"What are you *doing?*"

"What I should have done the first time I met him!"

"*Are you insane?*" Owen hisses. "We'd never make it out of here alive if you shot Malcolm."

"Well, Harper and I won't be alive for long if we go back empty-handed," I snarl, throwing him off me.

"That's why I brought you here!"

I don't listen. I don't pause to consider my next move. I just lunge for the gun.

Unfortunately, Owen has always been stronger and just a little bit faster. I don't get within a foot of the gun before I feel the scrape of a boot against my face.

He didn't kick me that hard, but the force is enough to make me lose my balance and slam face-first into the baseboard.

Harper gasps, and I shake my head to clear the sudden fuzziness.

Everything is upside down.

Owen snatches my gun off the floor, empties the chamber, and pockets the bullets.

"Calm the fuck down!" he growls. "You're going to get us caught. Everything will explain itself. Just sit tight for a second."

My cheek is inflamed where he kicked me, and my jaw feels as though I've been curb stomped. But I'm too pissed to show Owen I'm hurt, so I just stagger to my feet and lean back against the pillar.

I try to focus on Malcolm's speech, but I'm so furious I can hardly breathe. I can feel Harper's eyes on me, but I have no idea what she's thinking.

"We've come a long way in the last six months," says Malcolm. "We've salvaged the best technology . . . fuel . . . medicine. We've built the strongest civilian army this country has seen since the Revolutionary War. And someday very soon, we'll no longer have to live in fear."

The crowd erupts into applause, and my stomach clenches. Malcolm makes a humble-looking gesture that fills me with hate, imploring the crowd to hold its applause.

"I just confirmed myself that we successfully exterminated compound 119."

Then the crowd goes wild. People get to their feet, stomp, clap, and cheer. They're hugging and smiling, but it feels as though I left my stomach back at Cactus Ridge.

He can't have said what I thought he said. It isn't possible.

"*You* killed all those people at 119?" Harper breathes.

I glance over at her. Her face has gone stark white, and she's staring at Owen in utter disgust.

I can't believe it. This has to be some kind of sick joke. All the drifters down below — they're celebrating the deaths of thousands of innocent people.

"Why would you bring us here?" I spit in Owen's direction.

I don't look at him. I don't want to see him smiling along with the others as though they've made some big accomplishment.

"Just wait."

After several minutes, the crowd's cheers die down enough for Malcolm to make himself heard again. "Someday very soon, we'll no longer have to fear their soldiers who come out to kill.

We'll be able to raise our families without the need to run and hide. We'll have access to clean water . . . a steady source of power.

"The plan is in motion. Soon, 112, the largest and most militant compound in the country, will be wiped — off — the map!"

My breath catches in my throat. There's a very good chance I'm going to puke all over the church's plush blue carpeting.

I knew the drifters were working to bring down the compound, but I never imagined they'd be successful. That was before I knew they were responsible for 119 — before I'd seen hundreds of them gathered together celebrating our impending death.

I can't take it anymore. Throwing Owen one last bitter look, I stand up and grab Harper's hand. She murmurs something I can't quite make out, but I'm already pulling her down the stairs toward the lobby.

I hear Owen following us, and once we're enclosed in the stairwell, he yells at us to wait.

I quicken my pace. I can't even look at him right now.

"Hey!"

I feel the hand on my shoulder and react without thinking. I wheel around and swing at him with a wild overhand punch.

Any amateur could have dodged it easily, but I catch Owen by surprise, and my fist crashes into his face with devastating force.

"*Fuck!* What the hell was that for?"

"Are you serious? Were you in the same room just now?"

"Yes!" he snaps in a nasally voice, mopping the blood from under his nose with the back of his hand. "I was trying to show you why you don't need to fake my death. It's time for you to leave all that shit. Soon there's going to be nothing left of that place."

"You think I'm just going to stick around here and wait for you to murder an entire compound full of people?" I splutter. "I have *friends* back there, Owen! People I care about! Or is that just such a foreign concept to you that you can't imagine why I'd have a problem?"

I shove him hard in the shoulder, but he grabs me by the collar and gives me a look Dad used to have when he was really, really pissed.

I don't have enough distance for a good jab, so I throw a hook into Owen's stomach. He makes a pained gurgling sound in his throat and slaps me — actually *slaps* me — upside the head.

Harper is watching our exchange with a frantic look in her eyes, and I know she's got to be sick with worry over Celdon and Sawyer.

I'm stunned that our little scuffle hasn't brought a dozen members of Malcolm's congregation running to see what all the commotion is about, but I don't care. Right now, I feel as though I could take on an entire army of drifters.

Somehow, Owen gets me in a headlock, and it's as if I'm ten years old all over again. He drags me down the stairs and through the lobby as if I weigh nothing.

Harper is trailing behind him, whispering a nasty stream of threats, but he manages to shove me into a small chapel and trap me in one of the short pews. There's a miniature altar directly in front of me and a stained-glass cross less than two yards away, but Owen is looking at me in a way that says he wouldn't hesitate to deck me in a place of worship.

"Listen!" he splutters. "I knew this would be hard for you to handle, but it's happening! There's nothing you can do to stop it. The plan is already in motion. I just wanted to show you so you'd understand why you don't need to fake my death . . . and give you a chance to escape."

"What plan?" asks Harper.

"You don't need to know the details," he says, rounding on her with a cold look in his eyes. "All you need to know is to stay away."

"Why should we trust you?"

"Because you don't have another choice. Hell, *I* don't have a choice. This thing is happening."

By Owen's tone, I can tell he's done talking to Harper. He turns to me with that stern older-brother look, but I can detect hesitation in his gaze that makes him look years younger.

"There's always a choice," I mutter. "You've just made all the wrong ones."

"Eli —"

"What the hell did you *do*?" I ask, feeling my voice running a little higher than normal. "How did you introduce a virus that killed all those people?"

Owen sighs. He doesn't want to tell me, but he seems to be torn between giving away the drifters' plan and keeping me under control.

Finally, he caves.

"The Centers for Disease Control had a repository before Death Storm. All the nasty diseases with the potential to wipe out the human race . . . they have a frickin' library of them — well, *had*. The preserved viruses most likely died when the center shut down. You have to keep them frozen, or else . . ."

"Is this relevant?" I snap.

"Yes! It wasn't just Atlanta that had the viruses. About a year ago, Malcolm met a guy who'd worked for the CDC branch in Fort Collins. He said that before Death Storm, the federal government bought one of the compounds in the Rocky

Mountains and preserved a bunch of samples there in case the facility was compromised."

"And you found the samples."

Owen nods. "We sent a mole into the compound and stole one of the viruses the CDC was keeping under wraps. We weren't sure if the samples would still be viable. But we were able to infiltrate 119, and it worked."

"You killed *thousands* of innocent people."

"They aren't innocent," Owen growls. "None of us are innocent in this, Eli, but the compounds make it damn near impossible for the rest of us to live."

"What you did was mass murder."

"No. They were just casualties of war. And this *is* a war, Eli. The question is . . . whose side are you gonna be on?"

There's a long, strained silence. I glance at Harper and then get to my feet. "Not yours."

"What are you gonna do?" Owen asks to my retreating back. He sounds a little desperate — so unlike his usual cocky self. "You can't go back there."

"What do you mean?"

"Going back there would be suicide."

In that moment, everything Owen has made me feel lately — the hope and betrayal and disappointment — bubble up inside me. I can't take it anymore. I fly out of my seat.

Owen wasn't prepared for my storm of fury, so he doesn't move out of the way. I slam straight into his chest and pin him against the wall with my forearm.

"How could you do this?" I growl. "I *trusted* you."

My voice sounds very strange, and my face and throat are burning with bitter unshed tears. "I've been running around trying to figure out a way to save your ass so we could be a family again, and you go and get yourself involved in something like *this*. What am I supposed to do now?"

"Eli!" Harper snaps, grabbing my arm. "Be quiet! They'll hear you."

"I don't care."

I shove my arm harder against his throat. Owen's having a hard time breathing, but I don't loosen my grip. Part of me wants to let him pass out and hope he wakes up a changed man. But I'm done lying to myself.

"What the hell has gotten into you?" I whisper, all the disgust and anger leaching out in my voice. "We weren't raised this way. If Mom and Dad heard what you just told me, they'd die of shame."

I drop my arm and let him choke in a breath before stabbing my index finger into his chest. "You're a fucking disgrace."

Owen takes a moment to replenish his lungs, and when he finally speaks, his voice is angrier than I've ever heard it.

"*I'm* a disgrace? You talk about what Mom and Dad would say, yet you're gonna turn your back on *me*? Your own brother? For what? For a bunch of people who don't give a shit about you? People who'd kill you just like that?" He snaps his fingers together, but the chilling effect is somewhat lost by his loud gasps for air.

I swallow and meet his gaze with as cold a look as I can manage. "You're not my brother."

As long as I live, I'll never forget the look on Owen's face. He's staring at me as though I just ripped his soul out of his body.

Then he lets out a low, bitter laugh. "Not anymore, I guess."

He reaches into his front pocket and holds out a closed fist. When I don't reach for it, he jerks his hand at me. "Take it."

"What is it?"

"Just fucking *take* it, Eli."

Reluctantly, I hold out my hand. He opens his fist, and something hard and flat falls into my palm. It's the arrowhead he and Dad found, still warm from his pocket.

All I can think is, *What the fuck is he giving me this for?*

It feels oddly heavy in my hand — as though Owen somehow managed to transfer the weight of his disappointment to this tiny piece of flint.

"If you're smart, you'll go into hiding," I say. My voice sounds funny, but I refuse to feel remorse. "Stay out of range of the cameras. I'm going to report you terminated. That'll buy us both some time."

I want him to take the damn arrowhead back, but he's just standing there staring at me.

Finally, I shove it in my pocket and turn to Harper. She's giving me a broken look that exactly captures the way I feel, but I can't wallow right now.

Without another word, I grab her hand and pull her out of the chapel.

I don't look back at Owen. As far as I'm concerned, Owen Parker is dead.

twenty-five

Harper

Eli doesn't say a word the entire journey back through town.

The winding streets of faceless, empty homes are downright chilling after what we just heard. I picture rows of compartments standing vacant in much the same way — waiting for owners who will never draw another breath.

I keep expecting Eli to stop at an abandoned building to rehydrate or come up with a new plan, but he seems determined to put as much distance between us and the drifters as possible.

The afternoon sun feels as though it's baking us alive, and by the time we reach our cliff outside of town, I'm exhausted and dehydrated.

"We have to stop, Eli," I say, tugging on his arm to bring him back to earth.

When he turns toward me, I half expect him to be wearing the same "you're dead to me" expression he had in the chapel, but he just looks lost and a little confused.

"I need some water," I say. "So do you."

There's a long pause, and Eli nods slowly. "Yeah. Okay."

Relieved, I guide him into the shadow of the cliff and settle onto the ground to dig into my pack. Eli is still standing, staring off into the open desert as though he plans to make a run for it. When I hand him the water bag, he crouches down next to me and takes a long drink.

"So what's the plan?" I ask tentatively, still concerned that he might lash out at the only person nearby.

"We need to signal the compound," he says, wiping his mouth with the back of his hand. "We can't exactly walk back."

"I mean about the drifters — Owen."

Eli reaches into his rucksack and withdraws Owen's faded gray baseball cap. "I'll tell Jayden I took out Jackson's right-hand man," he says, brandishing the hat. "Hopefully Owen does what I told him to do."

I look from Eli to the hat, waiting for him to continue. When he doesn't add anything else, I say, *"That's* your plan?"

Eli looks taken aback by my incredulous tone, and I force myself to muster up a little patience and compassion.

"Eli . . . you can't count on him going into hiding. Even if Jayden believes you killed him, one wrong move from Owen and she's going to know you made the whole thing up."

"Well, what do you suggest?" he snaps. "I'm doing the best I can here, Harper!"

"I know . . ."

Eli lets out a guttural growl and digs his hand into a clump of weeds next to his foot. "Shit! I should have shot Malcolm when I had the chance."

"No, you shouldn't have. We never would have made it out of that place alive."

"But he's their leader. If I'd shot him, this could all be over."

I can tell he's furious with himself, but whether his frustration is truly about Malcolm or if he's regretting the things he said to Owen, I can't be sure.

"You don't really believe that, do you?" I ask. "You heard Owen. The plan is already in motion. And there are so many of them. If one got killed, there'd be twenty more just waiting to take his place."

"I still should have shot him."

"No. Listen. There's no point telling Jayden that Owen is dead. Just tell her what we know about the virus. That has to be worth more than one dead drifter."

"Tell her *what*, exactly? That we just sat there and listened to the drifters plot the compound's destruction and then walked out with no trouble? How are we going to explain how we found out where they were meeting? Or why we didn't take out Malcolm when we had the chance? She's going to think we were in on the whole thing!"

"Just tell her we couldn't risk getting killed in there . . . we had to get out so we could warn the board."

"No. We're sticking to the original plan."

"We can't just say nothing!" I splutter. "We could *save* them. We have to tell the board what the drifters are planning!"

Eli shakes his head. "Owen wouldn't have told us anything about it if there was any chance we could slow this thing down."

"We have to try!"

"I know . . ." He lets out an exasperated sigh, and I can tell he's giving it some serious thought.

Finally he seems to come to his senses. "We'll warn them, okay? Just let me come up with a plan first. I can't think straight right now."

I bite my lip. I don't want to delay warning the board even by a minute, but since we seem to have reached some sort of an agreement, I let it go.

"We'll find a way out," he murmurs. "I promise."

"What?"

"If the virus really has been introduced to the compound, we'll find a way to get out of there. You, me, Sawyer, Celdon, Miles . . . whoever we can take with us."

So *that's* what's on his mind. Oddly, I hadn't even thought about a contingency plan, but if someone in the compound is already infected, we're going to need one.

We can't afford to waste any more time, so I stand up and hold out a hand for Eli. The sun is still bearing down with oppressive intensity, but we need to find the rover to send up a distress signal.

The walk back to the vehicle is much longer than I remembered. It's parked right where we left it on the side of the road, and the back tire is completely deflated.

Eli reaches inside and hits the tiny red button on the dashboard, and an uneasy feeling creeps over me.

Was Owen right? I wonder. *Is returning to the compound tantamount to suicide?*

We don't know anything about the virus except that it killed thousands of people in a matter of weeks. We didn't ask any of the important questions. We don't know how it's transmitted or how quickly it spreads. We don't even know how the drifters introduced the virus to 119 in the first place.

Eli and I wait in strained silence for nearly an hour. I know we should still be watching for drifters, but after being crammed in a church with hundreds of them, one random straggler seems manageable by comparison.

Finally, I hear the soft *whir* of an engine.

Because the rovers are painted to blend in with the desert, I don't see the rescue vehicle until it's about 200 yards away.

My heart sinks when I see Seamus sitting in the driver's seat. He's clutching the steering wheel as though the thing isn't self-driving, and he's wearing a mask despite the vehicle's airtight seal.

When the rover slows to a stop, Eli steps around back so he won't get stuck riding alongside Seamus.

"Where are your masks?" Seamus asks incredulously when I slide into the passenger seat.

I look back at Eli, unprepared for this line of questioning.

"Uh . . . we lost them," he mutters, buckling his seat belt and avoiding Seamus's probing gaze in the rearview mirror.

"How did you lose them?"

"It's a long story."

Seamus doesn't look satisfied with this response, but he punches the "home" button on the dashboard. The rover hums a little louder, turns, and starts accelerating in the direction of the compound.

"No trouble on the way here?" I ask.

"No. Weird, huh? It's eerie when nobody's shooting at you out here."

I force a smile to hide my disgust, and a strained silence falls over the three of us.

I can't see Eli's face, so I can't tell if he's thinking about Owen, figuring out how to tell the board what we know, or trying to come up with a plan to get us out of the compound.

"So what happened to your rover?" Seamus asks.

"Sorry, Duffy," says Eli in a sharp voice. "Couldn't tell you even if I wanted to — not until we're debriefed, at least. And last time I checked, you aren't Jayden."

Seamus blanches, and I turn slightly so I can give Eli a warning look. I'm not Seamus's biggest fan either, but there's no reason to piss off Jayden's right-hand man.

"Just trying to make conversation," he says.

After that, time slows to a crawl. The ride back to the compound is infinitely longer than the trip out to the town, and when the tall silver compound finally comes into view, I don't think I've ever been so glad to see anything in my life.

The rover makes a clean sweep around the structure, and the hangar doors slide open automatically.

The tension seems to magnify in the small space as we wait

for the doors to close, and as soon as they do, a trio of med interns in hazmat suits shoots out of the side doors.

I'm relieved to see Sawyer is among them. I get out of the rover and move toward her automatically, and the others descend upon the vehicle to supervise Seamus's and Eli's decontamination.

Sawyer steers me out of the hangar into a much larger decontamination chamber. Half a dozen enclosed shower stalls are lined up in a row, and I realize this must be where the Ex-Con guys go after a long day of work. I shudder as the cold water pelts me clean and wait for the light above the next door to turn green.

Sawyer leads me through to the secondary chamber, where she strips me down to my shorts and tank and shimmies out of her hazmat suit.

When we're as clean as we can be, she punches a large blue button to retract the doors, and I plop down in the wheelchair waiting on the other side.

It propels me toward the megalift, and as soon as the doors close behind us, Sawyer lets out an enormous sigh of relief.

"Oh my god, Harper! I was so worried!"

"Why? What happened?"

Sawyer shakes her head so her hair whips back and forth. She looks more frazzled than usual — as though she hasn't slept in days.

"They've had us on standby for the last twenty hours! They received a message that your rover had been compromised, and they were talking about deploying an emergency rescue crew to bring you back. We were standing by in case . . ." She trails off for a minute, looking sick.

"I thought you were seriously hurt. I didn't like them sending you out in that thing in the first place."

"Hey! It's okay. I'm okay."

Sawyer's eyes are wide behind her glasses, giving her an almost cartoonish expression.

"When I went for Health and Rehab, I never thought I'd be waiting around to get horrible news about you." She purses her lips and stares at the corner of the lift, and I can tell she's trying not to cry. "This isn't what I signed up for."

That elicits a sharp pang of guilt in my stomach, and I reach up to wrap an arm around her. "I'm sorry you were scared. But honestly, this isn't what I signed up for either."

I'm just trying to keep the mood light, but Sawyer's face falls. "Oh god. I'm sorry. You're right. I'm such an idiot! Forget I said anything."

I bat her apology away. "It's okay."

The megalift dings, and the doors slide open to reveal a bustling tunnel in the medical ward. Sawyer moves to disembark, but Jayden is blocking our path.

"What the *hell* is going on?" she barks.

"Commander," I say in a curt voice, trying to filter out my own contempt.

Her gaze snaps onto me. "We need to talk."

"O-*kay* . . ."

"Now!"

Sawyer clears her throat behind me. "Um, Commander? I'm sorry, but I can't release Cadet Riley until she's been medically cleared."

Even though I can't see her face, I know Sawyer must be blushing profusely. She *hates* standing up to her superiors, but by god, Sawyer always follows the rules.

Jayden stares at her blankly, unaccustomed to having her authority challenged. Normally, she just intimidates people from other sections until they give her what she wants.

Her lips tighten as if she's sucking on her teeth, but she musters up a fake smile and gives Sawyer a tiny nod. "Of course. Silly me. I just jumped the gun a little, I guess. Please let me know as soon as she's available for questioning."

Then, to my utter amazement, Jayden turns and walks away. I bet she's going to lurk nearby to ambush Eli, but I never see where she goes.

Sawyer maxes out the speed on my wheelchair, and we slide into the exam room farthest from the waiting area. As soon as the door closes behind me, all the problems I'd been trying to deny come crashing down around me.

Eli made me promise not to say anything to anyone about the virus until he came up with a better cover story, but seeing Jayden reawakened all the anxiety I felt listening to the drifters' scheme.

"I need to tell you something," I say to Sawyer, glancing back at the closed door.

"Okay. Spill."

I take a deep breath and get out of the wheelchair, pacing to relieve some of my pent-up nerves. "We have a problem. You know that virus that wiped out 119?"

Sawyer nods. "I've been studying the exam notes to see if I can figure out what it was, but I haven't heard of any virus that causes those symptoms and moves that quickly."

"That's because the virus came from some government facility in Colorado. The samples should have just died when the lab shut down, but a bunch got transferred to one of the compounds in the Rocky Mountains before Death Storm."

"That would explain why none of the antiviral meds worked," says Sawyer. "They'd never seen that virus before. Hang on. How did it get from Colorado to 119?"

"The drifters planted it there to wipe out the compound."

Sawyer looks stunned and then panicked. "What do you mean?"

"I mean they purposely introduced the virus as a biological weapon. They're using it to bring down the compounds one by one."

I launch into the story of everything that happened on our deployment, and Sawyer listens with rapt attention, trying to absorb every detail. When I get to the part about spying on the drifters' rally, her eyes grow so wide it looks as though they might pop right out of her head.

Sawyer doesn't really understand how deadly the drifters are, but the idea of survivors is still so new to her that it seems impossible that there could be hundreds congregating twenty miles from the compound.

"Owen said we're next," I finish. "He said the plan was already in motion. *What does that mean*? Is the virus already here? Do you think somebody in the compound is infected?"

"It sounds like it," Sawyer breathes.

"At first I thought maybe he was bluffing, but it doesn't make sense that he would just let us leave unless he was confident that the virus was already here."

Sawyer looks a little sick and backs up so she can support herself on the exam counter. "What are you going to do?"

"I don't know! I have to tell someone, don't I?"

She nods slowly.

"But Eli wants to wait until we have a better story. He thinks it's going to look like we were in on it or something.

"If Jayden finds out we were there and didn't take out Malcolm, she's going to freak. The board's going to be looking for *someone* to pin this on, and Jayden will probably try to make it look like we're traitors so she doesn't get blamed."

"Plus there's the whole thing about you guys not actually

killing Owen."

"Yeah, there's that."

"God, Eli's plan sucks," Sawyer mutters, cracking her knuckles nervously and staring up at the ceiling. She's got on her analytical face, and I know she's still processing all the information — too shocked to offer any real solution just yet.

"How the hell did they introduce the virus to 119?" she asks, more to herself than to me. "Recon operatives are always kept in the medical ward for observation, and patient zero wasn't a Recon guy anyway. He was Health and Rehab."

Sawyer closes her eyes in concentration. "Even if the virus was passed from a Recon guy to someone in the medical ward, the Recon worker would have presented with symptoms first . . ."

"I just want to know what he meant when he said the plan was already in motion. I mean, do you think they plan to ambush the compound again? We have people patrolling the perimeter, so . . ." I trail off, slowly latching on to Sawyer's train of thought.

"Hang on . . . Patient zero belonged to Health and Rehab?"

Sawyer sighs loudly, probably frustrated that I interrupted whatever breakthrough she was so close to. "Yeah, he worked in the decontamination unit . . ."

Suddenly, Sawyer's eyes snap open, and a look of pure dread spreads across her face.

"Harper . . ."

"What?"

Judging by her expression, I can tell she's worked out some horrible conclusion that I just haven't been sharp enough to grasp.

"Patient zero worked in the decontamination unit."

"So?"

"So . . . the decontamination unit is how people usually smuggle pre–Death Storm contraband into the compound."

"People like Shane?"

"Yeah. People like Shane sometimes pay Recon workers to bring stuff back from the Fringe. They've cracked down on illegal smuggling recently, but sometimes Health and Rehab workers still let things slip through."

She lets out a shallow breath, staring at me with a look that can only be described as devastation.

"*What?*"

She swallows. "The plan the drifters put in motion . . . It was you and Eli."

Sawyer looks as though she's about to cry, and I don't immediately understand what she's saying. "Owen sent you back here because you already carried the virus in . . . and I helped you do it."

twenty-six

Harper

For a moment, I just stare at Sawyer. What she's suggesting is too horrible to fathom.

"That can't be," I murmur. "Owen wouldn't. He couldn't pass the virus to me and Eli unless he was infected himself."

"Yeah, he could have."

"How?"

Sawyer begins to pace, talking so fast I can hardly understand her. "Do you remember reading about the anthrax attacks of 2001?"

"No."

"Well, I do."

Of course.

"They used it as a case study when they taught us Health and Rehab's safety protocol for containing a virus. Anyway, back before Death Storm, somebody sent anthrax spores through the mail in letters.

"It's possible Owen got Eli to carry the virus into the compound on something small. Where did Eli get that necklace? He brought it back on your last mission along with a picture of his family. Did Owen give him that?"

I shake my head. "No. Eli found that stuff at his house, but Owen was already gone when we got there. He didn't even know Eli took it."

"Did Owen give Eli *anything* to carry back to the compound?"

I shake my head, wracking my brain. "His hat, but Eli asked for it . . ."

Then the realization hits me, and I want to throw up.

"The arrowhead," I whisper. "Oh, god. Oh god, oh god! Owen gave him an arrowhead just after Eli told him they were finished."

"And Eli brought it back with him?"

"I think so."

Suddenly my mind flashes back to the drifters we overheard at the tavern: *Last time, we didn't have a contingency plan.*

Were we *the contingency plan?*

Owen tried to get Eli to join the drifters, and when he refused, Owen found a way to use him anyway.

"Oh my god," I say again. "You're right. We were supposed to be the mules."

When I look up at Sawyer, her eyes are shining with tears. That's when the full impact of our discovery hits me.

"Do you think we've been exposed?"

"I don't know," she whispers. "Probably."

"You shouldn't be here."

"If it's airborne, it's already too late."

"But we don't know if it is, right?" I ask desperately, trying to hold back the tears burning in my throat.

"It's the only thing that makes sense. Otherwise, I don't know how 119 couldn't have gotten a handle on the outbreak."

"Well, what about Eli?" I ask, starting to blubber a little. "If anyone's infected, it would be him. You should tell him and Seamus and whoever they were with. We need to quarantine ourselves so we don't infect anyone else."

"Yeah. You're right." Sawyer is nodding profusely, falling

into business mode, but her hands shake a little as she taps her interface.

She waits for the call to connect, and after a few seconds, the stern face of a man appears in front of her eyes.

He's wearing a surgical mask and a look of intense irritation. I can't hear what he's saying, but judging by the deepening crease in Sawyer's brow, I'd guess he's yelling at her for disturbing him.

"Sorry. I'm sorry, sir," she says, summoning a steadier voice. "Listen. I'm in exam room twenty-eight, and I've got a possible code green. I have Harper Riley with me. We also need to isolate Eli Parker, Seamus Duffy, and any medical personnel who've seen them."

He yells something through his mask at her, and Sawyer bows her head. "Yes, I know. I know. Well, I don't want to cause a panic, but we may have identified the source of contamination."

Now the doctor on the other end of the line seems to be paying attention. By the looks of it, he's barking orders to the people around him before rounding on Sawyer and hanging up.

She looks stricken as she redirects her attention to me.

"What did he say?"

"We're being quarantined until they know for sure whether we're infected."

"What about the debriefing?"

Sawyer lets out an evil, half-crying laugh that I've only ever heard once when she failed a test in higher ed. "Tell Jayden to come at her own risk. I'd pay big money to see that woman die a slow, painful death with us."

"We need to warn anybody we came in contact with," I say. "If it is airborne, we could have already spread it to half the medical ward."

Sawyer gives me a shaky nod. "I know. They'll send up the Undersecretary of Health and Rehab once we're quarantined to determine what other precautions we need to take. That's protocol, anyway."

At a time like this, I'm so grateful that Sawyer is a nut for protocol.

It doesn't take long for the quarantine crew to find us. They burst into the room like a SWAT team, wearing dark green suits with heavy-duty air filtration masks.

They strap masks on me and Sawyer and steer us out of the room and down the tunnel toward a wing I've never visited before. Instead of depositing us in separate private rooms, they put us in a small ward with four beds.

One of the beds is already occupied by another med intern I vaguely recognize. He's got strawberry-blond hair and a dense spatter of freckles.

Then there's Eli. He's hovering near the door, looking as though he's about to start climbing the walls.

"What's going on?" he asks as soon as the doors slam shut.

I take a deep breath and glance at Sawyer, who looks miserable.

"Harper . . ."

By his voice, I can tell he's expecting something terrible, but it's not nearly as bad as the truth.

"Why are we here?" he asks. "They wouldn't tell me anything except that we couldn't leave this room. Where's Jayden? Did she already debrief you?"

"No."

"Then why —"

"We're being quarantined."

Eli's eyes dart from me to Sawyer and back to me. "What? Why?"

"Sawyer thinks . . . she thinks Owen played us."

"Played us?" Now he looks pissed off and confused. "Played us *how*?"

I hesitate, wishing I didn't have to say it out loud. "She thinks he let us come back because we were carrying the virus."

"Virus?" pipes the guy in the corner.

Everybody ignores him.

For a second, Eli just stares in stunned silence. I expect him to lash out at me, but he turns his fury on Sawyer. "You think my own brother would infect me and Harper with a virus and send us back to the compound to die? Are you out of your fucking mind?"

"Eli!" I yell.

But Sawyer doesn't shrink away from him. She straightens up and leans in to his outrage. "It's the only thing that makes sense."

"Owen didn't infect us with a virus! He'd have to be infected himself."

Sawyer is already shaking her head. "It's in the arrowhead."

"Arrowhead? How the hell do you know —" He turns back to me with an irate expression on his face. "You *told* her?"

"She asked if Owen had given you anything to carry back with you, and I said he had."

"It's just something he found with my dad when we were kids."

"Do you have it on you?" Sawyer asks.

"No! It's in my uniform —" He stops abruptly, as though he just remembered that he left the arrowhead in his pocket to be decontaminated and sent through the laundry service.

"It's not in the arrowhead," he says finally.

"Oh, wake up, Eli! Why would he give it to you after you ended things with him the way you did? He tried to get you to stay with him, and when you wouldn't, he made us the drifters' back-up plan!"

"There's no way in hell!" Eli bellows.

"Excuse me," the guy interrupts.

The three of us finally turn our attention to him, and he looks a little intimidated.

"Will someone *please* just tell me what's going on?"

"No," says Eli, waving off the intern. He turns back to Sawyer. "Do you realize what you've done?"

"Lay off," I snap, stepping between them.

That's when his expression changes to a look of pure betrayal. "I can't believe *you* went along with this."

"It's the only explanation that makes sense! Patient zero at 119 was medical-ward staff who worked in the decontamination unit. How do you think Shane gets all his pre–Death Storm crap into the compound, huh? Through the decontamination unit."

"You only think it makes sense because we haven't thought of anything else," he groans. "You were supposed to wait until I came up with a plan. I was handling things, but now that's all screwed up.

"What are we supposed to tell Jayden? That we were having a nice little chat with my brother and he told us all their evil plans? Oh, and then he gave me a poison arrowhead to smuggle back to the compound! How's *that* going to look?"

"I don't give a fuck about Jayden!" I snap. "This isn't about her or Owen. It's about saving the thousands of innocent people who have nothing to do with any of this."

Eli opens his mouth to protest, but I cut him off.

"And don't give me that crap about 'handling things.' You weren't handling *shit*!"

A stormy look flashes across Eli's face, and I'm suddenly

reminded of the fighter in him with all that buried rage. Then his expression evolves into something else. He looks . . . hurt.

I open my mouth to apologize, but before I can get the words out, a low beep sounds over the intercom.

"Miss Lyang. Miss Lyang. Kindly come through the door and be seated."

Glancing around the room, I see a door off to my left next to the bathroom. Sawyer throws me a puzzled look and opens it, revealing a smaller isolation chamber framed in glass. Through the window, I can just make out a slight woman in a taupe suit. That must be the Undersecretary of Health and Rehab here to interrogate us.

"Shut the door," she says over the intercom.

Sawyer obeys.

When the door slams shut, Eli seems to deflate. Rubbing his eyes, he sinks down onto the bed closest to the exit and sighs.

"Harper. When you talk to her, you can't mention Owen. I have to tell Jayden he's dead so she doesn't come after him . . . or you."

"Don't you think a deadly virus in the compound cancels out your little deal?"

He tilts his head to the side and gives me a look of disbelief. "It's Jayden. She'd kill her grandmother on Christmas if she thought she was plotting against her."

"Right."

We fall silent for a few minutes, and then he says, "I still don't believe Owen would do that to us . . . to me . . . to his own brother."

"Hey!" says a voice behind Eli, noticeably bolder this time.

I turn to look at the elephant in the room — the freckly intern with shocking green eyes.

"Sorry to interrupt, but I couldn't help overhearing you."

By the tone of his voice, he isn't sorry at all — he's pissed that he's stuck here with us. I would be, too.

"What the hell is going on? You're saying your *brother* is out on the Fringe and *he's* the reason we're being quarantined?"

Eli glowers at him, and the intern recoils.

I glare at Eli. "It's a long story. All you need to know is that there are some hostile survivors out there, and some of them are looking to bring down the compound with a virus."

The intern's brow crinkles. I don't like the look he's giving me — as though I'm some crazy girl who just messed up his day. "And how do you know all this?"

"Who *are* you?" I blurt, my irritation getting the best of me.

"Don't mind him," says Sawyer, breezing back into the room. "That's Caleb. He works with me. We're both going for Progressive Research."

"You knew about this?" he says, rounding on her. "That the people out there are trying to infect the compound with some kind of virus?"

"N-no."

But Sawyer is a terrible liar. She freezes on the spot and blushes from her neck to the roots of her hair.

"So why are we here when the others aren't?"

"Seamus and his retrieval specialist wore their masks the entire time, so neither one of them would be at risk of contracting an airborne virus," says Sawyer impatiently. She turns to Eli. "They want to talk to you next."

"Who's *they*?"

"Natasha Mayweather and Jayden."

Cursing under his breath, Eli gets up and crosses to the door. I try to send him a silent plea not to lie about Owen, but I know it's futile. Eli has already made up his mind.

"What did you say?" I ask Sawyer.

"Just what you told me . . . that you came into contact with a drifter after they'd been planning to bring down the compound with a virus. And that Eli has a habit of trying to smuggle pre–Death Storm relics into the compound. I put two and two together and figured you guys were a big risk."

"That won't get either of us in trouble or anything . . ." I mutter.

Then I remember I might be carrying a deadly virus. Getting written up for breaking deployment protocol is probably the least of my worries right now. "I *feel* fine."

I said it out loud without really meaning to, and Sawyer cracks a weak smile she sometimes uses to deliver uncomfortable news. "The incubation period for that virus is seventy-two hours."

"How do you know?"

"That's what Natasha said."

"How could she know that?"

Sawyer shrugs. "It was in the records from 119."

"That bitch. She knew all about the outbreak."

"I guess."

"What are you talking about?" blurts Caleb. "What outbreak?"

Shit. I keep forgetting we have an audience.

"Nothing," I say, hoping he'll just shut up and leave it alone. No such luck.

"One-nineteen? Do you mean *compound* 119? That's where they sent the recruits who opted out of their bids this year. Are you saying the virus is there, too?"

Sawyer and I have a silent conversation, and she gives me a tiny nod that says Caleb can be trusted.

"You can't tell anyone," I say. "It would just start a panic."

Caleb sinks back down on the bed, staring up at me with

those earnest, startling eyes. "There *was* an outbreak."

"Yes."

He shakes his head. "So what happened? Is there a cure?"

"No."

Sawyer and I exchange another look, and Caleb's expression grows more and more desperate. "What happened to them?"

I swallow. "Everyone at 119 is dead."

Caleb opens and shuts his mouth several times, and for a moment, I think he might burst into tears. It's becoming a very familiar reaction to me. But he just runs a shaking hand over his face and attempts to steady it on his knee. "That can't be right. We would have heard . . ."

Sawyer shakes her head once, and I start to wonder if this kid was equipped to handle the reality of the situation. He's not in Recon. He doesn't know what's out there — not really.

He doesn't know about the corruption in the compound or how he ended up in Health and Rehab. We probably just blew his mind.

Suddenly the door opens again, and Eli comes back in, looking frazzled.

"Everything okay?" I ask.

He nods. "Jayden bought it."

"I'm glad." My voice sounds flat, even to me. Lying to her is a stupid plan, but I guess what Eli says goes.

He stares at me for a second, and I can tell something has changed. He's no longer looking at me with that loving, protective gleam in his eyes. He feels betrayed and completely blindsided.

"You're next."

"Right."

I turn to go, but he grabs my wrist as though he meant to reach for my hand but thought better of it. The look in his eyes is unsettling — as though he's making one last request before washing his hands of me.

"Please, Harper. Just . . . don't say anything. I know I said a lot of stuff back at the church, but . . . even if this is his fault, he's still my brother."

"I know."

He gives me a gruff nod, and I pull open the heavy door and step inside the chamber.

To my relief, Jayden is gone. I guess she only cared what Eli had to say.

Natasha Mayweather, Undersecretary of Health and Rehab, is seated on the other side of the thick glass. She's a thin woman with graying black hair, sharp, beady eyes, and a tight, wrinkled mouth. She can't be a day over fifty, but she looks at least ten years older — probably from the stress of the job. Her eyes follow me from the door to the chair in front of her, oozing suspicion the entire way.

"Please have a seat, Miss Riley."

I sit.

"Miss Lyang told me she suspects that you and Mr. Parker may have come into contact with a virus while you were deployed. Do you know why she might think that?"

I take a deep breath, choosing my words carefully. I don't know exactly what Sawyer and Eli said, so I try to be as vague as possible.

"Yeah, I guess. Eli and I found the drifters' meeting place, and we overheard them talking about bringing down the compound with a virus."

"Where was the meeting place?"

"This big church."

She nods slowly. "And how did you know they would be meeting there?"

Damn, this woman is good.

"We knew the town would be crawling with drifters, but we didn't see anyone on the main strip. The church was the only place big enough to fit them all."

"Why did you expect there to be that many of them?"

I pause, and she seems to read my hesitation as concern for keeping deployment information classified.

"Don't worry about sharing the details of your deployment," she says. "The board needs this information. Even your commander had to give up what she knew."

I highly doubt that Jayden gave up *anything* she didn't want to, but I don't say that.

"Well, we expected there to be at least as many drifters as there were in the other town the last time we were deployed."

"And why did Miss Lyang think you and Mr. Parker might be carriers of the virus?"

My stomach clenches. This is the part I'd been dreading — the part Eli, Sawyer, and I should have talked about to make sure we had our stories straight. I can't tell her about Owen. I don't know *what* I'm going to tell her.

"They said in the meeting that the plan was already in motion," I say slowly, desperately thinking through the enormous lie I'm about to tell. "Eli stole something from a drifter's house a while back and sneaked it into the compound. He could have carried the virus in on that."

The undersecretary's mouth tightens. She doesn't believe me. "You think you could have brought the virus into the compound after your last mission?"

I shrug.

"So how is it that everyone you've come in contact with isn't showing symptoms? How is it that *you* are not showing symptoms?"

"I don't know. I don't know what the symptoms would even look like."

Her mouth quirks up around the edges. *Is that how this woman smiles?*

"Oh, I think you do."

"Excuse me?"

"Miss Riley, I'm not stupid. This . . . 'meeting' you attended was not the first you'd heard of this virus, was it?" She sits back in her chair and crosses her arms smugly. "You knew all about it."

"What?"

"Let's save some time and stop pretending you didn't take a little vacation to 119," she snaps. "An Operations worker was found unconscious on the supply train and was brought to the medical ward for treatment. He said he doesn't remember anything except getting a glimpse of a man matching the description of your dear friend Celdon. I know you were with him, which means you know the outcome of this virus."

I open my mouth to deny ever going to 119, but she holds up a hand to stop me.

"Please save your lies for someone with more time on their hands. We know you were there. The only reason we didn't bring it to Control's attention was to keep the situation at 119 under wraps. We don't want to start a panic."

I still don't know who "we" is, so I just wait for her to finish.

"You don't think you came in contact with the virus on your previous deployments. Something happened on this one . . . something none of you seems to want to share."

I cross my arms, determined not to let this woman wear me down. My brain is moving too slowly to think up some version of the story about the arrowhead that doesn't involve Owen.

"Come on, Miss Riley. I know better than to try to get the truth out of Mr. Parker. Insubordination seems to be something he enjoys. But I always took you for the sensible one of the bunch."

"Always?" I repeat, rolling my eyes. "What? In the last ten minutes?"

"You don't seriously think this is the first we've met, do you? Well, I suppose it's the first we've been formally introduced. But I've been following your case for years. Progressive Research takes the health of all Recon operatives very seriously — especially operatives who were part of the Fringe Program."

I clench my fists on the edge of the chair. She's baiting me to see what I know.

After several minutes, she grows impatient.

"Fine, Miss Riley. I can wait. Maybe a few days in isolation will give you time to think about how critical this information is to the thousands of people living in this compound — the thousands of people you're putting in jeopardy by refusing to tell the truth."

She gets up to leave, and her words trigger the toxic guilt that's been brewing in my stomach since we spoke to Owen.

"Wait," I hear myself say.

"Yes?"

I swallow a few times to wet my scratchy throat, hating myself as soon as I make the decision to ignore Eli's plea. "Something did happen on this deployment."

She turns back to me and raises an eyebrow. "I'm listening."

"We met with a drifter after the meeting."

"Who?"

I shake my head, determined not to betray Eli completely. "Just a drifter. I don't know his name."

"What did the drifter want?"

My mind is racing, and suddenly I have an idea. "He wanted to hand off something we were supposed to deliver to Shane." I squint, trying to think of Shane's last name. "Shane . . . Adams?"

"I know whom you're referring to."

"Anyway, we agreed to smuggle it in to settle my debt with Shane. I thought it was just a pre–Death Storm relic."

"What was it?"

"An old arrowhead."

The undersecretary hasn't moved her mouth once since I started spilling my guts, but her eyebrows are raised in a triumphant expression. "Thank you very much, Miss Riley. I won't forget that you cooperated, should I be called upon to testify at your hearing."

"My hearing?"

"Smuggling contraband into this compound is not something the board is likely to ignore, Miss Riley. It's a serious crime. That matter is beyond the scope of *my* duties, but I'm sure you haven't heard the last of this."

My heart sinks. Not only did I betray Eli, frame Shane, and invent an entirely new story, but I'm probably going to be arrested for something I didn't even do. Sure, I probably deserve to be arrested for *something*, but not this.

"I still get the feeling you aren't telling me everything," she muses. "But that's all right. I suspect you'll be more forthcoming if it turns out that you are infected. Once symptoms present themselves, most people have less than a week to live. But if we find a way to treat the virus, I'm sure you'll want to be at the top of the list to receive care."

I give her a withering look. Leave it to a board member to use a cure as leverage.

"Maybe a visit from Mr. Reynolds will help remind you of

what this virus is capable of."

"Celdon?"

"I was hoping you'd share what you knew. I brought along Mr. Reynolds as your reward. But I suppose he can also offer his perspective on the tragedy you witnessed."

She smiles brightly as though this is just a happy coincidence and heads out the door. She can't possibly know how much the visit to 119 affected Celdon, but like Jayden, the undersecretary seems to have an instinct for suffering.

A second later, a messy blond head of hair appears on the other side of the glass.

Celdon looks as though he hasn't slept in days. The deep purplish shadows under his eyes accentuate his unbelievably pale skin, and he looks more disheveled than usual.

"Hey!" After everything that's happened, I want nothing more than to reach through the glass and hug him. "Where have you *been*? I looked for you before we got deployed, but you weren't in Systems or your compartment. I messaged you, like, three times."

"I know. I'm sorry."

"I was so worried. Where were you?"

He sighs. "It's a long story. I'll tell you when you get out of here."

Celdon's gaze drifts around searching for hidden cameras, so I don't press the issue. Constance or the board probably has this room bugged.

"So . . . what's going on?" He lowers his voice. "They said you and Eli might have come in contact with the 119 virus."

"Sawyer thinks we carried it in here on this arrowhead Eli brought with him," I whisper. "But the drifters made it sound like the plan was already underway."

"You mean someone with the virus is already in the compound?"

"Could be. I can't say anything else right now."

"Right."

Celdon's leg jiggles nervously, and I want to ask him what's really going on. He looks even more run-down than usual, but it's his caginess that perplexes me.

Something doesn't feel right.

"Sawyer's in there with you now?" he continues, interrupting my train of thought.

I nod. "She came in direct contact with me right afterward. There's another med intern who was with Eli, too."

"That sucks."

"Do you think you could do me a favor?"

He nods, but it seems forced. "Yeah."

"Just . . . keep doing what you're doing for Eli, okay? And let us know if you . . . see anything."

"I will."

Celdon gets up to leave, and it looks as though the motion hurts his joints. "I gotta run. I'll see you later."

He touches the glass with his palm, and I place my hand directly over his. He gives me a half smile and turns to go, but I just stand there with my hand pressed against the window, trying not to cry.

I don't want to think that today could be the last time I see Celdon. I don't want to consider the possibility that I may never escape this room. But the choking fear and paranoia are starting to overwhelm my senses.

If we are infected, we only have a week and a half to live.

twenty-seven

Celdon

As soon as I'm out the door, I make a beeline for the emergency stairwell. Now that I know where all the cameras in the compound are hidden, I've found myself avoiding the megalift and high-traffic tunnels to minimize the chances that I'll be seen.

I only have five minutes to get back to my compartment, so I take the steps two at a time.

I shouldn't have risked visiting Harper. Any other day, she would have been able to tell something was up. And if anyone from Constance saw me, I'm going to be in trouble.

In less than twenty-four hours, I've already broken several cardinal rules. Rule number one: no fraternizing with old friends or family members until reeducation is complete.

What a load of bullshit. They just don't want anything interfering with their patented brainwashing program.

There's no written rule that says I'm not allowed to hack into security footage from the Fringe and use what I find to sabotage Constance's plans, but I'd bet that's a no-no, too.

I reach my compartment with two minutes to spare, sweaty and out of breath. My reeducation packets are delivered every hour on the hour.

First I receive a message to verify my identity that automatically erases itself from my inbox after thirty seconds. Then I receive a file that disappears from my hard drive after an hour. If I miss one, it's gone for good, and I can't afford any screwups right now.

Sliding into my chair, I pound in my computer password and reach for a cold box of takeout. Instantly, my monitors are blanketed by a dozen rotating security feeds from the Fringe and my message window.

The clock hits eighteen hundred, and a new message appears in my inbox from an unknown user. I open it.

The message is completely blank except for a long link. I already know it's malware, but I don't have any choice but to click and let it download onto my computer. The malware does its thing, and a tiny red light illuminates the top of my monitor.

A shiver rolls down my spine. I imagine some tech guy like me watching from Constance headquarters. He verifies my identity, and another message appears in my inbox.

There isn't any text — just an attached file. I click on it, and it immediately starts to download. A video appears, filling half my screen. It's a still shot of a lower tunnel, but the nondescript walls and doors make it impossible to tell which section it's in. The tunnel is completely empty, and the camera pans slowly from one door to the next.

A low monotone voice comes over my speakers, speaking in a rhythm that seems designed to put me to sleep.

Imagine a world where the last vestiges of humanity have been wiped off the planet. Your friends are gone . . . your colleagues are gone . . . you are gone. There's no one left to remember Celdon. There is no one left to remember the horrible atrocities that destroyed the last remaining pockets of civilization . . . no one left to remember the sanctuary of the compounds . . .

I roll my eyes. Constance has a flair for the dramatic, but at least it's personalized.

The threat is very real. While the board focuses on the horizon, where thousands of hostile survivors are plotting the compounds' destruction, we must turn our attention inward to more subtle threats we face on a daily basis . . .

These threats start small, but when magnified over days, years, and generations, they are poison to the order and stability that ensure the survival of the human race.

Acts of defiance, no matter how small, weaken the compound. When order unravels, the people you once trusted can be the biggest threat to your life and the future of humanity.

Constance has sent me twenty-four videos so far, and each one has been more of the same: Defiance in the compound weakens the compound. A weak compound is a threat to the survival of the human race. Constance saves humanity. Long live Constance.

My first order of business as Constance's newest lackey? Make better videos.

Through all the gloom and doom, I feel my eyelids start to droop. I reach for an Energel, but my hand just nudges half a dozen empty tubes, sending a few clattering to the floor.

I'm exhausted, but I can't fall asleep. If I miss one of Constance's reeducation lessons, they'll see that as a lack of commitment. They'll think I'm a slacker, which is exactly what I don't want. Slackers can't be trusted, and I need them to trust me completely.

To counteract the effects of the narrator's dull voice, I do a quick scan of the security feeds. Constance would definitely not approve of my extracurricular espionage, but I already feel as though I'm betraying Harper, and I refuse to drop the ball on the one thing she asked me to do.

She would *kill* me if she knew I'd joined up with Constance, but I have to know what happened to my mother.

I don't blame Harper for lying to me. The lie was much kinder than the truth. But if my mom really is out there somewhere, I have to find her.

To gain access to that information, I just have to go along with Constance's brainwashing program and behave myself. Once I'm in, I can find out *exactly* what they know and stay one step ahead of them if they try to take Harper off the map.

I just have to be convincing.

Watching footage of the Fringe isn't doing much to keep me awake. There's not a drifter in sight — just abandoned buildings, rusty cars, dirt, and tumbleweed.

But then the window changes to a new feed, and three figures appear in my peripheral vision. I freeze the feeds so the view doesn't change and enlarge the window.

Three men are walking down the street at a brisk pace. Two of them look alert and confident, but the third is definitely acting shady. He's wearing dark sunglasses and keeps glancing around as if he expects to be jumped at any moment.

His eyes bounce from building to building in a scanning pattern, and I realize he's checking the corners for cameras.

He knows.

The men stop at a building just out of the camera's line of sight. The other two seem to be speaking to someone standing in the doorway.

The third man's gaze travels higher, and then suddenly he freezes. I don't move or breathe. It feels as though he's looking right at me.

Somebody calls the man to the door. He steps up and raises his sunglasses so they can see his face. When the person in the doorway verifies his identity, the shady guy puts his sunglasses back on — but not before I get a good look at him.

He looks just like Eli.

My heart starts pounding harder. Owen is alive, and now there's video evidence. Not only that, but the camera got a clear shot of his face. Anyone who knows Eli would think this man was his twin, which is going to raise a lot of questions I'm sure Eli doesn't want to answer.

I have to warn Harper, but there's still another twenty minutes left on my reeducation video. Then I'll have maybe fifteen minutes before the next file arrives.

The red light is still glowing at the top of my monitor, which means someone in Constance is still watching me. They don't fuck around when it comes to monitoring their protégés.

I wonder how long it will take for someone to see this footage and notify Jayden. It's possible they have other things to worry about, but Harper made it seem as though finding the drifters' leaders was Jayden's number one priority.

I try to talk myself down, but I can feel the clammy sweat breaking out all over my forehead. I need to get a message to Harper and Eli.

I tap my fingers impatiently on the desk, waiting for the video to come to an end. Owen and his companions have already disappeared into the building.

What an idiot. I'm sure Eli warned him that he needed to act dead. And what does he do? He wanders right into range of the surveillance cameras.

Suddenly, I hear a dull beeping coming from just outside my door. Someone is letting himself into my compartment.

With a lightning-fast stroke of keys, I clear my monitor of every window except the reeducation video.

Less than a second later, my door flies open.

I'm on my feet by the time the intruder rounds the corner, and my fists clench automatically when I see Devon's smug face.

"Good evening, Celdon," he says in that falsely bright voice.

"Devon," I snarl. "Did knocking go out of style, or do you just want me so bad that you're letting yourself into my compartment now?"

The second I blurt it out, I know it was a mistake. Devon's creepily polite façade wavers, sending a ripple of anger down his smooth, tan face. It happens so quickly I could have missed it, but I know instantly that I fucked up *big time*.

"I'm not sure where this hostility is coming from," says Devon. "We're on the same team now."

"I know . . ."

"When you agreed to join us, you promised to put the bitter, angry Celdon to rest and focus on becoming a better version of yourself."

"Sorry," I mumble, trying and failing to sound sincere.

Devon sighs and shakes his head. "This is really unfortunate. You're deep in your reeducation now. We should be getting past this cynicism and negativity."

The guy looks so genuinely upset that Constance hasn't been able to break me of my angry, fucked-up ways that I almost feel bad that I'm not taking this shit seriously . . . almost.

Then I remember I'm trying to infiltrate a psychotic, eugenics-happy cult. It's probably a *good* thing that I'm having a hard time adjusting.

I'm so busy trying to arrange my expression to look contrite that my brain doesn't immediately register Devon's hand reaching into his pants pocket.

"Don't worry," he says, fiddling with something at his side. "We'll get you up to speed."

"Oh, yeah? Good, because —"

I never finish the sentence. Devon throws out an arm with unexpected speed and aggression and whips me across the face with a long, stiff object.

White-hot pain flares over my skin, and I double over before I realize what he struck me with. Fighting the painful throbbing sensation spreading from my cheek to my ear, I squint up at the long silver instrument in Devon's hand.

"We generally . . . try to avoid the use of force," he huffs, drawing his arm back again and whipping me across the other cheek.

A strangled yell escapes my throat, and now my entire face is on fire. I take a deep breath and force myself to stand, glaring up at Devon.

"It's all right to be angry with me," he says. "But this is for your own good."

It sounds as though he's reasoning with himself to justify striking me. What a nut job.

"I'm your benefactor, and part of that job is holding you accountable." He meets my gaze with a creepy look of determination in his eyes. "Celdon . . . I'm going to hold you to high standards because I believe in your potential."

He breaks into a crazed smile. "It's time to go."

"Go where?"

"Just a little field trip."

"But I'm not done with the video."

"We'll make sure it picks up right where you left off," he says. "Since you've . . . *fallen behind* in your assimilation, we need a physical intervention."

Cold dread seeps into my stomach. I've been here before, only I wasn't trying to convince Constance that I wanted to be one of them. I was their prisoner, and they tortured me for days.

I can't go back there again. I won't.

It isn't the pain that scares me. I can handle the pain and the insults and the humiliation. But I need to get a message to Harper, and right now Devon is standing between me and the door.

This is definitely going to delay my "reeducation." Hell, it's probably going to earn me a week in their torture room and twenty extra brainwashing videos. But I can't risk being stuck in the bowels of the compound with no way to get a message to Harper.

Letting out a wild battle cry, I launch myself across the room at Devon with all the force I can manage. Devon's a little bigger than me, but I'm taller. And even though he sees it coming, he can't get out of the way fast enough.

My hands clamp down on his throat, and the momentum from my leap knocks him backward.

Unfortunately, I haven't had much practice choking people with my bare hands.

I lose my balance, and we both crash into my beautiful glass coffee table. The sharp edges cut into my skin. Blood trickles down my arms and stains my slacks, but the fall isn't as painful as I would have expected.

Maybe the adrenaline is numbing the pain of the glass poking into my skin. Or maybe it's because Devon is receiving the worst of the lacerations as he squirms underneath me.

Then he lets out a guttural noise and swings out — hard.

For an overgroomed pretty boy, Devon packs one hell of a punch. I feel his fist crash into my cheek — bone against bone — and the shock and heat travel all the way down my face. I wind up and throw out my fist, feeling the power and a slight twinge of pain shoot up my wrist as I make contact.

Devon lunges to the side, and shards of glass cascade off his shoulders and back as he tries to buck me off.

Then I feel a sharp throttle to my gut, and Devon uses the opportunity to grab my neck and head-butt me.

There's no cartoonish *boink!* sound when our skulls collide, but for a moment, the room goes all blurry. There's a crackle of pinks and yellows in my vision before I fall forward onto my hands and knees.

Glass is cutting into my palms, but they're already so slick with blood that it barely registers.

Devon is no longer sprawled in front of me. All I see is the sparkle of bloody glass and the blur of carpet.

By the time I hear the *crunch* behind me, it's too late. Devon's arm encircles my neck, and his other fist puts pressure on the back of my head.

For one horrible moment, I feel my air passages close as he squeezes the life out of me. I smack his arm and jerk around, but Devon doesn't let go.

I keep fighting as the darkness closes in, but there's no air left in my lungs.

My last thought before passing out is that I really, *really* should have asked Constance to teach me their kung fu moves before I fought Devon Reid.

twenty-eight

Harper

The next two days are the longest of my life.

We aren't allowed any more visitors. When we arrived, the quarantine crew stuck little monitors to our chests, which means the doctors don't need to come by to take our vital signs. Apart from each other, the only human contact we get is the nurses who serve our meals.

Health and Rehab confiscated my interface when we were quarantined, so I can't message Celdon to see if there have been any new developments on the Fringe.

But the worst part is not knowing if we're infected. Every little sniffle or cough sets me on edge. The constant boredom makes me tired, but fatigue could also be a symptom of the virus.

When Eli tosses and turns in his sleep, I worry it's because he's feverish — not that he would tell me. He hasn't said more than a dozen words to me since we've been locked up together. He won't even look at me.

Then there's Caleb. He's the only real source of entertainment we have. If I haven't taken well to confinement, Caleb should be *institutionalized*.

Less than two hours after we were locked in the room, he came up with a plan to stay busy and keep from going crazy. He requested an interface for reading, but they just sent up a tablet and cut him off from the compound network, which meant none of us could use it to communicate. I guess the board didn't want to risk us telling people we may have introduced a deadly virus to the compound. Go figure.

As soon as we finished breakfast yesterday, Caleb started pacing back and forth. It's become his habit after every meal.

Part of me thinks exercise must be on the little prisoner schedule he made for himself — either that or he's just bored and anxious like the rest of us.

Sawyer is the only one who seems to be handling this well. She stares at Caleb as he paces back and forth across our small room and drinks lots of fluids. She takes her own temperature every two hours and even coaxed me and Caleb into letting her take ours. Occasionally, she'll strike up a conversation, but it always circles back to "if we make it out of here." After a while, we seem to reach an unspoken agreement that silence is better.

I'm relieved when our dinner arrives. We had *just* missed dinner when we were locked in here two days ago, which means fifty-three hours have passed without even a whisper of symptoms.

They send in a nurse in full hazmat gear to deliver our trays, and the smell of overseasoned institutional food fills the room.

The nurse is a blond woman I vaguely recognize. She's young, and her eyes dart warily between us as though we might suddenly morph into rabid dogs and maul her until she's infected, too.

Eli takes his tray without really looking at her, but the nurse's eyes follow him all the way back to his bed. I scowl at her when I take my tray, and she quickly averts her gaze.

Man, I really need to get out of here.

I try to focus on the food and instantly wish I hadn't. Even though it comes from the canteen, there's something different about the meals they send up to the medical ward. The rice is more like mush, and the protein cube is too salty and slightly cold in the middle. The vegetables are soggy, but I savor every bite and draw out the meal as long as I can. At least it passes the time.

I finish too quickly, and then it's time for Sawyer's temperature check and Caleb's stroll around the room.

At twenty-two hundred, I crawl into bed and turn out my light. Caleb and Sawyer follow suit, and I know we're all thinking the same thing: When we wake up, we'll only have a few hours to wait. Then we'll know if we're getting out of here or if we're going to spend our last days in the medical ward, battling an illness for which there is no cure.

A few feet away, Eli flicks off his light, but he doesn't lie down. I can see his silhouette in the shadows: He's just sitting there, staring into the darkness.

It's impossible to tell if he's worried about the virus, scared for Owen, or just angry at me.

I'm not tired yet, so I just lie there listening to the others' breathing. Sawyer's levels out after about twenty minutes, and when Caleb's loud, rolling snores fill the room, sleep becomes utterly impossible.

Eli still hasn't moved. He's propped up against the pillows with one arm thrown over his knee.

I can't take it anymore. I throw off my covers and roll off my bed. He doesn't turn to look at me, but he stiffens slightly and watches me approach out of the corner of his eye.

The four feet between our beds feels like an enormous distance, but I force my feet to shuffle toward him until I'm standing at the edge of the mattress.

"Hey," I whisper.

"What is it, Harper?"

His tone isn't harsh, but it still leaves a bitter taste in my mouth; it's almost indifferent.

"I just wanted to . . . talk to you."

"There isn't much to talk about," he sighs.

"I think there is," I say, fighting to keep the hurt out of my voice.

"You didn't talk to me before you jumped on Sawyer's paranoid bandwagon and got us locked up here, so I'm not sure why you want to talk now."

He still won't look at me, and that aggravates me more than anything.

"I didn't have a chance! It's not like I could just come and find you and risk exposing more people to the virus!"

"We aren't infected!" he splutters. "I can't believe you'd think he'd do that."

"I'm sorry, Eli. But it's the only thing that makes sense!"

"It doesn't make sense!" he snaps, whipping his head around.

Suddenly, I wish he'd go back to not looking at me. In the dim light filtering through the door, I can read the fury in his expression. It's almost like looking at Owen.

"My brother wouldn't try to bring down the compound if it meant killing me in the process. He only gave me the arrowhead to remember him by. He didn't contaminate it with the virus."

"Do you hear yourself? He and the drifters are releasing a virus in the compound . . . and you're *in* the compound."

"He didn't want us to come back."

"But he didn't stop you!"

I instantly wish I hadn't said anything. Eli is looking at me as though I physically struck him.

He takes several deep, angry breaths. "What would you

have me do, Harper? Turn him over to Jayden?"

"N-no. But I don't think you should put your life on the line when you're stuck in here and he's not. If he's not worried about Constance, maybe you should stop lying for him. He doesn't need you to protect him."

"He's not the only one I was protecting," he says fiercely.

Now there's a heavy guilt competing with my discomfort. "You still shouldn't have lied. If Jayden finds out —"

"I told you. I'm handling it."

"*How?*"

Eli's jaw tightens, and his gaze becomes so intense — so accusatory — that I have to fight the impulse to look away. "Damn it, Harper! Why can't you just *trust* me? Every decision I've made has been to protect you. How do you not get that?"

His words throw me off guard, but he's right.

When I finally speak, my voice feels very small. "I . . . I'm sorry."

"Whatever." He shakes his head, and it seems as though the fight's gone out of him. "Let's just get some sleep, okay?"

I nod and then realize he probably can't see me. I back away from his bed and settle down on mine, fighting the tears that are quivering in my eyes. I know our shouting has woken Caleb and Sawyer, which makes everything ten times worse.

If I felt bad before, it's nothing compared to how I feel now. I let Eli down — there's no denying it. He finally let himself care about someone, and I destroyed his trust.

I think back to our night in bed together, embracing skin to skin, and imagine what it would be like to have that all the time.

I could have had that. Eli was different around me — *we* were different — but I wrecked it.

When I close my eyes, a single hot tear leaks out and burns a path down my face.

The worst part about the whole thing is that I might not have any time to repair the damage. If we are infected, this could be the end: the end of me, the end of Eli, the end of us.

* * *

When I wake up the next morning, Caleb has already started his breakfast promenade back and forth across the room. There's a tray of cold oatmeal sitting at the foot of my bed, which means I must have slept right through the morning nurse's visit.

Sawyer is sitting up in bed reading from the tablet, and Eli is nowhere to be found.

I hear the shower cycle running on repeat in the adjacent room, and dread settles over me as I recall our argument from the night before.

It suddenly makes sense that Sawyer and Caleb didn't wake me when breakfast arrived. I can only imagine how awkward it's going to be with the four of us stuck together for another several hours.

"Morning," says Sawyer in a groggy voice.

"Yes, it is."

Sawyer picks up the thermometer from her nightstand and swipes it once over her brow.

"What's the verdict, doc?"

"Ninety-eight point six," she breathes. "Here, let me do you."

She reaches over and swipes the cold metal over my forehead, and we both wait for the thermometer to beep.

"Well?"

She lets out a big breath of relief, and a hopeful grin spreads slowly across her face. She meets my eyes, and I know everything's going to be all right. "Ninety-eight point four."

I let out a burst of air I didn't realize I'd been holding. We still have five hours to go to the seventy-two-hour mark, but it feels as though we just might make it after all.

"It's too early to tell for sure, but I think symptoms would have presented overnight if we were infected," says Sawyer.

"I guess we're gonna be all right, then."

She nods, but her grin slips slightly. "Is . . . everything *else* all right?"

She glances at the bathroom door, and I cringe.

"You heard all that, huh?"

"You guys weren't exactly quiet."

Caleb seems to quicken his stride, purposefully averting his gaze every time he paces in front of me.

"It's okay, Caleb. I know you heard, too."

He stops pacing, looking incredibly uncomfortable. "Yeah."

"So what's going on with you two?" Sawyer asks, handing him the thermometer and falling into girl mode.

"I don't know. Things were good. But he's really sensitive about the Owen situation, and he's upset that I didn't trust him."

"He does seem to have a pretty big blind spot when it comes to Owen."

I nod. "It's tough on him because Owen is the only family he has left. He assumes that just because he has a conscience, Owen must have one, too. But god, they're *so* different."

"Is Owen a warm and fuzzy teddy bear who's super polite and always shares his feelings?"

I snort. "No. He's like Eli, except he's a total asshole. He doesn't trust anyone. And he hates me. Sometimes I think he might do the right thing, but as far as he's concerned, the compounds *have* to be destroyed."

"The asshole thing must run in the family," Caleb mutters.

"Don't think we won't cut you out of this conversation," Sawyer snaps.

Caleb looks chastened, but I swear I see a slight smirk playing at the corner of his mouth. And when Sawyer turns back to me, she's *definitely* fighting a grin.

The shower stops running, and we exchange a meaningful look. A minute later, Eli comes out shirtless, drying his hair with a towel.

I try not to stare at his chiseled abs and chest too long, and Sawyer is blushing hard. Caleb looks annoyed.

We fall into a strained silence and wait for the hours to pass.

I wish Eli would let Sawyer take his temperature, but he's wearing an expression meant to fend off anyone who might come near him.

Around noon, I hear some commotion in the hallway and a nurse's bright voice yelling something down the tunnel. Then the door flies open, and a doctor I don't recognize comes in wearing a hazmat suit.

"How are we all feeling today?" he asks, glancing around at us through the blue wall of his interface projection.

"Fine," we all chorus.

"Well, that's a very good sign."

"We don't have a fever," Sawyer says, gesturing between us.

"I know. The vital signs our monitors picked up all look great. Do you have any other symptoms? Vomiting? Trouble breathing? Hallucinations?"

We all shake our heads.

"Well, that's enough to convince me that we're not dealing with a virus."

I breathe an enormous sigh of relief, and Sawyer and Caleb look at each other as though they might start making out any second. Something is *definitely* going on between those two.

The only person who doesn't seem overjoyed is Eli.

"So we can go?" he asks.

"Yes. Whenever you're ready."

Eli nods. Without another word, he pulls on his T-shirt and runs a hand through his hair. He glances at me once with an unreadable expression and then strides out of the room.

My heart sinks, and Sawyer throws me a sympathetic look.

I force a weak smile and turn to go, too, walking slowly to keep a little distance between myself and Eli.

I could still make it to training this afternoon, but instead of heading down to Recon, I punch the button for Systems to check on Celdon.

After being stuck in a room with Sawyer, Caleb, and Eli for two days, I'd really like to see a *different* friendly face.

As soon as I step off the megalift, the other lift beside it dings. I glance behind me to see who it is and almost throw up.

Celdon is standing in the lift, but he doesn't look like Celdon. A deep bluish-yellow bruise spans the entire left side of his face. His eye is swollen beyond recognition, and he's got a busted purplish lip. His blazer is ripped in several places and caked with a dark substance that looks like dried blood.

"What the hell happened to you?" I shriek, rushing up to him as he steps gingerly out of the lift.

He isn't holding his ribs, but he moves with such precise, robotic movements that I know he must have injuries I can't see.

"Can't talk about it," he groans. He limps past me down the tunnel toward his compartment and keys in. The sight of the place is astounding.

Trash and empty food containers cover nearly every surface, with the piles growing more dense in the three-foot radius around Celdon's desk. There's a pungent odor of rotten food mixed with sweat, and I'd bet Celdon hasn't cracked open the curtains in days.

But that's not the worst of it. Shards of broken glass sparkle like diamonds in the carpet, starting near the skeleton of his coffee table and exploding out from there. The white carpet is also caked with dried blood.

"Tell me what happened," I demand.

"I can't."

"Did Constance do this to you? Did they hurt you to get to me? Is this because we went to 119?"

Celdon sighs, and it looks as though the movement pains him. "No. It's not that."

"Then what is it?"

"I can't tell you."

"Why not?" I ask, feeling frustrated. Clearly Celdon is in trouble, but I don't know if it's the sort of trouble that comes from Neverland or from up above.

"It's just safer if you don't know."

I open my mouth to argue some more, but the stiff set of Celdon's jaw and the determined flash of his eyes says I'm not going to get anywhere today.

He drags in a deep breath, trying to hide his wince. "Listen. There's something unrelated to all of this that you need to see."

Before I can ask what it is, he crunches through the shards of broken glass and crosses to his desk. I stare at him, utterly perplexed, as he punches in his password and pulls up a dozen video feeds on three gorgeous ultrathin monitors. Then he opens an old file and swivels around in his chair to watch my reaction.

On screen, I see three men approaching the building where the camera is mounted. Two are walking casually as if they own the block, but the third seems nervous. He's wearing sunglasses and looks as though he doesn't want to be seen. His gaze darts along the street, traveling upward until he locks eyes with the camera.

He turns to say something to someone standing out of sight, lifting his sunglasses so the stranger can see his face.

Owen.

"This footage is from three days ago . . . after you and Eli returned from the Fringe."

A heavy, all-consuming dread settles in the pit of my stomach. Eli told Jayden that Owen was dead — even brought her Owen's hat as evidence — yet here's a clear shot of him.

Worst of all, Owen showed his entire face, and it's like seeing Eli's twin.

"I have to warn Eli," I croak, backing out of the room. "Thanks for showing me."

"Yeah."

Celdon moves as though he wants to follow me, but then something dark flashes over his face, and he stops himself.

I don't know what Celdon's gotten himself into this time, but I don't have time to worry about that right now. Clearly he doesn't want my help — at least not at the moment — and Eli and I are in *immediate* danger.

Jayden must have seen the footage by now. Even with so many feeds to watch, if Celdon spotted Owen, one of Constance's surveillance guys must have recognized him from the telltale scar on his arm.

There's a small crowd of people clustered around the megalift, so I head for the emergency stairwell and take the steps two at a time. I pass a controller and two Health and Rehab workers making out in a corner, but none of them pay me any attention as I fly down the stairs toward Recon.

By the time I reach the lower levels, I'm panting and breaking a sweat. I fling myself against the door and fly out into the tunnel, where a sea of gray-clad people are pushing their way toward the training center and Recon offices.

Cutting across the crowd, I head for the officers' tunnel and bang on Eli's door. He doesn't answer.

I forgot to claim my interface from Health and Rehab, so I have no way to message him. It's possible he's ignoring me, or he might have decided to catch afternoon training. I quicken my pace and head for the training center, hoping he'll at least listen to what I have to say.

It's past thirteen hundred by the time I get there, but the cadets and privates aren't split into their squads the way they should be. They're scattered across the training center in tight little clusters.

People are flitting from group to group, finding their friends and speaking in anxious voices. I can't make out what they're saying, but their expressions tell me something big must have happened.

A few lieutenants are trying to restore order, but it's a half-hearted attempt. They look just as unsettled.

The place is mass chaos, and the hubbub echoes loudly off the cinder-block walls. I catch the flash of a few interfaces. They all seem to be tuned in to the same news feed, but I can't read the headline in reverse.

I scan the crowd for Lenny's red hair before remembering she's probably still recovering in the medical ward. Luckily, Bear is easy to see over the crowd, and I widen my search around him for Eli.

Finally I spot him. He isn't barking orders at our squad or pulling on his irritated lieutenant face. He's walking toward me with purpose.

As soon as I see him, I know something is wrong. He looks

much too pale, and his blue eyes are flashing with panic.

I push my way through a knot of gossiping cadets to reach him, and he doesn't pay them any attention as he grabs my shoulders and pulls me close. I can feel his body heat in the small space between us, and his grip on my arms tightens.

I open my mouth to blurt out what Celdon discovered, but it's Eli who speaks first.

"We have a problem."

twenty-nine

Harper

My brain is working in fits and starts as Eli's words sink in.

"Wh-what's going on?"

He glances around at the people on either side of us and pulls me closer.

"It's all over the news," he murmurs, eyeing the blue glow of interfaces lighting up the crowd. "Two of the AWOL Recon operatives just returned to the compound."

"*What?*"

"Yeah."

"Well . . . where are they? Where have they been?"

"They're still being debriefed," he murmurs. "I'm not sure how this even got out. Someone in Health and Rehab must have leaked it to Information."

"Did you know either of them?"

He shakes his head. "Not very well. They were both privates, but they weren't even deployed together — that's what's so weird. Well, that and the fact that they've been missing for the past two months."

"How is it that they're back now?" I whisper. "Where have they been this whole time?"

Then it hits me.

"You don't think . . ." I shake my head, too horrified by my own best guess to voice it aloud.

Eli's been watching me carefully, and as soon as the possibility takes shape, my expression seems to confirm his worst fears. "Yeah, I do."

"They're carrying the virus," I whisper. "That's what Owen meant when he said the plan was already in motion. They've been with the drifters the entire time."

Eli nods, and dread washes over me.

"We have to warn someone!"

He drags a hand through his hair. "Yeah, I know."

"We have another problem, too," I say, suddenly remembering why I came to find Eli in the first place. "I just saw Celdon. He's been monitoring the feeds, and . . . Owen made an appearance after you told Jayden we killed him. He got caught on camera three days ago."

"*Three days ago?*" Eli's face tightens. "Are you sure it was him?"

"Yes. The cameras got a perfect shot. You'd have to be blind not to see that you two are related."

"Something isn't right," he mutters. "Jayden should have seen that footage by now, but she hasn't shown up to confront me about it."

"Have you been back to your compartment?"

"No. I came straight here."

"Maybe she's been busy . . ."

Eli shakes his head. His eyes dart around the training center as though he expects Constance to leap out and tackle us at any second. "We have to get out of here. Now."

For once, I don't argue. I don't ask questions.

Eli reaches for my hand — completely oblivious to the hundreds of people standing around — and pulls me through the crowd.

It's slow going. People are standing in tight clusters talking about the AWOL operatives, and many are so engrossed in their interfaces that they don't notice us trying to push past them.

Finally, we break through the congestion and make a beeline for the exit. We've almost reached the door when Eli freezes.

Jayden is standing in the doorway, flanked by two controllers. She spots me and Eli right away, but he doesn't let go of my hand.

"You two look like you're in a hurry," she says, glancing down at our interlaced fingers and back up to Eli's face.

"Harper's not feeling well," he says through gritted teeth.

"That's too bad," croons Jayden. Her eyes don't leave Eli's for a second.

"Can we go?"

"I'm afraid not."

Jayden jerks her head, and the controllers on either side of her start to encroach on us.

When they move, I see Warner Cunningham, Secretary of Security, standing next to Jayden. He's an imposing man with closely cropped brown hair, a hard jawline, and wolflike eyes. He's wearing one of the board's signature taupe suits, but he's got the Control insignia emblazoned on his breast pocket.

He takes a step forward and addresses me directly. "Harper Riley, you're under arrest for refusing orders, lying to your commanding officer, colluding with drifters, and smuggling illegal contraband into the compound with the intent to sell."

Before I can even move, I feel one of the controller's fat, sweaty hands on my wrist and the sharp slap of cold metal as he cuffs me.

Jayden is watching with an amused expression, and it takes me several seconds to form a response.

"What?" I splutter, trying to keep my other arm out of the controller's reach.

I don't plan on going quietly — even if that is a pretty accurate description of my crimes.

The secretary keeps speaking in that monotone voice of his. "You have the right to remain silent. Anything you say or do may be used against you in trial before the board.

"You have the right to representation. You may select your own representation or use the counsel Recon provides. You'll be taken to Control to be questioned and await sentencing."

Suddenly, Eli seems to unfreeze from his moment of shock. "What the hell is this?" he growls, stepping forward to shove the controller away from me.

"Parker, I would think *very* carefully about what you do next," says Jayden. "You are already in serious trouble."

"For *what?*" He sounds much more surprised than he should, given everything we've done.

Jayden turns to the secretary. "Well?"

Cunningham's upper lip twitches in irritation, but he nods. "Eli Parker, you're under arrest for high treason."

The second controller moves forward to restrain Eli, and this time he's too shocked to resist.

"What?" I yell, straining at the handcuffs and causing my controller to jerk forward. The metal digs into my wrists, but I keep lashing out at Jayden. Certainly Eli and I have committed our fair share of crimes, but treason is the most serious charge that can be laid against a compound citizen.

Jayden glances at me with a look one might give a misbehaving child and takes two steps closer to Eli. Her voice is low and deadly, but I'm close enough to hear.

"I must admit, it took me a while to figure it all out. It wasn't until I paid a visit to your compartment that I put the pieces together."

Cunningham is standing too far back to see, but out of the corner of my eye, I watch Jayden reach into her breast pocket and withdraw a tiny piece of wrinkled paper.

When she unfolds it, I can just make out the image of a much-younger Eli smiling shyly for the camera.

When Jayden speaks next, her whisper is barely discernible. "Oh the things we'll do for *family*."

Eli growls and jerks forward, nearly throwing his controller off balance. "This is bullshit! You had *no* right to go through my stuff."

By now we've attracted quite a lot of attention. People around us are watching the proceedings as though it's a drama staged purely for their entertainment. Bear, Blaze, and Kindra have pushed their way through the crowd, but several other controllers have materialized to hold back the spectators.

"I can do whatever I want," breathes Jayden. "Besides . . . we had to search your compartment to ensure you weren't hoarding any contraband that could be contaminated with a virus."

Eli throws me a confused look, and my stomach drops to my knees.

"You have the right to remain silent," the secretary repeats.

"He didn't do anything wrong!" I cry.

"Harper, don't."

"You have the right to representation."

"I was just coming to warn you," he growls at Jayden. "The AWOL operatives . . . *they're* the ones carrying the virus."

I don't know who he thinks will listen to us at this point, but I feel his desperation mixing with my own panic, compounding the severity of the situation.

"You'll be taken to Control to be questioned and await sentencing."

Suddenly, the controller yanks my arms back and shoves me in the spine. My shoulders strain at the pressure, and I have to take two steps forward to keep him from yanking my arms out of their sockets.

"Eli!" I yell. I don't know what I plan to say or do, but I'm overcome with the horrible feeling that we're about to be separated for good.

My charges are enough to land me in the cages for years, but high treason is punishable by death.

I jerk my head around to look at him, and our eyes meet over my controller's shoulder.

"Say whatever you need to say," he says desperately, straining at his cuffs. "I'll be all right. Just get yourself cleared — whatever it takes."

I feel the tears forming a lump in my throat, but I can't resist as the controller pushes me forward. I stumble down the tunnel, trying to stay tough for Eli and all the onlookers wondering whether or not we really were trying to bring down the compound.

I keep glancing over my shoulder to make sure Eli and his controller are still behind us, and every time I look, my controller bends my arms back harder until my shoulders are screaming in protest.

We all crowd onto the megalift, but my controller shoves me face-first into the corner so I can't make eye contact or talk to Eli. I hear them board, though, and a deep groan tells me the controller must have kicked him.

I squirm the entire trip up to Control, but there's no escaping my current position. Finally the lift dings, and when the doors slide open, the smell of urine and unwashed bodies seeps onto the lift.

My controller shoves me out into the tunnel, and I breathe through my mouth to keep the stench from overwhelming me. I squint around at the poorly lit receiving area and get a jolt of fear unrelated to whatever they're going to do to Eli.

I'm under arrest. They're laying charges against me, and I'm one hundred percent guilty.

I am so screwed.

The doors groan as they start sliding closed, but I don't hear Eli struggling behind me.

I wheel around, causing a painful cut to open in my wrist.

Eli's controller disembarked right behind me, but Eli isn't with him. When he shifts, I see why.

Eli is still aboard the megalift, flanked by Jayden and the secretary. Two large men dressed in black have replaced the controllers, and horror settles over me.

They're from Constance.

When I catch Eli's eye, I only have a second to read his look of terror. Someone lowers a black bag over his head, and the doors slam shut.

Author's Note

Thank you for reading *Outbreak*. This was the first book I wrote as a full-time writer, and I honestly thought it would feel different now that writing books is my job.

I don't buy into the idea that if you love what you do, you'll never work a day in your life. If you love what you do, you work *every* day of your life because you don't want to stop.

Luckily, writing this book didn't feel much different than it did when writing was just a side hustle for me. Every night when I go to bed, I'm already looking forward to waking up and working on whatever book I'm writing.

But once I started talking to readers about *Outbreak*, I could tell something had changed. Many of you were *waiting* for this book, which made me that much more excited to release it. I'm so grateful for your emails and your infectious enthusiasm. It pushes me to write faster and makes everything more fun.

One of the best things about being an author is the ability to share experiences with people and achieve a true understanding that's so rare in the real world. I put a little bit of myself (or people I know) in every character, so it's a relief when readers can empathize with their flaws.

Another perk of being an author is the excuse to learn about new scientific discoveries as I'm doing research for the books. I want to make things as realistic as possible, so I always try to ground fiction in reality.

Sometimes it's terrifying; other times, it's incredibly cool.

Recently, I stumbled upon some information about IBM's supercomputer Watson, which can digest and analyze an enormous amount of medical information, new research, and even human genome data. Watson is so good that hospitals are using it to diagnose cancer: It successfully diagnoses lung cancer 90 percent of the time, while regular human doctors are only correct 50 percent of the time.

This discovery further reinforced my belief that genetic data is going to play a big role in the future. Watson is great news for the fight against cancer, but I'm still a little wary about other potential applications of this technology.

IBM just acquired two startups to bolster its data analytics, which means the company gained access to one of the largest clinical data sets in the world (data from 50 million people!).

Now, maybe I'm just paranoid, but if a supercomputer has access to your health data and millions of others' data, I don't think it's too far-fetched to think that one day our genetic data could be evaluated when we apply for health insurance, jobs, loans, etc.

Sequencing a person's genome has already gotten significantly cheaper and faster. For $1,000, you can get your genome sequenced within 24 hours, and Oxford Nanopore Technologies is testing a super-cheap gene sequencer about the size of a flash drive.

The company hopes to one day bring the technology to consumers for mobile self-monitoring. (I don't know about you, but I couldn't help but picture people going on a date in the future and whipping out their phones to test their genetic compatibility.)

Another aspect of the book that's actually very close to reality is the idea that genetic mutation could lead to radiation resistance. Scientists have bred a strain of E. coli that can repair its own DNA after being bombarded with radiation. They think that human cells could eventually repair radiation damage the same way, and there is already a system that allows scientists to edit a genome.

And speaking of bleeding-edge medicine, how about bringing a patient back from the dead? The life-saving procedure the doctors performed on Lenny when she was rushed to the medical ward is a real thing.

Researchers at the University of Pittsburgh Medical Center are currently experimenting with a suspended animation procedure that literally brings people back from the dead. Surgeons drain the patient's blood and replace it with cold salt water to induce hypothermia, which slows cell death. This buys them a few hours to repair the patient's injuries and repopulate the body with blood.

If the procedure works, the heart starts beating again, and the patient regains consciousness within a few hours or days.

Okay — enough with the good news. Let's talk about the scary shit.

How is it that the Desperados got their hands on a deadly virus that absolutely no one can control? Even if the federal government relocated some virus samples to a compound before Death Storm for safekeeping, doesn't that seem like the sort of thing they would keep on heavy lockdown?

Unfortunately, biosafety level 3 and 4 labs make horrendous mistakes all the time.

Specimens go missing; infected research animals escape. What's even more terrifying is that the federal government doesn't even know where all these high-containment labs are. (Reporters have identified more than 200.) It should come as no surprise, then, that oversight of these labs totally sucks.

In 2014, officials unearthed some old boxes of smallpox samples in storage at the National Institutes of Health that everyone had forgotten about. Horrified by the NIH's poor housekeeping skills, the feds investigated some 4,000 labs and found poorly stored specimen that cause plague, botulism, and bird flu. Just recently, a Defense Department lab in Utah accidentally sent live anthrax to nine labs and a U.S. military base in South Korea. (Whoops.)

After gathering enough material to give myself nightmares for years, I concluded that it's very plausible for the drifters to get their hands on a fictitious virus that could devastate the compounds. I'm eager to explore how compound 112 will react to a potential outbreak in book four.

I'm also very excited to follow Celdon into the inner folds of Constance, see the viral outbreak from Sawyer's position in the medical ward, and maybe even get inside Owen's head to understand where his true loyalties lie.

As I was writing this book, it occurred to me that Harper and Eli could either be the best thing for each other or the worst. They push each other and comfort each other, but their strong personalities frequently lead to clashes that border on unhealthy. Harper is finally beginning to understand Eli, but they both still have a lot of hang-ups.

I'll be interested to see how they cope with separation in book four and if they can finally reach a point of trust and understanding that will make their relationship sustainable. Of course, I'm a sucker for couples that have true chemistry, so I'm rooting for them.

After reaching the end of book three where Harper and Eli are arrested, one of my beta readers pointed out that things look pretty hopeless for those two. I don't disagree, but I'll leave you with this: No matter how bleak things seem, there is always hope for resourceful, resilient people like Harper and Eli.

In my opinion, the best defense against a world that's barreling toward destruction is mental toughness and relentless curiosity. Don't assume that everything is fine. Don't assume that *somebody* has things under control. And always, always, always ask questions.

I hope you enjoyed *Outbreak* and that you'll help me spread the word by leaving reviews on Amazon and Goodreads. Reviews are the best marketing in the world because they help readers like you discover books by independent authors.

Visit my website at **www.tarahbenner.com**. There you can sign up for my mailing list to be the first to hear about book four or get in touch to tell me what you thought of *Outbreak*. I love getting emails from readers.

* * *

28922565R00223

Made in the USA
San Bernardino, CA
09 January 2016